# Dream Catcher

by Phillip Christian

*Copyright* © 2017 by Phillip Christian
All rights reserved.
ISBN: 978-1979960069

Any unauthorized reprint or use of this material is prohibited. No part of this book may be reproduced or transmitted in any form or by any means, electronic or mechanical, including photocopying, recording, or by any information storage and retrieval system without express written permission from the author/publisher.

> Elizabeth —
> To a fellow aspiring author — thanks for the encouragement over the years. Please accept this proof copy of Dream Catcher, but don't be too critical. It may not be the Great American Novel I set out to write so long ago, but it is American. I'd love to read with your own writing — I'd love to read what you've been working on.
>
> Phil

This book is dedicated to the memory of my mother, my father, my grandparents, and Yoopers everywhere

## Table of Contents

| | |
|---|---:|
| Prologue | 1 |
| Making Plans | 4 |
| Up North | 12 |
| The Straits | 20 |
| Dream Catcher | 28 |
| Iron Falls | 36 |
| Lake Cottage | 44 |
| God's Country | 52 |
| Rita and Ray | 60 |
| The Cave-in | 68 |
| Consequences | 75 |
| Change of Plans | 82 |
| Camping Out | 91 |
| The Boathouse | 99 |
| Bobber Lane | 107 |
| Ernie's Diner | 115 |
| The Bear | 124 |
| The Deer | 132 |
| Little Thunder | 140 |
| Boat Work | 149 |
| The Gibsons | 157 |
| The Storm | 165 |
| The Aftermath | 173 |
| Falls Park | 181 |
| Independence Day | 190 |
| Rescued | 198 |
| The Body | 207 |
| Hoops | 215 |
| Ghost Stories | 223 |
| Bobber's Cabin | 232 |
| Angie's Party | 239 |
| The Attack | 248 |
| Wounds | 256 |
| Missing | 264 |
| Break In | 273 |
| Confrontation | 280 |
| Loose Ends | 288 |
| Goodbyes | 297 |
| About the Author | 307 |

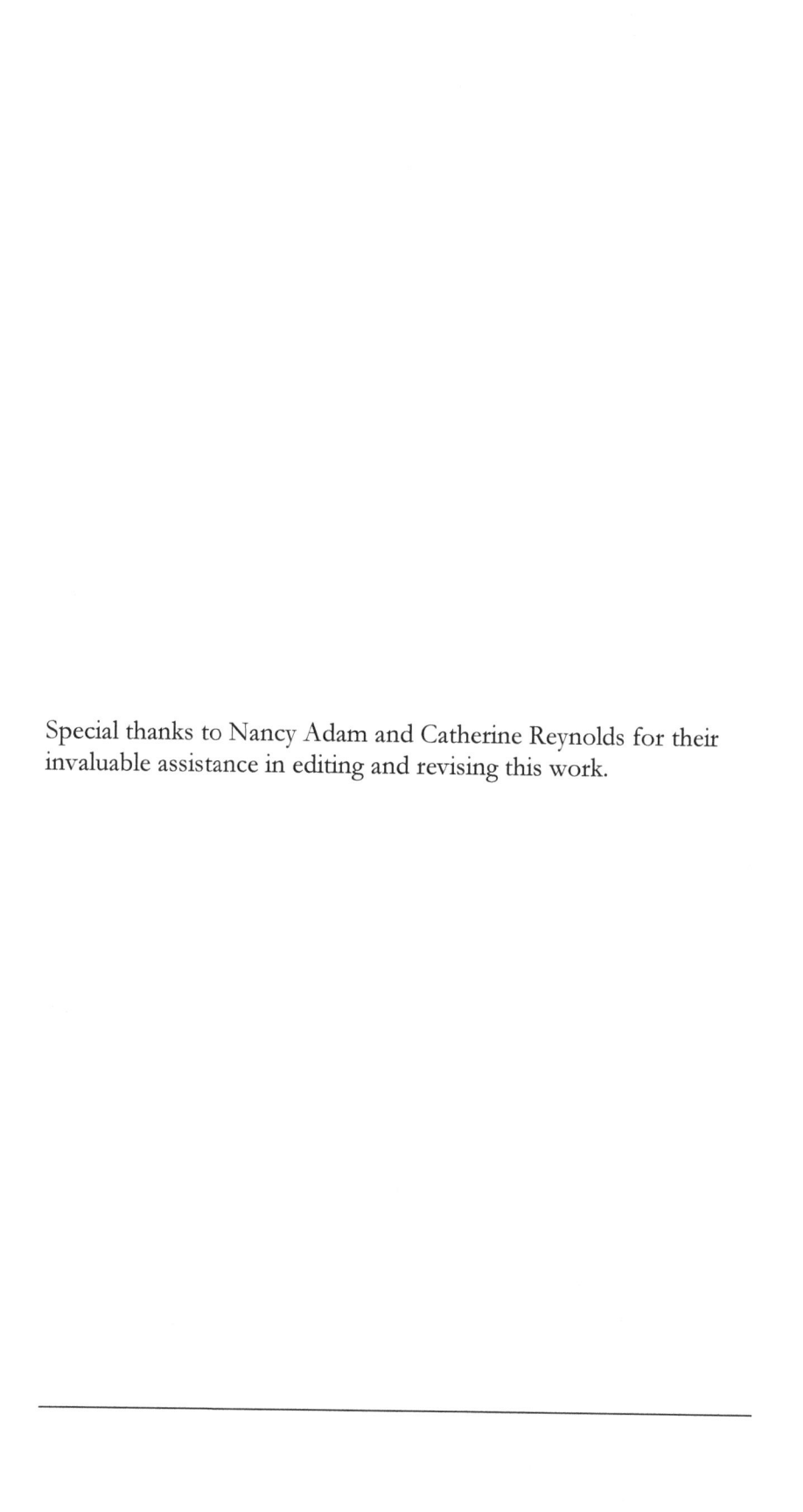

Special thanks to Nancy Adam and Catherine Reynolds for their invaluable assistance in editing and revising this work.

# Prologue

The storm came on suddenly, but not unexpectedly. The boy had been here before, many times, waiting for the storm to overwhelm him. Each time it was the same, yet each time it was different. No matter how often he had experienced the chill wind blasting his face or watched the storm moving inexorably forward, it never ceased to be new to him. It never ceased to terrify him.

Black clouds slithered along the Western horizon like a coiled serpent ready to strike. As the waves intensified, the small boat in which he sat began to heave and roll. Clear skies darkened, billowing clouds pushed in to cover the sun. Eerie cloud shadows created ghostly apparitions skittering across the surface of the water.

As the dark clouds swirled in, the color of the water beneath the boat began to deepen. The bright blue of the waves turned deeper and deeper in hue until no light at all was reflected from the cold black surface. The chill waters turned to ice, splashing frigid spray into the boy's face.

The storm advanced like an army, taking no hostages, canons of lightening blazing away indiscriminately at everything in their path. Lightning strikes in the distance illuminated patches of the landscape with brief flashes of brilliance. The birches and pines lining the shoreline suddenly took on a sinister, menacing aura, highlighted by the afterglow of the flashes.

Electricity filled the air. A tingling sensation filled his body. The hair on his head began to stick straight out. He knew that at any moment a bolt of lightening could strike him down.

He reached out, grasping for a paddle or an oar - anything he could use to propel himself toward the shore. But there was nothing. There was never anything. The shoreline had already begun to recede into the distance.

Pellets of hail bombarded the lake, turning the water's surface into a cratered war zone. The hail lashed at the boy's face and arms like tiny razors cutting into his skin. And when the hail finally subsided, it was replaced by the even more menacing threat of a torrential downpour. Rain began to drive down in sheets drenching the boat and its lone occupant.

The boy sat immobile, powerless to stop the storm's relentless approach. The boat beneath him began to creak and groan under the stress of the increasingly violent waves. He felt the surge of the whitecaps breaking against the fragile hull. He grabbed hold of the gunwales of the small craft trying to brace himself against the storm's fury. But a series of gigantic waves smashed the hull, one after another, sending the boy flying from his seat.

The boy thrust his arms into the turbulent waters, using his hands to paddle toward the shore, but the harder he paddled, the harder the wind pushed back, preventing him from making any progress.

Thick black coils of clouds now boiled across the heavens towards him. Lightening thundered and crashed on all sides. Flash after flash cut through the skies. The wind bullied and buffeted the small boat mercilessly, shoving it back and forth over the open water. The small craft was thrashed and battered by the huge waves. The constant roar of thunder assaulted his ears. Day had turned to night.

The wind began to howl, a mournful, haunting sound. Gusts of wind tore at the waves, whipping them into a frenzy of froth and foam. The boat beneath him began to moan, creaking and groaning under the stress of the torturous onslaught. Water rushed over the gunwales, slowly engulfing the small craft. The boy frantically tried to use his hands to bale out the hull, but it was no use.

He huddled down into the belly of the small craft seeking safety. A deafening roar filled the air. He looked up just in time to see a wall of water, towering over him like a huge hand, ready to reach down and crush him. The wave crashed into the side of the boat, smashing the hull, and splintering the wooden planks. The boy struggled to maintain his grip, but the wave overwhelmed him, tearing him from the relative safety of the boat. Abruptly, the boy flew over the side into the black, freezing waters of the lake. Tossed about like a piece of driftwood, he struggled to stay afloat, gasping for air. He tried to swim, but his arms felt like boat anchors pulling him down.

A dark indistinct shape broke the surface near him. He tried to make it out, but the looming presence vanished in the raging torrent. The boy struggled to keep his head above water. He grew increasingly aware that he was not alone. Something was in the water with him. He twisted his head around trying to catch a glimpse of whatever was lurking beneath the surface. He felt the presence drawing closer and closer. Something brushed his leg. He panicked, drawing in a mouthful of water, gagging him.

Suddenly he felt an unseen force grabbing at him, grasping his arms. He struggled to free himself, but the unseen force held him tightly. Something was drawing him down into the depths of the lake. He gasped, trying to take a deep breath before he disappeared under the surface, but managed only to choke on another mouthful of water. Then it was too late. His head was pulled beneath the surface. Deeper. Deeper.

# Making Plans

The boy screamed as loudly as he could. Again and again he screamed for help.

"David? David? Wake up. You're dreaming," the familiar voice summoned him from the depths of his terrifying vision. His mother. His mother was calling him.

David Bishop's eyes shot opened wide, his pulse still pounding. Slowly he began to recognize the familiar confines of his bedroom, leaving behind the terror of the dream world. He felt sweat running down his forehead. He reached up to wipe his brow with the sleeve of his pajamas.

"You were having a nightmare, but you're all right now," David's mother, Helen, tried to reassure her son.

Concern showed on Helen Bishop's face. She was a plain woman, more drab and colorless in appearance than she needed to be. She wore almost no makeup, and kept her dishwater blond hair pulled back in a bun. The black plastic sequined-rimmed glasses she wore on the bridge of her nose gave her the look of a dowdy matron rather than a loving mother who had just turned forty.

"You're safe at home," she comforted. "Nothing can hurt you here."

David listened to her soft, soothing voice drawing him back to wakefulness. It was morning. He was in his own bed, safe and unharmed. He tried to calm himself, taking deep breaths to relax. His mother stood over him, running her hand over the stubble of his short-cropped crew cut brown hair. "Are you all right, David?" she asked smiling. "You really had me going there for a minute, young man."

"I had the dream again," David tried to sound brave. "There was a storm up at the lake, and then something grabbed me and started pulling me under. It was so real."

"You know it's not real, David. None of it. You were having a bad dream-that's all." Helen removed her reading glasses, letting them dangle at the end of the chain she wore around her neck. "I hope you're not just using this dream thing as an excuse to get out of going on this trip."

She had a round, full face with pleasant features that betrayed her German ancestry. As a girl, growing up in Michigan's Upper Peninsula, her father often told her that she was the spitting image of her mother. But Helen had only faded photos and vague memories to judge the truth of that claim. Her mother had died when Helen was only thirteen, leaving her to be raised by her father.

Now she wanted to go home-she needed to go home, to visit, to rest. Her father, Carl, owned several small rustic cabins near Iron Falls, her hometown, and she had made arrangements with him to stay at his cottage on Spirit Lake with David. At least until things were settled.

"Mom, I don't want to go to the lake this year. It's not just the dream. If I go there something bad is going to happen, I know it."

Normally David didn't mind his family's annual journey north to his parent's hometown. Even the presence of his older cousins, Kyle and Kenny, didn't bother him all that much. Somehow he always managed to tolerate their belittling taunts and know-it-all attitudes. And he actually liked staying at his grandfather's cottage by the lake. Besides, the legend of the lake fascinated him. He had grown up knowing the story of Little Thunder, the ghost of the ancient warrior who still haunted the lake's crystal clear waters.

But this year was different. This year David's mother had decided to spend the entire summer - almost two full months - at the lake. And then the dreams had begun. The dreams that foretold disaster.

"Now don't be foolish," Helen said. "You're getting to be too old for such nonsense. Next year you'll be in junior high, for goodness sake. Is this any way for a seventh grader to act? You're just having bad dreams because you don't want to leave your friends here in LaSalle."

"No, Mom, I'm really scared. Please?"

"We've been planning this trip for weeks. Your grandfather is expecting us. He's fixed up the cottage for us and everything. Now start getting ready."

"But why do we have to be gone for so long? We always go for two weeks," David protested. He hated the idea of leaving LaSalle. He had already made plans with his friends. "How come we have to be gone all summer anyway? Can't I just stay here with dad?"

"You know you can't stay here. Your dad is busy at work. Besides I want you to have some time with your grandfather. He's not getting any younger, and I want you to get to know him better. Now go get cleaned up and dress. Breakfast will be waiting for you when you're done. You've still got to pack for the trip."

\*\*\*

At breakfast, David lingered over his bowl of Wheaties until the flakes grew soggy. Ever since team practice had started in March, David and his friends had thought about nothing but baseball. David played second base for the LaSalle Explorers, and the Explorers were in the thick of the 1957 Taylor County Little League championship race. But now his parents were forcing him to go on this stupid trip. If David left now, he would miss the chance to play for the title.

"You're wasting time," his mother interjected sternly. "Now get busy and pack before I get really angry."

"Ok, ok. I'll pack, but I still don't think it's fair," David said, knowing that there was no point in arguing. His mother refused to listen to him anyway. But maybe it wasn't too late, he thought. His friends wouldn't let him down - he was sure of it.

In his room, he pulled a tattered brown Samsonite suitcase out from under his bed, flipped open the latches, and lifted the lid. He pulled open his top dresser drawer and began moving an assortment of socks, tee shirts, and underwear into the empty case. Then he tossed in his Bermuda shorts, swimsuit, and a tattered old, gray sweatshirt. The case was filling up quickly.

He opened his closet, and began pulling shirts and pants off the hangers, throwing them unfolded into the suitcase. When he got to his new dress suit he hesitated. He knew that his mother would expect him to wear it to church every Sunday, but the wool blend was uncomfortable and scratchy. He really preferred his old blue blazer and dress slacks, even though they barely fit him any more. In the end he crammed both outfits into the case along with his patent leather dress shoes. By the time he'd finished, he could barely force the lid of the suitcase down and latch it closed.

David turned his attention to a large wooden storage chest at the foot of his bed. The chest contained a collection of Golden Books along with various pieces of sports equipment: a basketball, a football, several baseballs, a fielder's glove, and Mickey Mantle signature baseball bat. These were David's most prized possessions. He wasn't about to leave any of them behind. He grabbed a large bundle of baseball cards secured with a thick rubber band from the top of the dresser. Most of the cards were Detroit Tigers players - Al Kaline, Harvey Kuenn, Frank Bolling, and his favorite player, Ol' Paw Paw, Charlie Maxwell. He tucked the bundle of cards into the chest along with his Tigers baseball cap.

Next he needed to decide which music to take with him. David had gotten his own portable record player last Christmas, and even though the sound quality was not as good as his parent's Hi-Fi, at least he could play music he liked on it. After some discussion, his mother had agreed to let him take the player and a few 45s with him to the cottage. He sorted through his collection of 45-RPM records - Elvis Presley, Bill Haley and the Comets, Buddy Holly. He slid each 45 into its dust jacket, and carefully packed them into the chest.

During the entire process of packing, David kept listening expectantly for a knock at the door or a ring of the phone. Where were Jimmy and Al? Al Matthews and Jimmy Dewitt were David's best friends at school and his team mates on the Explorers. Why hadn't he heard from them yet? They had to come soon, he thought, otherwise the plan wouldn't work.

The plan was David's last hope of getting out of an entire summer banished to the north woods. Jimmy was the one who had come up with the idea, but it was Al who was key to its success. If Al didn't come through, the plan was doomed. But where were they? Why didn't they call? There was nothing David could do but wait.

By lunchtime, David began to worry. He had not heard anything from his friends, and it was getting late. He called Al's house, but the phone kept ringing. No one answered. He went into the living room and switched on the black and white TV, fiddling with the rabbit ears until the picture came in more clearly. WSPD, the NBC station in Toledo, was the only station people living in LaSalle could receive. Host Bill Leyden pointed to a woman in the studio audience, insisting that *It Could Be You!* David turned the TV off and went back to his room.

***

It was after three in the afternoon when David finally heard someone knocking at the front door downstairs. A few moments later, he heard his mother calling him, "David? Are you done packing? Your friends are here to see you."

He raced down the stairs to find Al and Jimmy waiting at the door.

"We're headed down to Martinelli's for some ice cream. Can David come?" Al asked. A born athlete, Al was deeply tanned from hours spent playing ball in the early summer sun.

"Please," David implored his mother.

"Well I suppose that would be all right. Just be back by dinner time." She reached for her purse, pulled out a dollar, and handed it to David. "Here's some money for ice cream, just bring me back the change."

It was only three blocks from David's house to the center of LaSalle. As the boys walked along the cracked sidewalk, past the boarded up Victorian mansion on the corner, they tossed a worn baseball back and forth.

"Well, how did it go?" David asked Al anxiously. "Did you talk to your mom?"

"Yeah. She said it was ok with her if your parents agree. It would be great. You could stay with us during the day while your dad's at work."

Their plan was simple. David would remain in LaSalle with his father, while his mom drove up North alone. Then he could ride up later in July when his dad left to join his mother at the lake cottage. That way he'd still be able to play ball with his friends. But in order to make his plan work, David would have to convince his parents that he could take care of himself. That's where Al came in. David would stay with Al and his family during the day while his dad was at work, then go home with his dad at night. The plan was flawless, but first David had to get his parents to agree.

At the main four corners, the boys crossed the street in front of the bank and continued walking by the Rexall Drug Store and Goldman's Dry Goods to reach Martinelli's restaurant. Over sodas, the three discussed David's options and prospects for staying in LaSalle.

"So, when you gonna ask your mom and dad about staying here in LaSalle?" Jimmy pressed David. A bout of rheumatic fever as an infant had left Jimmy with a weakened heart and a tendency to be slightly overweight. Consequently, Jimmy did not play for the Explorers, but served as the team's manager.

"I'll talk to them tonight at dinner,"

"We're counting on you, buddy," Jimmy said, putting his arm around David's shoulder. "Everybody knows you're the best second baseman in town. If you can't play, we'll just have to put Eddie on second, and he throws like a girl."

On the way home, David and his friends rehearsed the arguments he could use to convince his dad. David prospects of staying in LaSalle depended on persuading his father that his plan would work. Whatever Donald Bishop decided, his wife would agree to, even if she did so grudgingly.

***

By the time David returned to his house, it was already after five. A dark blue Chrysler with "Prescott Manufacturing" stenciled on the driver's side door sat in the driveway behind the family Chevy. David's father, Donald, was managing supervisor at Prescott, a company making truck frames for GM. Though it was against company rules, Donald often borrowed the company car for his own use.

As David entered the house through the back door, he found his mother busy preparing dinner in the kitchen. He continued through the dining area to the living room, where he knew he would find his father reading the *LaSalle Tribune*. Everyday his father's routine never varied. He came home, put on his slippers, got the paper from the front porch, sat down in his easy chair, put his feet up, and read the paper until dinner was ready.

"Can I talk to you for a minute, Dad?" he asked cautiously, hesitant to interrupt his father. When he was younger, David and his father had spent a lot of time together, playing catch or working in the yard. But now that he was older, David seldom saw his dad. Donald was too wrapped up in his job to take time for his wife and son.

"Is it important? I'm kind of busy right now."

Donald Bishop looked exactly like the typical middle-class businessman he was. The sleeves of his white Arrow dress shirt rolled up to the elbows, his collar unbuttoned, his wide blue and red striped necktie hung loosely around his neck. A thinning crop of brown hair flecked with gray skirted his balding head.

"It's about the trip..." David started.

"Look, David, I'm tired right now," his father interrupted. "It's been a long day. Can't this wait till after dinner? Go get ready to eat. We'll talk after supper, ok sport?"

Throughout dinner David waited for an opportunity to talk to his father about his idea, but each time he was about to bring up the plan, his father started talking about something that happened at work.

Dinner was over before the subject of the trip finally came up. After they finished eating, David's father took two *Chesterfields* from the pack in his shirt pocket, lit both with a single match, and handed one to his wife. He took a deep puff, and then looked over to address his son.

"Ok, bud," he said addressing David. "What's this I hear about you not wanting to go with your mother?" Donald asked.

Suddenly, all of David's carefully planned arguments escaped him, and he looked blankly at his father. Finally he blurted out, "I want to stay here with you, Dad. Mom can drive up now, and I can come up with you in a few weeks."

"'Fraid not kiddo," answered his father, taking a puff of his cigarette and inhaling deeply. "I have to work all day at the plant. There'd be no one here to watch you, and you're too young to take care of yourself."

"I am not. I'm twelve. I can take care of myself just fine," David replied defiantly. "And besides, Al's mom said I could stay there while you were at work."

"Al's mom? Since when did Al's mom have anything to do with this? Did you talk to her about this?" Helen asked confused.

"No, really. I didn't talk to her - Al asked her if it would be all right. You can call her if you don't believe me."

"I'm not calling anyone, young man," his mother stated emphatically. "This is a family matter, and the decision has already been made. I'm leaving tomorrow morning, and you're coming with me. Do you understand me?"

"But it's only a couple of weeks. Just till the end of Little League season…"

"Look, we've been through this before," his dad replied, his voice beginning to show his irritation. "You'll just have to go with your mother. I'm sure they have Little League up in Iron Falls too."

"I'll bet they don't even know how to play baseball up there," David replied stubbornly. "I'm not going. You can't make me!"

David's father lost his patience, his face growing red with anger. "You're going with your mother, and that's the end of it," he shouted. He threw his napkin down on the table, pushed his chair back, and stormed out of the room, ending the conversation.

"It's not fair," David yelled, breaking into tears. "I hate you!" Angrily he pushed his chair away from the table, ran up the stairs to his room, rushed in, and slammed the door behind him. The decision had now been made, and David knew that he had no choice but to comply with his father's orders. He sulked for most of the evening. Fully clothed, he lay down on top of his single bed, fuming, unable to sleep.

It was well after midnight when he heard the voices coming from his parent's room. Subdued at first, his mother and father had begun another one of their "discussions." In the Bishop household, "discussion" was the polite euphemism that David's parents used for their periodic fights. Over the past few months, these discussions had escalated from occasional quarrels, to more frequent arguments, to all out shouting matches. David frequently lay awake listening to the harsh insults filtering through the paper-thin walls. Though indistinct, their bitter words penetrated David's consciousness.

David pulled a pillow over his head to muffle the sound. Even after the talking stopped, he lay awake wondering what would come next.

## Up North

The night passed slowly. David slept very little. He did not dream at all. He glanced at the clock next to his bed to see what time it was - almost three o'clock. He checked again at four, and then at five, before finally getting up just after six. He dressed quickly and made his way downstairs to the kitchen, where his mother was already busy preparing breakfast.

"Good morning, Mom," he said coming up beside her to give her a kiss on the cheek.

"My, my, you're up bright and early, young man," she replied. "You must be feeling better." There was no sign in her voice that she was upset by whatever had transpired between her and his father the previous evening. "Are you all ready to go?"

"I didn't sleep very well last night," he replied evasively.

"Did you have the dream again?"

David thought for a moment. If he told her the truth, that he had heard his parents arguing, she would be even more upset. So he lied. "Yeah, I had the dream."

"Well, you can always take a nap in the car on the way," his mother said sympathetically. "Now sit down and have some toast and eggs. Your father will be down in a minute. We've got to get going if we want to make the Straits by dinner time."

Breakfast was eaten in almost complete silence. David watched his parents closely. They barely spoke to each other, and seemed to be avoiding eye contact.

After breakfast, David's father directed him to take the suitcases out to the family car. He hauled the bags to the car, and threw his own suitcase along with his mother's into the trunk of the yellow and green two-tone Chevy Bel Air sedan, and slammed the trunk lid shut. His mother had packed a basket of snacks and a picnic lunch, which he placed, carefully on the floor in the back seat. When everything was ready, Donald walked with his wife and son to the Chevy to say goodbye.

David watched as his father reached out to grasp his mother's shoulders, pulling her close. As Donald leaned in to give his wife a parting kiss, Helen turned her head so that the kiss became a brief peck on her cheek. Donald released her shoulders and stepped back slightly. "Be sure to call as soon as you reach your dad's, all right?" he instructed his wife. "Just let it ring four times then hang up. I'll know it's you."

David parents had worked out a code to save long distance charges when they were apart. Rather than answering an incoming call immediately, they would wait four rings. If the caller hung up, they would know everything was all right. It the phone rang more than four times, it was someone else calling, and they would answer.

Donald bent down to hug his son. "Take care of your mother, all right, David?"

Donald waved briefly to David as Helen backed the car out of the driveway, then he turned and walked back into the house even before the Chevy drove off down the street.

***

Muted shades of pink and purple colored the ribbons of clouds in the eastern sky over LaSalle as Helen turned the corner from Grove Street onto Main. She drove past the bank, the Rexall Drug Store, Goldman's Dry Goods, and Martinelli's where David and his friends had walked the day before. The streets were practically deserted. The pedestal clock in front of the bank indicated that it was just before seven.

Helen took a sip of coffee from the large brown mug she had filled just before leaving the house. David looked at her, trying to guess her mood.

They drove past the newly completed LaSalle High School building. In three more years David knew he would be entering the school as a sophomore, but until then he and his classmates would be relegated to the old junior high school building.

In the right corner of the new high school, stood a huge cement block engraved with the year "1957." David and his father had been present at the dedication ceremony, where the mayor had helped seal a time capsule into the school wall behind the block. Inside the capsule was an odd assortment of items, some of which David and his classmates had helped to select. His favorites included a Davy Crockett coonskin hat, a plastic disk called a Wham-O Frisbee, a Wiffle ball, a pair of two-toned saddle shoes, a 45 copy of Elvis Presley's number one single "All Shook Up," and a walking-spring device known as a Slinky.

According to the inscription on the time capsule, it would not be opened again for fifty years, not until the year 2007. By then David would be as old as his grandfather. He could not imagine ever being that old.

As they reached the outskirts of LaSalle, they passed the Prescott Plant. Smoke billowed from the smoke stacks of the factory, as it did practically twenty-four hours a day. The seven o'clock shift-change had just taken place, and the night shift were piling into their cars and heading out of the parking lot toward their homes. In another hour David's dad would be heading for the plant.

What was going on between his parents, David wondered. They argued almost all the time now. He felt that his dad loved him, but sometimes it was hard to know that for sure. And now this trip. David wished he could turn back time to when he was younger. He had been happy then, and so had his parents. Then they had done everything together, as a family. Now he was not sure about anything.

"Cat got your tongue?" Helen prodded her son. "You're not very talkative today. A penny for your thoughts."

David smiled, but said little. "You'd be wasting your money, Mom. I guess I'm just not awake enough to talk yet."

"Well, if you change your mind, let me know. It's a long drive to the Straits, and I could use some company."

***

The route from LaSalle to Michigan's Upper Peninsula led along US 223 through Adrian to US 127 then north toward Lansing. Traffic was light as she drove through the seemingly endless fields of corn that formed a checkerboard along Michigan's southern border with Ohio.

At first, David kept busy doing crossword puzzles and connect-the-dots in the newsprint activity books his mother had purchased for him before leaving LaSalle. When he tired of the books he watch the scenery pass by. David sat solemnly starring out the passenger side window at the rapidly changing landscape.

Nearing Lansing, however, rows of post World War II tract houses, sprouted up along the highway. As Helen drove toward the heart of Michigan's capital, the trickle of traffic became a steady stream. Helen had hoped that by arriving in Lansing after rush hour she would avoid the traffic and congestion normal around large urban areas, but nearing the city limit, new road construction caused traffic to slow almost to a halt.

She tapped the steering wheel nervously, frustrated by the lack of progress. Traffic inched forward. She extinguished the butt of her still glowing cigarette in the Chevy's ashtray, and reached into her handbag for another *Lucky Strike*. David countered by rolling down his window completely, hoping the light breeze would clear the car of the fog of smoke. It took more than an hour for them to plod haltingly through the maze of roadwork and mid-morning shopping congestion, moving haltingly from one traffic light to the next.

Once she reached the outskirts of the city she pulled into a Mobil station to fill up with gas and stretch her legs. "I need to use the bathroom, Mom," David exclaimed as they pulled up to the pump.

"Go ahead, but be quick about it," Helen replied. "We won't be stopping long."

By the time he returned, the station attendants had already filled the tank, checked the oil, and the air in the tires. As he got back into the car, Helen looked over at her son, concern showing in her face.

"David? You've still hardly said a word since we left LaSalle. Are you feeling all right, darling?"

"Yeah, I'm ok. I just don't have much to say, that's all."

"Well if you're not going to talk, how 'bout turning on the radio, and finding a station we can both listen to."

David clicked on the Chevy's am radio and waited for the vacuum tubes to warm up. He turned up the volume only to hear the static of a local LaSalle station, now miles away in the distance. He began to fiddle with the tuning knob, trying to find a nearby station that was not all news. David knew that his mother favored singers like Patti Page and Teresa Brewer, or crooners like Frank Sinatra and Bing Crosby. But sometimes she would listen to songs by the Everly Brothers or Elvis Presley, and those were the songs David preferred. With a twist of the dial, Buddy Holly's *Wake Up Little Susie* replaced *Tammy* by Hollywood star Debbie Reynolds.

As the traffic congestion of Lansing faded in the distance, the miles began to roll by more quickly. Not far from Lansing's growing suburbs US 127 merged with route 27 coming up from Indiana. The landscape began to change, the burgeoning housing developments giving way to more farmland, planted with corn, wheat, and alfalfa.

Farther north these flat farmlands gradually turned into low rolling hills - moraines carved into the rocky soil by retreating glaciers thousands of years before the first European settlers arrived. It had been the glaciers that created the shape of Michigan's mitten, carving out the Great Lakes and the two peninsulas that formed Michigan's unique profile.

***

By the time they reached Houghton Lake, it had been over two hours since his mother had stopped for gas near Lansing. David squirmed in his seat, now both tired and hungry.

"Mom, when are we gonna stop?" he complained. "We've been driving a long time and I'm starving."

"Well, so, the silent one speaks. I was beginning to think you'd lost your voice." For a few moments, Helen paused to consider the situation. "I'll tell you what," she said at last. "I'll stop and fix us some lunch, if you'll promise to keep me company and talk to me. Is it a deal?"

"Yeah, sure, Mom," David smiled. "I could do that."

"Great - keep your eyes open, and we'll stop at the next picnic area you see."

David kept watch as his mother drove. It was not long before he found what he was looking for. "There it is - there's a pull off coming up in a half mile," he announced enthusiastically.

Helen noted the direction her son was pointing, pulled off into the roadside picnic area, and parked the Chevy in the shade of a large oak tree. The day had already become uncomfortably hot in the midday sun. "Go ahead and take the picnic basket to the table. I'll get the cooler." When they traveled, David's mother always prepared a basket for the road, packing sandwiches, cookies, fruit, and ice-cold punch for lunch. David grabbed the basket and took it to a table in the shade of another huge oak tree.

Helen threw a tablecloth over the top of the rough-hewn table, spreading it smooth with her hands. She took the basket from David and opened the top, pulling our several sandwiches wrapped in wax paper, a box of Ritz crackers, a jar of pickles, and a bunch of grapes. She unwrapped one of the sandwiches and handed it to David. "It's bologna and cheese. Go ahead - there's a jar of mustard and knife in the basket."

As he rummaged in the basket for the knife, David spotted a bag of New Era potato chips crunched into the corner. "Can I have some chips, Mom?" he asked.

"Sure. I was saving them for the ferry ride, but if you're hungry, go ahead."

He gulped down the sandwich greedily, saving the chips until he had finished. He completed the meal by devouring several oatmeal cookies Helen had made especially for the trip, and washing them down with a large glass of fruit punch flavored Kool-Aid.

"Well, you must be feeling better. Do you feel good enough to tell me what's going on? You haven't said more than two words to me all day. Why don't you tell me what's bothering you, sweetheart? Is it about what happened last night?"

"I'm sorry about last night, Mom."

"Sorry? You don't need to be sorry."

"Yes I do. I told dad I hated him. I don't really hate him."

"I know you don't, honey - and so does he. It just slipped out, that's all. We all say things we don't really mean when we're angry."

"But isn't that why you and dad were fighting last night? I heard you."

"You heard? What did you hear, David?"

"You and dad were yelling. I couldn't understand what you were saying, but you sounded like you were mad at each other."

"I'm sorry we disturbed you, dear. Is that why you didn't sleep last night?"

"Yeah, I guess so."

"No bad dreams?"

"No, not last night. I just couldn't sleep, that's all. I thought you were fighting about me."

"No, no. Of course not, David" Helen said, reaching out to stroke his hair. "It's just that your father and I have been having some problems lately."

"Is that why we're taking this trip without dad?"

"In a way," Helen said thoughtfully. "We both need some time alone - to think things out. When your grandfather called and invited us up, I thought it might give us both - your dad and I - the time we need."

"Are you and dad going to get a divorce?"

Helen looked over at her son, now genuinely surprised. She

thought that she and Donald had been able to conceal their marital problems from their son. "What ever gave you that idea? We just need some time that's all. We'll work things out. You'll see." Helen began to repack the remaining food. "Why don't you finish up and we'll get back on the road."

***

When they finished eating and returned to the car to resume their drive, neither David nor Helen pursued their lunchtime conversation. There had been much left unsaid, but neither of them wanted to confront the real issues involved. Instead they discussed other matters: David's coming school year, the nearly completed Mackinaw Bridge, and whether the Detroit Tigers had any chance to win the American League pennant. David's mood brightened as the miles slipped by.

Helen continued to follow US 27 as it pushed northward. Semis and trucks vied with passenger cars for space along the two-lane blacktop road. Often traffic slowed to a crawl as tank trucks and Greyhound busses blocked faster traffic in a hurry to reach destinations far from Detroit's hustle and bustle. Speed traps located in villages and small towns lining the route further impeded progress, often slowing movement to a snail's pace. Near Camp Grayling military base, a convoy of olive drab trucks and jeeps, fifty or sixty vehicles long, held up traffic for almost an hour, enraging motorists.

By the time they reached Gaylord, David was ready for a stop at the Sugar Bowl Restaurant, one of his favorite places to get homemade ice cream. Every year on the long trip north, David's parents would stop for double-dip cones. His parents always got plain old vanilla, but David preferred strawberry. They sat on a bench in front of the restaurant, licking their ice cream to keep it from dripping, until only the wafer cones remained.

Returning to their car, David suddenly began to feel the effects of the long day on the road. "Mom, I'm kinda tired. Would it be all right if I took a little nap?" he asked.

"I'm surprised you made it this far," she agreed. "Why don't you sleep in the back the rest of the way? We should be at the Straits in an hour or so."

David got into the backseat, trying to make himself comfortable by propping himself up on pillows set against the locked passenger door. When he was younger he had been able to stretch out on the backseat, his feet never touching the opposite door. Now, however, he had to keep his knees pulled up toward his chest in order to conform his growing body to the space constraints of the car's interior. As the journey resumed, he could feel the motion of the tires rolling along the road beneath him.

He put his head down on the pillow and pulled a plaid wool blanket over his legs. He watched out the side window as the miles slipped by. Mile after mile, pine and spruce forests lined the sculptured green hills. David felt himself drawn into the hypnotic rhythm of the passing landscape. He began to relax. Slowly his eyes closed, and within moments he was asleep.

David found himself once again adrift on the placid waters of Spirit Lake when the storm hit. As before, gigantic waves lashed the small boat, sweeping him into the turbulent waters. Something moved in the waters around him as he fought to stay afloat. Everything was moving in slow motion. Then he felt himself being pulled down into the watery abyss.

But once again he heard his mother's voice calling him, pulling him back. Saving him.

"We're here David. We've arrived. We're at the Straits of Mackinaw," she said.

## The Straits

The Straits of Mackinac was land's end, the point at which Lakes Michigan and Huron touched. Located at the tip of Michigan's "mitt", Mackinaw City thrived on souvenir sales, fudge shops, smoked fish, pasties and endless lines of cars. David liked the fudge, but he didn't like the inevitable, interminable lines waiting for the ferries.

Car ferries constituted the only means of transporting people and goods from one side of the Straits to the other. As they arrived at the ferry terminal, attendants directed Helen to park the Chevy at the end David saw that cars were lined up row after row, far out into the massive parking lot. One of the older ferries, the *City of Petoskey*, was beginning to board. He watched as cars drove onto the aging vessel in a steady stream. His family had traveled aboard the *Petoskey* many times. It was small and cramped.

David was hoping to travel on the *Vacationland*, the newest, most modern ferry carrying cars and passengers across the Straits. As the *Petoskey* pulled away from the dock, David watched the horizon, waiting for the *Vacationland* to arrive. He knew that this might be one of the last times he would ever cross the Straits on a ferry. The age of the ferries was about to come to an end. By autumn the long lines of cars waiting at terminals would be a thing of the past. After years of planning and construction, the magnificent Mackinaw Bridge was nearing completion. When it opened, the ferries would cease to exist. Beautiful ships like the *Vacationland* would become extinct - like the dinosaurs, David thought.

But until the bridge opened, there was nothing to do but wait for the next crossing. The stifling heat of the day made sitting idly in the car oppressive. David opened the passenger door to let in some air. Car-to-car vendors paced the long lines of cars hawking smoked fish, soft drinks, and ice cream. Helen bought a chunk of smoked fish and two ice cream bars. David picked needle-sharp bones out of the fish, savoring the delicate smoked flavor as ever-present sea gulls circled overhead waiting for stray morsels of bread or fish. After consuming all of the fish he could eat, David quickly devoured his ice cream before it had time to drip away.

At last the gleaming white vessel sailed into view. The

*Vacationland* glided into the dock almost silently, and then at the last minute gave out a tremendous blast from the ship's horn to signal its arrival. David continued to watch until the huge transport ship tied up and the signal was given for cars to begin boarding. Helen started the Chevy, following the line of cars across the ramp onto the main deck and into the belly of the powerful craft.

***

As soon as the car was parked below decks on the ferry, a deckhand ran up and grabbed a chain anchored to the deck, and hooked it to the axle under the car. No one was allowed out of the cars until the attendants signaled that they could leave. The instant the deckhand gave the go ahead, David opened the passenger door, scrambled out of his seat and began to run across the sheet metal deck plates.

"Don't run!" called his mother. "And wait for me."

He waited, and together they made their way through the maze of cars to the narrow stairways leading to the upper deck.

Another loud blast of the ship's horn announced that the ferry was about to leave the dock. As the ship moved out into the channel of the Straits, the waves began to buffet the hull, rocking the huge ferry from side to side. David could feel the motion churning his stomach as he watched the horizon move up and down through the porthole. The *Vacationland* rolled heavily through the Straits as another huge whitecap struck the hull. A wave of nausea swept over David. He ran his hand through his hair, sighed deeply, and squirmed restlessly on the plastic seat of the bench.

The passenger lounges were furnished with Spartan accommodations - long narrow straight-backed benches covered with Naugahyde. The quarters weren't meant to be luxurious, just adequate for the half hour crossing from Mackinaw City to St. Ignace. The room was full of people. Some were reading newspapers or paperback books to pass the time on the brief journey. A few had lunches in brown paper sacks or just some cookies or snacks. Helen took a seat on one of the narrow benches and pulled a copy of **Saturday Evening Post** magazine out of her bag and began to read.

David sat nervously on the bench next to his mother trying to ignore the cloud of cigarette smoke filling the room. An acrid, bitter fog of smoke engulfed the youth. He was used to the hazy smoke cloud and foul smell, but today the smell was making him feel queasy.

Helen put down the copy of the **Post**, took a *Lucky* out of her handbag, and proceeded to light it. She drew the smoke deeply into her lungs with a satisfied expression on her face, and then exhaled, blowing smoke directly at David. He choked slightly, trying to use his hand to fan away the fumes.

Reaching to pick up her magazine, Helen noticed how pale David had suddenly become. "Are you all right?" she asked with a mother's concern.

"I'm fine, mother," David managed to cough. He had to suppress an urge to heave the contents of his stomach all over his mother's neatly pleated flower print dress. "Just a little upset stomach," he said pulling himself upright in his seat. "I think I had too much smoked fish back at the ferry dock."

Helen flicked an ash from her cigarette into an ashtray beside the bench. "I warned you about the fish," she said. "I told you not to eat so much."

Again the ship swayed, and again the nausea rocked the boy. He struggled to control his heaving stomach, not wanting to show his mother how sick he really felt.

"I think I'll be ok if I can just get some air," he assured her. "I'll just go out on deck for a few minutes till I feel better."

"Do you want me to come with you," she asked.

"Naw, you wait here. I'll be all right. Really."

David rose unsteadily to his feet, and staggered toward the hatchway in the bulkhead leading out onto the fore deck. The motion of the ship made David lurch forward from side to side like a drunken sailor as his mother watched uneasily. She wanted to help, but knew that it would be better if she let the young man take care of this problem on his own. She sat and watched as David struggled to push the heavy hatch door open against the stiff wind blowing through the Straits.

***

It took all the strength he could muster for David to force the massive metal door open against the steady breeze off the Lake. The wind felt even stronger and colder as he walked out onto the deck. Few passengers had been brave enough to venture out in the cold harsh winds blowing across the waters. On a calm day the deck would have been teaming with passengers eager to point and gawk at the vast expanse of the Mackinaw Bridge.

Already the newly constructed approaches to the bridge reached far out into the frigid waters of the Straits from both shores like giant fingers. Between these fingers, twin towers reached up over 500 feet into the sky. Massive cables of twisted wire, stretching over 7,000 feet from pier to pier, connected the towers. And now the latest additions, large sections of roadway trusses hung from the cables, balanced precariously from the towers like arms of a giant teeter-totter.

David watched as a huge barge maneuvered another enormous section of truss into place beneath the north tower. When the last sections of roadway were in place, and the bridge opened to traffic in the fall, the Mackinaw Bridge would become the longest suspension bridge in the world.

Today, the only other people David could see on deck were a man and woman standing at the rail and gazing out at the "Mighty Mac" as the bridge had become known. The man held up a Brownie camera, lifted the viewfinder, looked down to frame the shot, and snapped his picture. The woman looked as if she would rather have been inside the cabin than out on deck.

Feeling increasingly ill, David made his way to the rail. Another surge of nausea racked his body, twisting his stomach into a knot and causing him to gag. He knew he wouldn't be able to contain the urge to heave much longer. He leaned over the rail as far as possible, retching violently, uncontrollably. As he did, the winds picked up, blowing the vomit back onto the deck, landing in part on David's tennis shoes.

Embarrassed, David looked up, checking to see if anyone around him had noticed. The man and woman who had been standing by the rail were now walking away, the man's arm wrapped around the woman shielding her from the bitter winds. They were too preoccupied keeping warm to notice David. He looked in the other direction. No one was around. David felt relieved and stooped down to wipe off his shoe.

\*\*\*

"You all right, son?" The voice came from behind him, startling David. He turned to see a rugged looking man wearing a stocking hat and plaid wool-hunting jacket staring at him with concern. The man appeared to be about his mother's age, and not much taller than David himself, but with a lean muscular build, like an athlete.

"I think I ate some bad fish," David mumbled apologetically trying to cover up his unease and embarrassment.

"Hey, it happens, kid," said the man holding out a clean handkerchief to David. "You should'a seen me last weekend. I got so shitfaced I couldn't see straight. Almost tossed my cookies myself."-

The man's vulgar language surprised David. He wasn't used to adults swearing in front of kids. Once and a while David's dad said 'damn' or 'hell' but only if he thought no one else was around, and David had never heard his mother use bad language.

David took the handkerchief from the man and wiped the residue from his mouth. He folded the kerchief to enclose the soiled section of cloth, and then handed it back to the man. "Sorry about the mess," he offered lamely.

"No problem," the man replied. "My name's Tom, Thomas Wainwright," he said, "but folks round here call me Little Tom."

"You don't look that little to me," replied David.

The man laughed. "Yeah, well, lots of guys up here have nicknames. Kinda goes with the territory. What's yours?"

"No nickname. I'm just David - David Bishop. What do ya mean nicknames 'go with the territory'? What territory?"

"You're looking at it," said Tom pointing toward the skeleton of the Mackinaw Bridge. "Over there - the bridge, you know? Most of the guys I work with have some sort of nickname."

"You mean you built the bridge?" David exclaimed, his interest heightened. David considered himself something of an expert on the bridge, having watched it take shape on his family's annual trips to the U.P., but he had never before actually met anyone who had worked on the immense span.

The man laughed softly shaking his head. "Well, I must admit, I had some help. A lot of folks worked on that bridge. I'm just one of the crowd."

"My dad says that once the bridge is open the ferries are going to be a thing of the past - 'as dead as the dinosaurs' he says," David quoted.

"Yeah, the way I see it, the bridge is the future of this state," Tom replied in agreement. "It's going to bring us all together

-Yoopers and down-staters. It'll put the Upper Peninsula on the map." 'Yoopers' was the euphemistic term people who lived in Michigan's Upper Peninsula, or U.P., used to identify themselves.

"My mom doesn't think so. She doesn't think the bridge is safe. She talks like she's an engineer or somethin'. She swears that she'll never drive across the bridge."

"People who think the bridge is dangerous don't know what they're talking about," Wainwright said. "That bridge is one of the safest in the world."

"I think that the real reason Mom won't cross the bridge is cuz she's scared of heights. She thinks she'll get blown off."

"Tell your mom she doesn't have a thing to worry about. Wind blows right through the bridge. They designed it that way. When the wind blows, it goes right through the grates. When you're up on the towers, you can barely feel it sway at all."

"You've been up there - on the towers I mean?"

"Yeah, me and a few hundred other guys," Tom said modestly.

"Weren't you scared up there?"

"Hey, the first time I went up one of those towers, it scared the crap out of me. But you get use to it."

"My dad says one of the workmen fell from one of those towers into the wet cement at the base, and they just left him buried in there."

"Yeah, I heard that one too, but don't believe everything you hear," Tom replied. He looked uncomfortable continuing the conversation. Instead he tried changing the subject. "Sounds like you and your folks come up to the U.P. a lot," he said.

"Yeah. We - me and my family - come up here at least once a year. Sometimes more. My parents are from Iron Falls, that's over near the Wisconsin border."

"I know where that is - along US 2. I drove through there a couple of years ago. Are you traveling with your family now?"

"Just my mom." David glanced back toward the waiting room where he had left his mother. The man followed David's eyes, looking through the porthole where a rather plain looking woman sat smoking a cigarette and reading a magazine. "Is that her?" he asked nodding toward the figure inside.

"Yeah, that's her," David verified. "I'm going to spend the summer with her at my grandpa's cottage on the lake. He owns some cabins a few miles from Iron Falls. My parents and I go up there every year, and it's always just the same. My dad's supposed ta come up later."

"You don't seem very happy about going," the man sounded curious. "I take it this trip wasn't your idea."

"Not really," David said hesitantly. He was still not sure he could trust the man standing before him. "My grandfather owns some cabins on a lake, and there's not much to do up there. Just fishing - that's all my grandpa likes to do. My parents and I go up there every year, and it's always just the same. The lake's pretty nice, but... well..."

"But you don't want to be away from your friends all summer - is that it?"

"Yeah, especially since I don't know anyone up there," David responded.

"Hey, I know the feeling," Little Tom said sympathetically. "Everytime I have to go to a new job site, I end up making friends all over again."

"Mind if I ask you a question?" David asked tentatively, beginning to let his guard down a bit.

"Go ahead, shoot."

"Did you ever have bad dreams?"

"Bad dreams? You mean like nightmares? Sure I have 'em once and a while. Everybody does."

"Does everybody have the same dream over and over?"

"You're having some kind a nightmare, eh? What kind of dream is it?"

"It's really awful. I'm all alone in a boat up at my grandpa's lake when this huge storm comes up. The boat starts to get tossed around, and I get thrown into the water, then something starts chasing me..."

"Sounds kinda scary. You want to get rid of those dreams? What you need's a dream catcher."

"Dream catcher? What's that?"

"The Indians up here use them to ward off bad dreams like yours. They hang them by their beds at night to make sure that they only have good dreams."

The horn of the *Vacationland* sounded two loud blasts drowning out Tom's comments. "We'll be docking in St. Ignace in a couple of minutes."

"Yeah, well, I'd better get back inside. My mom'll start to worry if I'm gone too long."

"Are you feeling ok now?" Tom asked the boy.

Since he had started talking to Tom, David hadn't thought at all about being sick. "Yeah, I'm ok. Sorry I threw up and everything."

"No problem, David," Little Tom held out his hand toward the young man. "It was very nice to meet you. Maybe the bridge will be open by the time you come back. And remember what I told you about getting a dream catcher, ok?"

David shook the man's hand and smiled. "Ok, thanks." He turned and went back into the cabin area.

By the time he reentered the ship's lounge, his mother was just finishing her magazine article and was snuffing out the butt of her cigarette in the ashtray beside the bench. "Time to go now, David," she said. "We have a long trip ahead of us."

"I know, Mom," replied David sadly.

He turned to take one last look at the bridge through the small porthole above the bench. It would be a long time before David would see the bridge again. Over two months. By then Tom and his coworkers would be almost finished. Maybe the bridge would even be open when they came back. Already it seemed like he had been gone an eternity. David took a last glance then turned to follow his mother down the narrow stairway to the car-park deck two floors below.

# Dream Catcher

It was already late afternoon by the time the Vacationland docked in St. Ignace. As David and his mother returned below decks to their car, Helen seemed concerned about her son. "You're looking a bit peaked, David," she said. "Are you feeling all right?"

"I'll be ok, Mom," he replied. "I'm just a little woozy from the boat ride, that's all. Do you think we'll be stopping soon?"

"I was thinking that we could stop here in St. Ignace," she answered, "if that's all right with you."

"That would be great, Mom," David said, a look of relief crossing his face.

"Good," she said. "We can get a room at the Birch Bark - it's close to downtown. Once we get settled, we'll grab a bite to eat and get a good night's rest. In the morning we'll both feel better."

St. Ignace was one of David's favorite towns in the Upper Peninsula. He knew the town's history practically by heart. Founded in 1671 by Father Jacques Marquette, Saint Ignace was a center of trade between the French and Ojibwa natives who once inhabited the straits area. In modern times, St. Ignace had become the gateway to the Upper Peninsula - the jumping off point for tourists heading for the Soo Locks, Pictured Rocks, Tahquamenon Falls, and nearby Mackinac Island.

As Helen drove off the ferry and turned toward town, David could just make out the outline of Mackinaw Island in the distance. David loved the island. It reminded him of happier times. Visiting Mackinaw Island was like traveling to an earlier time and place. No cars were permitted on the island, making it a haven for pedestrians and bicyclists alike. Before becoming Michigan's first state park, Mackinac Island had briefly been America's second national park.

When he was younger David's parents would often stop at the island on their annual pilgrimage to Iron Falls. David wished that this were one of those earlier trips - he wished he could go back to a time when his parents loved each other and they were a real family.

The Birch Bark Motel wasn't one of David's favorite places, but he had to admit it was within easy walking distance of the heart of downtown St. Ignace. Built in the thirties, the motel was showing its age, but still provided clean rooms with reasonably comfortable beds close to the attractions of downtown St. Ignace.

By the time David and his mother arrived, only a few rooms remained vacant. There were no more rooms with two beds available, so they checked in to a large varnished pine room with one double bed and a hide-a-bed sofa. The couch would serve as David's bed for the night.

After unpacking, David and his mother walked into town, stopping at the Burger Basket Café where David ordered a double cheeseburger with fries. "Can we go to Indian Village?" David asked his mother as he gulped down a huge mouthful of hamburger.

David's mother scowled in disapproval. Although Indian Village billed itself as a museum of Indian lore and folk art, much of the store's merchandise represented an odd assortment of authentic native crafts and cheap imported novelty items.

"Why do you always want to go to that awful place?" she asked. David's room in LaSalle was already filled with drums, bows, and beaded baskets from previous trips. "Wouldn't you rather see some real artifacts - like the ones at the Father Marquette museum?" Father Jacque Marquette had been one of the first Europeans to explore the Great Lakes region, and his story inspired a storefront museum in St. Ignace celebrating his life. But Helen's arguments fell on deaf ears. David was determined to go to Indian Village. Ever since talking to Little Tom onboard the *Vacationland*, David wanted nothing more than to get a dream catcher of his own.

***

Above the road along State Street, an Indian brave stood resolutely shooting brightly colored neon arrows toward a long narrow metal building covered with cedar bark shingles. Near the brave, a neon teepee announced the entrance to the *Indian Village*, a St. Ignace landmark as long as anyone in the area could remember. According to locals, the building had been built on the exact spot where missionary Father Marquette landed in 1671.

Now only two or three canvas, cone-shaped teepees occupied the grounds, standing before a long, narrow bark covered building. David knew that teepees had been used by Plains Indians, not the natives of Michigan's North Country. Still, the Indian Village was David's favorite store in the entire Upper Peninsula.

A mannequin made up to look like a cigar store Indian stood on the porch of the building, inviting visitors to enter. The mannequin was dressed as an Indian brave in buckskins with a full feather headdress. Like the teepees outside, the brave's attire was more suitable to the Great Plains than to the wilds of Northern Michigan. David followed the brave's posed invitation to step inside. The interior of the building consisted of a series of white birch posts supporting walls papered with strips of birch bark. The walls were adorned with a fearsome display of stuffed deer and bear heads, along with garish black-velvet paintings depicting stern-faced braves, eagles, and wolves.

Shelves and tables were filled to overflowing with a vast assortment of genuine and not-so-genuine Indian artifacts. Real handcrafted items like deerskin moccasins, beaded necklaces, and hand-thrown pots sat on shelves next to Davy Crocket coonskin hats and Japanese made tom-toms with rubber drum heads. David searched through aisles filled with cowboy hats, plastic six-shooters, and rubber tipped spears bearing the label 'Made in Japan.'

After making several trips up and down the rows of trinkets and souvenirs, he stopped at a display of spider webs strung across circles formed of bent willow branches. Each web was formed from thin strips of knotted animal hide with feathers, horsehair, and beads woven into a web. The web formed a perfect circle except for a hole at the center.

"Are these things dream catchers?" David asked the clerk behind the counter pointing to the display of willow webs.

"Yeah, that's right - dream catchers. You interested in buying one?" asked the clerk. He looked more Italian than Indian.

"Maybe - I'm not sure. A guy I met on the boat told me about them and said I ought to get one. But he didn't say how to use 'em. What do they do?" David asked.

"The web's supposed ta catch bad dreams. Sounds kinda stupid, don't it? But people'll believe most anything you tell em, huh?" The clerk reached up and took one of the webs down from its hook, showing it to David.

"Do they really work?" asked David, examining the dream catcher closely.

"Hey, how do I know, kid? Like I told ya, I don't believe in all this stuff. I just work here. All I know is people hang 'em on the wall as decorations, like art or somethin'. So, you want one or not?"

"Mom," David called across the store to his mother who had stopped before a display of moccasin slippers. "Can I get one of these?"

Helen walked over to examine the object in her son's hand, taking it from him with some reluctance. "And what exactly is this thing?"

"It's a dream catcher, Mom. It'll help me sleep better tonight. Really."

"I don't know - it sounds like some superstitious nonsense to me," she replied.

"Please," he implored her.

"Well... How much is it?" she asked the clerk behind the counter.

"That one's fifteen," the clerk said. "Made by Chippewas with deerskin, hawk feathers and beads."

Helen sighed. "Fifteen dollars? I don't think so. Not for a few feathers and some string. Isn't there something more practical? How bout a beaded wallet, or a nice belt?"

"We got this other one. We get 'em from Japan I think. They're not as nice - knotted with braided string and goose feathers. They're only five bucks.

"Please, Mom," David pleaded. "I won't ask for anything else. I promise."

"Well, I suppose," she said slowly, a sure sign that she was giving in. "But you don't need hawk feathers and deerskin. The one with goose feathers and string will do just fine."

Helen opened her purse and handed the clerk a five-dollar bill. "This is it, young man. You're done. Understand?"

David smiled at his mother. The clerk folded plain brown wrapping paper around the dream catcher and secured the package with Scotch tape and a piece of binder twine. As they turned to leave, the clerk reached behind the counter and handed David a piece of paper with some printing on it. "Here, kid, take one of these. It tells all about 'em - how they work and stuff."

David examined the sheet that the clerk had handed him. Next to a crudely drawn picture of a dream catcher, the title read "The History and Use of Dream Catchers." David neatly folded the paper and put it in the back pocket of his Levi's.

"And let me know if it works, eh?" added the clerk. "Maybe I should get one myself," he laughed as David and Helen walked out of the store.

*** 

When they returned to the motel, David could not wait to unwrap his purchase. He ripped the wrapping paper off the circle of willow branch, and held the web up to the light so that he could see the interlaced pattern of knotted cords. The clerk at the Indian Village had not been much help in finding out how to use the dream catcher, and David hoped that the instruction sheet would be more useful. After placing the dream catcher carefully on the table, he reached into his back pocket and removed the paper the clerk had given him.

His mother walked to the table and picked up the woven circle of string and beads. "Well, it sure doesn't look like much," she stated, shaking her head. "I hope it wasn't just a big waste of money."

"No, mom. It'll work really. It says here that the Indians from around here were the first ones to use dream catchers. There's even a legend about 'em. This old lady named Spider Woman took care of the kids of her tribe. When the kids grew up, they started to go off on their own, so the old woman showed 'em how to make dream catchers to protect their children from bad dreams."

"And just how is this thing supposed to protect you from bad dreams, anyway?" his mother asked.

David continued reading. "It says you're supposed to hang it over your bed. Then when you go to sleep, the bad dreams - nightmares and stuff - get caught in the web. But the good dreams pass right through the hole in the center and slide down the feathers to the dreamer. Then in the morning, the rays of the sun burn up all the bad dreams that are caught in the web. I bet this'll get rid of my bad dreams. Can I hang it over my bed tonight, mom?"

"I guess it won't do any harm, but where are you going to put it? I don't see any empty dream catcher hooks on the wall."

He looked for a place to hang the web over the hide-a-bed where he was going to sleep, but the only nail on the wall already held a picture of an angry looking bear painted on a slice of a pine tree coated with thick yellowed varnish.

"Can I put it up on the wall instead of that bear picture, mom," David asked.

Helen looked at the pine plaque hanging above the couch. "Well I'll have to admit, that picture is really hideous. But I don't think taking it down is such a good idea."

"It's just until morning. I'll be real careful, and I'll put everything back the way it was - I promise."

"Well, ok, go ahead," she said tentatively. "But everything goes back in place first thing tomorrow."

David removed the picture of the bear, and hung the dream catcher on the empty nail. He brushed his teeth, changed into his pajamas, and went to bed.

For several minutes, he stared up at the feathers dangling from the webbed hoop of the dream catcher. David wanted to believe that the dream catcher would help, but what if his mother was right? What if it was just a silly superstition?

"Time for bed," Helen said, walking over to the light switch by the front door of the cabin. "We've got to get an early start in the morning." She flicked off the light switch, leaving the room in the dark. "Sweet dreams," she said.

"Good night, mom," David replied.

***

At seven a.m. Helen, prodded David to wake up. "Come on, sleepy head, time to rise and shine," she coaxed. "How did you sleep, honey?"

David rolled over and rubbed his eyes. "I slept great, mom. I told you the dream catcher would work." As promised, he took down the dream catcher, packed it away, and returned the ugly black bear to its place on the wall above the hide-a-bed.

He helped his mother pack the few items they had removed from their bags, and put the bags back in the trunk of the car. By 7:30 they were back on the road headed west toward Iron Falls. US 2 cut across the U.P. from St. Ignace in the east to the mining towns of Bessemer and Ironwood in the west. Along the way numerous roadside attractions dotted the route, enticing road weary travelers to stop for a while and spend a few dollars on one diversion or another.

Helen drove west along US 2, passing the Straits Viewing Tower, where for a nickel you could climb a series of staircases until you reached a platform offering glimpses of bridge construction and mile after mile of towering evergreens stretching as far as the eye could see. The souvenir store at the foot of the tower offered a vast assortment of shells and rocks native to regions hundreds of miles from Lake Michigan's shores.

Just beyond the tower stood the entrance to the Mystery Spot, a strange location hidden in the woods where things were not what they seemed. Huge billboards sporting giant sized question marks begged travelers to visit this unique place where "the laws of nature are suspended." There was a house were you could climb straight up a wall, a floor where a basketball rolled up hill, and a chair where a person could balance on a narrow plank supported only by the chair's rear legs. Though he was still several inches shorter than his father, David had once stood next to his dad on this gravity-warped spot and looked his father straight in the eye.

A few miles from the Mystery Spot, a sign announced, "Only 250 miles to Perkins Café. Best food in the U.P." Iron Falls' restaurateur, Merle Perkins, had paid to have the signs erected along US 2 to drum up business in the early 1940s. His business boomed. Since then, the signs had become a fixture of Upper Peninsula lore, enticing travelers to "Stop in and Dine with Us." For David, the signs served as a measure of their progress toward his grandfather's home, and his exile to the wilderness. The sign was only the first of many.

From the Straits, US 2 followed the contours of Lake Michigan from Point Au Chenes past Big Bay de Noc to Little Bay de Noc. Hugging the shoreline, the drive was one of the most beautiful in the state, providing magnificent views of pine forests against a background of azure blue waters. The towns lining Route 2 testified to the diverse history of the Upper Peninsula. Naubinway, Manistique, Rapid River, Gladstone, Escanaba, Norway, Iron Mountain, and Spread Eagle dotted the highway, providing outposts of civilization in the wilderness of pine forests that spread across the landscape like a shaggy green carpet.

Helen stopped frequently to relieve the monotony of being the lone driver, giving David a chance to walk along the beach and dip his feet into the chill waters of the lake. She paused beside the road at the Cut River Bridge, allowing David to hike to the bottom of the deep, scenic ravine to touch the water and hike back up while she waited in the car. By the time he returned he was exhausted, crawling into the backseat of the Chevy and napping all the way to Escanaba.

In Escanaba, his mother stopped at a white cinder block building on the edge of town that advertised "FRESH PASTIES" in hand painted letters on a sign projecting from the top of the building. She bought two of the pastry covered meat pies and directed David to join her at a picnic table next to the building.

The pasty came wrapped in newspaper, and David unfolded his package to reveal an oval loaf-like pastry pie. The pie was filled with diced potatoes, onions, and chunks of beef. It was generally acknowledged that Cornish immigrants had brought pasties to the Upper Peninsula, and they soon became a favorite food of the iron and copper miners. By bundling the hot meat and potato pies in a towel in the morning, the pasties provided miners with a warm lunch at noon. Authentic pasties contained rutabaga, though downstaters and other "foreigners" preferred carrots. David ate his pasty covered in catsup, but pasty purists also considered this culinary heresy.

West of Escanaba, US 2 turned away from Lake Michigan into the depths of the great north woods. Lands flattened by retreating glaciers yielded to rocky outcroppings marking the beginnings of iron country.

"Only 200 miles to Perkins," read a sign by the side of the road. "Only 150 miles…," read another. "Only 100 miles…," "Only 50 miles…," "25 miles…," then "10 miles…" David continued to watch the signs as they flew by along the roadside, counting down the miles until they would finally reach Iron Falls and the final sign in the sequence, indicating the end of their long journey.

## Iron Falls

"PERKINS CAFÉ - YOU'RE HERE!" The sign was painted in bright, bold letters, almost completely covering two stories of a red brick building in the middle of Iron Falls' Main Street. The building and the small café it housed seemed a real anti-climax after the seemingly endless barrage of signs hyping the eatery along US 2. David had dined at Perkins only once, and did not particularly like their food. All the vegetables tasted like they came from cans, and the meat in his roast beef sandwich had been tough and cold. As his mother drove slowly past the front of the café, David could see only one or two patrons sitting at the counter.

The main street of Iron Falls could have been the main street of any of hundreds of small Michigan communities. At the intersection of 1st and Main, the city's only stoplight regulated traffic, allowing local vehicles to merge with the flow of cars moving steadily through town on Highway 2. On one corner of the intersection stood the First National Bank, housed in an imposing building built during the thirties to reassure investors shaken by the hopelessness created by the depression. Opposite the bank stood Broderick's Department Store, with full-view plate glass windows displaying the latest 1957 summer fashions, and just down the street was the Red Owl grocery store.

Iron Falls had not changed since David's first memory of the town when he was just two or three years old. Though he did not know it, the town had not changed appreciably since the late nineteen hundreds. Despite periodic grand openings and going out of business sales, the brick and mortar buildings that formed the heart of the city remained unchanged. By the 1950s, buildings that had been modern marvels in the 1890s were showing the ravages of age - paint fading and peeling, walls beginning to crumble.

Iron Falls existed because of the iron mines punctuating the landscape of Falls County. In the late 1800s and early 1900s, miners from Cornwall, Denmark, Sweden, Finland, and Norway flocked to the Upper Peninsula, bringing with them their skills and families. In return for service in the mines, the mining companies built communities, known as "locations," which provided housing and other essentials to miners and their families.

Among the families coming to Falls County just after the turn of the century were Donald Bishop's parents, Douglas and Elizabeth. Lured by the promise of a better life in America, Douglas and his young bride had packed up their meager belongings and moved from the rugged coast of Cornwall to the frigid forests of Michigan's Upper Peninsula. Though he never found great riches, Douglas did find a home in America, and raised a fine family - two sons, Donald and Roger, and a daughter, Rita.

David still missed his grandfather and grandmother. Growing up, his favorite memories of Iron Falls centered on his visits to their small two-story home in the Jasper Location. If he tried hard enough he could still recall the smell of fresh baked bread and cookies permeating Grandma Bishop's kitchen. And Grandpa Bishop had been the one who first taught him how to cast a fly rod into a trout stream.

But that was before the accident at the mine. His grandfather's leg had been crushed by falling rock, and the injury forced his early retirement. After that Douglas Bishop retreated from the outside world. And, according to David's Aunt Rita, he began to drink too much.

Then five years ago, David's Uncle Roger, a Pan Am pilot living in Arizona, invited Douglas and Elizabeth Bishop to come live with him and his family. "The sun is just the thing to help dad," he had insisted. The move had been made over the vocal protests of David's grandfather who vowed never to leave his home. Only two years later Douglas Bishop died of a heart attack, and his wife Elizabeth passed away six months later.

Now the only relatives David had left in Iron Falls on his father's side of the family were his Aunt Rita, her husband Ray Peterson and their boys Kenny and Kyle.

Of course, on his mother's side of the family, there was still Grandpa Carl. Carl Wertz had been a harness maker in Germany before immigrating to Wisconsin in the early 1900s. When he married, he brought his bride north to establish a small harness shop in Iron Falls. The shop was located on a quiet side street, away from the bustle of downtown. Helen drove the Chevy down Main Street and turned onto Oak, pulling up in front of an unassuming, drab two-story brick and stone building. A sign above the door identified the shop as *Wertz Upholstery and Leather Goods*.

The lights were out inside the shop, and a window shade was drawn down over the door. A sign hung from the shade proclaimed the store to be "CLOSED".

"He's probably around back," Helen said, "but why don't you check the door just to make sure."

David got out of the car, went up to the door, and tried the handle. Locked. All the lights were out. He held his hand over his eyes to shield the glare, and peered into the window. Inside he could just make out the silhouette of a wing-backed chair that had been partially recovered in an elegant floral pattern. Near the chair stood a wooden rack holding an ornate western style saddle, resplendent with silver buckles and accents. David couldn't see anyone in the shop.

"He's probably in the back," David told his mother as he got back into the car. Helen drove around the corner to the rear of the building. The rear of the upholstery shop faced on a broad residential alley, essentially splitting a single, long city block in two. From the rear, the shop appeared to be a two-story residence. David opened the gate of a small fenced-in yard bisected by a short sidewalk leading to the back porch entry to his grandfather's apartment.

When Helen was young, the family had lived on the second floor of the two-story building, and Carl had used the entire ground floor as his workshop and showroom. When her mother died, she took over as the woman-of-the-house in addition to completing her studies at Iron Falls High School. After she moved to Chicago at nineteen to begin work as a stenographer, Carl decided that he no longer needed the entire second floor as a living area. He added a rear stairway and outside entrance to the second floor residence, converting it into an apartment, while he moved into modest accommodations on the first floor, at the rear of the shop area. This arrangement gave him some added income, but provided little room for entertaining guests.

***

As David opened the gate in the peeling white wooden picket fence, a lazy golden haired retriever-spaniel mix stirred from her sentry post on the back porch in front of the door and began to growl protectively. "Hey, Lady, you remember me don't you?"

"Be careful, David, Lady may not remember you," Helen cautioned. But even before the words were out of her mouth, the dog began running up to the youth, wagging her tail and barking happily.

"Lady, lady, come here," a gruff, gravely man's voice with a slight German accent called from the doorway. A short stocky man with a round wrinkled face, thinning gray hair, and a white mustache stained yellow by tobacco walked forward to greet his daughter and grandson. "Lady, heel," he commanded, and the dog obediently returned to the man's side and fell in behind him.

Carl wore a faded plaid shirt crossed by two wide black suspenders, which held up a pair of baggy brown Carhartt work pants. Both the pants and his worn tan work boots were permanently stained by multiple spills of the leather dye he used in his shop. Between his teeth, Carl clenched the stub of a well-chewed Havana cigar.

"Soon you will be as tall as I am," he said to David, reaching out his stained, calloused hands to pull the boy forward into an uncomfortable hug.

"You had a good trip, ya?" he said turning to his daughter, leaning to give her a warm hug and a kiss on both cheeks. He motioned his guests to follow him into the house.

He held open the wooden screen door as David and Helen entered through a utility room littered with boxes of newspapers, empty milk bottles, and discarded pieces of upholstery fabric. A bank of hooks above the boxes held heavy canvas winter coats, and a pair of rubberized fishing waders.

Beyond this storeroom lay the kitchen. Except for a dense cloud of smoke hanging in the air, Carl's kitchen could have been part of a museum display. The fog of bluish-gray haze of smoke billowing from Carl's cigar mingled with the fumes from the combination wood and gas stove Carl still used for heating and cooking.

David inhaled deeply. His favorite memory of his grandfather's shop was the smell. The fragrance of the smoke from the stove and cigars mingled with the aroma of rawhide and freshly cut leather drifting in from the front shop area.

"Come, come sit down," Carl said pulling out two slat back wooden chairs from the oak drop leaf table near the door. "You must be exhausted from your drive." He crushed his cigar butt into a glass ashtray that already contained five or six stubs. Even after he crushed the cigar, smoke continued to billow from the still glowing embers of tobacco.

He walked over to a steel percolator steaming on a gas burner attached to the side of the wood stove, and poured himself a cup of dark, rich coffee.

"Would you like a cup, Helen?" he asked almost as an afterthought.

"Yes, please," she answered. Carl took a cup off a hook hanging from the bottom of a shelf, poured a second cup, and handed it to his daughter.

"Are you hungry? Let me get you something to eat." Carl opened his refrigerator. Like his stove, Carl's refrigerator was a relic of bygone days. It was a dingy white enameled box, held several inches off the floor by four curved steel legs, and crowned by a curious barrel-shaped condenser assembly. David thought the old white monstrosity looked like Robbie the Robot from the movie *Forbidden Planet*. Carl still referred to it as his "ice box" even though the minuscule freezer compartment was barely large enough to hold an ice cube tray.

Carl pulled out a box of crackers and two small packages wrapped in waxed paper. "Would you care for some cheese, perhaps?"

David could smell the contents of the first package even before his grandfather unwrapped the paper. "Do you like Limburger, David? Or perhaps something a bit more mild." He opened the second small package to reveal another white cheese. "Maybe you would like this goat cheese better, ya?"

To David, cheese wasn't cheese unless it was yellow. "Do you have any Velveeta?" he asked.

Carl looked puzzled. "Velveeta? I do not know this kind of cheese. I'll tell you what - you eat some salami and crackers now, and I will buy some Velveeta the next time I go to the store. I know you like salami." Carl put out plates and cut thick slices from the large stick of salami.

David snacked on crackers and salami while his mother and grandfather talked. Lady nestled under the table at David's feet. Every now and then David slipped a piece of meat under the table to the dog, even though his grandfather frowned on feeding Lady table scraps.

Soon David's plate was empty, but the conversation continued. He was bored and uncomfortable. He began to fidget noticeably in his chair. "Honey, are you all right?" Helen asked concerned. "You look tired - why don't you go lie down on Grandpa's bed and read for a while?"

"Maybe there is something else David would like better, ya?" Carl looked at his grandson. "Stand up David. Let me look at you."

David stood beside the table, as Carl looked on thoughtfully. "It looks like that belt we made you last summer is all ready too small," he said. "Would you like to work on a new one while your mother and I talk?"

\*\*\*

Carl led the boy through the curtain that served as the only door between the shop and his living quarters. Beyond the cloth barrier lay an odd mixture of wild western gear, cobbler's tools, grotesque, medieval-looking contraptions, and sleekly designed pieces of furniture. As they entered the shop, Carl threw on the light switch, illuminating a maze of machinery, half completed projects, and unsold inventory, with bits of leather and fabric strewn across the floor.

Leather working tools were everywhere - leather dies, mallets, chisels, tack pullers, needles, scissors, and shears. Larger machines, like a kick press for setting grommets, stood bolted to the floor.

A stack of variously dyed cowhides was piled high on a cutting table, taking up an entire corner of the workroom. A drafting table that Carl used to design custom leather goods, complete with T-square, compass, rulers, and a variety of pencils, stood in another corner. Next to it sat a heavy-duty sewing machine capable of joining pieces of leather for handbags or wallets.

David loved the organized chaos of the workshop. He walked through the maze of equipment to the doorway leading to the front showroom. There he saw an assortment of goods for sale - belts, purses, sandals, handbags, wallets, holsters, belts, and gun cases. On the far side of the showroom sat an oak saddle rack, a stand made up of wooden slats attached to a frame on wooden legs, used for displaying trophy saddles and custom made bridles and halters. When he was a little boy, David remembered getting up on the saddle and imagining riding across the plains, like the cowboy heroes of his favorite television shows.

David went over to the saddle and ran his fingers across the intricate tooling stamped into the leather. It was a shame that his grandfather seldom got a chance to use his skill, David thought. Carl was a craftsman who, in the Middle Ages, would have been considered a master. But times had changed. In the 1950s only hobbyists rode horses. Farmers and merchants had long ago traded their horse drawn plows and wagons for tractors and panel trucks.

When the demand for leather goods declined, Carl turned to upholstery as an alternate source of income. Many of the tools he had used to create leather goods were easily adapted to cut and sew furniture fabric. Now Carl spent most of his days repairing and reupholstering ottomans, sofas, and wing chairs. He used his knowledge and skills to remove broken springs and weave webbing on wooden chair frames. The work, though not as demanding, was steady, and in its own way, rewarding. The income from the upholstering business had allowed him to own the building he worked in, to buy the cabins at Spirit Lake, and indulge his love of leatherwork.

The old man took David over to a table with scores of leather straps already cut into belt width slices. "Go ahead. Pick one out," Carl prompted.

David picked out a fine strip of light brown leather about a foot longer than he needed and handed it to his grandfather. "Good! You remembered what I taught you. Do you also remember how to start your design?"

"Yes sir. Wet the leather with a sponge, draw a guideline down the center of the belt, pencil in the pattern, then hammer the stamp designs into the leather."

"And if I leave you in here by yourself?"

"I'll be fine, Grandpa. This will be the best belt ever."

Carl knew from past experience that he could trust his grandson with his tools. David carefully laid out his design, marked the leather, and used various stamps his grandfather kept on his shop bench to hammer in the pattern. The work was tedious and exacting. Several times David's hand slipped as he stamped the belt, creating minute flaws in the pattern. But David knew that these imperfections would not be noticeable on the finished belt.

As he worked, David could hear his grandfather and mother continue their conversation well into the evening.

There was much to tell, and Carl's strong dark coffee kept both father and daughter engaged despite the lateness of the hour. When daylight began to fade in the kitchen, Carl rose to turn on the overhead light. Helen used the opportunity to check her wristwatch. It was already after eight.

"My gosh, Dad," she exclaimed, "look at the time. I had no idea. We still have to drive out to the cottage and get things unpacked."

"It is getting late. Why don't you and the boy spend the night here with me? You can use my bedroom. I will set up a folding cot in the workshop for the boy, and I will sleep on the couch. Tomorrow after everyone is well rested we will go to the cottage, ya?"

The idea of staying in town appealed to Helen. She was exhausted and needed rest. She walked to the doorway separating the kitchen from the front shop to inform David of the decision.

"David," Helen called. "Are you about finished yet? It's bedtime." David looked up from his work, amazed that the time had passed so quickly. He had completed only about one third of the design, and wanted to work on the rest. Reluctantly, he put away his tools, cleaned up the workbench, and turned out the lights in the shop. There would be plenty of opportunities to finish the belt. It was going to be a long summer.

## Lake Cottage

"Lady! Lady, come here girl," Carl commanded as he held open the passenger door to his weather-beaten, wood-paneled Ford station wagon. The vintage 1948 Super Deluxe wagon, built in nearby Iron Mountain, had begun to show its age. The varnished wooden panels on the doors had peeled badly, and the weatherproof roof fabric sometimes leaked.

Lady remained steadfastly at David's side, seemingly unwilling to leave the boy. "Go ahead, Lady, get in," urged David prodding the dog forward. "It's ok, girl. I'll see you out at the lake." The dog looked at the boy but did not move.

"She's really taken to you, David. She's not usually so friendly to people she does not know well. I think she wants you to come with her."

"Can I, Mom? Can I ride out to the lake with Grandpa and Lady?"

"It's all right with me, if it's ok with your grandfather," Helen replied.

"Of course it is all right. Lady, back seat," Carl ordered. This time the dog ran from David's side, jumping into the back of the station wagon and barking for David to move into the vacant passenger's seat.

The tan leather seat was tattered and covered with dog hair. David brushed the seat off with his hand and got in the car.

As Carl started the car and pulled out in front of Helen's Chevy, he glanced over at David. "So did you sleep well last night?"

"It took me a while to get comfortable, but after that I slept just fine," David lied. His back ached from sleeping on the sagging, lumpy cot. And his eyes still burned from the thick fog of smoke that filled his grandfather's shop. Even the dream catcher hung over his bed did not help him sleep.

By the time they had driven two or three miles out of town, the cookie cutter rows of the mining sub-development housing had begun to give way to the dense green forests which covered ninety percent of the U.P.

As they rounded a broad curve in the road, a brightly painted billboard appeared reading "Thank You for Visiting Perkins Café -

Come Again Soon." Just beyond the sign stood a simple white cinder block building on the right side of the highway surrounded by a dusty gravel parking lot. A sign attached to the peak of the roof read "*Ike's Market - Bait and Gas*." A covered portico extended from the front of the building, housing twin gasoline pumps, and a five-pointed star mounted above the pumps proclaimed it to be a Texaco station.

Opposite Ike's, a narrow gravel road marked with a simple wooden arrow labeled "CR 10" turned away from the highway and wound through the dense undergrowth, quickly disappearing into the forest beyond. Carl turned down the road, closely followed by Helen.

They drove several miles until they reached a fork in the road where a four by five wooden sign read "Spirit Lake Cabins." Beneath the words, a peeling painted arrow pointed the way down a two-track side road to the left. Carl turned off the main road and onto the gravel path, kicking up a cloud of dust as he did so. After traveling along the road for approximately half a mile, Carl pulled the station wagon off the track and into the driveway of a pleasant one-story cottage.

***

Carl's cottage was a modest wooden lake house with white lap siding sitting on a low hill overlooking the lake. As soon as the station wagon pulled into the drive, a short, stout woman with a round face opened the cottage door and came out to greet the visitors. Her intense, coal black eyes and bronze complexion gave her an exotic, almost Asian appearance. She wore her long, straight black hair in a bun at the back of her head.

"Maddie, you remember my grandson David, ya?" Carl said. David reached out and shook her hand. Maddie was Carl's housekeeper and resident manager of the cabins. David judged her to be in her early forties, though he was not good at telling a person's age from their appearance. She was a short plump Indian woman who David had met on previous trips to the lake. He realized that he had never heard his grandfather, or anyone else for that matter, ever mention Maddie's last name. She was quiet and reserved, but she fascinated David because Maddie was the only real Indian he had ever met.

"And Helen," Carl now addressed his daughter, "you already know Maddie. She has cleaned the cottage and gotten it ready for you. She will make sure you are comfortable when I'm not here."

"I'm sure that won't be necessary, Dad," Helen stated flatly without reaching out to shake the shorter woman's hand. "We'll get along just fine." For some reason David did not understand, his mother seemed to dislike Maddie. Helen never talked directly to her, always directing her comments to Carl, and never looking directly at the stoic Indian woman.

Maddie seemed not to notice the snub. "If you don't need me, I've got work to do on Cabin #4," She replied quietly.

"Good," Carl said in approval. "I'll walk down with you. There is some work I need to do on the dock. It will give Helen and David a chance to unpack and settle in." He pulled a gold pocket watch from his overalls, and checked the time. "I should be done in about two hours. How would you like to go fishing with me when you finish unpacking, David? Maybe we can catch some supper, ya?"

"Sure, ok, if it's all right with mom. It won't take long to get unpacked," David replied.

"It is settled then. Come down to the lake when you are finished. You can tell me what you have been doing since I saw you last while we fish, ok?"

***

In order to make room for David and his mother, Carl had already moved the majority of his belongings to the back of the harness shop in town. The cottage's kitchen was immaculate, dishes neatly shelved, stove cleaned and polished, and table with a bright bouquet of daylilies.

"Well, at least she left the place in decent condition," Helen remarked critically, allowing David to conclude that the 'she' in her comments referred to Maddie. "I expected much worse."

"Mom, why don't you like Maddie?" David asked. "She's always been real nice whenever we come up here. And grandfather says he couldn't run this place without her help."

"You're just too young to understand, David," his mother responded. "She's just a gold digger, and I don't know why your grandfather is so gullible. The whole thing is ridiculous. It's a disgrace to have that woman around all the time. He's become the laughing stock of the whole town. He's just an old fool."

"But what's wrong with grandfather having someone help out?"

Helen looked at her son, recognizing that she had said too much already. "Of course it's all right, David. Your grandfather needs someone to help him here. I just wish he'd have chosen someone more suitable, that's all."

"Well, I think the place looks great," David stated, "and it doesn't smell all musty and smoky like it usually does when we get here." David went into the living area, noting the sparse furnishings. An uncomfortable looking wing-backed chair sat opposite a small wood burning stove, the only source of heat for the room during the cold winter months. A large burgundy overstuffed couch sat against the wall between the doors to the two bedrooms.

David noticed a stand in the corner with what looked like a record player with a wooden cover. He went over to the stand and lifted the hinged oak cover. Inside he found what looked like a turntable, but the record on the spindle was a quarter of an inch thick and looked really old. Then he noticed that there was no electrical cord from the machine and a crank handle extended from the right side of the turntable box. "Hey, Mom, is this Grandpa's record player? It looks like some kind of antique or somethin'. I don't think it will play my 45s at all."

"Well, aren't you glad you brought along your own player?" his mother said brightly.

"Yeah, sure. But... Mom? Do you think Grandpa'll ever get a TV out here?" he asked.

"No honey, Grandpa probably won't ever have a television. Besides, he wouldn't be able to get reception out here in the woods even if he had one," his mother answered.

David frowned.

"Oh, don't give me that hang dog look, young man. Things aren't that bad. You can always listen to the radio. And besides, now you'll have plenty of time to get some reading done this summer. So why don't you go unpack and set up things in your room the way you want them? It might make you feel more at home here."

Dejectedly, David grabbed his suitcase in one hand and the portable record player in the other and headed into his room. Situated just off the living area, his room was not large - perhaps ten by ten - with a single window and a closet in the far corner. He looked around the room for power outlets, but found only one, on the wall near the door. A reading light on a nightstand was already plugged into one socket.

He moved the record player to the stand and slid it onto a shelf under the lamp. He plugged it in, put a record on the spindle, and watched as it dropped down onto the turntable. "Day-Oh, Day-ay-ay-Oh," cried Harry Belafonte from the monaural speaker, filling the cottage with the calypso melody.

Next to the nightstand stood the single bed where he would sleep. It had a headboard and footboard made out of pine logs matching the pine paneling on the walls of the cottage. When David sat down on the bed, the mattress sagged down in the middle and the springs squeaked. He bounced once or twice to assess the extent of the squeak and the amount of sag. The bed would be soft, he decided, but not as bad as the cot at his grandfather's shop.

He threw his suitcase onto the bed, clicked open the snaps holding it closed, and looked inside. On top of his folded clothing was the dream catcher he had purchased in St. Ignace. Examining the wall above the bed, he found a small metal hook already extending from the pine paneling. "Perfect," he muttered to himself as he reached up to hang the dream catcher in place.

He knew that the dream catcher would help him sleep better, even if the mattress sagged and creaked.

David finished unpacking even before the two hours Carl had allowed were up. His clothing was hung neatly in the closet, and his underwear and socks were packed away neatly in the drawers.

When he was done, he called his mother into the room. "See, Mom, I put everything away," he beamed, "can I go down to the lake now and see if Grandpa's ready to go fishing?"

"Go ahead, but be careful, and make sure to wear a life vest," Helen gave her son a quick hug and watched as he ran out the door.

***

David ran all the way down the path to the lake. When he arrived, he found his grandfather just coming out of the boathouse carrying an overloaded tackle box in one hand and two bamboo fishing poles in the other. "Are you ready to go?" he said shifting the cigar stub hanging from the corner of his mouth from one side to the other. "The fish are waiting. Grab that can of bait and come along."

David picked up the can, and followed his grandfather past a weather beaten picnic pavilion and then past a line of guest cabins toward the boat dock. Lady ran ahead and jumped into the boat first. As David boarded the rickety boat, his grandfather lifted a weathered five horsepower Mercury outboard from its resting-place on a sawhorse next to the dock. The lettering partially worn off the side, read 'Merc--y'. Oil stains streaked the housing and the paint had pealed off the shaft. With some difficulty Carl carried it down to the boat, dropped it onto the mounting board at the stern of the craft, and clamped it in place.

The old man primed the motor by pouring a small amount of gas into a small cup at the top of the engine. He pulled the cord wrapped around the starter once, twice, then three times. The engine stammered briefly, belching out three puffs of black oily smoke, then fell silent. Undaunted, Carl tried again, adjusting the choke before yanking the cord once more. Again clouds of black choking smoke billowed up. The engine sputtered hesitantly, spit, coughed, and finally roared to life.

"Good," Carl muttered. "It starts. We go catch some dinner now, ya?" With that he removed the rope loop from the post at the end of the dock and pushed off. Shoving the handle of the engine hard to port, Carl swung the nose of the bass boat around and headed out into the choppy waters of the lake. Even at full throttle, the rickety craft made scant headway running against the wind. The ancient 5-horse outboard sputtered along, barely moving the craft forward.

David sat at the bow as the old vessel plodded steadily along. Several other small fishing boats zigzagged across the lake, each headed toward its own 'secret' spot. Most of the other vessels breezed past Carl's boat as it plodded along. Many had twenty or thirty horsepower engines and could skim over the surface of the lake, their owners smiling and waving as they passed.

"The first time I came here to fish, your mother was just a girl," Carl said. "Every Sunday after church I came to fish with my good friend Benjamin Martin. He is the one who built the cabins."

"You didn't always own the cabins?" David said surprised.

"Oh, heavens no. Benjamin built them long before the war."

"Then how did you get them, Grandpa?"

"When Benjamin died," Carl explained sadly, "there was no one to take over for him here, so the cabins began to fall apart. I hated to see that happen. I did not have much money, so I took out a loan on the shop to buy the property. For years, every dollar and every minute I could spare went into rebuilding this place. That was a long time ago."

"Back when Little Thunder lived here?" David asked.

Carl laughed. "So, do I really look that old?" He reached out and rubbed his grandson's head. "No, no, Little Thunder and his people lived here long before my time."

"But is there really a ghost? Is it true? Is the lake haunted?"

"Little Thunder was real. He was a leader of his people," Carl explained. "But I'm afraid the story of his spirit is just a legend."

"You don't believe in the spirit, Grandpa?"

"If you ask me, the spirit is nonsense. It is nothing but a tale invented to scare superstitious tourists. But I am not the one you should be talking to about Little Thunder. You should ask Maddie. She believes in the spirit. It is part of her culture. You should ask her - she will tell you."

*** 

Carl maneuvered the old bass boat into the shallows at the tip of the point, arriving at a spot near a patch of lily pads. He cut the engine and allowed the boat to coast to a stop. He lifted the rusted iron anchor and dropped it overboard, taking care that the anchor rope did not get tangled or caught on the poles or oars. Picking up the two bamboo poles, he separated them, handing David the shorter of the two.

"This one should be about right for you, hey?" he said as David reached out to take the pole from his grandfather.

Carl pulled the can of worms over to his end of the boat, reached in, felt around, and removed a large fat wriggling night crawler. Deftly he folded the worm accordion style, skewering it on the hook. This was done with neat precision, using skills acquired from years of practice, like some ancient ritual that was completely foreign to David.

He pushed the can back in David's direction. David timidly reached in with two fingers and daintily extracted the first worm he touched. The worm felt cold and damp. Taking the hook in his left hand and the worm in his right, he attempted to push the barb of the hook through the center of the worm. The punctured worm writhed and squirmed in his hand, until it wiggled loose. Reaching for the fallen worm, David only managed to stick his finger on the barb of the hook.

Carl, who witnessed the whole scene, smiled. "You put the hook through the worm, not through the finger," he laughed. Without further comment he took the pole from David and scooped another worm from the can with his stubby calloused fingers. "Here, let me show you." Effortlessly he folded the worm onto the hook, working the body back and forth, impaling it securely through the barb.

"There, you see," he held the baited hook up to the boy. "That way the worm can not wriggle back off. Now we catch some fish, ya?"

Carl tossed his hook over the side and motioned for David to follow his lead. For several minutes the two fished in silence. Before long Carl had managed to pull in several small perch, but David still had not had even a nibble.

Finally, David felt a slight tug at his line. "I think I have a bite," he told his grandfather proudly.

Carl moved to help David pull in the fish on his line. David began to enjoy being out on the lake. He soon landed another perch, this time removing the hook from the wriggling fish himself. By the time they headed in they had five pan-sized perch and three small blue gills ready for dinner.

# God's Country

"David, hurry up, will you?" Helen knocked on David's door. "We're going to be late. It's almost ten. Service begins in less than an hour and you're not even dressed yet."

"I'm almost ready, mom. Just give me a couple of minutes."

David opened the chest of drawers, pulled out a white dress shirt with collar stays. He put on the shirt and went to the closet for a tie. Being careful not to mess up his hair, he slipped his suit jacket on over his shirt and looked at himself in the mirror. Not bad, he thought.

"Well, come on out here and let me take a look," his mother called through the door.

David opened the door and stepped out into the living area.

"Goodness," his mother laughed when she saw him. "What on earth were you thinking? Where did you get that old pair of pants - and that ridiculous clip on tie? Where's the new brown suit I bought for you in Toledo?"

"It's hanging in my closet. But I hate that suit - the wool is way too scratchy. Besides, what's wrong with what I have on?"

"Well, for one thing, you've outgrown that old suit. Those pants are two inches too short. You certainly can't go to church looking like that. And why aren't you wearing the striped tie your dad gave you?"

"You know I can never get the knot straight. This clip on looks ok."

"You look like Pinkey Lee in that silly tie. You'll have to change before we go. Now hurry - and don't forget to put on your dad's tie."

David moped as he returned into his room. Moving quickly, he pulled off his old clothes, and changed into the brown suit his mother had picked out for him. As soon as he pulled on the pants, the rough fabric began to itch and scratch. When he had finished, he popped off the clip on tie, and wound his father's tie under his collar. Carefully he tied the four-in-hand knot just as his father had taught him. He checked the mirror. The tie wasn't straight. He tried again and again, but somehow the front of the tie always came out shorter than the back.

"Mom, I can't get this stupid tie."

"Well, come out here and let me help you with it," Helen

offered. When he opened the door, Helen reached out and loosened the knot on the tie, adjusting it so that the ends were of equal length. "There, that's better. Now put on your jacket and we'll get going?"

"Ah, mom, why do I have to wear my coat? It must be almost 100 outside. I'll roast."

"Don't exaggerate, David. It's not that hot out - you won't roast. Look, I'll make you a deal - if any of the rest of the men at the service take off their jackets, you can remove yours. Deal?"

"Yeah, sure, I don't really have a choice, do I?" David said, slipping on his jacket.

Helen gave herself a last check in the mirror, her simple pink dress accented by a single strand of pearls. After touching up her ruby red lipstick, she slipped the tube back into her white patent leather clutch.

"Ok, I'm ready," she said. "Let's go." Together they rushed quickly out the back door, got into the waiting Chevy, and drove off down the dusty dirt road.

***

Religious preference in Iron Falls was decided primarily on the basis of ethnic origin. The Catholics, by far the largest religious group, comprising over half the population, included Iron Fall's residents of Irish, Italian, French, and Polish decent.

Next in order of numbers were the Evangelical Lutherans, who stuck to the rigorous fundamentalism of Martin Luther's frugal simplicity. The Lutherans included the Swedes, Norwegians, Fins, and Germans like Carl. As a girl Helen had attended the Lutheran church with her father. She still recounted tales of her strict upbringing as a Lutheran and the fire-and-brimstone sermons she was forced to attend.

Welsh and Cornish iron miners, like Donald's parents, Douglas and Elizabeth, brought with them the Methodist and Presbyterian tenants of John Wesley and John Knox. Though these denominations were rooted in the same fundamental Protestant belief system as the Lutherans, to Helen they seemed more open and forgiving than the faith of her childhood. Therefore, when she married Donald, she readily adopted his Presbyterian religion as her own, much to Carl's chagrin.

After hearing his mother's stories of sin, hell, and eternal damnation, David was happy that she had decided not to remain a Lutheran. His dad always said there wasn't a lick of difference between Lutherans and Presbyterians in God's eyes anyway.

Now whenever they visited Iron Falls, the Bishops went to the Iron Falls Presbyterian Church, while Carl continued to attend Lutheran services.

The Iron Falls Presbyterian Church was an impressive white frame building surrounded by high arched stained glass windows. Crowning the edifice was a towering spire housing the church belfry. The church bells had already begun tolling their call to prayer as Helen pulled into the parking lot next to the church. Mainly arriving by foot, parishioners streamed into the temple of worship from all directions.

While regular church members greeted each other, shaking hands near the huge oak entrance doors, David and his mother slipped into the church practically unnoticed and took a seat near the rear of the nave. Before taking his seat, David removed his suit jacket and hung it loosely over the back of the pew. He looked over at his mother, but she didn't seem to notice. Slowly the rest of the pews began to fill, until only a few stragglers remained standing.

As the processional ended, the minister rose and moved to the lectern. The minister, Reverend Joshua Goodall, was a short stout man in his early forties with a round friendly face and a black robe draped down over his protruding stomach. He reminded David of Friar Tuck from the movie *Robin Hood.*

"Please rise and join the choir in singing 'How Great Thou Art,'" the minister requested. As a single entity, the congregation rose, and opened their hymnals. Suddenly, the massive pipe organ blasted out the first notes of "How Great Thou Art", and the choir led the parishioners in a boisterous, if sometimes off-key rendition of the traditional hymn.

As the last chords of the organ faded into the upper reaches of the sanctuary, and the parishioners settled back into their seats, the Reverend Goodall returned to the podium. He pulled a pair of reading glasses from the stand, unfolded some papers, cleared his throat and began to speak.

"After my graduation from seminary," the minister started in a booming voice, "I received my first assignment. 'You're lucky, son,' the bishop told me. 'You're going to God's Country.'" This comment caused a woman in the rear of the nave to chuckle softly.

"Now, being a small town boy from rural Georgia," the minister explained, "I thought I was already in God's Country." Again there were a few scattered giggles among the parishioners. "Then the bishop explained where God's Country was, and I almost turned in my collar." Now several people began to laugh.

"Well, despite my reservations, I came," he continued, "and by gosh, I soon found out why they call it God's Country up here - because God it's beautiful, and God it's cold." This comment elicited a burst of laughter from the congregation, and even brought a smattering of applause. "Well, I've lived here for nearly twenty years now, I can tell you that you truly are God's chosen people." Reverend Goodall went on to describe his feeling that God held the Upper Peninsula and its inhabitants in special regard.

The sermon was too long, too wordy, and definitely too boring. In David's mind the same could be said of every Sunday service he had ever attended. Over the years he had established several proven methods for keeping himself from falling asleep during the sermon, like counting the pieces of blue stained glass in the sanctuary windows, or reading the words to songs in the hymnal backwards. But the Iron Falls preacher was even more monotonous and dreary than most ministers David had encountered. Several times during the service Helen had to poke him with her elbow to keep him from nodding off in his seat.

A rousing chorus of "What a Friend We Have in Jesus" brought David back to life, just before the benediction that ended the service. David followed behind his mother as the congregation filed out of the nave. Together they walked out of the dim dark church into the bright light of a beautiful summer Sunday.

***

"David? Helen? Is that you?" David knew the voice immediately. Sharp with a sing-songy lilt, the voice belonged to his Aunt Rita. Rita Peterson was his father's sister, and one of the last persons David wanted to see.

David looked toward his mother to see what she would do. Helen had never been on good terms with her husband's family, and only tolerated Rita because she was her sister-in-law. Helen cringed slightly. Acting as if she had not heard the summons, she took

David's hand, and led him quickly away from the voice.

"Helen? Helen Bishop? It is you. What on earth are you doing here?" The voice was closer now, almost directly behind David and his mother. No longer able to avoid contact, Helen turned around to face the inevitable confrontation.

Rita stood barely taller than David, but her high spiked heals gave the illusion that she was much taller. She wore her dark brown hair short in tight Toni-permed curls, accented by a pair of garish starburst-shaped rhinestone earrings. A matching costume jewelry necklace hung around her neck, detracting from her frilly bright turquoise summer dress.

The boy stood at her side reached up to wipe his long auburn hair out of his eyes. He looked restless and distracted, as if he longed to be somewhere else. The boy was David's cousin, Kyle. Though Kyle was almost a half-foot shorter than David, he was a few weeks older, and when they were together, Kyle always treated David like a little kid.

"Helen, why didn't you call? How are you? How long has it been anyway?" The words came out of her mouth in a stream, leaving no time for reply or comment. Rita was just as David remembered - frilly, frantic and flaky. Every trip to the U.P. inevitably included at least one mandatory visit to Aunt Rita and Uncle Ray's. David always dreaded these visits.

"Kyle, you remember your Aunt Helen," Rita prompted. In response, the boy nodded toward his aunt.

Having acknowledged Helen, Rita turned her attention to David. "David, my, my how you've grown. Kyle, you remember David don't you? Say hello."

"Hi ya, Davy. How ya doin'?" Kyle extended his hand. David accepted his cousin's handshake reluctantly. David hated the nickname 'Davy,' and Kyle knew it.

"When on earth did you get in?" Rita resumed her questioning. "I didn't know you were coming. Why didn't Donald call? Where is he anyway?"

"Donald couldn't make it," Helen replied. "Busy at the plant, you know. We just got in a couple of days ago. I was planning to call of course, but things have been so rushed. Donald's coming up in a couple of weeks - as soon as he gets the chance."

"Oh it's a shame he couldn't come up with you. He works too

much, just like my Raymond, you know. He needs to relax more. Besides, I don't get a chance to see my baby brother nearly enough these days. So it's just you and David, eh? Where are you staying, anyway? You know we have an extra room out at the house."

"Oh, we wouldn't think of imposing. Besides, Dad's letting us have the cottage out at the lake while we're here."

"Ray will be so disappointed when he finds out he missed you."

"Ray's not here? I hope he isn't ill," Helen said concerned.

"Well, to tell the truth, Ray wasn't feeling very well this morning, so he just dropped us off before the service," Rita answered.

"Then you still aren't driving, I take it," Helen queried. Rita was one of the few adults David knew who had never learned to drive. As a result, she had to rely on her friends, neighbors, and most of all her family to deliver her to her many social engagements.

"Oh, my, heaven's no. I told Ray when he breaks down and buys an automatic, I'll learn to drive. But you know Ray - stubborn to the end. He'll never admit that the stick shift is a thing of the past. So I guess he'll just have to keep on carting me around. In fact he should be here by now. He was supposed to pick us up right after the service." She checked her watch. "He must be running late. I wonder what's keeping him?"

"And what about Kenny? I don't see him around either. Is he here?" Helen continued. "Why he must be a senior this year."

"Oh, that Kenny. He just couldn't seem to wake up this morning. Ever since he turned seventeen I just don't know what I'm going to do with that boy."

***

As they stood talking, an old black Ford pickup pulled up to the curb in front of the group, and squealed to a stop. The truck's running boards were almost rusted through and the grill was missing from the front of the vehicle. The right front fender had been reconstructed with plastic body filler, sanded smooth and spray painted with a fine coat of gray undercoating.

Behind the wheel was a tall, lanky youth with a cocky attitude and a sly smile. He wore his hair in a greased-back ducktail.

"Kenny? What are you doing here?" Rita greeted her oldest son, obviously confused. "Is everything all right at home?"

"Yeah, no problem, Mom. Dad just asked me to swing by and

pick you and Kyle up. Are you ready?"

"Ready? Ready for what? You don't think I'm riding home in that, do you?" she asked indicating the cramped cab of the truck.

"Hey ma! Have a little respect," Kenny said defensively. "This truck's a classic."

"Well, classic or not, I'm still not riding in it. Where's your father anyway?"

"He said he was in the middle of something, and asked me to come."

"Then for heavens sake why didn't you drive the Pontiac?"

"'Cause that's what he's busy workin' on. He's changing the oil."

"On Sunday morning? I thought he wasn't feeling well."

"Guess he got better. So, are you comin' or what?"

"Just hold your horses, young man. I certainly hope you don't expect me to sit on that filthy seat in my best Sunday dress."

Kenny did not answer, but glared angrily at his mother. The situation seemed to be getting tense, and both David and Helen felt uncomfortable witnessing the bickering between mother and son. "Maybe I can help," Helen interjected. "Why don't I give you a lift out to the house? That way I can say hi to Ray."

"Oh, Helen, I wouldn't want to put you out," Rita feigned reluctance, though delighted with the offer. "The lake's way over on the other side of town."

"It's no problem. We're meeting dad for lunch after his service is out, and that won't be for another hour."

"Oh, Helen, you're positively a lifesaver. I know Ray's gonna be just as pleased as punch to see the two of you," she continued.

"Good, then why don't you come with me," Helen directed. "I'm parked over there, in the far corner of the lot. David, you can ride in the back with Kyle and let your Aunt Rita ride in front with me."

"Hang on. I've got a wonderful idea. Why don't David and Kyle go with Kenny? That way David can get reacquainted with his cousins, eh?"

Kenny gave his mother another dirty look. "Ok, Davy boy, you can come, but you have to ride in the middle," Kenny said.

David cringed. He didn't like his older cousin much. On previous visits Kenny had taken every opportunity to embarrass and humiliate him. "I don't think there's room for me, Mom," David looked to his mother for help.

"I'm sure it will be all right," Helen responded unsympathetically. "You go ahead and we'll meet you there."

"Hop in, but don't touch anything, understand? And don't get in the way," Kenny added.

Given little alternative, David got into the truck straddling the transmission hump and trying to avoid the gearshift lever. As Kyle hopped into the passenger seat, Kenny got behind the wheel, squeezing David between them.

"A beaut', isn't she? A '49 Ford. Got her for a song. Did the work on her myself. See this fender?" Kenny said pointing to a newly reconstructed truck panel. "I did all the Bondo-ing, sanding, and rubbing myself. Couple coats of lacquer and it'll be better than new, eh?"

"Next year I'm gonna redo the interior. The whole nine yards... new seat, a radio, maybe even a tach." David had no idea what a 'tach' was, but pretended to be impressed anyway.

Kenny turned the key in the ignition. The starter ground as the engine turned over, but failed to start. "It'll catch," Kenny reassured his passengers. "Just give it a minute. I think it might be flooded." David smelled gas fumes seeping through the floorboards.

Kenny adjusted the choke, put his foot to the gas, and turned the key again. This time the engine roared to life. Kenny threw the truck into gear, let his foot up off the clutch, and gunned the engine. He squealed the tires as the truck shot out of the parking lot and down Iron Falls Main Street.

# Rita and Ray

"Hey Kyle, reach into the glove box and get a Camel for me, will ya?" Ken ordered his younger brother.

"If mom catches you smokin' around the church, she's gonna kill you," Kyle warned.

"Shut up, and get me a smoke," Kenny snapped back. "It's not like I'm smokin' in church anyway. Mom'll never know unless you say something to her. And I know you wouldn't do that, would you?"

"It's your funeral," Kyle said, reaching into the truck's glove compartment and pulling out a pack of Camels. He tapped the pack against the dash and offered it to his brother.

Kenny pulled out a cigarette, put it to his lips and pushed in the truck's cigarette lighter. "So, how long you and your ma gonna be around?" he said to David.

David squirmed uncomfortably between the two brothers. He wondered how his aunt had failed to notice her son's smoking habit. Ken's clothing reeked of cigarette smoke. "For the whole summer," he replied. "Mom says it'll help me get to know Grandpa Wertz."

Ken lit the cigarette, and inhaled deeply. "Wow, the whole summer, huh? You're gonna be bored shitless, if you ask me. Ain't nothin' happenin' out at that lake where you're stayin' unless you like fishin'."

David grabbed the edges of the car seat as his cousin breezed through a red stop light without seeming to notice.

By the time Ken had smoked his cigarette almost down to his yellowed fingers, the truck reached the Peterson house. From the road, David saw that his mother and Rita had gotten to the house ahead of them, and were already talking to a tall, dark-haired, muscular man dressed in jeans and a dirty white tee shirt. Uncle Ray looked exactly as David remembered him.

Kenny also spotted the threesome standing in the driveway. "Oh, shit, they'll see me," he exclaimed tossing his still glowing cigarette butt out the driver's side window. Frantically he began waving his free hand around to clear the air in the cab.

He wheeled the truck into the driveway, making gravel fly in all directions. Almost before the truck skidded to a stop behind Helen's Chevy, Kyle slid out the passenger door. David scrambled out of the truck behind Kyle, glad to be safely on solid ground again. From what he could hear of the conversation, Ray was already in the process of defending himself for failing to pick up his wife as he had promised.

"Honey, look I'm sorry, ok? It won't happen again, really" Ray apologized.

"Don't you 'honey' me, Ray Peterson," Rita berated her husband. "What on earth were you thinking? If Helen hadn't come to my rescue I might still be standing in front of the church. Sometimes I just don't understand you."

"Christ, Rita, I sent Kenny, didn't I? I would'a come myself, but I had trouble with the damned oil pan plug."

"You knew I was waiting for you," she charged. "How could you be so inconsiderate?"

"Ok, ok, I screwed up. I admit it. But right now we have guests. Can't this wait till later?" Ray wiped his calloused, greasy hand on his overalls and extended it to his sister-in-law. "How the heck are you anyway, Helen?"

Helen accepted his outstretched hand hesitantly, careful to make sure he did not make contact with her pastel pink dress.

"And who can this strapping young fellow be?" Ray said turning his attention to his nephew. "It can't possibly be little David can it? Let me have a look at you." Ray grabbed David's hand, shaking it vigorously. "Jesus, you must have grown a foot."

"Now watch you language, Ray. You don't want David here to think we use profanity around the house, now do we?" Rita scolded.

"Oh for God's sake, Rita, I'm sure the boy's heard worse," Ray responded.

"That's not the point, dear," she persisted. "By the way, Reverend Goodall asked about you after the service today."

"I hope you told him I died," Ray answered sarcastically.

"I did nothing of the sort. I told him you were sick - you were sick weren't you? Anyway he said he'd keep you in his prayers this week. He's a wonderful man, Ray, and I don't understand your attitude toward him."

"That phony's more interested in his collection plate than he is in his parishioners, if you ask me."

David smiled. Uncle Ray was David's favorite relative - probably because his uncle didn't act like the rest of the adults he knew. Uncle

Ray was tough and blunt, and liked hard physical labor - all qualities David's father lacked.

"Anyway, it's good to see you, both," Ray tried to move the conversation back toward their guests. "Where's Don anyway?"

"He couldn't come. Too much work at the office," Helen replied.

"That's a shame. I wanted to tell him what my Packers are going to do to his Lions this year." Like many football fans in Michigan's U.P., Ray had transferred his team allegiance from the distant Detroit Lions to the much closer Green Bay Packers.

"You mean like they did last year," quipped David teasingly. The Lions had finished second in the NFL West the previous season, while Ray's Packers had finished dead last.

"So your old man's been brain washing you, eh? Well, this year's gonna be different. The Pack's gotta new stadium and a couple of young guys, Bart Starr and Paul Hornung. They'll turn things around, just wait and see."

"Ray, please. I'm sure Helen didn't come all this way to hear about the Packers," Rita scolded.

"Oh, Rita, I'm sure Helen doesn't mind," Ray replied unfazed. "Hey, why don't we go inside? I'll clean up and we can talk. You two are staying for supper aren't you?"

Helen looked surprised, but Rita's face lit up at the suggestion of her guests staying for dinner. "Ray, what a wonderful idea! I should have thought of it myself. It won't be anything fancy - just ham and mashed potatoes with canned corn, but it will give us a chance to catch up, eh?"

"That's very generous of you," Helen replied evasively, "but we can't really. Dad's expecting us to stop by the shop after church."

"Oh, I forgot. Carl still attends the Lutheran service doesn't he?" Rita's tone expressed her disapproval. "Well, I'm sure he won't mind. Just tell him you're eating out here," she pressed. "In fact, why don't you invite him to join us? If he's still on that awful raw milk and goat cheese diet of his, I'm sure he could use a good home cooked dinner for a change."

"That's awfully kind of you, Rita, but..."

"But nothing. It's settled," Ray replied cheerily. "Come on in the house. You can give him a call right now."

Ray clasped David around the shoulder, propelling the entire group toward the house. "And why don't you take that damned tie off - you make me uncomfortable just lookin' at you." David gladly complied, loosening the tie's knot, pulling it off, and shoving it in his pant's pocket.

***

When she had finished her call, Helen placed the receiver back in its cradle on the phone. "Dad sends his regards," she explained, "but says he won't be able to make it. So I guess it'll just be David and me for dinner. I told dad that David and I would meet him back at the shop after we eat. "

"Wonderful," said Rita. "Why don't we take a look at the rest of the house while Kyle and Kenny get changed." Both Kyle and Kenny looked relieved to be excused from the room.

"A lot of things have changed since you were here last," Ray said as he led Helen and David through the dining area and into the living room.

The Petersons lived in a modern ranch-style home with cozy fireplace, three bedrooms, and brick patio just off the dining room. Ray had done most of the construction himself, with Kenny's help, hiring only the electrical and plumbing work out to friends who freelanced after their shifts were over at the mine. It had taken him almost five years to complete the house but with the exception of some landscaping and trim work he was now finished.

David and Helen got the full tour - kitchen, four bedrooms, living room, one and a half baths, and even the unfinished basement. Although Ray had done the construction, Rita had done the decorating, and her influence permeated the dwelling. Pinks and pastels dominated the color scheme of most of the rooms, and flower prints were splattered across all the furnishings.

"Rita's in charge of all our decorating," he explained, stating the obvious. "But there's one room I won't let her touch. Wait till you see this," Ray enthused, leading them into a small space just off the living room. "This is my den - or as your Aunt Rita calls it, my sanctuary," Ray teased his wife. "She says I spend more time in here than I do in church."

"It isn't funny, Ray. The Good Book says, 'Thou shalt have no other god before me,' and just look at this room - it's like a shrine or something."

Entering his uncle's den, David stood amazed. Ray had turned team loyalty into a personal obsession. David began to understand his Aunt's comment about the room being a shrine. He had indeed transformed his den into a memorial to the Green Bay Packers. Pictures of players and team pennants were hung everywhere on the walls. Books on, and by, Packer players filled the bookshelf.

"Did you see the antenna tower in the back yard?" Ray asked. David nodded, indicating that he had indeed seen the tower standing in back of the Peterson home. He could hardly have missed the massive structure, rising almost fifty feet into the air, dwarfing the adjacent house. "I can pick up broadcast signals from Menominee and even Green Bay - once and a while. So I can watch the games now when reception is good."

"Mostly what he watches is a screen full of snow," Rita snapped. "Every Sunday in the fall he's out there fiddling around with that darned antenna. He has time for television, but he can't make it to church."

"Maybe if they showed the Packers after the sermon, there'd be a reason to come," Ray replied sarcastically. "Rita thinks I worship the Packers," Ray laughed.

"Ray, it's true. Just look around. You've got a picture of that quarterback - that Tobin Rote fella - on the wall like he was the Messiah. I don't see any pictures of our Savior anywhere in here. I swear, the only praying I've seen you do in the last year is for the Packers to win."

"Just because I don't go to church every Sunday doesn't mean I don't believe in God. I just prefer watching the Packers to standing around gabbing with a bunch of hypocritical, holier-than-thou old maids. The way you talk it's like I worship the devil or something. It's just football for Christ's sakes, Rita."

"Don't you bring the Lord's name into this," Rita chastised her husband. "Come the reckoning you're going to have to answer for your blasphemy, Ray Peterson."

"For cryin' out loud, Rita. Don't throw one of your hissey fits in front of our company." Ray protested.

Rita glared at her husband. "Helen," she said, "I don't know about you, but I've about had it with all this football talk. Come on, we've got women's work to do." Taking Helen by the elbow, Rita led her out of the room and back toward the kitchen.

\*\*\*

After his mother and Aunt Rita left, David's attention was drawn to an old black and white photo hung on the wall next to the picture of the Packer quarterback. It was a wide panoramic photo taken in front of the Jasper mine showing row after row of miners, most of them unrecognizable, their faces covered with ore dust and grime.

"Are you in this picture, Uncle Ray?" David asked.

"Yeah, that's me carrying the pick next to the ore car," he pointed to a dirty figure in the foreground. "And that's your grandfather - Grandpa Bishop - there next to me. That was taken before the accident. Boy, we both look young there, don't we?"

Like most men in Iron Falls, Ray had spent almost his entire life working in the iron mines. He had begun as a trainee at the Jasper Mine while he was still in his teens, and worked as a miner ever since. Now, at forty, after spending almost half his adult life under ground, he had been made foreman of a work crew. His job had given him enough money to move out of the company housing project and build his dream house.

David studied the photo more closely, just making out the similar eyes and smiles of his grandfather and uncle beneath the layers of grime and ore dust.

"I've got something you might like to see," Ray said opening the bottom drawer of the mahogany desk searching for something in a pile of papers. "Here it is," he said, pulling out a small rectangular book with a worn brown cover. He placed the book on the desk so that David could see.

The book consisted of numerous pages of what looked like black construction paper bound together with a shoelace strung through two holes in the binding. Pictures were mounted in the book with small triangles at each corner. Beneath each photo, carefully printed with white ink, was a caption describing who, where, and what the picture contained.

"Uncle Ray? What are those donkeys doing down in the mine?"

Ray stood looking over the boy's shoulder at the grainy black and white photo. "Those aren't donkeys. They're mules. The company used to use mules to pull the ore cars back to the surface."

"Did they actually live down in the mines, Uncle Ray?"

"Yup, sure did. They built stables right down there in the tunnels. At least that's how your Grandpa tells it. They were still using mules when he started at the Jasper mine."

"Did you ever see mules in the mines, Uncle Ray?"

"I never saw 'em myself. By the time I started, electric motors had replaced mules."

David turned the page of the album. Picture after picture showed miners, dirty, sweaty, and tired, wearing ore-stained overalls and hard hats, carrying picks and shovels, surrounded by shear walls of rock. The pictures said things like "Shift change," "Drilling a new vein," and "Up from the underground." As he turned the pages, David noticed one thing the miners had in common - none of them looked very happy.

He turned the page again and saw a picture of a group of miners standing at the entrance of the Jasper mine. But this picture was different. All the men in the picture were smiling and laughing. In the midst of the crowd stood David's grandfather. The caption read, "40 years in the mines and still working."

"Your grandfather spent forty years mining ore and not so much as a scratch," Ray said. "He was all set to retire before the accident, you know."

"Were you there when it happened? The accident I mean." David asked.

Ray suddenly looked uneasy. "Yeah, I was there. We all were. Something happened - a cave-in in tunnel three. Nobody's exactly sure what went wrong. Your grandfather was trapped along with four others."

"So how'd they get out, Uncle Ray?"

"It took 'em till the next day before they could get a crew down to 'em. I volunteered to go, but they said I was too personally involved. By the time they got down there, their air was almost gone. Two of the guys were ok - not a scratch on 'em. Your Grandpa wasn't so lucky. He got caught when the timbers supporting the crosscut collapsed. The roof gave way trapping his leg. Shattered it in at least a dozen places. Took doctors three surgeries just to get it back to where he could walk again."

"You said there were four miners trapped. What happened to the other man?"

Ray looked thoughtful. He reached over David's shoulder and flipped through several pages of the album until he found the picture he wanted. David studied the faded photo of a thin dark complected miner with a scruffy beard of stubble on his chin. The only thing remarkable about the picture was that it was unremarkable, looking much like all the others in the album.

"His name was Pete Johnson," Ray said. "Cave-in caught him full-on before he could react. Didn't have a chance. They brought his body back to the surface on an ore cart. He was one of my best friends at the mine. I was a pall bearer at his funeral." A deep sadness fell over Ray, darkening his mood. "That's enough shop talk," he said taking the album off the desk and returning it to the drawer.

He ushered David out of the den and down the hall toward Kyle's room. "Come on, let's see what your cousin's doing," he said. Ray ignored the '*Keep Out!*' sign hung conspicuously in the center of Kyle's door, and opened it without knocking.

Kyle was busily engaged in using plastic glue to piece together a scale model of a 1954 Corvette at a desk along one side of the room. He had changed out of his church clothes and was now dressed in a plaid short-sleeved shirt and denim jeans.

"Listen, Kyle, I've got some things to finish up on the car before supper," Ray stated. "Why don't you and David go outside and play ball or something for a while before we eat, ok?"

"But dad," Kyle moaned in protest, "I'm kinda busy right now..."

"No buts, Kyle," Ray ignored his son's angry stare. "Now get going before I get mad." Without waiting for a reply, Ray turned and walked out of the room, closing the door behind him.

## The Cave-in

"Asshole," Kyle muttered under his breath. He threw the plastic hood of the Corvette model he was working on against the wall, almost breaking it.

"What?" David said assuming that his cousin was talking to him.

"Oh, not you," Kyle explained. "My dad. Sometimes he's just such a jerk. He could see I was busy. Sometimes I really hate him."

"Hey, look, we don't have to play ball if you don't want," David said apologetically. "I think your dad just wanted to get rid of me."

"Naw, it's not your fault," Kyle said, calming down slightly. "It's ok." He picked the Corvette hood up off the floor and put it back in the parts box on top of his desk. "Look," he said, "I'm about done here anyway. Why don't we go out and toss a ball around for a while. I don't mind. I haven't had much chance to play ball this summer and I could really use the practice."

Kyle removed a fielder's glove he had hung on the post of the footboard on his bed and headed out the door. "Come on. Let's go. You can use my brother's glove. He keeps it out in the shed."

David followed Kyle out of his bedroom and down the hallway toward the dining room. "Hey, Mom, we'll be out in the back until we eat, ok?" Kyle called out in the general direction of the kitchen. He pushed open the sliding glass doors that led to the brick patio at the rear of the house and headed outside.

"Dinner'll be ready in about an hour, so don't wander off. Do you understand?" Rita shouted after the departing boys just before the door slid shut.

They crossed the patio, skirting several tulip-backed lawn chairs set around a glass-topped umbrella table. A flagstone path cut across the lawn leading to a well-tended flower garden decorated with peonies, zinnias, and roses. At the end of the path, in the far corner of the garden, stood a small metal shed. Kyle flipped open an unfastened pad lock loosely hooked through the hasp and opened one of the double doors. He entered the shed, returning moments later with a scuffed up old baseball and a well-worn glove.

"Here's Kenny's glove," Kyle said flipping the mitt to David. "He won't mind - he never uses it anymore anyway." Kyle moved away from David, to the far side of the yard. "Let's see if you're any good," Kyle said. He threw the ball hard toward his cousin.

David easily snared the ball in the webbing of his glove. "Nice arm," he said. "Do you play much ball up here?"

"Naw, just a few pick-up games with my friends. Kenny and me used to toss the ball around once and a while, but ever since he got his truck, he doesn't stay around here. He's always hangin' out with his friends."

"How bout your dad? Do you and him ever play?" David grasped the ball with a split finger grip and threw it back.

"Pop? The only baseball he's interested in is listening to the Tigers on the radio." Kyle again pitched the ball forcefully at his cousin, then squared up waiting for a return throw. "He's usually to tired to do anything when he gets home from work anyway."

David went into a long windup before firing the ball back toward his cousin. "I think I might have upset your dad when I was talking to him."

"Why? What did you say?"

"I ask him about Grandpa's accident. He showed me an old album of pictures and I think it must of bothered him."

"Yeah, he doesn't talk much about what happened that day. I'm surprised he said anything at all."

"Do you ever worry about something happening to your dad - I mean after what happened to Grandpa Bishop?"

"Sometimes, but dad knows how to take care of himself. He says what happened to Grandpa was just bad luck anyway."

"Do you think you'll ever work in the mines?" David pitched the ball back to Kyle.

"Me? Hell no. I'm gonna be a stock car driver. It's too dark and creepy underground."

"You mean you've been inside a real mine?" David asked. "What's it like?"

"Well, I've never been in a mine exactly," Kyle replied evasively. "Only workers are allowed down there. But Kenny and me checked out the mine cave-in down on the old county road awhile back."

"Cave in?" David said, his curiosity aroused.

"Yeah. The road collapsed a few years ago. They were supposed to fill it in last year, but the county ran out of money. It's pretty scary when you get up close."

"You mean you can walk right up to it?"

"The police put up a barricade, but the fence is broken down so anybody can just walk in."

"Really? How deep is the cave-in anyway?"

"I don't know - at least a hundred feet - maybe more," Kyle exaggerated.

"You're kidding, right," David said.

"Hey, if you don't believe me, you can check it out yourself. It's not far."

David paused uncertainly. "We better not," he replied. "Your mom said to stay around here before dinner."

"Don't worry. We've got plenty of time if we leave right now. It's only a half-mile or so from here - across Gleason's field. You said you wanted to see what a mine was like. This is your chance."

"But I've still got on my church clothes."

"Come on, chicken." Kyle dropped his glove and headed back toward the shed. "Follow me, I'll grab a flashlight. You'll love this, it's really neat."

***

Gleason's field was a large pasture surrounded by a barbed wire fence. The two boys plowed a path through the waist high field of switch grass, past patches of lupine, thistle, black-eyed Susan, goldenrod, and Queen Anne's lace. Scores of grasshoppers scattered as they pushed through the grass.

"How much farther is it?" David said swatting at a horsefly buzzing around his head.

"Not far now. Just try to keep up, eh?"

As he stepped out of the tall grass, David spotted the biggest bull he had ever seen in his life standing in a clearing no more than a hundred yards away. He stopped dead in his tracks.

"Kyle, watch out..." he yelled, panic edging into his voice.

Kyle looked at the bull, and laughed. "Don't worry 'bout him," he reassured his cousin. "That's Brutus. He's harmless."

Kyle led David across the field toward a hole in the fence. He climbed through the hole motioning for David to follow. "Watch the barbs," he cautioned. David angled his body through the hole, careful not to catch his shirt or pants on the jagged wire.

After continuing through the woods for another ten minutes, they reached a shallow stream. Kyle leaped across easily, urging

David to follow. David jumped but landed awkwardly on the edge of the water. His foot twisted and his shoe slipped into the muck. The shoe made a sucking sound as he pulled it out.

"Crap," he exclaimed wiping away the mud with a handful of grass.

"Don't worry. They'll look fine once the leather dries."

Finally, after following a rutted path through a dense stand of maples and birch, they arrived at an area overgrown with brush and weeds. The remnants of a two-lane asphalt roadway disappeared into the undergrowth. Yet another fence blocked passage, and a barricade placed across the road indicated that 'No Trespassing' was permitted.

Ignoring the sign, Kyle made his way over the broken fence into the barricaded area.

"I don't think we should be here," David said cautiously.

"Oh come on, you sissy," Kyle urged.

Reluctantly David followed his cousin across the fence. Up ahead, a gaping hole had opened up consuming the asphalt and roadbed around it. "What is this place?" David asked.

"It's a sinkhole. One of the old mine tunnels collapsed right under the county road. They built a detour around it, but they never did fill in the sinkhole. Cool, eh?"

David drew back. "I don't know," he said. "It looks kinda dangerous."

"Naw - it's ok. Just stay close to me," Kyle instructed.

As they came closer, David stopped, reluctant to get too close to the edge. "How did it happen, anyway?"

"One night a couple'a years ago, a woman came barreling down this road. Suddenly, POW! The road just opened up in front of her. She slammed on the breaks, and tried to swerve out of the way, see? But it was too late. BLAM! She nose dives right into the pit. The pavement gave way under her, and down she went - fifteen, twenty feet. SPLAT! Deader than a doornail."

"Geez, that's terrible. She died, for real?"

"Sure did. They didn't find her till the next day," Kyle explained. "It made the headlines of *The Falls Herald* for days. Even the *Detroit News* sent a crew up here to cover the story."

"Is she still down there?"

"Naw, they hauled her out right away, but they still haven't sealed the shaft. It goes straight down." To prove his point, he threw a rock into the black chasm. After several long seconds, the sound of a splash echoed from the mouth of the opening.

"Sounds like there's water down there," David observed.

"Probably a whole lake," Kyle offered. "Dare you to look over the edge."

"I don't think so. It doesn't look very safe to me."

"Come on, scaredy-cat. Nothin's gonna hurt you," Kyle challenged, edging toward the opening and shining his flashlight down into the blackness.

Hesitantly David crept toward the edge. The rock and soil around the top of the pit were unstable and slid beneath his feet. There was no rail and nothing to hang on to. He was afraid that he might lose his balance and fall.

"They say that even walking by like this, or any noise could cause another cave in - like SHOUTING," Kyle purposely yelled as loudly as he could. David stepped back from the edge, but Kyle only laughed. "Got ya that time."

Suddenly there was a low rumbling sound from the pit below. Kyle stopped laughing. "Oh, shit," he exclaimed as the ground began to move under him. His feet slid sideways. Dirt and gravel began to tumble into the opening.

Seeing his cousin sliding toward the hole, David acted instinctively. He reached out, grabbing Kyle's arm and yanking him back with all his might. The boys tumbled backwards onto the gravel as the piece of roadbed Kyle had been standing on disappeared into the abyss below.

"Shit that was close," Kyle stammered picking himself up off the ground and brushing off the dust. "Thanks, I owe you one."

David saw blood oozing from a cut over Kyle's eye. "Geez, you're hurt. Are you ok?"

"Yeah, I'm fine," Kyle replied, reaching to wipe away the blood. "How bout you? Looks like you tore up your pants pretty good."

David looked down. His white dress shirt was covered with fine brown dust. His dress pants had a two-inch rip in the left knee, and blood was seeping into the fabric. David bent over and saw that he had suffered a small gash on his knee.

"Crap, these are my good clothes. Mom'll kill me when she finds out what happened."

"Don't worry," Kyle said reassuringly. "Nobody'll ever know cuz we're not going to tell 'em. But you've got to promise to keep your mouth shut. Promise?"

"Do I really have any choice?" David said uncertainly.

"Good. Then when we get back just let me do all the talkin', ok?"

\*\*\*

Kyle moved rapidly back across the field and through the meadow toward the Peterson home. David tried to keep up, but his knee had begun to throb and he started to favor his right leg as the pain increased. "Hey, hold up, will ya?" he yelled ahead. "Don't go so fast. I don't know what you're in such a hurry for anyway."

"I told you - everything will be all right. Just remember, let me do all the talking."

As they neared the rear of the Peterson house, David saw Rita, Ray, and Helen sitting on the metal lawn chairs around the umbrella table in the middle of the patio. They were sipping what looked like lemonade. The umbrella had been raised over the table and turned slightly to block the sun's glare. Kenny sat to one side of the parental grouping, sprawled out on an aluminum chaise lounge.

"Where have you two been? Dinner's getting cold," Ray called out to the two approaching figures. "Get your butts over here right now!"

As the boys came closer, their condition became more apparent to those seated at the table. The cut over Kyle's eye had opened slightly, and a trickle of blood ran down his cheek. David appeared to have been in a fight. Splotches of dried mud covered his shoes and blood stains streaked his torn pants.

"My gosh, are you all right?" Helen called out concerned about her son's appearance.

"Yeah, it's just a little scratch. I'm ok," David assured her.

Kenny showed little sympathy for his brother's condition. "Oh, man, you're really gonna get it for this one," he laughed.

"All right, young man," Rita addressed Kyle critically. "I want an explanation, and I want it now."

"It was an accident, Mom. Really!" Kyle exclaimed. "We were cutting through Gleason's pasture when that bull of theirs took off after us. I must have tripped. Anyway I fell down and cut my head. Davy helped me up, but the bull kept charging. We had to dive over a barbed wire fence to get away, but David ripped his pant on the barbs as we dove over. We made it just in time."

"What on earth were you two doing in Gleason's field anyway, young man?" Rita asked.

"We were taking the shortcut over to Township Park. Davy wanted to see where we play ball, so I said I'd show him." David tried not to look surprised by his cousin's account of the 'accident.' "Hey," Kyle continued, "it could have been worse. That bull almost got us both."

"I can't believe you'd be that careless - and with your cousin along, for goodness sakes. What were you thinking?"

"Come on, Rita, take it easy. The boys didn't mean any harm," Ray countered. "It was just an accident. I always knew that bull was trouble. Wait till I see Harold. I'll give him a real piece of my mind."

"Helen, I'm so sorry about this," Rita stammered apologetically to her sister-in-law. "If I'd had any idea…"

"Don't blame yourself, Rita. You couldn't possibly have known," Helen responded.

"All right, I guess the damage is already done," Rita concluded. "You boys go get cleaned up. Look in the medicine cabinet for some bandages. And Kenny? Go and see if you have a pair of pants that will fit David."

Kenny looked perplexed. "Why can't he wear Kyle's pants?"

"Because David's too big to wear Kyle's clothes. Now do as I say," Rita ordered.

David breathed a sigh of relief. Kyle's story appeared to have worked. Helen looked at him skeptically as he walked by, but said nothing. He knew that he hadn't heard the last about his part in the afternoon's fiasco, but for the moment he was off the hook.

"And make it fast," Rita called. "Dinner's in ten minutes."

# Consequences

A tense silence accompanied Helen and David on their ride back to Carl's upholstery shop. David squirmed uncomfortably in his cousin's clothes as Helen tapped the steering wheel impatiently.

Dinner at the Peterson's had proven uncomfortable for everyone involved. Throughout the entire meal, Rita had continued to apologize to Helen for her son's behavior. Each time she did, David looked over at Kyle, who seemed unconcerned about their misadventure. For his own part, David just wanted to crawl under the table and hide.

Though he had been relieved when the dinner finally ended, David dreaded the confrontation with his mother he knew was inevitable. Helen had remained quiet throughout the entire meal, but David knew she was fuming inside. Now that they were alone in the car, driving back into town, David once again braced himself for his mother's questions.

"Mom, can I explain..." he started.

"Save your explanations, young man," Helen replied curtly, "There's nothing you can say to me right now."

Helen pulled the Chevy around to the rear of the upholstery shop. Lady ran up and jumped on David as he emerged from the car. "Down, Lady," he pushed her away. "I don't feel like playing right now."

"Here," Helen said handing the torn pants to her son, "take these in and show them to your grandfather. I'm sure he'll want to see how you treat your Sunday-best clothes."

David moved awkwardly toward the back door to the shop. Even with the cuffs rolled up, his borrowed pants dragged on the ground as he walked.

In the kitchen, Carl sat behind the table, the Sunday *Herald* spread out in front of him, the stub of a cigar clenched between his teeth. The slam of the screen door made him look up over his reading glasses. "Tisk, tisk," Carl scolded noting David's condition. David was embarrassed.

"Well, are you going to tell your grandfather what happened?" Helen prompted.

David felt trapped by the lie Kyle had created. "Well," he started,

"Kyle and me were out in this field behind his house, and this big bull chased us. We had to jump over a barbed wire fence to get away. I guess that's when I cut my leg and tore my pants."

"You're a terrible liar, young man," Helen charged. "I hope you know that the cost of replacing your suit is coming out of your allowance."

Carl reached out and took the torn pants from David's hands. "Let me see how much damage has been done."

"Well, they won't be like new," he said after checking the tear, "but I can sew in a patch to hold them together until you get back to the lake. It will only take a few minutes."

Carl led his daughter and grandson through the curtain into his workshop. In the scrap pile, he found a piece of fabric which almost matched the color of David's suit pants. He sat down behind the rugged industrial sewing machine, set the tension, and lowered the presser bar into place, firmly securing the pant leg against the machine bed.

As he worked, a faint whistling sound cut through the air from the direction of the kitchen. "Ah, my water is hot. I was just about to make a cup of tea when you arrived."

"Don't get up dad," Helen offered. "I'll get it. You still take milk and sugar, right?"

"Please. It's very kind of you. The tea is on the shelf above the stove."

Helen made her way through the curtain into the kitchen. Carl waited until she was out of hearing range before he addressed David.

"So now that your mother is gone do you want to tell me what really happened?" he said.

"I told you. It was an accident."

"An accident? Yes. But that tear was not caused by barbed wire. How did it really happen, eh?"

David knew that he couldn't fool his grandfather any longer. "Well, Kyle took me over to see this old collapsed mine shaft," he said, relieved to finally be telling the truth.

"Mine? But all the abandoned mines around here have been boarded up."

"It was a cave in, Grandpa. Kyle took me to a place where the road fell in a couple of years ago. He said it would be ok."

"Ya, ya, out by Route 11. I know the place. It was a terrible accident - I remember." Carl raised his eyebrow, expressing his concern. "So what happened when you reached this cave in?"

"Kyle got a little too close and the ground began to give way. I grabbed him but we both fell. I must'a cut my leg and torn my pants on the gravel."

"It sounds like you were lucky to have come out of it with only a scratch, ya?"

David nodded his agreement. "But now Mom says I'm gonna have'ta pay for a new suit, And I only have about five dollars saved up."

"Well, then you have to tell your mother that you will earn the money you need."

"But I don't have a job, Grandpa. Besides, I don't know anybody up here who'd hire me."

Carl thought for a moment before responding. "You know me, ya?" he said. "You will go to work for me. I am sure there are things you can do to help Maddie out at the lake. I will pay you for your work. That way you will be able to earn enough to repay your mother. How does that sound?"

"All right, I guess," David replied, finding a hint of hope in his grandfather's offer.

"Good, then it is settled," Carl said, handing the patched pants back to David. "Here are your trousers. Why don't you go try them on while I tell your mother about our plan."

***

"That's a lovely Dacron worsted blend. Just feel the fabric." The salesman at Broderick's Department Store gestured for Helen to come closer and examine the material. "Very light and cool in this hot weather we've been having lately."

"I'm not sure," Helen said examining the cut of the jacket her son was trying on. Helen had readily agreed to the plan Carl and David had proposed to pay her back for a new suit and shoes. Now, she had insisted on coming into Iron Falls early Monday morning to find a replacement for David's ruined suit. "The sooner we find a new one," she had explained to David, "the sooner you'll know how much you owe me."

David stood at attention, looking almost as stiff as the mannequins posed around him. "It looks pretty expensive, mom," he complained.

"Not if you consider it's a genuine Botany 500," the salesman said. "It's really quite reasonable at only $44.95."

David's heart sank into his shoes. He would be paying for the suit until he graduated from high school.

"It's very nice. But I don't know about the narrow lapels," Helen hesitated.

"It's very fashionable, madam. Ivy League." The clerk, a balding man with white hair, peered over his wire rimmed glasses. "We can barely keep them in stock." Wearing a white dress shirt with the sleeves rolled up, a black bow tie, and red vest, the man looked more like a railroad conductor than a store clerk.

"I'm sure it's very stylish," Helen replied, "but we were looking for something a little more traditional."

David took off the jacket and handed it back to the clerk. "How 'bout one of these, mom?" he said moving toward a nearby rack of suits marked 'SALE.'

"Oh, I don't think so, honey," his mother answered dismissively.

"Actually," the clerk spoke up, "I might have something you'd be interested in." He went to the rack and pulled out a conservatively cut light blue suit with pinstripes. "I just marked it down this morning - we're no longer carrying this brand, and I need to make room. But it's a very fine quality wool blend."

The clerk held the suit draped over his arm so that mother and son could inspect it.

"Are you sure it's in David's size?" Helen asked. "It looks a little big to me."

"Why don't we let the young man try it on?" The sales clerk helped David slip into the jacket. To Helen's surprise, the jacket fit fairly well.

"Let's see how the trousers fit," the salesman said. He handed David the pants and showed him to the fitting room.

When David returned, his pants dragged on the floor as he walked. The salesman rushed up to roll up the cuffs.

"Don't worry about the length. A few alterations will take care of that," the clerk explained. "That way, as he grows, you'll be able to let out the seams."

Helen looked her son over thoroughly. "How much are you asking?"

"Let me see. That suit was originally forty dollars, and it's marked thirty. But if you're interested, I can give it to you for $24.95. That's well below our cost, and a real bargain, I can assure you."

"Can we get it, mom?" David interjected, suddenly seeing an opportunity to save some money. "It's a little big now, but I'll grow into it."

After deliberating briefly, Helen made her decision. "All right, we'll take it, providing you can have it ready by next Sunday."

"I'm sure that won't be a problem," the salesman said as he knelt down and began making marks on the fabric with a small piece of wedge shaped chalk. As David shifted uncomfortably, the clerk jotted down his measurements - neck, shoulders, sleeves, chest, waist, and inseam - on the notepad he kept at his side.

When he finished, he stood up and said, "Will there be anything else, madam?"

"That blue and gold tie, on the mannequin in the window, how much is that?" Helen asked.

"Excellent choice, madam. That's pure silk. And only $2.49."

"But mom, I don't need a new tie," David protested.

"Well you should have thought of that before you and your cousin went off chasing bulls, or whatever happened out there in that field."

"But it's not fair. I just tore my pants and you're making me buy a whole new suit and tie and everything."

"Ok, I'll take care of the tie," Helen relented. "But you still owe me for the suit."

The clerk pressed the keys on the mechanical cash register and pulled the handle. He tore the receipt off and handed it to Helen. "That will be $28.54 with tax," he said.

Helen took out her wallet and gave the clerk two twenties. "You can pick the suit up anytime after ten on Thursday," the clerk said, returning her change. "And thank you for your business."

***

David had never been to a job interview before. But now, as he sat at the kitchen table in the cottage surrounded by three adults, he suddenly began to feel nervous and uncomfortable. His mother had called the meeting, inviting his grandfather and Maddie to join them, in order to discuss a plan for David to repay the money he owed. He had never seen his mother so serious and determined.

"All right, David, let's see," Helen started writing numbers down on a small pad of paper in front of her. "You owe me $24.95 plus tax for the suit, and then there's the cost of your new dress shoes..."

"Mom, do I really have to pay for the shoes too?" David complained. After leaving Broderick's, Helen had insisted on stopping at Mason's Shoe Store. That stop had added another $8.26 to David's mounting debt for a pair of black Buster Brown shoes.

"We already talked about this. You have to learn that your actions have consequences. Those old shoes of yours were a mess. They'll never be the same. So it's both the suit and the shoes, do you understand?"

David nodded meekly.

Helen resumed her calculations, drawing a circle around the sum as if in emphasis. "So the grand total is $34," she said. "How much did you say you have saved up?"

"You know, Mom," David replied dejectedly. "Just five dollars."

"Ok, you give me the five dollars, and that means you still owe me $29."

Carl looked on sympathetically. "Well, you know my offer still stands," he said. "And Maddie agrees that there is plenty of work for you to do around the cabins."

David looked toward Maddie, but the short stout woman remained silent, saying nothing.

"Exactly what kind of work would I be expected to do, Grandpa?" he asked.

"Well, let me see. To start with, there are some boards on the dock that must be replaced, the boathouse has to be cleaned out, and the beach chairs could use a fresh coat of paint. I'm sure there are other things, but that is enough to get started, eh?"

"Sure, Grandpa. That doesn't sound too bad. But, well...," David fumbled for words, "There's just one other thing I was wondering, ah..."

"You want to know what you will be paid, eh? What do you think would be fair?"

"I don't know. I was thinking maybe a dollar an hour?"

"Minimum wage?" Helen asked incredulously. "And just what makes you think you're worth that kind of money? Most boys your age are lucky to make fifty cents an hour."

David looked disheartened. "Fifty cents? It'll take me till Christmas to earn enough to pay you back."

"Well, let's see. I want to be fair," Carl stepped in. "So what if we do this - I will pay you fifty cents to start, ya? And if you show me that you are a good worker after one week, I will raise your pay to seventy-five cents. All right?"

David tried to calculate how much he would have to work in his head. Working four hours a day for a full week at fifty cents an hour he would earn ten dollars. It would take him at least three weeks to make enough to pay back his mother. Unfortunately he had little choice but to accept the offer.

"It's a deal," David stated holding out his hand. "I can start right now if you want."

Carl took David's hand and shook it, sealing the agreement. "My, my! Anxious to get started, eh? Before you start I'll need to pick up some supplies. We'll need some paint and nails. And besides you are still not walking around too well."

"But I thought I could start today. Isn't there anything I can do right now?"

Carl scratched the coarse gray stubble on his chin. "I don't know," he said. "What about you, Maddie. Can you think of anything David could start on today?"

"There's that pile of firewood George Davis dropped off last week," she answered. "It still needs to be sorted and stacked. I suppose David could stack the wood up out by the shed."

"How about it, David? Are you ready to get to work," Carl asked.

"Mom, is it all right with you? I'll be careful, I promise."

"I don't see why not," she said.

"Ok, just let me change my clothes and I'll get started."

## **Change of Plans**

"Maddie? Maddie? Hello?" David stood on the porch of Maddie's cabin. Her small house stood, half hidden by trees, set apart from the rest. The cabin had been the first one built on the property, and was slightly smaller and more secluded than the others. Many of the summer guests never realized that it even existed. Carl provided the cabin to Maddie as partial compensation for her work as his manager.

The door stood open just a crack. David tapped softly, but no one answered. He looked around. The lake stood still and serene in the early morning light. All the guest cabins were quiet. No one's up yet, David thought.

"Maddie? Are you in there?" David called out again, peeking in through the crack in the door. Still no answer. Where was she? She must have been expecting him. Maybe she had forgotten.

For the past two days, David had stacked firewood, fixed broken dock boards, pulled weeds around the cabins, and picked up junk littering the beach. In return, he had earned almost three dollars toward his goal of repaying his mother. Today Carl wanted him to help Maddie repaint the wooden chairs outside the guest cabins. But where was she?

He pushed the door open slightly so that he could look inside. He had never been in Maddie's cabin before. He took a tentative step into the kitchen. Unlike Carl's upholstery shop, the air inside Maddie's cabin smelled good. A potpourri of cinnamon, cloves, orange peel, and rose flowers sat in a wooden bowl on the log table near the door. The mixture released a fragrant odor that permeated the small structure.

David looked around the dimly lit interior. The main room was sparsely furnished. A hand woven rug covered the rough-hewn wooden floor. Embers from a small fire still glowed in the fireplace. David began to feel uneasy being inside Maddie's home without her permission.

An iron kettle simmered on the wood cook stove while a half-empty cup of black coffee still steamed on the table. Maddie must be close by, he thought.

He stepped tentatively into the cabin and walked over to the table. A small knife with an oddly shaped tip sat near Maddie's coffee cup. David had never seen one like it before. He picked it up to examine it more closely. The blade was about five inches long and curved at the tip. The tang of the blade had been wedged into an angled piece of tree limb forming a handle. The haft had been carved to resemble a duck's head and was lashed onto the blade using a binding made of rawhide.

"It's called a crooked knife," Maddie's voice called from behind him.

David turned to see Maddie standing in the doorway holding a wicker basket containing some asparagus, a few carrots, and a handful of freshly picked peas. "It looks old," he said of the knife.

"You're right," she replied. "That knife is very old. My grandfather made it and he gave it to my father who gave it to me."

"What's it for, Maddie?"

"Here, let me show you." Maddie put her basket of vegetables down on the table and took the knife from the boy's hand. She turned the blade inward and slowly drew the blade toward her body as if shaving a piece of wood. "My people used knives like this to carve canoe ribs, sled runners, and snowshoes. I keep it to remember and respect my ancestors," she said.

"Can I try it, Maddie?"

"Perhaps another day, David," she said shutting the knife away in a drawer under the counter. "Right now you have work to do." She led him outside unto the porch where he saw a screwdriver, two cans of whitewash, and several paint brushes sitting beside the door. Maddie picked up the screwdriver and brushes and put them into a small hand bag she carried over her arm.

"Grab those paint cans and come with me," she ordered. Grabbing a paint can in each hand, David followed her down the path toward the beach.

The sun was just breaking through the tree branches behind the cabins, giving the lake a warm hazy glow in the morning mist. A robin dropped to the ground pulling a worm from the soft moist soil. For the moment at least, the thought of the work that lay ahead seemed secondary to David's excitement at having returned to the lake.

\*\*\*

Though Carl and Maddie referred to the structure as 'the pavilion,' in reality it was an open-air picnic shelter with a gabled roof and cement slab floor.

When they reached the pavilion, Maddie stopped and motioned for David to put down the paint cans on a picnic table that stood in the center of the shelter. Around the perimeter of the pavilion sat a row of dingy wooden beach chairs with fading paint.

Maddie handed David a screwdriver and paint brush then took a seat on the picnic table bench. "Ok, let's see how you are as a painter," she said.

David used the screwdriver to pry the lid off one of the cans, dipped his brush into the paint, and began spreading the watery whitewash liberally onto one of the chairs. He was glad his mother had found some old work clothes for him to wear. Paint spattered everywhere - on his tee shirt, on his pants, and even on his face.

While David painted, Maddie removed some yarn and a half finished scarf from the hand bag she carried and began to knit. David soon realized that her idea of helping was to sit and supervise.

After he had been painting for about fifteen minutes or so, a commotion just offshore attracted David's attention. Two men David didn't recognize were guiding Carl's sputtering old bass boat carefully toward the dock. The men coasted to a stop, coming to a rest against the dock's tire bumpers before tying the bow line to the mooring post.

"Morning Miss Madaline," the older of the two men hailed as he came ashore carrying a string of perch and blue gills. "Tell Carl thanks for the use of the boat. They're really biting out there this morning. Caught our limit already. Who's your new helper?"

"This is David Bishop, Carl's grandson," Maddie responded.

"Nice to meet you David," the man said. "I'm sure we'll be seeing more of you around here." The two men took the string of fish and headed away toward the line of cabins.

"Who was that, Maddie?"

"That's Mr. Livingston and his son. They're from Dearborn. They come up here for a week every year to fish."

Within the next hour, several more guests emerged from their cabins. An elderly couple came out of cabin three, got into a Hudson sedan, and drove off in the direction of Iron Falls. Then, a few minutes later, a young couple appeared from cabin one, taking their three year old for a walk along the beach. The little girl waved to David and smiled as she passed by the pavilion. But none of the guests were remotely close to David's age.

"Is there anyone my age staying in the cabins, Maddie?"

"I am afraid not just now, David," she replied. Maddie saw the discouraged look on his face. "I hope you are not too disappointed," she said.

"My cousin told me I'd be bored to death staying out here all summer," he replied.

"There will be plenty of time for you to find friends your own age, eh? Perhaps next week when your grandfather's friends arrive from Milwaukee..."

David looked up, his interest aroused. "Grandpa didn't say anything about his friends coming. Do they have kids my age?"

"I'm not sure, but it's possible. They will be staying in cabin five. That cabin has three bedrooms. You should ask your grandfather about it."

"I really hope so, Maddie. It would be nice to have some friends while I'm here."

***

David returned to the cottage, entering through the back door. He kicked off his shoes and walked over to the refrigerator. Pushing aside his mother's Canada Dry ginger ale, he pulled out a cold bottle of Nehi orange.

"Hey, Mom, I'm done painting," David said beaming with satisfaction. "Maddie said I'm a good helper, but she doesn't have anything else for me to do today."

Helen looked at her son affectionately. "You've been working so hard the last couple of days, David, and I'm very proud of you," she said. "I've made spaghetti and meatballs. Go get washed up, while I set the table."

David could barely keep his head up during dinner, only managing to finish part of his supper. "I'm really beat," he said. "If it's ok with you I think I'll go to my room and read for awhile."

"You've had a long day. Why don't you get some rest, dear. I'll talk to you in the morning."

In his room, David opened the box containing a collection of classic novels his parents had given him the previous Christmas. The collection contained *Little Women*, *Black Beauty*, *Treasure Island*, *Huckleberry Finn*, *Tom Sawyer*, and *Robin Hood*. He picked up the copy of Robert Lewis Stevenson's *Treasure Island* he had been reading since the beginning of summer.

Removing his shoes, he hopped into the squeaky single bed, and propped his feet up. He switched on the lamp sitting on the stand next to the bed. His eyes strained to make out the words in the dim lamplight. Still, David remained glued to the page, fascinated by Jim Hawkins escape from the nefarious Long John Silver.

He had been reading for almost half an hour when the phone in the next room began to ring. The phone was on its third ring before he heard the click of his mother's high heels approaching across the hardwood floor. "Don't get up. I'll get it myself," Helen called through the door.

David went back to his reading, but found it hard to concentrate. He could hear his mother's indistinct voice filter through the thin walls. "Hello? Oh, it's you," she answered edgily. David wondered if it was his father calling. He put down the book, trying to hear the indistinct words as they filtered through the door. At first he caught only bits and pieces of the conversation, but as his mother's voice became more and more agitated, he could understand most of her words.

"That's not what I said," Helen tried to contain herself. There was a pause. "What do you mean by that?" she said, clearly irritated now. Another pause. "Well, my time is valuable too!" her voice flashed with anger.

A long silence followed. David crept closer, putting his ear to the door. "I can't talk now," he heard his mother whisper. "He's right in the next room." David strained to hear more, but his mother's voice had grown quiet again and he could no longer make out her words. He reached over and switched off the reading light.

Slowly and gently he grasped the doorknob and turned it cautiously, fearful that the latch would snap open and give his presence away. There was a slight click as the lock opened and David froze holding his breath. But his mother continued to talk softly, unaware of the disturbance.

David pushed the door open just a crack, allowing a narrow shaft of light to penetrate the room. He peeked out and could see his mother sitting with her back to the door only a few feet away. Again she paused.

"You can't do that," she snapped into the receiver. "I won't let you." She tapped her foot nervously as she listened to the caller. "But we just got here," she replied. "It's not fair to David." David flinched at the mention of his name. What did all this have to do with him, he wondered.

"I know we need to talk but…" Helen hesitated. "All right, fine," she agreed at last. "If that's the way you want it, I'll see what I can do. We'll talk about this when I get there. Goodbye." It was only after the call ended that David heard his mother sob for the first time. He closed the door slightly, but continued to watch through the crack.

Helen continued to cradle the phone in her lap, tears streaming down her cheeks for several minutes before hanging up. Finally, visibly shaking, she placed the receiver back in its cradle and walked away in the direction of the bathroom. David pulled the door shut and climbed back into bed.

He lay awake for a long time, listening for the sound of his mother returning to her room. But in the end, fatigue got the best of him and he drifted off to sleep. His sleep was restless and troubled. Several times during the night he awoke thinking he heard the sound of weeping drifting through the darkened cottage. His dream catcher dangled over the bed, unable to keep the bad thoughts from slipping through its web.

*** 

Lady's bark pierced the morning air, startling David awake. He groaned and rolled over, pulling a pillow tightly over his head. He had not slept well and the noise made his head throb. The barking started again, this time followed by his grandfather's voice. "Lady! Lady, come here!"

David rubbed his eyes and sat up in bed. He got up, went to the window, and raised the shade. A thin curtain of fog blurred the trees across the drive, but he could see no sign of his grandfather or Lady. He slipped into his pants, pulled a clean tee shirt on over his head, and headed out into the living room. As he passed his mother's room he saw that her suitcase lay open on the bed.

As soon as he saw his mother's face, David knew that he had not dreamed the previous night's conversation. Although she feigned a smile, her eyes showed her hurt and sadness. They were still red and puffy from crying, dark circles betraying her lack of sleep.

"I thought I heard Grandpa's voice," he said. "Was that Lady barking?"

"I'm sorry we woke you," Helen replied. "Your grandfather came early this morning. He's outside taking Lady for a walk. They'll be back in a few minutes."

"Why's Grandpa here? I thought he wasn't coming back till Saturday. Is something up?"

"That's what I want to talk to you about, David. I need to take a little trip."

"What's going on? Is it about dad? Are you going back home?"

His mother looked surprised, but at the same time relieved that she no longer had to keep up a cheery façade. "Can't fool you for a minute, can I?" She walked over and sat down next to David on the sofa, taking his hand into her own. "Something unexpected has come up at home, and your father thinks I should come back down until we can straighten things out."

"You mean we won't be able to stay here all summer?" David's voice pretended disappointment, masking his real excitement at the idea of returning to his friends in LaSalle. "We just got here. Won't Grandpa be upset?"

"I called your grandfather this morning and explained the situation to him," Helen replied. "He understands why I have to go back. But David," she said gripping his hand tighter, "there's something else, and I'm not sure you're going to like it."

David looked up at his mother, sensing the change in her tone. "What is it?" he asked.

"I need to go back alone, honey. You'll have to stay here with your grandfather. He'll take care of you while I'm gone. Your father and I will come back and get you as soon as things are settled - it won't be more than a week or so..." Tears began to run down her cheeks.

David could barely comprehend what his mother was telling him. His mother was abandoning him. David stood in disbelief as the finality of her decision began to sink in.

"Don't look so upset," Helen said. "It won't be so bad. It'll give you a chance to know your grandfather better. You can swim and fish. It'll be fun. Come on and cheer up, now."

Fun was the last thing staying alone with his grandfather for even a few days meant to David. "That's no fair," he bellowed. "I can't stay here alone. There's nothing to do up here. Mom, you can't leave me all by myself."

"I'm sorry, David," his mother sobbed softly, beginning to cry once more. "I have to do this, and you can't go. You'll be all right. I promise."

"When are you going, Mom?"

"I'm leaving today, just as soon as I finish packing and put the bags in the car."

***

By early afternoon, a light drizzle had begun to fall from a uniformly gray sky. Carl took Helen's bags and put them in the trunk of the Chevy as she prepared to leave the cottage. David refused to help, waiting in the kitchen with Maddie.

Helen shook the rain off her plastic poncho as she returned to the back door. "Ok, I guess I'm as ready as I'll ever be," she said.

"David? David? Come out here and say goodbye to your mother," Carl called into the kitchen.

David ran to the screen door, almost in tears. "Please why can't I go with you, Mom? I won't be any trouble," he pleaded.

"We've already been over all this," Helen said. "I told myself I wouldn't cry. I'll call as soon as I get home. I want you to promise me you'll pay attention to your grandfather and do whatever he says. He's in charge now, ok?"

David consented reluctantly, his eyes welling with tears.

"Now don't get all long faced on me. You're almost a man, and I want you to show me how grown up you are."

David had never been away from his parents for longer than a single night. Now he would be staying alone with his grandfather, until his parents returned for him. And there was no guarantee when that would be.

Helen got into the Chevy and started the engine. Tears flowed freely down her cheeks. "Now be a good boy while I'm gone. It won't be long. I'll get back up here as soon as possible." Turning to Carl she held out her hand. "Thanks for taking care of David, Dad. I love you both and I'll call as soon as I get to LaSalle." She rolled up the window, and pulled the car away from the cottage.

David watched the Chevy as it splashed through the puddles

along the rain drenched cabin access road. After a few moments the car disappeared into a curtain of rain and his mother was gone. David ran into the cottage, slamming the screen door behind him.

"What's your hurry, young man," Maddie called as he brushed past.

David did not reply, but rushed into his room. He pounded his fists angrily into his mattress, sobbing uncontrollably. But Helen could no longer hear his heartfelt cries. She was already headed down US 2, back toward the Straits and the Lower Peninsula - far from the sadness of her grieving son.

## **Camping Out**

David lay in his bed staring at the ceiling. Except to use the bathroom, he had not come out of his room since his mother's departure. He did not remember falling asleep, but guessed it must have been very late. Now it was morning. He heard sounds outside his room coming from the kitchen, and opened his door slightly to look out. He sniffed the air. The smell of sausage frying in a pan beckoned him.

Still groggy from sleep, he made his way to the kitchen. His grandfather was already sitting at the table eating. "Smells good, ya? Why don't you pull up a chair and join me?" Carl tapped the seat of the empty chair next to him invitingly.

As David sat down at the table, Maddie brought a plate of pancakes and sausage from the stove and placed it before him. He took a small bite of pancake. It tasted good. He was famished.

"So, you had quite a day yesterday," Carl said. "How are you feeling this morning?"

"I'm ok," David said taking a bite of sausage. "I just miss mom and all my friends back home."

Carl watched as his grandson lingered over Maddie's pancakes. "I know it must be hard for you, stuck out here with no friends your own age," he said. "But perhaps things will be better soon, ya?"

"Do you really think so? Maddie said that you were expecting some friends of yours from Milwaukee."

"Ya, ya. Nathan Gibson and his family. They are coming for the 4th of July holiday. I've convinced them to stay for the full two weeks of Nathan's vacation this year."

"Do they have any kids, Grandpa?"

"I believe Nathan has a son and a daughter."

"Really? How old is the boy?" David asked taking another bite of pancake.

"I am not sure - a bit older than you I think. But you must be patient. They will not be here until the end of next week."

Disappointed, David wiped his mouth with his napkin and pushed his plate away. "What am I supposed to do till then?" he asked dejectedly.

"Well, perhaps you can work on earning the rest of the money you owe your mother, eh?" Carl suggested. "Why don't we take a walk down to the lake? I can show you the work I want you to do on the boathouse. You can get started today, if you are feeling up to it."

"What do you mean, Grandpa?" David asked confused. "Mom's gone now and that changes everything. When she and dad get back, I'll talk to them about it."

"And what will you do until then, eh? You must do something, no?"

"I've got my books and my record player. Maybe I can learn to fish like you."

"I'm afraid it is not going to be that easy," Carl replied.

"Sure it is. Mom'll understand."

"Maybe she will, but while she is gone, I am in charge. Your suit has already been ordered, and someone will have to pay for it. I will take care of the bill, but then you will have to pay me back."

"I never wanted to buy that stupid suit anyway," David protested. "It was all mom's idea, and she isn't here anymore."

"No, she has gone," Carl agreed, beginning to loose his patience. "But she also left you in my care, eh? So if you are going to live in my house, under my roof, then you are going to live according to my rules."

David realized that he could not back down. "You're not my father," he screamed. "You can't make me do anything." He jumped up from the table, and rushed back to his room, slamming the door and bolting it behind him.

***

"David? Open the door please. I want to talk to you." It had been almost an hour since David barricaded himself in his room.

"Go away. I'm not coming out," he growled back.

"You can't stay in there forever. It's a beautiful day."

"I don't care. Leave me alone."

"I have decided that you are right," Carl continued in a low, even voice. "I can not make you go to work if you are not willing."

David was skeptical. It wasn't like his grandfather to give up so easily. "You mean I don't have to help out at all?"

"No, you may do as you wish. I will talk to Maddie and make sure she does not bother you again."

David opened the door slightly to peek out. Carl stood just

outside the door puffing on his cigar. "You mean I don't have to do anything if I don't want to?"

"That's right. Nothing unless you decide to help. In the meantime, get your things ready. I'll help you move out of your room."

"Move out? What do you mean?" David expected Carl to do something, but he never considered the possibility that he would be asked to leave.

"Since you are not interested in helping out around the cabins, I'm afraid you are not going to be able to stay here."

"Does that mean you're going to take me home?"

"Goodness, no. I cannot afford to leave Iron Falls right now. There is so much work to do, and I have no one to help me, ya?"

"So what are you going to do? Call my dad?"

"No, that won't work either. Your mother left you in my care, and I wouldn't want her to be disappointed. No, I have something else in mind."

David looked at his grandfather suspiciously. "What are you going to do?" he asked.

"When I was very young I learned that only workers get paid," Carl said relighting the stub of his cigar. "If a man does no work, he gets no pay, ya? Since you refuse to work, then you should not be paid."

"What do you mean, Grandpa? Our deal was just so I could earn enough to pay for the suit and shoes."

"Yes, yes, that is true," Carl said. "But there are other things. You live in my house. You sleep in my bed. You eat my food. It is only fair that you work for your keep."

"But you told Mom you'd take care of me..."

"And so I will, but just not in this house," Carl said matter-of-factly. "Until you change your mind, you will sleep in a tent in the yard. I will get the tent out and set it up while you get your belongings together. When you are done, I will help you move. Living in a tent should not be so bad, ya?"

"You mean you want me to camp out? Like in the Boy Scouts?" David suddenly began to see his punishment as an adventure. "That'll be fun."

"Very well, if it is all right with you, come along and we will get started on your new accommodations, ya?"

Carl led David to a closet near the front door, opened it, and pulled out what looked like a roll of blankets. He handed the bundle to David. "Here is your sleeping bag, and there is a pad rolled up with it. You can take it outside while I get the tent." David put his nose close to the rolled bag. It had a musty odor as if it had been sitting in the closet for a long time.

Carl reached up and pulled a large canvas duffel bag from the top shelf. He turned and walked past David without saying a word, opened the screen door in the kitchen and walked outside. David followed Carl out to see what he was going to do next.

He watched as Carl unclipped the clasp at the top, opened the bag and pulled a bundle of khaki canvas out. Carl placed the bundle on a level section of ground and unrolled it. The tent unfolded in two pieces, which Carl laid out on the ground, one with the snap fasteners facing up, and the other with the fasteners facing down. David recognized the pieces of canvass as the two halves of a pup tent like the ones the army had used during the Korean War. Carl lined up the fasteners along each side and began to snap the two halves together.

Reaching back in the duffel bag, Carl pulled out two wooden tent posts and a bag of stakes. He picked up a flat rock about the size of his fist and used it to pound stakes in at the two front corners of the tent.

"All right, now I need you to help. Come here if you want a place to sleep tonight." David walked over to the still flat tent. His grandfather pushed the spindle of one of the poles through the front side grommets and motioned for David to hold the pole. He pulled the guy line taunt and pounded a stake into the ground holding it in place.

With the front secured, Carl turned his attention to the other end of the tent, repeating the previous steps, and securing the rear guy line with another stake. Completed, the tent formed a triangular prism, with the bottom side open to the ground. "I can't sleep on the grass," David protested. "I'll catch cold or something.

"Don't worry. I have a ground cloth right here," the old man said, reaching into the duffel once more, producing a canvas tarp, and tossing it to David. "Spread that out on the ground and your sleeping bag will keep nice and dry." Carl looked up at the gray clouds moving in overhead, adding, "Unless it rains, of course."

"It won't rain. And I'll do just fine in the tent," David said defiantly.

David was sure that his grandfather was bluffing. He wouldn't make him stay outside all night. Still the old man was pretty set in his ways. If his grandfather was serious, so was David. He would wait it out as long as he had to. He had camped out before in the Boy Scouts. This wasn't any different. He'd show his grandfather and Maddie.

"Very well, then. I will leave you to finish setting up your tent. Maddie will call you when supper is ready."

***

Supper was at six. Maddie summoned David, calling him through the screen door. "Come on in and get cleaned up. Food's on the table."

By the time he washed for dinner, the table was already set, and Carl had seated himself. Maddie brought a plate of pork chops, string beans, and mashed potatoes steaming from the stove and set it in front of Carl. "Your creation looks wonderful as usual," he told her. She returned to the counter where she picked up a plate with nothing but a peanut butter and jelly sandwich on it. This she placed in front of David.

At first David just looked at the sandwich without saying a word.

"So you need to eat something, ya?" Carl urged.

David glared at his grandfather, then took his butter knife, cut the sandwich in two, and took a big bite. "I love peanut butter," he enthused. "This is going to be great. I get to do what I want and eat my favorite food too."

"I'm glad you are enjoying your dinner. Of course you will not have to eat only peanut butter. I think for breakfast tomorrow Maddie will make you some oatmeal, and for lunch, how about a bologna sandwich? What do you think about that?"

"That'll be great. I love bologna," he said, taking another big bite of his sandwich.

After he had finished his meager meal, David waited as Carl and Maddie finished their dinner. Then he watched as Maddie brought out an apple pie, and placed a generous slice on a small plate for Carl. David waited as his grandfather devoured the pie without saying a word.

"Would you mind if I go out to my tent and read for a while

before bed?" David asked after everyone had finished.

"Not at all," Carl said. "As I told you before, you are welcome to do as you please." Carl got up from the table and walked over to the Hoosier cupboard next to the stove and opened the drawer. He pulled out a black metal flashlight, tested it by turning it on momentarily, and then held it out to David. "It won't be long until it is dark," he said. "Here's a light for you to read by. You will need it."

***

Outside, in the twilight of the evening, David settled into an old swaybacked canvas folding chair next to his tent and put his feet up on a large flat rock nearby. He was able to read for only about fifteen minutes or so before the daylight began to fade and the seat on his chair began to get uncomfortable.

He decided to walk down to the lake and watch the sunset before turning in for the night. Waves rippled gently across the surface of the lake. David watched as the sun dropped lower in the western sky, peeking out from a bank of low hanging clouds.

Around nine o'clock the sun began to sink below the western horizon, turning the clouds pale shades of pink, then orange, and finally violet. David watched as the skies darkened and clouds moved in, obscuring the sun's last rays. It appeared that a storm was coming. Still David was certain that his new home in the pup tent would protect him.

The remaining light of day had faded by the time David returned to his tent site. This is just like Scout camp, he thought. He took out the flashlight his grandfather had given him, turned it on, and set it on a pile of wood pointed toward the tent so that he could see what he was doing. First, he took the ground cloth and spread it to the edges of the tent. Then he pulled the flaps down over the rear entrance and fastened the snaps. At the front of the tent, he folded the flaps back on each side for ventilation. When he had finished, David unrolled his sleeping bag, spreading it out over the ground cloth.

He laid down on the bedding to test it out. The ground felt hard and rough. He removed the sleeping bag, pulled back the ground cloth, and removed a couple of pebbles which poked through the fabric layers. He tried the bed again. Not too bad, he decided. Just to be on the safe side, he tied his dream catcher to the top of the tent post outside the tent. He stepped back to look at his work with satisfaction. This wouldn't be such a bad experience after all.

David took the flashlight and retreated into the tent, making himself as comfortable as possible on the lumpy bedding. He tucked himself in and switched off the flashlight. Blackness surrounded him. He closed his eyes, attempting to sleep.

Something scurried past the tent in the darkness. It made a scratching sound just beyond the canvas wall.

"Lady? Lady?" David called into the night. "Is that you?"

The noise retreated into the darkness. David waited for it to return. He listened intently. A dog howled in the distance. No, not a dog, David decided. A wolf. Definitely a wolf. Another howl, this time closer.

A gust of wind blew through the pine branches overhead. The weather had changed. An owl hooted in a nearby tree, then nothing.

David gazed into the darkness. Vague shadowy shapes danced past the gap between the tent flaps. He closed his eyes trying to sleep. But sleep eluded him.

Crickets began to chirp in the bushes, providing a soothing night chorus. Finally, the wind gusts began to die down and the ghostly shapes stopped moving across the tent door. Within minutes David was fast asleep.

***

The flaps on the tent fluttered in the wind. Leaves rustled uneasily in the trees. A branch cracked far overhead. Something fell to the ground not far from the tent. Half asleep, David stirred from his brief slumber. He rolled over, wondering about the time. Midnight? One? Two? He pulled the sleeping bag up over his head.

A drop of rain splashed against the canvas, then another. Soon the drops were falling with a regular cadence against the thick olive drab fabric. The rhythmic tapping became a constant drumming, then a raging torrent. David pushed open the tent flap and saw a rivulet forming near the opening. A drip began to fall from the tent canvas above him onto the ground cloth. David swiveled his body and angled the sleeping bag away from the drip. A shallow puddle began to form in the center of the ground cloth.

David rolled against the wall of the tent. Moisture began to seep through from each point at which he had made contact. He switched on the flashlight. He saw nothing but cold and damp. The flashlight began to flicker and dim as the batteries died. He felt more miserable than he had ever felt in his life.

He waited for a lull in the storm, then pulled a blanket over his had and ran for the back door of the house. The cottage was dark. He banged on the door for a long time.

"Grandpa? Grandpa, let me in," he called against the din of the storm.

A light came on in the kitchen. Carl's face appeared briefly in the window, and then disappeared. David heard the lock on the door click and then the door opened just a fraction.

"So?" Carl inquired as if asking the wind a question.

"I want to come in," muttered the soaked youth.

"No more camping out?"

"I give up. Just let me in - it's pouring out here."

Carl opened the door and let David enter. "We will get you to work on the boathouse first thing tomorrow morning," he explained.

David said nothing, but continued toward his room. It was one thirty in the morning. Dawn was just a few hours away.

Phillip Christian

## **The Boathouse**

"I think it might be ruined," David said examining the rain soaked pup tent he had abandoned the night before. He was thankful he had made the decision to sleep in the warm shelter of the cottage. The storm had passed during the night, but puddles still dotted the landscape and the tent canvas remained sopping wet.

"Nonsense," Carl answered, dragging David's waterlogged sleeping bag from the tent and spreading it out over a loosely hung clothesline. "It will soon begin to dry."

"No, not the sleeping bag, Grandpa. My dream catcher. I think it's ruined." David reached out and removed the drenched talisman from the tent post. He looked at the broken web he held in his hands. The twine holding together the ends of the willow loop had come untied, and strands of the interlocking webbing had begun to unravel. The paint on the goose feathers ran together into a brightly colored blur.

Carl took the ruined amulet from his grandson. "And what is this?" he asked examining the crudely made object.

"It's my dream catcher. The man at the store said it would keep bad dreams away. But now it's broken."

"Another of Maddie's superstitions, eh?"

"Maddie? No, I don't even think she knows I have it. Mom got it for me."

"Bad dreams, eh? You should not believe such stories. Too bad it did not keep away the storm," Carl joked.

He saw the disappointed look on his grandson's face. "Perhaps it is not so bad," he said setting the dream catcher on the porch. "I am sure it can be fixed. I will take a look at it later, all right?"

"Yeah, I guess so," David answered dejectedly.

"So are you ready to get started? Follow me and I'll show you what to do." Carl led David and Lady along the path down to the beach, past the cabins, stopping in front of the boathouse.

Carl's 'boathouse' was in reality a small one car garage, located under a massive oak tree near the water's edge. As far as David knew, there had never been a boat in the boathouse. The building's peeling paint and moss covered roof told a story of years of neglect. A rusted basketball hoop just below the peak of the roof clung tenuously to the weather beaten clapboard siding.

As they approached, a small, furry animal darted into a hole under the foundation of the building. "Muskrat," Carl said with a laugh. "They live under the floor. Lady chases them, but they just swim away. Let me show you where to start."

Carl moved around the boathouse to a cross-braced carriage doors, unlocked a padlock from the hasp and slid the squeaking doors aside. He flipped on the light switch. A single bulb in a green and white enamel fixture came on, illuminating the dingy, dilapidated interior.

David glanced around in disgust. Cobwebs trailed from the rafters. Dirt blanketed the grimy cracked cement slab floor. The six-paned windows had a coating of soot and filth that blocked most of the sunlight. There were piles of animal droppings in the corners. A stack of life jackets had been thrown into one corner. Something had chewed a hole in one of them, scattering stuffing across the floor. Five or six bamboo fishing poles hung from nails pounded into the wall studs. Hand tools and coffee cans filled with a variety of screws, bolts, nails and other hardware filled a workbench beneath one of the windows.

Carl gestured to the piles of broken, out dated, and unwanted junk. "You can start by straightening things up in here," he said. "I need you to clear out this entire area by the time I get home this evening."

"But Grandpa, this place is a mess," David complained. "There's a ton of stuff in here. What am I supposed to do with it all?"

"It is part of your job to decide what has value and what does not. If it is worth keeping, make a place for it inside the boathouse. If not put it in a pile and we will haul it away." Carl opened a small closet next to the workbench. "You will find everything you need in here - broom, mop, bucket, brushes, rags, and cleaners." Carl handed David the broom.

"But this place is filthy," David protested. "It'll take me forever to clean all this stuff up."

"It looks like a lot now, but once you start, you will be surprised how fast the work will go. And remember, the work must be done by the end of the day. Until then, if you need anything just ask Maddie, all right?"

Carl looked down at Lady who sat at his feet. "Lady," he

commanded, "stay here and keep David company." Obediently, the dog lay down on the deck and put her head on her paws. "Now I will leave you to get started. You will do just fine."

***

Carl was wrong. The work did not go rapidly at all.

First there was the problem of the lights. David couldn't see anything in the dimly lit old building. He rummaged through the utility closet until he located a box of light bulbs, using them to replace two burned out lights in the overhead fixtures. Once the lights were in place and he could see exactly what he was up against, he formulated a plan of attack. If he was lucky he might finish by the time his grandfather returned.

A tattered orange life jacket sat in one corner the room, its stuffing strewn across the floor. Mice had used the stuffing as a nest. David grabbed a broom out of the closet and began to sweep up the jacket stuffing along with the rest of the dirt and debris. Clouds of dust billowed into the air choking him. He stopped sweeping and fashioned a crude dust mask from what looked to be a clean rag he found on the work bench next to the door. The mask helped, but he still had to wait for the dust to settle before he could continue.

Beneath the window ledge stood a workbench. Tools were piled high - hammers, wrenches, nails, screwdrivers, and hand saws, all in a jumble. David cleaned off the top of the workbench. He located a wooden toolbox on a shelf under the bench and began sorting, cleaning, and storing the hand tools away. Next he sorted piles of nails and screws into groups, putting them into little jars on a shelf above the workbench.

Once this was done, he used a board and a handful of nails to hammer together a rack for hanging up shovels and rakes. He took the step ladder he had found in a dark corner of the room and used it to move several large boxes of Christmas ornaments into the boathouse loft.

Now the real work began. Piles of rusted car parts, broken fishing gear, garden tools, boat parts and boxes of outdated newspapers and magazines lined the interior walls. Sorting and reorganizing the mounds of refuse proved tedious, but in the process David found a few useful items hiding amid the debris. A hammock, a folding lawn chair, an incomplete croquet set, and a broken stepladder, all held his interest momentarily. At the bottom of a box of mildewed newspapers he found an old pair of U.S. Army surplus binoculars. He dusted of the lenses with the tail of his tee shirt and lifted them to his eyes, focusing on a cabin across the lake. He rotated the center adjustment knob until the line of trees across the lake came into focus. Deciding that these might come in handy someday, David hung them on a hook by the door.

In the midst of the pile he spotted something more interesting. Half hidden among the gears, cylinders, and transmission parts, stood a rusted but serviceable bicycle. He pulled the grimy old bike out of the pile and propped it up against the boathouse wall where he could examine it more closely. The bike was in rough shape, but fixable. David smiled to himself. With just a little work, he could be mobile.

***

By the time he had finished cleaning and rearranging the castoff items, the morning was almost over. Maddie arrived at the boathouse just before noon carrying a lunch basket covered with a linen towel over her arm. "I see you found my old bicycle," she said. "I had forgotten all about that rusted old thing."

"It was buried under a pile of junk," David explained. "Do you know if it still works?"

"Not very well, I'm afraid. I haven't used it for years. I'm afraid it's not in very good shape."

"Would you mind if I tried to fix it up?"

"I don't see why not," she replied. "It would be nice to see it running again."

"Thanks, Maddie. I'll get it working good as new - you'll see," David said.

Maddie walked to the open door of the boathouse and looked inside. "Looks like you've been busy," she said. "Your grandfather will be pleased. I'll bet you're hungry after all that work, eh? Why don't you take a break and we can have some lunch." Maddie led the boy to a picnic table under the shelter of the pavilion. She put down the basket and took out a sandwich and bottle of Coke, handing them to David. He lifted the bread on top of the sandwich.

"It's bologna," she explained. "You said last night that you love bologna." She sat down on the bench beside the boy, saying nothing, just watching him eat. She made David nervous.

He had almost finished his sandwich and Coke before he finally worked up the courage to speak. "Maddie?" he said. "Can a dream catcher be fixed?"

"A dream catcher? How do you know about dream catchers?"

"My mom got me one at a souvenir shop in St. Ignace. It helps me to sleep sometimes, but it got left out in the rain last night."

The stout little native woman looked skeptical. "Dream catchers are very powerful medicine," she said. "They are not souvenirs or toys."

"Grandpa says he can fix it."

"Your grandfather can not fix what he does not understand. He thinks that our ways are foolish."

"You mean like the spirit of Little Thunder? Grandpa says that whole story was made up to scare tourists." David paused looking out at the lake. "Maddie?" he said. "Is there really a ghost out there?"

"Yes, there is a spirit," she replied matter-of-factly.

"Really?" David said. "You're not kidding, are you?"

"The Spirit is not a joke, David," she replied flatly. "The *manitou* of Little Thunder has existed here for over one hundred years."

"Manitou - what's that?"

"It is what white people call the spirit," she said. "All things have a manitou - plants, animals, people. The manitou is as real as you or me."

"Aw, come on, Maddie. You don't really believe that, do you?" David tried to show his bravest face. "You're just sayin' that stuff to scare me. There's no such thing as ghosts - Grandpa says so."

"Your grandfather doesn't believe because he is too white. He only believes in what he can touch. That's the way white people think," Maddie replied disdainfully. "He doesn't believe in the spirit world."

"You've known Grandpa for a long time, haven't you?" he asked, taking a bite of his sandwich.

"Since before you were born."

"How did you meet him, Maddie?"

"The first time I met your grandfather was when my husband went to work for him."

"Your... your husband?" David said confused. "You're married?"

"*Was* married. My husband used to work for your grandfather.

His name is Peter - Peter Girard. He's part French and part Ojibwa. Peter used to help Carl run the harness shop."

"What happened? Did he die?"

"No... he's not dead. He's too stubborn to die. He lives over by Baraga. I even heard he ran for tribal council there. Maybe he won. Maybe not. It's all the same."

"So if he's still alive, why don't you live with him?"

"Peter drank," Maddie stated bluntly. "We argued, and he left."

"My parents argue all the time," David said sympathetically.

"It's not good for two people to fight all the time," Maddie sighed sadly. "But now it is time to get back to work," she added, bringing their conversation to an end. "We both have things to do this afternoon." She began to gather up the utensils and plates, putting them back into the basket.

When she finished, she turned to go, then paused briefly. "Bring your dream catcher to me later," she said. "Maybe there is something I can do to help."

***

By four o'clock in the afternoon David was exhausted, but the boathouse was clean and the piles of junk had been neatly sorted and stacked along the interior walls. He looked around with a degree of satisfaction. Now he just hoped that his grandfather would be equally pleased.

Having completed his assigned task, David turned his attention to Maddie's old rusty bicycle. The bicycle was in worse shape than he had first thought. The frame was corroded and the chain dangled loosely over the drive sprockets. It would need a ton of work to get it back into riding condition.

He was still looking over the old bike when Lady began to bark. David turned around to see Carl's station wagon coming up the drive. Getting out of the old Ford, Carl walked toward David, eyeing the old bicycle as if appraising a valuable antique. "And what's this?" he asked. "What have you uncovered? A hidden treasure perhaps?"

"It's Maddie's. She said I could use it if I can fix it, but it's in pretty bad shape."

Carl took a closer look, rubbing his chin thoughtfully. "It looks like you have your work cut out for you all right," he said. "Perhaps we can work on it together, eh? But right now, I want you to show me what you have done today."

David gave his grandfather a brief tour, explaining everything he had done. He showed him the piles of newspapers, broken lawn furniture, and miscellaneous car parts waiting to be hauled away. Then he took him inside the boathouse explaining how he had organized the tools, cleaned up the shelves, and tidied up the cartons.

"You've done an excellent job," Carl observed when they finished. "I could not have done better myself. But now it's time you learned why I had you do all of this work, eh? Come along and get in the car. We need to take a little ride."

"Where are we going, Grandpa?" David asked.

"We're taking a drive over to Ike's Market. There's something there I want to show you."

*\*\*\**

David got into the passenger seat of the station wagon, and Carl drove the short distance along the gravel road to *Ike's Market*. *Ike's* was located on the corner of US 2 and Spirit Lake Road. Lake residents who were short on fuel or bread could find both at *Ike's* along with a liberal dose of Ike's opinion on practically any topic.

Carl pulled under the overhanging portico, stopping next to a gas pump topped by a red, white, and green milk glass Texaco globe. Carl rolled down the driver's side window. Moments later, a young man, wearing the official Texaco green uniform, ran up to the station wagon. The attendant looked to be no more than eighteen or nineteen years old. "Howdy, Mr. Wertz," he greeted. "You want me to fill 'er up?"

"I don't know, Frank. If Ike keeps raising his prices, I won't be able to afford a fill up," Carl laughed. "Twenty-five cents a gallon, eh? Well, I suppose... go ahead."

Carl and David waited as the attendant filled the station wagon, gently squeezing the nozzle to coax the last few drops into the tank. "That'll be three bucks," he said. "Want me to check the oil?"

"Not today, thanks. Just put it on my bill, ok, Frank? Is Ike around?"

"He's inside, Mr. Wertz. He's been expecting you. He said to tell you to pull around back. I'll run in and tell him you're here."

Carl pulled the station wagon away from the gas pumps and around the corner of the building.

"So what's the big secret, Grandpa?" David asked. "Why are we here?"

"Just be patient," Carl said. "You will see soon enough."

He drove past a whitewashed barn at the rear of the store and pulled up along side a trailer hidden in the shadows of a willow tree. A canvas tarp covered the trailer, concealing whatever it carried.

Carl got out of the station wagon, walked over to the trailer and began to loosen one of the ties holding the cover in place. "Give me a hand with this tarp," he said, motioning for David to do the same.

When the ropes had been loosened, Carl grabbed a corner of the tarp and tugged it off. Beneath the canvas tarp sat the inverted skeleton of a small speedboat, perhaps fifteen or sixteen feet long. The empty shell had neither bottom nor sides, but was simply a framework of wooden slats bent around a series of upright supports.

"What good is a boathouse without a boat, eh?" Carl smiled.

But David was not impressed. Apparently his grandfather's big surprise just meant more work for him. The long summer had suddenly gotten a lot longer.

Carl could see the disappointment written across his grandson's face. "Not what you were expecting, eh?"

"Not exactly. What is it anyway?"

"That's our next project, David. When it's finished it will be a 16 foot Chris Craft Barracuda runabout. I bought it and the trailer from Mr. Eisenberg. That's why I asked you to clean out the boathouse today. I needed you to make room for it. I thought we could work on it together." Carl saw that David looked skeptical. "Well, what do you think?"

"Looks like there's a lot of work left to do. Are you sure we can do all of this ourselves?"

"I know it looks like a lot of work," Carl replied, "but it will go faster than you think."

David sighed in resignation, and then a slight smile crossed David's lips. "That's what you said about cleaning out the boathouse," he laughed.

## **Bobber Lane**

As David and Carl stood talking, the back door of *Ike's Market* slammed shut, and Ike Eisenberg appeared, walking cheerfully toward them. Dressed in a white grocer's apron, dress shirt and black tie, Eisenberg was a stocky man in his early sixties with a salt and pepper beard framing his jovial, friendly face.

"Howdy gentlemen. I've been expecting you," he greeted. "I see you've already got her uncovered. She doesn't look like much now, but when she's finished, she's goin' to be a real beauty. David, I know you and your granddad'll do right by her."

David noticed that Mr. Eisenberg talked about the boat as if it were a woman. "Gee, I don't know Mr. Eisenberg. I've never built a boat before."

Eisenberg turned toward the unfinished framework of the Barracuda. "When I started putting her together, I figured I could do it all myself, but you really need two people. I got the frames tacked onto the fixture all right, even managed to get the stem and keel fastened to the frame, but that's about it. I got so busy running the store I didn't have time to finish. The frame has been sitting here on this trailer for almost a year. I'm hoping you two will take it from here."

"Tell you what, Ike," Carl said. "When we get finished, you can have the first ride. And you can use it whenever you want."

"I know she's going to a good owner," Eisenberg continued, "but I still hate to see her go. The parts crate is in the barn. Why don't I give you a hand loading it before I change my mind about selling her to you?"

"Come on David," Carl urged, "give us a hand."

Eisenberg opened the barn door to reveal a large crate with the scripted words '*Chris Craft*' stenciled along the side. Carl and Ike Eisenberg positioned themselves at opposite ends of the crate while David moved to the center. The long narrow crate proved to be heavier and more awkward than it at first appeared. The three men struggled before finally managing to maneuver the heavy crate out of the barn. Because the skeleton of the Barracuda already occupied the trailer, the three men struggled to lift the parts crate up onto the station wagon's roof rack. It took several tries before they succeeded in maneuvering the box into position and strapping it down.

"Is that everything?" Carl asked breathing heavily from the effort.

"Yup, that's it," Eisenberg replied. "Everything - hardware, trim pieces, bench seats, decking - it's all in there. They pretty much thought of everything."

"You go ahead and back the wagon up to the hitch and I'll give you a hand with the trailer," Eisenberg said. "Then I better get back inside and tend to my customers."

David watched as Carl backed the station wagon up to the trailer tongue, maneuvering carefully to ease the coupling over the ball. Within minutes, he had the trailer tongue securely latched onto the ball hitch, and they were ready to go.

"Well, David, I think you deserve a little reward for all this hard work, don't you?" Eisenberg said. "Why don't you come inside with me and help yourself to a cold bottle of pop while your grandfather ties down the load, eh? Pick out whatever you like. It's on the house."

***

Two large plate-glass windows, one displaying a large Pabst Blue Ribbon beer sign, the other advertising Chesterfield cigarettes, framed the entry door. David pushed open the door setting off a small bell positioned above the entryway. Near the door stood a long counter upon which sat a huge brass National cash register.

On the wall was a framed portrait of President Dwight Eisenhower. Poised above the portrait hung a large banner reading "I LIKE IKE!" David had always liked President Eisenhower because he shared the President's middle name - David.

The entire store was only twenty-five or thirty feet wide with aisles barely wide enough for two people to pass each other between the shelves of food. David made his way down the aisle on the left, to a pop cooler near the door. He reached in and pulled out a bottle of orange Nehi soda.

As he pried the cap off the bottle using the bottle opener attached to the cooler, a commotion broke out. Angry voices emanated from the rear of the store. A woman holding a box of Kellogg's Corn Flakes in the next aisle looked to see what was happening, and then quickly moved to get away from the uproar.

David moved cautiously around the corner of a large pyramid display of Green Giant canned vegetables so he could see what was causing the disturbance. At the end of the aisle he saw an old man dressed in shabby work clothes being confronted by a blond teenager wearing a tee shirt and blue jeans. The boy wore a ducktail, dark sunglasses, and had a pack of cigarettes rolled up in his shirt sleeve. David had seen posters of James Dean from the movie *Rebel Without a Cause* and figured the boy was trying to imitate him.

"Get away - leave me alone," the old man growled at the teenager.

Two other boys, dressed almost identically to the first, came up behind the old man and stood behind him, blocking his retreat. "Hey Terry, who you got there?"

"Look who I found. It's our old buddy, Bobber Lane," said the boy named Terry.

The boys surrounded the strange old man, taunting him. "What ya up to, Bobber?" one of the two boys asked.

The old man did not reply but tried to walk around his young antagonist. But the boy continued to stand in the man's path, making it impossible to get around him. "What's wrong, Bobber? Cat got your tongue?" the boy goaded his victim as the older boys chuckled. Bobber continued to mutter and mumble under his breath.

Suddenly, the boy came forward until he stood just inches from Bobber Lane. He reached out and grabbed the old man's bag, dumping much of the contents onto the market floor.

"Well, what have we here? Been shopping, huh?" the boy pulled a loaf of bread out of the bag and held it up for the rest of the group to see. "Butternut," he informed his companions. "Let's see if it's as soft as they say it is," he called, as he squashed the bread into a ball with his hands.

Bobber reached out and tore the bag containing what remained of his groceries angrily away from the slender youth. "You give me that, you little hoodlum."

"Oh, Bobber's angry," the boy laughed in mock fright. "Hey guys, I'm really scared. After all, everybody knows what a dangerous man Bobber Lane is." He turned back to face the fuming man. "Isn't that right Bobber?" he teased. "Everybody knows you're crazy as a loon, don't they boys?"

"Sure," one of the other boys replied. "Bobber Lane, Bobber

Lane, he only has half a brain." Terry began to recite. He was immediately joined by the entire group, chanting in unison, "Bobber Lane, Bobber Lane, everybody knows he's insane."

"Hey, get away from him!" The entire group turned to see Ike Eisenberg coming from behind the counter with a baseball bat in his hand. As he came forward, Ike kept tapping the bat against the heel of his empty hand. "You boys leave him alone," Ike called out as he approached.

"Hey, Mr. Eisenberg," Terry once again took the lead. He held up his hands, palms out as if to ward off the old man's anger. "Hey just slow down there. We were just having a little fun. We didn't mean any harm."

"Fun? Is this what you call fun? Don't you boys have anything better to do than bother my customers?" He brushed past the group of boys, placing himself between Bobber Lane and his detractors. "Get away from him - leave him alone before somebody gets hurt." It was obvious by the way he swung the bat menacingly that if anyone got hurt it wouldn't be him.

"Hey, man, don't get all bent out of shape. We were just helping ol' Bobber here out." Terry turned to the ragged old man. "Isn't that right Bobber?" Bobber glared menacingly at the cocky youth, but said nothing.

"Maybe you ought to do what Mr. Eisenberg asked you to do." Carl interjected as he arrived from the front of the store. "Why don't you and your friends just walk out of here, get in your car, and drive away."

Suddenly finding themselves out flanked, the boys changed their attitude, becoming more contrite and less belligerent. "Look we don't want any trouble," Terry offered defensively. "We were just kidding around." He held his hands up in a gesture of compliance, and began backing away from Bobber Lane. "We'll leave quietly. Come on, guys," he motioned his buddies toward the door. "Looks like we're not welcome here anymore."

"What are you waiting for," Ike demanded, tapping the bat on a display shelf hard enough to rattle some jars of peanut butter. "Go on. Get out of here now, before I call the police."

Moving quickly, the boy and his friends headed out of the store. Ike went to the front window and watched them as they went over to a beat up old Chevrolet and got in, laughing all the way. The

Chevrolet roared to life as the driver threw the transmission into reverse, spun around throwing up a hail of gravel, and roared off down the road in a cloud of dust.

The strange disheveled old man seemed upset and shaken by the incident. "You ok Bobber?" Ike asked him. Bobber appeared not to have heard the store owner, choosing instead to continue looking into his shopping bag as if taking inventory of his groceries.

"David, help Mr. Lane pick up his things," Carl instructed. David reached down and began picking up cans of baked beans, jars of dried beef, and boxes of Ritz crackers and stuffing them into the bag of groceries.

Mr. Eisenberg helped put a fresh loaf of bread into the top of the bag and patted Bobber on the back. "No charge today, Bobber. These are on the house."

Carl turned to the old man. "Did you walk here?" he asked. The ragged man nodded in affirmation. "Come on Robert. Let me give you a lift back to your cabin." He looked at David and motioned toward the full sack of groceries. "David could you please take Mr. Lane's things out to the car."

\*\*\*

They drove a mile or two back toward the lake past the park, turning right onto an unmarked single lane road leading into a dense patch of woods. From the distance they had driven along the road, David guessed that the cabin must be very close to his grandfather's property. The road followed a split rail fence for perhaps a quarter of a mile or so to a small log shack set back in a secluded inlet on the lake.

David hopped out of the station wagon and took a good look around. Bobber's shack was no bigger than one of the Spirit Lake Cabins, but not nearly as well maintained. Moss grew from the ancient shingles clinging tenuously to the roof, and a thin wisp of smoke trickled from the weathered brick chimney. Two small four-paned windows with cracked and peeling caulking bracketed either side of the rough-sawn timber front door. A huge pile of firewood stood stacked along one side of the porch.

As David waited, Carl walked around to the passenger side of the station wagon and opened the door so Bobber could get out. "All right, Robert," Carl said. "You're home, safe and sound." Taking the old man's arm, Carl guided him toward the porch, past a row of large wooden boxes.

It was the first time that David had noticed the boxes. Each container was about four feet tall and three feet square. David walked over to one of the containers, and looked inside. The box contained what looked like dirt.

"What's in here?" David asked his grandfather.

"They're worms," Carl explained. "Robert runs a worm farm."

"Worm farm? How can you farm worms?" David asked, mystified. "Don't they just live in the dirt?"

"Mr. Lane supplies the bait for most of the fishermen in the county. He supplies crawlers and worms to Ike's and most of the other bait shops in the area."

"Go ahead. Put your hand in," the curious old man invited. David hesitated. As he watched, the earth on the top of the pile began to writhe and churn.

Bobber giggled at the young boy's squeamishness. "They don't bite," he laughed and thrust his own hand deep into the black mass, withdrawing a fistful of wriggling, squirming nightcrawlers.

As they were talking, a curious tan and brown tabby cat strode up to David and rubbed itself affectionately against his leg.

"That's Captain," Bobber explained. "He usually doesn't take kindly to strangers. Must like you though." David stooped down and stroked the back of the cat's neck as it rubbed against his hand and purred contentedly.

"Mr. Lane?" David said cautiously. "Is your name really Bobber?"

The old man laughed. "My given name's Robert, David, but folks have called me Bobber as long as I can remember. I always kinda liked the name, you know, Bobber like a bobber on a fishing line."

"David, why don't you go get Mr. Lane's groceries out of the car and take them up to the house," Carl said.

The cat followed along as David walked to the back of the station wagon, opened the hatch, and pulled the sack of groceries from the storage compartment. Somewhat reluctantly, he followed the old man to the front door. Hesitantly he stepped through the door into the dark interior of the cabin. Bobber took out a match and lit a kerosene lantern sitting on the oak table in the center of the room. "Go ahead and set that bag on the counter," he said. "Sorry about the light, but I just never got around to getting electric out here."

David set down the bag next to the wood-burning cook stove, and took a look around. Bobber's cabin was sparsely furnished. An old platform bed sat along one wall and a small table with two chairs hugged the other. A large oak desk in the far corner of the room seemed out of place in the cramped quarters. Behind the desk, stood a full-length bookcase packed with an assortment of volumes of various shapes, sizes, and thicknesses. A kerosene lamp and a fragile looking pair of reading glasses rested on the desk next to an open volume of poems.

"Well, if you don't need us for anything else, we better get going," Carl said. "You sure you will be all right, Robert?"

"Yeah, sure. Those boys wouldn't of hurt me anyway, you know. Just full of mischief, that's all."

David quickly made his way back outside, into the light. He hopped into the station wagon and waited as his grandfather said goodbye to Bobber Lane and got into the driver's seat. As Carl turned the station wagon around and pulled away from the shack, David turned back to see Bobber Lane disappearing into the distance.

"All right, David," Carl said as they drove away. "What's bothering you? You seemed tense and uneasy all the time we were at Mr. Lane's cabin."

"I'm sorry, Grandpa. It's nothing really. It's just those boys - the ones back at Ike's? They were chanting something about Mr. Lane, and I was... well I just wondered if it was true."

"Exactly what did they say about him?"

"Well, those boys said he's crazy. They said he's insane, like he's retarded or something."

Carl suddenly became serious. He kept his eyes fixed on the road ahead as he talked. "David," he said firmly, "let me assure you, there is nothing wrong with Mr. Lane. He is not retarded, and he is not insane. Just because he lives by himself doesn't make him crazy. He is a good and honest man. Those boys lied. They do not know Robert Lane, and they care about nothing but themselves. Do you understand?" Carl glanced over at David looking for a response.

"I understand, Grandpa" David answered.

"Good, then let's get back to the cottage," Carl said. "It is almost time for dinner and I am starved."

When they arrived at the lake, David opened the door as Carl backed the station wagon up to the boathouse. Once the trailer had been unhitched, the two pushed it into the boathouse and unloaded the parts crate from the roof of the station wagon.

"When are we going to start working on putting it all together, Grandpa?" David asked.

"I'll be starting first thing tomorrow morning," Carl replied, "but you get the day off."

"Really?" David said hopefully. "I don't have to work tomorrow? I thought you wanted me to help."

"I do, but not this weekend," Carl responded. "I'm afraid your aunt has other plans for you."

"Aunt Rita?" David's earlier enthusiasm was suddenly replaced by apprehension. "What does she want?"

"She called earlier this morning. She knows your mother went back to LaSalle, so she wants you to spend the weekend with her family. I'll drop you off around noon and your uncle will bring you back Sunday after church."

"How did she know Mom wasn't here?"

"Your aunt is very good at knowing other people's business, eh? Anyway, she wants to see you, and you know how hard it is to say 'no' to her."

"Do I have to go? I'd rather stay with you and Maddie. We can get started on putting the boat together."

"It is only for a couple of days, ya? There is no rush on the boat. The work has waited this long, it will wait just a bit longer. We will have plenty of time to work on the Barracuda when you return. Now let's close up the boathouse and head back to the cottage. We both need to get cleaned up for dinner before Maddie sends out Lady to look for us."

## Ernie's Diner

Even before he arrived at his cousins' house, David regretted saying he'd go. By the time Carl dropped him off at the Peterson's late Saturday morning, David was sure he'd made a mistake. His doubts were confirmed when Aunt Rita greeted him at the back door.

"Oh, you poor dear boy," she lamented as if David had just been orphaned. "You must be feeling just awful." Unexpectedly, she moved toward him, enveloping him in a smothering embrace.

Extricating himself from her arms, David looked around embarrassed, half expecting to hear his cousins' laughter. "Where is everybody?" he asked.

"Kyle's in his room and Kenny's out in the garage working on his truck," Rita replied. "Your uncle's out on the patio grilling up some brats for lunch. Why don't you head back there and join him while I slip into the kitchen and grab the baked beans, eh?"

When David arrived on the patio, his uncle looked up from the grill. "Hey, David. Great to see you. You're just in time for lunch. Are you hungry? Why don't you help yourself to some chips while I dish you up a brat?"

"Has Rita started her interrogation yet?"

"Interrogation?"

"Grilling you about your mom and dad. She just has to know everything that's going on." Ray served up one of the still sizzling brats on a bun and handed it to David. "Don't let her get to you, ok?"

Rita's probing, began almost as soon as she returned from the kitchen with baked beans and potato salad. "You poor thing," she moaned. "I can just imagine how hard it must be for you. You must be anxious to know when your parents are going to come and get you, eh?"

"Yeah, It'll be nice when they can come up," he answered.

"And have you heard from your folks? Have they said anything about what's goin' on?"

"Now, Rita, don't bother the boy," Ray said, munching on a handful of chips. "I'm sure if he knew anything he'd tell you. Besides, its really none of our business, now is it?"

"Nonsense. We're all family here, Ray. I'm sure David doesn't mind. I'll tell you what, David, why don't we give your dad a ring as soon as we're done eating. I'm sure he'd love to hear from you."

Excited about the prospect of talking to his parents, David rushed through the meal, and then waited until the Peterson clan finished.

"All right, then," Rita said, "Let's make that call." She led David into the house and dialed 0 to get the long distance operator on the line. After several unsuccessful attempts, the call went through, and Rita handed her nephew the receiver. The connection was not very good, and David had a hard time hearing over the static.

"Hi dad."

"Hey kiddo, how you doin'?" his father asked.

"Ok, I guess" David replied. "I'm helping grandpa put together a boat kit he bought. It's a lot of work, but it will be neat when we put it in the water."

"A boat, huh? I'd like to see it. You'll have to show me when I get up there."

"I miss you guys," David said. "When are you coming up?"

"Soon, pal. Real, real soon, I promise."

"Is Mom there?"

"Not right now. But I'll tell her you called. She'll be disappointed she missed you."

"So are you and Mom getting a divorce?"

The directness of David's question startled Donald. "Did your Aunt Rita tell you that?" he asked.

"No, I just wondered, you know..."

"Listen, I guess you know something's been going on between your mother and me. We're still trying to work things out down here. But it'll all be over...," the voice on the phone crackled and began to break up.

"What? What did you say? The connection's bad."

"I said... get through this..." His father's voice gradually began to return. "You'll see. I'm beginning to lose you on this end too. Maybe we should wrap it up for now. This long distance call must be costing your Uncle Ray a fortune anyway. But, you hang in there, ok? We'll see you soon."

"Dad? I love you."

"Love you too, kiddo. Goodbye." There was a click, and the dial tone returned to the line.

The call disappointed David. He'd hoped to hear that his parents would be coming soon, but there had been nothing in his father's voice to suggest that to be the case.

"Do you want to talk about it, dear?" Rita pressed, still grasping for information.

"No thanks," David replied, much to Rita's chagrin. "I'll be all right." He began to sulk around the Peterson's home. Soon, his melancholy began to pervade the entire Peterson household.

Ray suggested watching a Tigers game on television, struggling with his antenna rotor to zero in on Van Patrick's broadcast of the game. But the prospect of watching the Tigers get blasted by the Baltimore Orioles did little to brighten David's spirits.

***

Much to Ray's delight, the Tigers managed to squeeze by the Orioles two to one, though the game did little to brighten David's spirits. The game had just ended when Kenny burst into the living room, his clothes still soiled with oil stains from working in the garage.

"Hey, Dad, I'm finished workin' on the truck," he announced "can I go down to Ernie's Diner to meet the guys?"

"If you're gonna drive your truck those lights better be working," Ray said.

"Rewired 'em this afternoon. So, can I go?"

"I don't see why not," Ray responded.

Rita shot a damning glance at her husband, and then turned toward Ken. "Just a moment, young man," she challenged. "You're not going anywhere tonight. Or have you forgotten? We have a guest."

"Yeah, I know, Mom. But I promised the guys I'd meet 'em at Ernie's Diner."

"I don't think so, Ken," Rita replied. "I thought after dinner we could all play some cards. You play pinochle don't you, David?" Rita asked. "How does that sound?"

"I'm afraid I never learned how, Aunt Rita," David replied. "It's ok with me if Ken has some place he wants to go. Really."

"See, Mom, David doesn't mind. Come on, Mom, you got to let me go."

Suddenly Rita's eyes brightened as an inspiration occurred to her. "Why I have a wonderful idea, Kenny. Why don't you take your brother and cousin with you? You can all eat at Ernie's."

"I don't think so, ma," Ken protested. "I don't want them tagging along."

"Listen, young man, if you're going then I want you to take your brother and cousin. I'll bet David hasn't been to Ernie's Diner yet. You can show him around."

"But Mom! That's not fair. They're just kids," Ken protested.

"Either they go or you don't. Make up your mind, dear."

"Ok, fine, but we'll need some money if we're all gonna eat there."

"All right, here's a five," Rita said pulling a five-dollar bill from her purse. "That's more than enough to feed the three of you."

"Ok, I'll take 'em, but as soon as we're done eating, I'm bringing 'em home." Kenny took the money and headed out the door. "Come on, we're taking the truck," he said without waiting for his brother or cousin. Not wanting to be left behind, Kyle rushed to catch his brother, motioning for David to follow.

"Hurry up and get in," Ken ordered the younger two boys when they reached the Ford. "I don't have all day."

David hopped over the rusty running board and slid into the middle of the bench seat, and Kyle jumped up beside him. David squirmed to get comfortable on the hard bench seat. The stuffing showed through where the fabric had worn so thin that the threads had split apart. When both boys were in place, Kenny slammed the door hard to latch it, then walked around to the driver's side and got in.

The Ford's shift lever extended up through the floor of the truck, and David pulled his knees back out of the way so that Ken's hand would not make contact with his legs when he put the car into gear. A puff of white smoke belched out of the tailpipe as Kenny eased the shifter into reverse and backed out of the driveway.

***

Though Ken never seemed to move too fast around the house, he accelerated down the two-lane highway as if he were being chased by demons. David reached down to clutch the seat and held on. Just as they reached the Iron Falls city limits, however, Kenny downshifted and put on the brake to slow the car to a modest thirty-five miles an hour. "Cops wait out here to nail speeders," he explained to David as if apologizing for his reduced velocity.

He rolled through the center of town, past the Red Owl Market, Perkin's Café, and the Rexall Drug Store, before turning down Maple Street and pulling to a stop in front of a modest white cinder block building with a large neon sign glowing with the words "Ernie's Diner."

Ken got out of the truck first and went around to pry open the passenger side door. David followed Kyle out, and together the three walked around to the front of the building. Two oversized plate glass windows revealed a brightly lit interior lined with numerous booths, a few scattered Formica tables, and a soda fountain manned by a freckle-faced counter attendant.

Ken went in first, nodding to the boy behind the counter. The counter attendant looked to be about the same age as Ken and was dressed in a soiled white apron with a white 'soda jerk' cap on his head. A cigarette hung from his lips. He took a drag off the cigarette, and set it on the Formica counter next to several burn marks left by previous ash embers. "Hey, Kenny," the attendant greeted. "How's it goin, man?"

"Cool, man," Ken responded. "How 'bout you, Walt?"

The youth at the counter threw up his hands. "Same old shit," he sighed. "What'cha gonna do?"

"Where's old man Green?" Kenny asked. "He's not stupid enough to leave you in charge now, is he?"

"Naw, he's in the back - gettin' supplies out of the storeroom. You lookin' for the guys?"

"Yeah, that's right - they here yet?"

"Booth in the corner, as usual," the soda jerk replied.

As Kenny led his cousins toward the corner table, one of the boys turned to greet them. "Hey, Ken. What's happenin'?" he said.

David recognized the boy immediately. It was Terry, the boy who had quarreled with Bobber Lane at Ike's Market. He was dressed almost the same way he had been then - slicked back hair, sunglasses, and a tee shirt. The two other boys sitting with Terry were the same two who had been with him at Ike's. "Who's the kid?" Terry asked referring to David.

"He's my cousin David," Kenny replied. "Him an' Kyle are tagging along tonight."

"Your cousin, eh? Well, cousin David, I'm Terry," the boy said introducing himself. "And this is Jeff and Mike," he indicated the two other boys. Terry leaned forward, staring intently at David. David began to feel uncomfortable under the steady gaze.

"Haven't I seen you somewhere before?" Terry asked. "I know - you were at Ike's the other day. You were hanging around with old man Wertz."

"He's my grandpa," David replied. "I'm staying with him out at the lake."

"Your gramps was sure pissed off," Terry mocked, causing his friends to laugh.

"Yeah, he was upset because you guys were bothering Mr. Lane."

"Mr. Lane? I never heard old Bobber called Mr. Lane before. That just doesn't seem right. Not after what he did."

"What do you mean?" David asked. "What did he do anyway?"

"You mean you don't know? That old coot is a dangerous man. He's a killer, you know," Terry drew his finger across his throat like a knife. "Killed his own son. Now he's nutty as a fruitcake."

"Really?" David said in awe. If what Terry said was true, he had been at the home of a killer. "He didn't seem that bad to me."

Ken took the last seat at the bench next to Terry, leaving no room at the booth for David or Kyle. "Hey, where we supposed to sit?" complained Kyle.

Ken pointed toward a vacant table on the far side of the room. "Why don't you two sit over there," he ordered. "Get whatever you want, and don't bother me. I'm gonna talk to the guys."

Left alone, Kyle tried to get the waiter's attention, but he was too busy talking to Terry and his friends to notice. It was several minutes before the attendant finally made it over to take their order. "What'll you guys have?" he said to Kyle.

"I'll have a small malt, fries, and a burger with the works," Kyle ordered.

The waiter took down the order and turned to David. "I'll have the same thing," decided David. "Only I want my hamburger plain."

"Plain?" asked the counter attendant.

"Yeah, just plain - no pickle, catsup, mustard, onion, or anything. Just hamburger on a bun."

"Whatever you say," replied the attendant, then added, "You want Cheez Whiz on that?"

Cheez Whiz on a burger was a new idea to David. His mom usually put a slice of Kraft on the hamburgers she made at home, but Cheez Whiz was even better. "Go ahead," encouraged Kyle. "Try it - it's great."

"Why not," David agreed.

When the food came, David realized that the hamburger was the best he had ever tasted. The Cheez Whiz dripped down over the sides of the burger making it seem to melt in his mouth. Kyle poured a big pool of catsup on his plate, and then used his French fries to scoop up the red goop before popping them into his mouth. David scowled at his cousin's strange eating habits. Like everything else, David preferred his fries plain.

\*\*\*

David and Kyle were still finishing their burgers when the group of older boys got up from their booth and moved across the room toward them.

"Come on, let's go - we're out'ta here." Kenny ordered the two younger boys. "Me and the guys are gonna go down to Mickey's and shoot some pool, so I'm gonna drop you at the house."

"Hey, Ken, ease up, will ya?" Terry interjected. "Let the small fry finish their meal. We got plenty of time. Besides I haven't had a chance to get to know your cousin here. Isn't that right Davy boy?"

Terry slid uninvited into the seat beside David, crowding him and blocking his retreat. David put down his hamburger, suddenly losing his appetite. "So, you're from down state, eh?" Terry challenged, tossing one of David's French fries into his mouth and leaning in close to the younger youth.

"Detroit?" Jeff asked.

"No, LaSalle - it's down by Detroit."

"LaSalle, eh? Wasn't that some kind of car or something?"

"The town was named for the explorer, not the car," David explained.

"You do any hunting down there?" Terry asked.

"Hunting? My dad hunts for pheasants in the fall. And up north for deer sometimes."

"Bet you don't have any bears down there where you live, do you kid?"

"Bears? No, nothing like that. I visited the Lincoln Park Zoo in

Chicago and saw the bears there last year with my folks," David said defensively.

"The Zoo?! We're not talking about tame old zoo bears. You know, Kenny, I'll bet your cousin would love to see some genuine wild bears. How bout we take him out to the dump and give him a real thrill, eh? We can shoot pool any night."

"Geez, I don't know Ter," Ken replied with obvious reluctance. "I don't think so. Mom wants us home early."

"We won't keep you out late - I promise. Besides, it's been a long time since we had new blood out at the dump. And Davy wants to go check out the bears, don't you Davy boy? "

"Dump? There are bears at the dump?" David asked skeptically. "Can you get very close?"

"Sure, sometimes they come right up to the truck, don't they Ken?" Terry glanced over at Ken, urging him to follow his lead.

"I'll give Mom a call and see if it's ok for Kyle and Davy to go. But she said to be home early," Kenny told the group. He headed off to use the pay phone next to the MEN'S room at the rear of Ernie's Diner.

"Look, me Jeff, and Mike are goin' out to the truck. Catch up with us as soon as you make your call," Terry said getting up to leave. Jeff and Mike followed close behind.

"Hey, which one of you deadbeat's is payin'," shouted the gray haired owner, Ernie Green, who had now replaced the counter attendant behind the cash register. "You guys owe me four dollars and fifty six cents. Come on, cough it up."

"Don't get your tail in a knot, old man," Terry snapped back. "You'll get your dough. Get it, Mike."

Mike flipped a five-dollar bill on the counter and headed out to join his friends. Ernie Green swept the money into the cash register and turned to Kyle and David. "And what about you two? Who's payin' for your burgers?"

"My brother's on the phone," answered Kyle. "He'll take care of it when he gets back."

"Make sure he does," the owner threatened before returning to cleaning up the counter area.

"Asshole," Kyle muttered to David.

Kyle was just finishing the last of his fries when Kenny returned to the table. "Ok, everything's set, so let's get a move on," Ken told his brother. Kyle wiped his mouth on his shirttail and got up to join his brother and the other boys heading for the door, but David remained seated at the table.

"What's the problem small fry? Let's go," his cousin commanded.

"I don't think this is a good idea, Ken. My Grandpa doesn't know where I am, and I don't want him to worry." David objected.

"Our dad knows where we're going, and your gramps doesn't have to know anything about it. You comin' or not?"

"No..., but, well, do I have any choice?"

"Geez, nothin's gonna hurt you. You got my word. Besides, you're stayin' over tonight anyways, right? So what the heck? Live dangerously. What do you say?"

"All right," David conceded. "Let's go."

## The Bear

"You guys hop in the back, eh? Terry and me'll ride up front," Kenny told the group as they walked to the rear of the truck. He unhooked the chains on the tailgate and dropped it down. Kyle climbed up followed by Jeff and Mike. "Go on, get in," he prodded David to follow the others. Reluctantly David scrambled up onto the flatbed looking for a comfortable place to sit.

Kyle, Mike and Jeff were already seated on the metal bed of the truck, facing backwards, their backs against the cab of the truck. There was no room for David to sit with them, so he was forced to make a place for himself. He picked up the toolbox Ken kept handy for emergency repairs and slid it over so that he could sit down. The box felt cold and hard but seemed preferable to sitting directly on the truck bed.

"We got a couple of stops to make, then we'll be on our way," Ken told the others as he lifted the tailgate and used the support chains to clip it closed. Once Terry was seated, Kenny started the truck and drove off down the street.

"Ken probably wants to pick up some smokes and brews before we go out to the dump," Kyle informed his cousin. "Bet your grandfather wouldn't let you ride with us if he knew about that, eh?"

Ken pulled away from Ernie's Diner and continued down Maple for two blocks before taking a left on River Street and coming to a stop in front of a vacant building. David wondered why they had stopped. He looked up to see Terry talking to an older man with a scruffy looking beard and ragged clothes. Terry handed the man some money and the older man turned toward a liquor store two doors down. "Ted buys for us," Mike explained. "Ken gives him an extra buck so he can get a bottle of Thunderbird."

In a few minutes the ragged man returned carrying a case of Stroh's beer, a carton of Camel cigarettes and a bottle that looked like wine.

"Here you go," Terry said, swinging the case of beer up onto the flatbed. He flipped open the cardboard case and took out a couple of longneck bottles. Bracing the top of one of the bottles against the tailgate latch, he used a quick flick of his wrist to snap the cap off. He took a swallow of beer. "Nice and cold," he observed.

Terry opened the second bottle and handed it to Ken. "This should keep us till we get out to the dump," he said. "Just one more stop to make."

The truck continued down side streets and back alleys into a rundown residential neighborhood. David watched as Terry got out of the cab and went into one of the nicer houses on the block, returning moments later carrying a bulky cardboard box. He slid the box onto the bench seat between himself and Ken, and climbed back into the cab. "Ok, we're ready now, let's party," he called out to the group sitting in the open truck bed.

***

Ken drove out of the city and headed down back roads deep into the woods. David couldn't see where the truck was headed, but he could feel every bump and rut in the road. Ken seemed incapable of driving around any obstacle, but instead drove directly through potholes and over rocks and branches. It took no more than a half-hour to drive to the entrance to the dump, but to David it seemed an eternity.

"A little rough, eh," Kyle said noting David's discomfort. "It won't be long now. We're almost there."

The rocky ride continued along increasingly bone-jarring roads, until Ken turned down a small dirt access road marked "Falls County Waste Disposal." Ken drove into the dumping ground, until he reached a crater shaped depression in the ground. David looked around the crater. There were two or three other cars parked around the edge, all of them occupied by teenagers about Ken's age. The stench of decomposing refuse drifted up from the mass of decaying garbage in the pit below.

Ken found a gap in the circle of cars around the crater, pulled straight in, then turned around so that he could back up to the edge. "All out," he called, hopping from the truck cab and walking around to the back. He gulped down the remainder of the Stroh's he'd been drinking and pulled another bottle from the case in the back. Jeff, Mike, and Kyle hopped down from the truck bed to join Ken on the ground.

"Is this where the bears are," David asked.

"They'll be here. They always come," answered Mike as he reached into the cab to pull out the carton of Camels Ted had gotten for them. He took out a pack, opened it, and offered a cigarette to each of the boys standing around the truck. When he reached David he held the pack out and said, "Smoke, Davy?"

"No thanks," David declined.

"He doesn't smoke," Ken explained. "Old man Wertz wouldn't like it."

"Well, at least have a beer, eh?" Jeff said tossing an unopened beer toward David. David just had time to react, catching the bottle before it smashed against the body of the truck.

"Sure, why not," David responded trying to show the others that he was not as naïve as they suspected. He knew that this was a challenge, and that he would have to meet it to be accepted. Back home in LaSalle David's dad would sometimes offer him a sip of beer or a taste of rum and coke on special occasions like Christmas or his birthday. But only a taste. *Drinking stunts your growth,* his mother would warn jokingly. Once, when his parents were visiting friends, David had sneaked some whiskey from his father's liquor cabinet under the sideboard in the dining room. But the Seagram's whiskey was too strong for him straight and he had ended up spitting it out in the sink.

David had never been offered a drink outside of the confines of his home with his parents nearby. He stared at the unopened bottle, the cap securely in place, wondering what to do. "How do you open this thing?" he asked.

"Here let me show you a little trick," Terry said coming up and taking the bottle from his hand. Just as he had done earlier, Terry used the tailgate latch and a quick snap of his wrist to pop the cap off the bottle. Terry handed the open bottle back to David.

"That's pretty neat," David said, accepting the bottle from the older boy. He tipped his head back, bringing the bottle up to his lips and taking a small sip. The older boys laughed and nodded as if David's drinking beer with them somehow made him a member of their private club.

\*\*\*

The area around the crater was completely dark now, and the only illumination came from headlights aimed down into the garbage filled pit. Several of the teens held flashlights that they shined around the area in seemingly random patterns. Taking their beers with them, the older boys wandered away from the truck to join their friends. David understood now that for them the main attraction at the dump was not bears, but the opportunity to hang out with their friends.

Left alone standing by Ken's truck, David took another drink of beer. The beer had a somewhat bitter taste - not what he was expecting. Not nearly as good as rum and Coke, he thought. At first he sipped the beer tentatively, but became bolder as he drank more. He was still upset about the conversation he'd had with his father earlier in the day. Somehow the beer made him feel better.

Finishing the beer in his hand, David tossed the empty bottle down into the bear pit below. He heard the bottle smash into an unseen rock, shattering the stillness of the night. He looked at the case of beer, now half empty, sitting in the bed of the truck. No one was around. He reached in and grabbed another beer out of the case. What if somebody saw him, he wondered. Probably nobody would notice, he thought, and if they did they wouldn't care.

Unable to duplicate Terry's feat of opening the bottle on the truck frame, David looked around the cab of the truck until he found an opener on the floor and pried the top off the bottle. Nobody had seen him sneak the beer from the case. Self satisfied, David sat down on the fender of the truck and swigged down the beer, now less self conscious about his drinking.

Before long, David had finished that bottle as well and reached into the case to grab his third beer.

"Hey, take it easy with the brew, man," the sound of Kyle's voice startled David, almost causing him to drop his beer. "You'd better slow down. It'll mess you up real good and I don't think you want to show up at your Grandpa's tomorrow with a hangover."

"Just one more won't hurt," David insisted, prying open the bottle and taking a sip.

"It's your funeral," his cousin conceded, joining David in sitting on the tailgate of the truck.

David quickly consumed half the bottle, wiping his mouth with the back of his hand. He looked down over the edge of the pit. The stench emanating from the decomposing garbage made him feel slightly nauseous. "So where are the bears anyway?" he muttered.

"You might not see them, but they're around," Kyle replied. "Just listen."

David pushed himself up off the tailgate, but felt suddenly light headed. He listened attentively. At first there was no sound. A faint rustling in the darkness, then the sound of tin cans banging together.

Kyle reached into the cab and pulled a flashlight from behind the seat. "Check this out," he said directing the beam of the flashlight down into the pit. Two dots of reflected light glowed up from the pitch-blackness below. David strained his eyes, peering into the shadowy half-light. He could barely make out the silhouette of a bear rummaging through the piles of discarded trash. Her eyes shown with an eerie yellow glow in the light's beam. More movement came from the huge heap of refuse. A cub emerged from the heap licking the inside of an ice cream carton.

"You mean we drove all the way out here to see one mangy old bear and a cub?" David said trying to sound brave. "That old bear doesn't look so scary to me."

"Don't get too brave, there Davy," Ken said returning to the truck for another beer. "If baby bear's down there with mom, daddy's bound to be around here somewhere."

David took an unsteady step forward, but suddenly felt light headed. He braced himself against the bed of the truck. "I don't feel so good," he said. "Maybe I'd better sit back down for a minute." He sat down on the truck's tailgate again.

"You look kinda pale," Kyle noted. "You gonna be ok?"

"Sure, I'll be fine," he said. "I'm just a little dizzy. I'll be ok if I just sit here a while."

"Well, you don't look too good to me," Ken pressed. "Why don't we take a little walk? It'll help clear your head," he said.

"Hey Kyle, let me borrow that flashlight," Ken said reaching out to help David get to his feet. Ken led David away from the group along the two-track dirt path. David staggered along behind his cousin, barely able to keep up.

"Don't feel bad - me and my buddies have all been in your shoes. Just breathe deep. The air'll clear your head," Ken said in a comforting voice, putting his hand on David's shoulder. "Take your time. If you have to heave, just stop and bend over."

The two continued along the path, moving farther and farther away from the group of boys waiting by the truck. The path led up a low ridge and, as David and his cousin descended down the other side, the truck disappeared from view and darkness enveloped them.

***

After walking for a few minutes, David began to feel somewhat better. "Shhhh," Kenny said, suddenly stopping dead in his tracks and motioning for David to be still. "Something just moved up there," he said, indicating the area ahead of them with his flashlight beam.

"Where? I don't see anything," David said anxiously, suddenly aware of how isolated they were from the rest of the group.

"Over there - by that tree," Kenny said pointing his flashlight toward a clump of bushes near what appeared to be a tall pine about a hundred feet away. "Look! There it is again," he exclaimed excitedly.

David strained his eyes in the direction his cousin pointed with the flashlight, but only darkness met his gaze. "I can't see anything. There's nothing out there," he added trying to convince himself. "Com'on let's head back. I'm feelin' better now."

"No, I'm gonna go check it out," Ken said, walking a few paces into the shadows. "You just wait here for me. I'll only be a minute. You're safe here. Don't worry."

Before David could object further, Ken moved quickly into the blackness, leaving David on his own. Darkness now surrounded him on all sides. The dirt path had disappeared into the night. As he watched, Kenny's flashlight began to recede into the distance. "Kenny, come on back," he called out toward the shadows.

The flashlight beam continued to move away. A moment later it disappeared entirely.

"Kenny?" David called out, his voice wavering slightly. There was no answer, just a chorus of crickets

He called out again, only louder, the fear now evident in his voice.

"What's the matter," Kenny called back from the darkness. "You all right?"

"Sure. I'm ok," David replied somewhat reassured. "You comin' back now? The others'll be expecting us."

"Yeah, I'll be right there," Ken yelled back. "Looks like you were right. There's nothing over here."

David strained his eyes to see into the darkness, until at last he made out a dim glimmer of light in the distance. As the light grew stronger, he began to make out the faint silhouette of a figure illuminated in the glow.

"GRRRARRGH!" Without warning a deep terrifying growl shattered the darkness, causing the crickets to go still. In the distance, David watched as a second shadow appeared, looming over the first figure. The flashlight beam jarred up into the air, and back down toward the earth. The light flared up again, then disappeared. Almost at the exact same instant Ken's blood curdling scream pierced the night air. David stood paralyzed with fear. He could hear thrashing and crashing noises growing louder. "Bear! Oh my god, it's a bear! Get help quick!" Ken screamed out. "Jesus, it's got me!"

Panic seized David. Without thinking, he spun around and began to run blindly into the night, hoping he was headed in the right direction. Still unsteady from the drinks he had consumed, he raced as fast as his legs would carry him back along the darkened path. He caught his toe on a rock or branch in the road and stumbled forward, falling to his knees in the gravel. Quickly he got back to his feet and sprinted forward. "A bear! A bear!" he yelled hoping someone would hear. "It's got Ken. Please someone, help please."

David had almost reached the knoll of the hill when the darkness suddenly exploded in a blaze of light. Six miniature suns simultaneously appeared in front of him, shining directly into his eyes, and blinding him. He brought his hands up to his face, covering his eyes. "Is that you Terry?" he shouted trying to see into the glare of the headlights before him. "Come quick - it's Kenny. He needs our help."

At first he heard nothing in response, except the sound of his own labored breathing, but slowly he became aware of another sound - a faint hint of laughter. As he continued to move up the hill toward the lights, the laughter became more distinct, and David began to make out the silhouettes of people lining the hilltop, looking down at him.

"Hey Davy, did you find your bear?" Terry's mocking voice called from behind the headlights. "Did the big bad bear scare the poor little boy?"

"But Ken needs help," David pleaded. "There's a bear..." The crunch of gravel behind him sent chills down David's spine. He spun around to face the oncoming threat. What he saw was Kenny's grinning face, beaming as he walked into the headlight's glare.

"What's going on?" David's said gradually becoming aware of the trick that had been played on him.

"We got you good, eh?" Ken laughed as he came up and put his arm around his cousin's shoulder.

David stood unsteady and confused, feeling the effects of the earlier beers. "But I saw you. There was a bear..."

"Here's your bear," Ken said pointing his flashlight toward Jeff who had also moved up from the shadows. Over his arms Jeff was carrying a very frightening but very dead bearskin rug. "It belongs to Terry's dad. That's why we had to stop at his house - to pick it up."

David's confusion was turning into anger.

"Come on Davy- no hard feelings, huh? Get in the truck and I'll drive you back to the house." Sheepishly, David did as his cousin asked, carefully avoiding eye contact with the other boys in the group. "Wait till I tell dad about this," Ken laughed. "He'll crack up."

## The Deer

"The Lord that delivered me out of the paw of the lion, and out of the paw of the bear, he will deliver me out of the hand of this Philistine," Reverend Goodall quoted from the pulpit of the Iron Falls Presbyterian Church. The minister looked out over the congregation, his gaze falling on David, who sat firmly wedged in the pew between his two cousins. Though the passage referred to the biblical David's encounter with Goliath, David felt sure that the minister was talking directly to him.

He fidgeted in his seat, pulling at the collar of his shirt. When Rita made arrangements for David's visit, she had insisted that he accompany the Petersons to church on Sunday. She had even made him bring along the new suit his mother had picked out for him before she left. Though the suit felt stiff and uncomfortable, it was the humiliation of the previous evening that really made David squirm.

Kenny leaned over and poked him in the ribs. "Looks like even Reverend Goodall knows about you and that old bear, Davy boy," he whispered.

David sank down into the pew as low as he could go. Every face in the sanctuary seemed to be focused on him. Every eye turned in his direction. They all seemed to be mocking him. By now everyone at church probably knew about the bear. He was sure of it. Pretty soon the entire town would know.

His uncle had been the worst. "Hey, Davy, don't be em-bear-assed", Ray had chortled after learning of the prank from Kenny the previous evening. "Sometimes when things seem un-bear-able, you just have to grin and bear it." Ray laughed so hard at his own joke that he almost fell out of his chair.

Thankfully Ray had once again found an excuse to miss the Sunday service. But the presence of Kyle and Kenny more than made up for his absence. "Hey, man, you're not still sore about last night are you?" Kenny whispered.

"Why don't you mind your own business," David snapped.

"Leave your cousin alone," Rita interceded, reaching over to poke her son's arm. While Ray had considered the entire bear incident to be a joke, Rita didn't find it one bit funny. When she had learned of the incident, she was mortified. What had Kenny been thinking taking David out to the dump in the first place?

Reverend Goodall continued his sermon, exhorting David's victory over the giant Goliath. David wondered if his biblical namesake had ever had to endure a family like his. Right now, he just wanted to go home, back to the lake.

***

The mandatory after-church dinner at the Peterson's proved to be a tense, anxious affair. David sat glumly at the table, glaring at his cousins, while his Aunt Rita berated her sons and Uncle Ray tried to remain detached from it all. But it was only after the dinner had ended that the underlying tension began to reach the surface.

"All right, Kenny, now I want you to drive David back home," Rita told her son. "And when you get there I want you to apologize to Mr. Wertz for the way you treated your cousin."

"Ah, Mom, do I have to," Kenny cried out in his most pained tone.

"Yes you have to," replied his mother in a calm but firm voice.

"But why?"

"Because I said so," she commanded, more firmly now. "Do you understand me young man?"

"This is real crap," Kenny replied. "I didn't do anything wrong. It was just a stupid joke."

"Watch your mouth, young man. Now get going before I get really mad, eh."

"Com'on," he called to David. "Let's go if we're goin'." Kenny grabbed the keys from a hook by the door and headed out, barely giving David enough time to catch up before he reached the truck.

Almost as soon as David slid into the passenger's seat, Ken hit the gas. The pickup flew backward down the driveway and skidded out into the road. Kenny accelerated toward Iron Falls, but just before reaching the city limits, he swerved sharply onto a gravel side road. "Hang on, Davy," Kenny called out above the road noise. "We're takin' the shortcut."

Ken kept his foot planted firmly on the accelerator as the road became bumpier and curvier, winding through sunlit fields and cow pastures until it eventually reached the shores of Spirit Lake. The road twisted and turned, tracing the contours of the lake over low rolling hills, following the path of a long forgotten Indian trail.

Kenny barreled down each slope, gaining speed as he went. Just to heighten the experience, Ken pulled his hands off the steering wheel at the top of each knoll and threw them in the air. "Just like riding a roller coaster, eh?" he yelled at the top of his lungs as the Ford plunged down each hill.

"Stop it Kenny," David pleaded, "I'm going to be sick. This isn't funny."

"Hey, sure it is. Just relax. Nothing's going to happen."

Abruptly, the road vanished into a thick cover of pine trees and white birch. Kenny continued to accelerate through the tunnel of trees. The affect of driving from the blinding sunlight of the open field into the dark shadow provided by the tree-lined canopy was like driving into an unlit cave.

In the few second it took David's eyes to adjust to the dim light, the buck appeared. It stood squarely in the middle of the road, jerking its head around to look at the oncoming truck. Kenny must have seen it at the same instant. "Oh, shit," he exclaimed, slamming his foot down on the brake pedal.

For a brief moment both Kenny and the buck tried to guess which way the other would turn.

They both guessed wrong.

Kenny veered to the left, into the oncoming traffic lane. At the exact same instant the buck reversed course and leapt into the air to escape back into the woods. The deer was quick, but not quick enough to make it past the front fender of the pickup.

The deer smashed squarely into the passenger side front fender directly in front of David. Everything appeared to be happening in slow motion. David saw the buck coming toward him, seemingly within inches of the windshield. He heard the sickening sound of the buck's hindquarters being crushed. The deer bounced into the air, careening away from the truck.

David flew forward toward the dashboard. Instinctively he threw his hands out, bracing himself for the impact. His hands hit hard against the dash but his head continued forward. He saw the glove compartment flashing toward him an instant before he felt the impact. The blow caught him in the mouth, just missing the ridge of his nose.

As the truck jerked forward and slammed to an abrupt stop,

David's head snapped back. For several moments the engine roared, then it began to sputter and cough. Suddenly the motor died and everything went quiet.

***

It took a few seconds for David to regain his composure and realize what had happened. The silence was broken by Kenny's shrill scream.

"Oh, fuck," cried Kenny as he hit the brakes hard in reaction to the jolt of the deer mangling his front fender. "Motherfucking shit," Kenny continued cursing as he threw his door open. "Where the shit did that fucker come from?" Quickly moving to the front of the truck, Kenny gave his entire attention to the state of his truck, completely ignoring both David and the injured deer. "Jesus, oh Christ, look at my grill! Fucking god-dammed deer!"

David tried pushing the passenger side door open with all his might, but it would not budge. Rather than fight the door, he slid across to the driver's side and jumped out. Suddenly he felt a little bit dizzy, deciding to sit down for a minute. He staggered slightly as he sat on the running board of the Ford to catch his breath. Putting his hand to his mouth, he noticed for the first time that he was bleeding. He licked his upper lip with his tongue, tasting the saltiness of his own blood.

Kenny stood at the front of the pickup, ranting and raving, while the deer lay four or five feet beyond his door, still thrashing in the dense foliage. Looking up, Ken saw David walking unsteadily toward him from the passenger side of the truck. A single drop of blood flowed down the side of David's face, dripping onto his clean white tee shirt.

Ignoring David's distress, Kenny remained focused on the mangled front of his vehicle. "Look at that mess," he agonized. At his cousin's insistence, David examined the damage. The grill had been folded in several places and the newly bondoed fender was now re-crumpled. "Did you see what that fucking, shit-ass deer did to my truck? This will cost a fortune to fix."

David wanted to point out that if Kenny had not been speeding down a twisty, dangerous lake road, none of this would have happened. But in Kenny's present mood, David knew the only thing to do was agree with his cousin. "It sure is a mess, all right," he replied, his words slightly slurred by his rapidly swelling lip. "Too bad."

The injured buck began thrashing around in the underbrush to the front right of the Ford. For the first time since the collision, David turned his attention toward the wounded animal. He did not know how to judge a male deer's age, but he knew the buck must be young judging from the short antlers just barely protruding from the animal's skull.

The buck had fallen not more than ten yards from where Kenny and David now stood. Its hindquarters were twisted and wrenched in an unnatural position, the rear legs sticking out from the torso at almost right angles. David looked into the deer's eyes. They showed pure terror: terror at being unable to run, terror at being unable to move its hind legs. Again and again the traumatized animal tried to stand. And each time it fell, bellowing and snorting its anger at defeat. David sensed the animal's frustration and bewilderment. The deer's brain no longer controlled its extremities.

"What's gonna' happen to the buck?" David asked expectantly.

"What the fuck do I care what happens to it. Goddamned fucker should be dead after what it did to my truck." Kenny's lack of compassion did not surprise David, but he could not take his eyes off the young buck. After each successive attempt to stand, the deer had less and less fight left in it. Slowly it sank back into the bed of pine needles around it, still snorting and wheezing.

"Hey, will you leave that cock-sucking deer alone and get back over here," Kenny yelled at David. "Help me straighten out this fender, will you?" The fender had been pushed into the tire, making it impossible to move the truck. David forced his gaze away from the wounded deer and saw that Kenny had begun to pull the frame of the truck away from the tire.

Kenny motioned for David to come around to the left side of the truck and help him pry the fender away from the wheel well. David grabbed a hold of the frame around the tire and began to tug at the body as his cousin used a crow bar from the back to pry the fender out. Between the two of them they managed to get the fender pulled out enough from the tire so that Kenny could get into the cab and turn the steering wheel, pointing the front tires forward once more.

Once his assigned task was completed, David returned his

attention to the wounded buck. The deer had become quieter now; its violent thrashing replaced by labored panting. The puddle of dark red blood seeping into the ground beneath the buck had become a pool now, as the life drained away from the dying animal. The initial surprise and horror in the deer's eyes had been replaced by a resigned melancholy. David stood riveted by the buck's side.

"Will you forget that damned deer and get back in here?" Kenny shouted from the driver's seat. He began cranking the engine, trying to restart the truck.

But David did not move away. Instead he knelt down beside the deer, moving slowly so that the buck would know it had nothing to fear. The deer did not move. Carefully David stroked the animal's flank. The pelt was soft and warm to the touch. "It's gonna' be all right, fella," David whispered softly. "Nobody's gonna' hurt you."

David could feel the animal's breath. The deer's breathing remained steady but shallow. David continued to stroke the buck gently. The deer seemed to quiet and settle more deeply into the bed of grass and pine needles. David looked up toward his angry cousin sitting in the truck.

"Ken, we can't just leave him like this. He's gonna' bleed to death," David pleaded.

"Well, what do you want me to do?" shouted Kenny. "I don't have my goddamned gun here or I'd shoot the bastard." Kenny leaned briefly on the truck horn, causing a short but deafening blast. At the blare of the horn, the deer panicked, lunging forward and throwing off David's comforting hand.

"Stop the damned honking," David screamed at his cousin. "You're scaring him!"

Kenny was rapidly losing patience with his cousin. He was about to drive off and leave David and the deer in the dust, when another truck pulled up behind Kenny's Ford.

***

"Geez," exclaimed the driver as he walked along side Kenny's truck, examining the damage. "That deer really tore you up, didn't he?" The man, about thirty, wore a dirty pair of worn coveralls over a faded blue work shirt. On his head he wore a green 'John Deere' hat, proclaiming himself to be a local farmer. He walked up and assessed the front-end damage. "Is she still drivable, or do you guys need a lift somewheres?" he offered.

"It'll move ok," replied Kenny, "but it's gonna cost a mint to get her patched up again."

"Sure is a mess," sympathized the farmer. "You was lucky though. Friend of mine hit a deer out on US 2 last winter - totaled his whole goddamned car. He was fit to be tied. Good eaten though. That doe fed his family for a month." The farmer seemed to have a glimmer of an idea, as he looked toward the dying buck. "What about this one?" he asked. "You guys gonna' skin 'im out?"

"He's still alive," David said reproachfully.

"Won't be for long though," replied the farmer. "You ask me, somebody ought'ta put 'im out of his misery. You want me to do it?"

"Do you have to kill it?" David pleaded.

"What's it matter? Damn things gonna die anyway," Kenny muttered.

"It's for the best," the man replied. "I'll get my rifle." He walked calmly back to his truck, opened the cab, and pulled a rifle from behind the seat. He cradled the gun in the crook of his arm as he returned to the scene of the accident. "This animal's suffering. A bullet's quick and painless. Now step back out'a the way, boy."

David remained squatting beside the deer. "He's scared," David said.

"I'll do it clean," stated the man, noting David's obvious concern. "You best not watch. Why don't you go stand over there?" he pointed back toward where Kenny was watching. "Just look away when I tell you. He won't feel a thing."

David looked once more into the eyes of the buck. The big deer seemed almost resigned to his fate. Tears began to roll down David's cheeks as he patted the deer once more to reassure it, then stood up and walked toward Kenny.

"Ok, now," stated the man with the rifle. "Turn away, and brace yourself. This might be a bit loud if you're not used to the sound of a rifle shot."

David turned and closed his eyes waiting for the shot to come. For almost a minute nothing happened. Just as he was about to turn to see what was taking so long, David heard the rifle being cocked and, almost immediately thereafter, the sharp report of a rifle shot. Even though David had prepared himself, the explosion of the rifle made him jump involuntarily. He whirled around to look once more at the young buck. It lay still now, eyes still open, staring blankly, tongue protruding from its mouth.

"Hey, kid," the man yelled over to Kenny. "Help me heft this guy onto the bed of my pickup, will ya? I might be able to salvage some venison from all this, if you don't mind."

"Sure, whatever," replied Kenny.

David walked over to the lifeless carcass of the deer and again knelt down beside it. Tears continued to stream down his face. He ran his hand once more over the soft coat of the buck. The body was still warm. Kenny grabbed the deer by the front legs while the farmer took the twisted rear quarters. Lifting on the count of three, they swung the carcass up onto the pickup bed.

"Sorry you had to see this," the farmer told David as he sheathed the rifle in a mount across the rear window of his truck cab. "But don't take it too serious. This sort a' thing happens all the time, ya' know?"

The farmer slid in behind the wheel of his truck and slammed the door. "Sure I can't do anything else for you boys?" he asked again. Kenny waved him off. "All right, you take care now," he stated as he started the truck. With a wave of his hand, the farmer backed up, turned around, and headed back in the direction from which he'd come.

"Let's go," Kenny urged. He jumped back into the cab of the Ford, cranked the starter and urged the truck back to life. David barely had time to run around to the passenger side of the truck before Ken kicked it open and motioned for David to get in. As David jumped in and pulled the door shut behind him, Ken hit the accelerator, tearing off down the road again.

David turned around and looked back through the rear cab window trying to take one last look at the site of the accident. But as Kenny drove away, the site quickly receded into the distance, and soon David could see nothing in the dense forest undergrowth to remind him that the deer had ever existed.

## Little Thunder

The deer lay still and cold, lifeless, its body blocking the path ahead. David stood transfixed, only a few feet from the buck, unable to move. The sight filled him with dread. The sun filtered through the trees, causing eerie shadows to flicker across the body. There wasn't a sound in the forest, not even the singing of birds. Where was Kenny? Where was the man with the gun? No one else was anywhere around. What was going on?

Cautiously, David stepped closer. He moved slowly around the body until he could clearly see the young buck's face. Blood oozed from the deer's nostrils, and the tongue protruded unnaturally from his mouth. The deer's eyes were closed. David knelt down and reached out to touch the buck's side. He stroked the soft and velvety flank. The body was still warm. David felt an indistinct movement beneath his hand. The deer was breathing - faint and shallow, but breathing nonetheless.

Suddenly, the deer's eyes flew open. David stepped back, startled. The deer's glassy, glazed eyes began to clear. It turned toward David. He recognized the same helpless, pained expression he had seen on the buck's face at the moment Kenny's truck had slammed into it. The deer snorted and struggled to stand. The unnaturally deformed rear legs began to untangle and straighten. The deer looked around as it rose unsteadily to its feet. It took a few awkward steps, trying to find its footing.

Tenuously the deer stumbled away down a narrow path, almost completely covered by weeds. The path led away from the main trail into the woods. David wondered why he had never noticed the trail before. For just an instant, the deer stopped and looked back, as if waiting for David to follow. He watched as the deer disappeared into the woods.

David started after him down the path. He pushed his way through the undergrowth and made his way toward a grove of nearby trees. He followed the trail into the overgrown forest. But the deer had already vanished. Up ahead, David could just make out a faint flicker of light. The radiance drew him onward. He moved toward the distant glow, but as he did, it seemed to recede even deeper into the woods.

At that moment David woke up. With a start, he sat up in bed. The light and the deer had both vanished. The dream troubled him. He looked up at the unraveled dream catcher draped limply over his bed. Though Carl had tied the ends of the willow branch loosely together, the net was still tangled and gaps permeated the webbing. He pulled the broken talisman from the wall and tossed it in the waste basket. It was worthless. His dream protection was gone.

***

"Hello? Is anybody home?" David called through the screen door of Maddie's cabin.

"Come in," she replied, "the door's open."

He entered her kitchen timidly, only to find Maddie sitting at her kitchen table drinking coffee as if she had been expecting him. "He came to you, didn't he?" she asked in a quiet voice.

"Who came?" he replied. "What are you talking about, Maddie?"

"The deer. He came to you in your dream didn't he?"

"My dream? How did you know about that?"

"Because I saw him too. He came to me in the night. He said he would visit you. So tell me what happened, " she said. "Tell me what you saw."

"First, I saw the deer lying there dying," he said, "just like I told you and Grandpa yesterday when I got home." David closed his eyes as if visualizing the dream. "But in my dream Kenny wasn't there, and the deer... he started to come back to life. His eyes opened and he just kinda stared at me. Breathing slow and gentle. His eyes were soft and sad. Then he got up and went into the woods and disappeared. Maddie, I don't understand, why would the deer come in my dreams?"

"When you touched the deer, you made a special bond with him," she said. "It was the manitou of the deer that returned to you in your dream. When a spirit comes in a dream, there is a reason."

"But why did he come to me? What does he want?"

"That I do not know," she answered. "You must discover why he came for yourself. Deer is watchful. He is a creature of peace. He knows when danger is coming. Maybe he is trying to warn you of some danger. That is what he did when Little Thunder summoned him in his vision."

"Little Thunder? You mean a deer spirit appeared to Little

Thunder?"

She got up from the table and moved around to stand by the window behind David. She pointed to a strip of land along the north end of the lake. David tried to follow her finger. "You see that spit of land jutting out where Falls Creek enters the lake? My people once had their village there."

"Yeah, that's over by Falls Park. I've been there with my dad," David said. "It's kind of creepy. There's a whole bunch of spirit houses where dead Indians are buried, and an old birch bark canoe that was supposed to belong to Little Thunder."

"That is the very canoe they found on the lake the day after he vanished," Maddie explained.

"Vanished? Little Thunder just disappeared?" David asked, his interest growing. "You mean like a magician? He just vanished?"

"No, not like that. Magicians are just tricksters. They don't have real magic. Before the white people came, my people had real magic. That's mostly gone now. But Little Thunder did not disappear by magic. One day he was just gone. Nowhere to be found."

"Oh, come on Maddie, people just don't disappear. That only happens in the movies. "

"Maybe, maybe not," Maddie responded. "Some people believe, some do not believe. It is their choice. All I know is what is told in our stories."

"What stories, Maddie?"

"Our stories are very old, far older than I am. They are as old as the earth itself," Maddie stated. "I heard them from my father, and he heard them from his father. That is how our history is passed down. Father to son, mother to daughter.

"Our legends and stories are like your history books," she continued, "but instead of writing them down, we retell the tales, or sing them in chants, and we remember what we hear. They are as real to me as the leaves on the trees, or the birds in the air."

"Is one of your stories about Little Thunder? What happened to him anyway?"

Maddie settled back in her chair as if her story would take some time to tell. "To understand the story of Little Thunder, you must understand something of the story of my people," she said. "The stories are intertwined. First I will tell you a little bit about my people. Then you will begin to see who Little Thunder was."

***

She closed her eyes as if trying to imagine another time and place in her mind. "Try to think of the lake with no houses or cottages on its shores," she said. "No roads cut through the pines slicing the land into pieces. No telephone wires strung like spider webs from pole to pole. Only sparkling rivers, crystal clear lakes, and forest as far as the eye could see. In the old times my people occupied all these lands."

"Yeah, "David exclaimed excitedly, "I learned about the Indians in school. They were here even before Columbus."

"Not Indians," Maddie corrected. "Indians come from India. My people are natives of this country. Our small band was just one of many tribes who lived on this land."

"Tribes?" David said. "You mean like the Sioux or Cherokee? Sitting Bull and Crazy Horse were both Sioux. Which tribe do you belong to, Maddie?"

"The Sioux and Cherokee lived on the plains," she explained. "I am an Anishinabe. The name means first people. The white men call us Ojibwa or Chippewa."

"Was Little Thunder an Amish... an Anishen... was he a Chippewa too, Maddie?"

"Little Thunder was also an Anishinabe. His tribal name was Animikeeg," Maddie explained. "He was said to have been a very wise man, but not very handsome. He had three wives - but only one at a time. His first two wives died of a white man's disease - probably small pox. So he married his third wife. They were still together when he disappeared."

"Disappeared? What happened to him, Maddie?"

Maddie thought for a moment, then continued with her narrative. "Before I tell you the story of Little Thunder, you must first understand how our people once lived on this land. Our men were hunters and trappers. They were also fishermen who caught sturgeon and trout. In the summer, we grew corn and squash. In the fall, we harvested wild rice and made sugar from the syrup of maple trees. Our village stood at the other end of the lake, where the county park is now. My people hunted and fished the forests and rivers from Lake Superior to the Wisconsin border."

"Were there white people living here then, Maddie?"

"Not at first," she replied. "The first white people to come were the French trappers. They hunted and lived like us. We thought all white men were like them. But then the missionaries came. They wanted to make us Christians. They wanted us to believe in their god, so they set up schools and taught our children white ways. After the missionaries, the English arrived, and after them came the American settlers. It was during that time that Little Thunder was born."

"At first the American settlers did not want our land. They said our land was not good for growing crops. But that was before the white men found copper."

"Copper? Like what they make pennies out of?"

"Yes, and copper wire. After they found copper, they found iron under our land as well. The white men wanted these things. And they wanted the wood from our forests. So they wrote treaties and told us we must sign. Our people did not understand what they were being asked to do. The whites told us that we would still be able to fish and hunt. But all they wanted was to steal our land.

"Our leaders met in council to decide what we should do. Some said we too should take what the treaty offered. They thought that if they agreed, that they would be left in peace. Others did not trust the white men's promises. They said that if we agreed to the treaty, we would be left with nothing.

"Because Little Thunder was a wise warrior, esteemed by all in our tribe, his opinion was highly respected. He was one of the tribal elders…"

"What's that?" David interrupted. "You mean like a war chief or somethin'."

"We call our leaders *gimaa*. They are elected by the tribal council. You get all your ideas of how Indians lived from radio and television. My people did not live like the Indians on *Hop-a-long Cassidy*. They didn't dress in feathers and war paint all the time. The chief, or *gimaa*, led the tribal council to make decisions for our people."

"Like the Congress in Washington?"

"More like a city assembly," Maddie answered. "Anyway, Little Thunder was one of the council elders, and the council waited for him to speak before making their final decision.

"Before he talked to the council, Little Thunder wanted time to consult the spirit world. So several days before the council was to meet, he set off with his brother, Twelve Trees, toward Power's Rock. That spot was considered sacred to our people. Together the two brothers paddled across the lake to set up camp and await a sign from the spirit world.

"For three days, Little Thunder maintained his vision quest while his brother kept vigil. Without food or water, both day and night Little Thunder waited without sleep for a sign from the gods. On the third day, he broke his silence. He told his brother that Deer had appeared to him and warned him not to let his people be bullied into giving away their heritage. He told his brother to return to their village, saying that he would be back by nightfall, in time for the council meeting.

"That evening, the tribal council met to discuss whether to accept the terms of the treaty. They awaited the words of Little Thunder, but by dusk there was still no sign of him, though Twelve Trees assured them that he would be there. The council sent one of the warriors down to the shore to watch for Little Thunder's canoe, but all he saw coming across the lake were the churning black clouds of an approaching storm.

"As the young brave kept his vigil, the storm clouds grew darker and more menacing. Lightning flashed, cutting through the darkness. During one of the flashes, the brave thought he saw Little Thunder paddling his canoe steadfastly toward the shore. Eagerly he ran off to tell the council that Little Thunder would soon arrive.

"In the council lodge, the debate over the treaty had reached an impasse. Supporters seemed to have the upper hand, arguing that the tribe would only suffer more indignity at the hand of the whites if they held out. Treaty opponents had all but given up, when suddenly Little Thunder burst into the council lodge, drenched in water, dripping from head to foot.

"The lodge became strangely silent as the great warrior stepped forward to speak. Boldly Little Thunder explained what Deer had told him. They were warriors, he reminded them, not timid sheep to be herded into new pastures. He said that he had had a vision, and seen our people scattered and destroyed if they gave up their land. He said that in his vision he saw whites digging up the land to steal treasure from the ground, and tearing down the forests to build cities. In the end, the Anishinabe would exist no more.

"When he finished talking, Little Thunder turned and walked out of the lodge. After he left, the council made its decision. When they had finished, Twelve Trees hurried from the meeting to find his brother and tell him of the result of the vote, but Little Thunder was nowhere to be found. No one had seen Little Thunder come to the council lodge, nor had they seen him leave.

"The mystery remained as the next morning dawned bright and clear after the storm. Little Thunder was not in his lodge, nor had anyone seen him, and his canoe was missing. A great search was begun, with all the warriors looking for their brother, but without success. Then, as the morning became afternoon, one of the young men of the tribe returned across the lake paddling Little Thunder's canoe. He had spotted it floating in the reeds at the edge of the marsh. But there was no sign of Little Thunder anywhere.

"Little Thunder was never seen again. Some say that he simply chose to leave the tribe rather than see his vision become reality. Others think that it was not Little Thunder, but his ghost who appeared before the council that night. They say that his body was lost in the storm, and it was his spirit that made it to shore.

"Nobody knows the truth, but there are those who claim Little Thunder still haunts these woods. Some claim to have seen him gliding across the lake in his canoe, paddling eternally to reach the shore."

"That's a great story, Maddie," David conceded. "But you don't really believe that there's a ghost haunting the lake do you?"

"It's not important what I believe," Maddie replied, pausing to sip her coffee. "It is what *you* believe that matters. You wouldn't be so certain Little Thunder is just a myth if you ever saw him. A lot of people have come up here thinking like you do, until they see for themselves. Then they become believers."

"Have you seen him, Maddie? Have you seen the ghost?"

"No, I have never seen him," Maddie's answer seemed to carry a degree of disappointment. "No one knows when Little Thunder will appear or to whom. Some have seen him in the morning mist, or maybe as the shadows are falling at sunset. Others see him paddling his canoe across the lake during a storm or just after. It is never the same."

"And what about Little Thunder's vision," asked David. "What did the tribal council finally decide to do?"

"Oh, the council heeded Little Thunder's vision. His words had swayed the council, and the vote to reject the treaty was nearly unanimous. They refused to sign the treaty, but the other bands of Anishinabe did sign. The L'Anse, the Lac Vieux Desert, and the

Wisconsin bands had all signed away their homelands. Soon only our small band was left.

"But in the end it made no difference anyway. The white men came and took what they wanted. They pushed my people onto reservations and finally forced them to leave. Only a few of us remain here today. We are scattered here and there, on small pieces of land. It is good that Little Thunder never saw what was to come. He would have bowed his head in shame."

A sudden sadness seemed to fill Maddie, draining the energy from her body. Slowly she got up from the table. "That is enough of our story for today," she told David softly.

"Before you go, I have something for you," Maddie said reaching into the basket she kept by the table. She pulled out a willow hoop webbed with rawhide, and decorated with a broach made with porcupine quills. Below the broach hung a cluster of hawk feathers. She handed the beautiful dream catcher to David, smiling.

"You made this?" David exclaimed, astonished.

"I carved the hoop myself using my grandfather's crooked knife," she said.

"Its beautiful," David replied, admiring the delicate craftsmanship.

"It's to help bring you good dreams. Perhaps now Deer will return to guide you in the dream world, as he did Little Thunder."

Maddie turned and left the kitchen. Even after she had gone, David continued to feel her sadness. If she could believe so strongly, perhaps there was some truth to her tale.

***

David hung Maddie's dream catcher on the wall hook and stepped back to assess its position over his bed.

"It is very beautiful," he heard his grandfather's voice. "Maddie must think very highly of you to give you such a gift, ya? Do you think it will help?"

"Help? What do you mean, Grandpa?"

"With your dreams. Maddie tells me you didn't sleep so well last night. Something about a bad dream?"

"I dreamt the deer came back to life. It kinda shook me up. I just can't forget the look in his eyes. It was as if the deer was pleading with me, asking for me to save him. But I couldn't do anything to help."

"What happened to the deer is not your fault, David. You mustn't blame yourself."

"I know that, but my dream still bothers me. Maddie says that the reason the deer came to me is because he was trying to tell me something. She even gave me a new dream catcher to help keep away bad dreams."

"I see, and what else did Maddie tell you?"

"She told me the story of Little Thunder. She said that a deer came to him in a vision and told him not to sign the treaty with the white men. That was the same night he disappeared. But the Indians lost their land anyway, and his spirit still haunts the lake."

Carl looked at David skeptically. "And you believe that is what happened?"

"Sure, I believe Maddie, if that's what you mean," David replied. "It's true isn't it?"

"It's all superstitious nonsense," Carl said. "They are just stories, nothing more."

"But Maddie said..."

"What Maddie told you is wrong. I want you to understand that I care very much for Maddie. In many ways she has been like a second daughter to me. But just because I care for her doesn't mean I agree with everything she says or does. Maddie was brought up differently from you or I. She believes that ghosts and spirits are real, and that dreams have special meaning."

"But its not just the dream, Grandpa. I saw the deer die right in front of me."

"It's only natural for you to be upset about what you saw, David. It is even normal for you to have bad dreams. But there is nothing supernatural about what happened. It was an accident - nothing more. Death is a part of nature. I'm sure that as time passes you will understand the truth of what I am saying."

Carl put his arm around David's shoulder sympathetically. "You've had a tough week. Why don't you take the rest of the day off. Tomorrow we will begin working together on the Barracuda," he said. "It will help take your mind off of all this nonsense. Besides, my friends the Gibsons will be arriving in a few days. I'm sure once you meet their children and get to know them, you will begin to feel better, ya?"

## Boat Work

Carl had already moved the Barracuda out of the boathouse, uncovered the boat frame, and was getting out the hand tools by the time David arrived to begin work in the morning.

"Ah, good morning sleepy head. So how do you feel today, David?" Carl greeted.

"Better, thanks Grandpa," David replied. "I must'a slept in." David avoided telling his grandfather that his new dream catcher was probably the reason for his sound sleep.

"Well, come along then," Carl said. "Let's get started."

"What do we do first, Grandpa?" David asked.

Carl pulled out the dog-eared copy of the Chris Craft assembly instructions Ike Eisenberg had given to him and handed it to David. "Here is the instruction manual. Ike said everything we need to know is in here."

David examined the tattered booklet, flipping through the pages and glancing at a few of the illustrations.

"You see? Ike has put a check after each step he completed. We will start where the check marks stop."

David paged through the instructions until he found the last check mark in the manual.

"Looks like the next step is to put on the transom. What's that, Grandpa?"

"The transom is the wall at the back of the boat where the outboard is attached, David. Go ahead and hold the transom in place at the stern while I drill holes through the keel." As they worked, David began to learn the parts of the boat he was helping to build.

"Go on. Glop lots of that caulking compound on the canvas strip. That's it. Now push it down against the keel while I screw it down tight. There, that should make a nice watertight joint."

David did as Carl instructed, applying the caulk to the joint and holding it in place while his grandfather screwed it in place. "Good job, David," Carl said when the transom was securely in place. "By the time you leave here to go home, you'll be a real boat builder."

David smiled. He appreciated the compliment, but still wondered about his grandfather's feelings toward him. "Grandpa?" he said. "Were you upset when mom left me here with you?

Sometimes you act like I'm just in the way. Would you rather that I just went home?"

"David, when your mother first asked me to let you stay here, I wasn't sure that it was such a good idea. I have lived alone for so long... I wasn't sure how things would work out with just the two of us."

"Is that why you acted so mean at first? I really thought you didn't want me around."

"You are right. Things did not go very well after your mother left. I even thought that I had made a mistake letting you stay."

"That night you told me I'd have to stay outside... You really scared me. Sometimes you still do."

"Me?" his grandfather laughed. "You don't need to be afraid of me? No, no. David, I want you to know that I love you, and I would never do anything to hurt you. Never."

"But I don't understand. If you love me, then why do you seem so angry?"

"At times I may seem strict, but that is only because I want what is best for you. That is the way I was raised by my father when I was a boy in Germany."

"You mean your father was strict too?"

"My father believed in firm discipline. Sometimes he would even take a belt to me. He could be harsh, but I never forgot what I learned from him. But over time I learned to respect my father, just as you and I have come to respect each other, eh?" David nodded. "Now I am most grateful we have this chance to get to know each other."

***

David heard the sound of a powerful outboard engine approaching, and looked up to see a sleek, trim powerboat speeding toward shore at full throttle. He watched as the boat threw up a huge plume of spray just before the skipper cut the engine and the boat coasted in toward the dock. At the helm was a middle-aged man wearing a white yachting cap. Seated next to him was an attractive girl wearing her bright red hair in a stylish ponytail. David couldn't tell for sure, but guessed that the girl was roughly his own age.

As the gleaming craft came within hailing distance, the skipper throttled down. "Ahoy there, Carl," the man called out over the roar of the engine. "Permisssion to come ashore?"

A smile crossed Carl's face. "Well, well, if it isn't Jake Bradshaw," he answered back. "It's been a while."

"Saw you boys hard at work and thought I'd stop and see what was going on," the man called out.

"Our new project," Carl answered. "It's a Chris Craft Barracuda. Bought it from Ike Eisenberg. It's a work in progress. Not all of us can afford a beauty like that cruiser of yours, Jake." Carl knew that Jake Bradshaw's pride and joy was his Dorsett Catalina, a sleek streamlined 17-foot fiberglass runabout.

"She is a beauty, no doubt about it," Bradshaw replied pridefully. "But then again there's nothing wrong with a Chris Craft," he added as an afterthought. "Mind if Angie and I come ashore and take a look?" he asked. Without waiting for an answer, Bradshaw maneuvered the boat in close to the bumpers on the dock. The huge cabin cruiser dwarfed the tiny boat ramp. Once the boat had come to rest against the tire bumpers, the girl jumped out and tied the craft off to the mooring post.

"Please, come over and take a look," Carl told him. "Perhaps you could offer some advice, eh?"

Bradshaw climbed over the gunwale of the Catalina and down onto the rickety dock. The girl followed Bradshaw as he strode over to the trailer where Carl and David stood waiting.

Bradshaw began to inspect the barebones framework of the Barracuda as if examining an unfinished work of art. "Very nice," Bradshaw said. "Plywood sides, I see," a note of disdain in his voice. "You might think about fiberglassing the hull. Space-aged stuff, you know. Strong and light weight. They say it's the future of boating."

"I'm not in your class yet, Jake," Carl replied. "I think plywood and marine paint will hold up just fine. Besides, I want David to learn the traditional methods, eh?"

"Well, I'm sure you know best. In any event it looks like a lot of work."

"Oh, it won't be that bad. I'm sure David and I will have it in the water by the end of summer."

"David? That must be this fine young man here," Bradshaw said.

"That's right, you two haven't met. Jake, I'd like you to meet my grandson, David Bishop. David, my neighbor, Dr. Jacob Bradshaw. Jake owns the big summer house out on Prospect Point."

"I'm glad to meet you, Dr. Bradshaw," David responded politely. David had seen the house on the point many times in the years his family had been coming to the lake. His father had once told him the house belonged to "a big shot doctor."

"How long will you be staying with us, David?" Bradshaw asked.

"Till my folks pick me up later this summer," David said.

"Well, then you should get to know Angie here. You must be about the same age. I'm sure you'll have a lot in common." Dr. Bradshaw turned to the girl standing next to him. She was extremely pretty with bright red hair tied in a bow at the back. She wore sequin-studded sunglasses, bright red lipstick, and a pink sun dress. "Did you hear that, dear," Dr. Bradshaw said, "David will be around all summer." The girl rolled her eyes and looked away.

For several minutes David and Angie stood by uncomfortably as the two elder men talked about boats, fishing, and the weather. Angie seemed particularly impatient, constantly fidgeting and pulling at her hair until at last her father decided it was time to leave. "Well, we'd better be going and let you boys get back to work, but if you need anything," he chirped, "you know where to find me. I'll look forward to seeing the results. Come along Angie," he told the girl, "time to go."

Angie brightened at the prospect of leaving. She ran ahead of her father, untying the Catalina from the dock before her father even arrived back at the boat. Once Dr. Bradshaw was back on board, it took only moments before the engines ignited and Jake Bradshaw and his daughter disappeared across the lake in the direction of Prospect Point.

After they had gone, Carl turned to his grandson. "Well David, what did you think of the Bradshaws, eh? Angie is a pretty girl, don't you think?"

"I guess so." David replied honestly. "But she sure didn't act very friendly."

"She's just shy, David. Angie hasn't been the same since her mother died a couple of years ago. But I'm sure if you got to know her you would find that she's a lovely person."

"Maybe, but she didn't act like she was interested in making friends."

"Give her a chance. You'll see. Now let's clean up here and get ready for dinner."

***

Little by little, as they continued to work on the Chris Craft, David began to learn the skills of a boatwright. "Now that we've got the transom in place, we can start bending the chines around the frames."

"Chines? What are those?" David asked.

Carl picked up a long strip of wood from the parts carton and handed it to David. "The chines support the side and bottom panels. Here, take this chine and hold it down while I bend it around the frame and screw it in place." Starting at the bow, David held each chine while Carl drilled and screwed it onto the frame. By the time all the chines had been mounted, David was beginning to feel like a real boat builder.

As the days went by the Barracuda began to take shape. After caulking the joints, the plywood side panels were put into place, securely fastened with brass screws starting at the bow. Next they added the bottom battens, narrow strips of wood used to add strength and make the framework more rigid. David held each batten in the frame slots as Carl fastened them down with screws. By the end of the week they had finished installing the side panels and battens, and were ready to screw down the bottom panels to form a watertight hull.

"Well what do you think, Maddie?" David asked proudly when Maddie arrived to bring them lunch. "Maybe you should have just built a canoe instead," Maddie said teasingly. "It would have been easier."

"Please don't joke about this," Carl replied. "David might just think you're serious."

"You know I am just kidding," Maddie explained. "You two have done a wonderful job. But now it is time to eat."

After lunch Maddie went back up to the cottage while Carl and David resumed work on the Chris Craft.

"Grandpa," David said, "the other day you told me that Maddie was like a second daughter to you. Did you really mean that?"

"Certainly, Maddie holds a very special place in my heart."

"Do you think that's why mother doesn't like Maddie?"

"Whatever do you mean? Your mother has always been very respectful of Maddie."

"She acts that way when you're around, but she doesn't really like her."

"My goodness, I certainly hope not. I never thought about it. You know how much I love your mother. No one could ever take her place."

"Does mom know what happened between Maddie and her husband?"

"Maddie told you about her marriage?" Carl asked, obviously surprised by David's knowledge. "What did she say?"

"Not much. Only that they are not together anymore."

"I'm surprised. She does not share her personal life with many people."

"She told me her husband drank. She said that was why they broke up."

"She told you about that too, eh? It was not just his drinking, David. Sometimes Peter did not treat Maddie the way he should have."

"You mean he hit her?"

"He hurt her, yes. When I learned what was happening," Carl continued, "I told Peter to leave and never return. It was then that Maddie started to work for me - first in the shop, and later as my manager. When she needed a place to stay, we fixed up a cabin for her."

"Do you think mom and dad'll end up like Maddie and her husband?"

"Do you mean will they get a divorce? What makes you think that?"

"That's why mom went back to LaSalle, isn't it? I knew something was wrong between mom and dad even before we left home. They just weren't getting along - they fought all the time. Sometimes I heard them shouting at each other after they thought I was asleep." David paused before continuing. "They just wanted me out of the way so I wouldn't see what's going on between them, didn't they?"

"Whatever happens between your mother and father, you must not think that it is about you," Carl answered. "I know both your parents love you very much. They just need some time to work things out."

"But what if things don't work out? What happens then? Who

will I live with?"

"I'm not sure what is going to happen, David. No one can know these things for certain. But I know that your parents will do what they think is best for you."

"I want to go home. I want to see my friends and have everything just the way it was before." David was almost in tears now.

"No one wants to keep your family together more than your parents. You must believe that. But as I told you earlier, things do not always happen the way we would like."

"Give them time. I'm sure they will be back to get you sooner than you think."

"I bet if mom knew the whole story about Maddie and her husband, she'd feel differently about her."

"Maybe she would. And maybe you are getting to be a very wise young man."

"You have done very well since your mother left. Don't you think it is time I gave you that raise I promised? How does seventy-five cents an hour sound, eh?"

"Thanks Grandpa. That would be great."

\*\*\*

As the week progressed, David found himself increasingly immersed in the Barracuda project. The work kept him occupied and he began to enjoy the routine. Although he still regretted having no one else his own age nearby, he no longer felt bored or anxious about his mother's decision to leave him alone with his grandfather.

Once the bottom had been screwed down, David helped Carl flip the hull of the Chris Craft over. In order to avoid having to again recruit extra workers to move the craft, Carl had rigged a series of ropes and pulleys from the rafters of the boathouse to lift and rotate the hull. David watched as Carl looped ropes through the block and tackle system to eyebolts he had attached to the Barracuda's empty shell. "When I tell you, lift and pull your side toward you," Carl said. The block and tackle rigging made it possible for Carl and David to easily raise the frame and flip the hull over, lowering it gently back onto the trailer right side up.

With the hull now in place, Carl seemed to relax. "Good, now it's time to install the seats."

Once the hull was flipped upright, they screwed the seats in place against the mahogany seat risers along the frame. They then attached the coaming clamp, a strip running along the inside of the top of the frames, so that they could fit the deck panels and begin to screw them down.

"Boy, I never would have believed it when we started, but this thing is actually beginning to look like a real boat."

"Just a few more pieces of trim and we'll be ready to go. We will be ready to start painting before you know it."

"I can start tomorrow if you have the paint..."

"Slow down, David," Carl said. "There will be plenty of time for painting, but first we need to finish up with the cover boards and fender rails. Listen, you've done a great job working on the Chris Craft, but maybe it's time for you to take a break. You said you wanted to fix up that old bicycle you found in the shed. Why don't you take off tomorrow and get started?"

"Really? Are you sure you won't mind if I don't work on the Barracuda?"

"Of course not. Besides the Gibsons will be arriving tomorrow...."

"Tomorrow? Really?" David exclaimed. At last there would be someone his own age at the lake.

# The Gibsons

A small drop of red paint ran slowly down across the Schwinn nameplate. David used his finger to wipe the paint away, then cleaned his finger off on his tee shirt. There, the painting was done. Now all he had to do was wait for the Rust-Oleum to dry and reassemble the bike's chassis. He would be riding by the beginning of the week.

"Boy, you're a real mess."

David jumped at the sound of the unfamiliar feminine voice. He turned to see Angie Bradshaw standing at the corner of the pavilion carrying a crumpled brown paper bag. She was dressed for a beach party, wearing a swimsuit covered by a robe, and sandals.

"Gee whiz, you scared me half to death," David said wiping his hands on his paint spattered pants. "What're you doing here anyway?"

"Sorry if I startled you," she replied. She pointed toward a small boat tied up at the dock. "Dad let me borrow his fishing skiff. He still won't let me take the Catalina out by myself. I cut the engine and coasted in. Guess you were too busy to notice."

She took a critical look at the Chris Craft, sitting on its trailer. "Shouldn't you be working on the boat instead of messing with that old bike?" she said. "At this rate you'll never get it done this summer."

"Grandpa and I have been working on it all week," David snapped back defensively. "He said I could take the day off to work on the bike. Don't worry, the Barracuda will be in the water long before I leave."

"Hey, kid, don't get all bent out of shape. I didn't mean anything by it."

"I'm not bent out of shape, and I'm not a kid either. I'm twelve."

"All right. All right. Take it easy. I only meant you're doing a pretty good job for someone your age." She looked at him skeptically. "Twelve, huh?" she said disdainfully. "What grade you in? Sixth? Seventh?"

"I'll be in seventh grade, if you really want to know."

Angie could not suppress a look of superiority. "I'll be sixteen in a few days. I'm a sophomore this year, but most of my friends are juniors and seniors. My boyfriend's seventeen. I really don't have many younger friends," she added. "There's probably nobody around here your age, eh?"

"It's not so bad. I keep busy."

"Too bad my cousin Amy's vacationing in Minnesota with her family. I could have introduced you. She's ten."

David was getting tired of Angie's smug, condescending attitude. "Look, if there's nothing else, I've got work to do, ok?"

"Actually, there is something else. I'm here on a mission. My dad wanted me to drop this off for your grandfather. Is he around?"

"He's at work in town. Won't be back till after four. I can give it to him if you want."

Angie handed the plain brown paper bag to David. The bag was heavy. Heavier than David expected. "What's in it?" he asked.

"My dad said it's a present for your grandfather. He said it would look good on that boat you're working on.'"

David opened the bag and pulled out an oddly shaped object wrapped in newspaper. He unwrapped the paper to expose a chrome sailing ship figurine."

"It's the hood ornament off my dad's old Plymouth," Angie explained. "He found it when he was cleaning out our garage. He says your grandfather should mount it on the front of your boat, like a figurehead. It's supposed ta bring him good luck, or something."

"Thanks. I'll give it to Grandpa when he gets home tonight."

***

The sound of a car crunching down the gravel driveway made Angie stop talking and look back toward the cabins. A sleek, newer model, gold and white Cadillac sedan eased slowly down the drive, carefully avoiding potholes.

"Wow, who owns the Caddy," Angie asked. "Looks like they're loaded."

"Probably Grandpa's friends the Gibsons from Wisconsin," David replied. "They're supposed to arrive sometime today."

"They sure have a cool car," she said.

The Cadillac continued down past the boathouse as both Angie and David strained to get a peek inside the huge car. Before they could get a good look, the car turned away, moving slowly along the rutted drive before pulling into the parking space in front of Cabin #5. When the driver's door opened, a large Negro man wearing

Bermuda shorts and a flowered Hawaiian shirt got out and walked around to the passenger side.

"Must be their chauffeur," Angie said, obviously impressed. "You're Grandpa's friends must have money, eh?"

"I don't know. I never met them, but Grandpa says they have a couple of kids about our age."

The man held the passenger door open as a petite, neatly dressed woman wearing sunglasses, a flowered sleeveless blouse and capri pants got out. A moment later the rear driver's side door opened, and a tall muscular boy wearing jeans, tee shirt, and Milwaukee Braves baseball cap emerged. On the opposite side, a pretty, slender girl in a polka dot sun dress got out of the car. Like the car's driver, all the passengers were black.

"Wow, they're Negroes," Angie exclaimed. "That guy isn't their chauffeur - he must be your grandfather's friend. Did your grandfather tell you that his friend was a Negro?" she asked. "I bet he didn't, did he. I can tell by the look on your face."

"No, he just said the man was some guy he used to work with in Milwaukee."

"God, this is so cool. There aren't any colored people here on the lake. My friend Doris went to school in Flint before her folks moved up here last year. She said almost half the kids in her school were Negroes. She said she even kissed a colored boy once. Can you believe it?"

David shrugged his shoulders noncommittally.

"Look," Angie said. "There's a boy and a girl. He's kinda cute for a Negro. I wonder how old he is."

The boy looked about Angie's age or maybe a little younger, David thought. His hair was close cut and his facial features were broad and severe.

"The girl looks about your age," she continued. Dressed in a one-piece red striped suit, the girl had dark ebony skin and wore her carefully braided hair in pigtails that hung down her back. She had a pretty face with laughing eyes and dimpled cheeks.

The driver moved to the rear of the car, using the key to open the trunk. He began pulling large Samsonite bags out and set them beside the car. The boy picked up two of the larger bags, and headed into the cabin. The girl took a smaller bag and followed her brother.

"Why don't we go over and say hi?" Angie offered. She began to walk away, then stopped when she realized David wasn't following her. "You commin' or not?" she said.

"I don't think that's such a good idea," David replied.

"Why not? You have to introduce yourself sooner or later."

"Maybe later. Look, you go if you want, but I've got work to do."

"Work? You haven't been working very hard so far. Come on. What are you afraid of? They won't bite. I'll bet they're nice."

"I don't know," he hesitated "They might not want to be bothered."

"Chicken! Suit yourself. You can stay here if you want, but I'm going over to say hello. Maybe they'll want to go for a swim after their long ride." Without waiting for a response, Angie walked off toward the Gibson cabin.

***

David watched from the cover of the boat house as Angie went over and introduced herself to the Gibsons. Her freckled, redheaded complexion stood in stark contrast to the dark skinned newcomers. The man reached out and shook her hand warmly as if they were old friends. The woman called for her two children to come back out of the cabin and meet their guest. The boy grinned broadly as he trotted down the steps to greet the attractive girl, while his sister seemed shy, merely waving hello from the cabin porch. Angie smiled in David's direction as if to say, 'I told you so.' David looked away, feigning disinterest.

He returned to work painting the bicycle, pretending to ignore the activity at the Gibson's cabin. But despite his best attempt to disregard the new arrivals, the laughter and brief snatches of conversation filtering down to him continued to be a distraction. After exchanging pleasantries, the two older Gibsons disappeared into the cabin, leaving their children alone to get better acquainted. Once their parents had gone, Angie led the younger Gibsons down toward the dock, disappearing behind a wall of shrubs and white birch trees along the shore.

David felt cheated. Somehow he had been counting on the new arrivals to save him from the boredom and monotony of life at the lake. Now he felt left out. Why hadn't he just gone over and introduced himself as Angie had suggested? Did the boy like baseball, he wondered. Could they swim? Maybe the boy knew something about bicycles.

He continued to hear voices coming from the direction of the dock, but trees blocked his line of sight. If he was going to find out what was happening, he would have to move closer. He noticed a small stand of pine trees on the embankment directly above the Gibson cabin. From that vantage point he would be able to see everything that went on below. He took the binoculars off the hook by the boathouse door, and headed quickly up the slope behind the cabins, being careful not to reveal his position.

He made his way to the stand of pines, and found a good hiding place, concealed in the high grass. He took a seat on a large, flat rock and focused his binoculars on the group of young people sitting on the dock near Angie's runabout. The boy and two girls seemed to be enjoying themselves, totally unaware of David's presence. Even with the binoculars, however, he could not quite make out what they were saying. He just watched in silence, wishing secretly that he were part of the group.

At one point the boy looked up the hill in David's direction, and David felt sure he had been spotted. He wanted to run, but knew if he moved, he'd give away his hiding place for sure. Instead he held as still as he could, waiting for the boy to look away.

After several minutes, the boy got up from his beach chair and headed toward the cabin. "I'm going to get a drink," he called out loud enough for David to hear. "Anybody want anything?"

"Get me a Coke, TJ," answered the girl. "And get Angie one too."

TJ - that must be the boy's name, David guessed. He watched as the boy disappeared into the cabin.

As the two girls remained sitting on a bench talking, David grew uneasy. After waiting for more than five minutes for the boy to return, he began to feel foolish. What a waste of time, he thought to himself. Why was he sitting in the bushes spying on people he didn't know anyway? Tired of waiting, he got up and turned to leave.

"What you lookin' at?" a deep voice boomed nearby. David stumbled forward, losing his footing. He looked up to find the Gibson boy standing directly over him. The boy's face was etched with anger.

"Nothing, that is I... I was only..." David fumbled for words, suddenly fearful.

"You were only what? Huh, you little shit? What are you doin' up here spying on us? How long have you been watchin' us anyway?"

The boy's easy profanity frightened David. "I wasn't spying - really," he lied. "I was just looking for Angie. Angie Bradshaw. I thought she might have come up this way."

"And what the hell would she come up here for? Don't lie to me, you jackass. Who are you and what are you doin' here? The truth this time."

"My name is David... David Bishop. My Grandpa owns these cabins. I was fixing up an old bike down by the boathouse, and I just wanted to know who was moving in, so I came up here to take a look."

"Well, I hope you got an eyeful, 'cause you've seen all you're going to. Now get out and don't let me catch you around here again, do you understand me?"

"Yes, sir," David replied shaking.

"And if you come anywhere near my sister, I'll personally tear you limb from limb. Understand? Now get the fuck out of my sight before I decide to kick the crap out of you."

David ran stumbling through the bushes, making his way through the branches and brambles toward his grandfather's cottage. He didn't dare look back.

***

At dinner David sat quietly at the table, hardly touching his food. The incident with the Gibson boy had unnerved him. He had no desire to explain the confrontation to his grandfather or Maddie. But by the time dinner was over, when Carl and David returned to the boathouse to work on the Barracuda, the subject could no longer be avoided.

"So," Carl said, "I see the Gibson's arrived today, ya?"

"Yeah, they drove in this afternoon," David replied noncommittally.

"I had a chance to talk to Nathan when I arrived," Carl said. "It was good to see him again. He told me that you already met his son."

"He did?" David replied nervously. "What did he say?"

"Only that his son ran into you on the path in back of their cabin. Did you get a chance to meet his daughter as well?"

"His daughter? Nope," David replied, remembering the boy's warnings. "I didn't see her. I don't think she was around."

"What's wrong, David. Why the long face, eh?"

"I don't think Mr. Gibson's son likes me very much," David volunteered.

"What makes you say that?"

"Well, he just didn't seem very friendly, that's all."

"Perhaps he feels uncomfortable coming here. After all, the Gibson's come from Milwaukee. That's a big city. Life here at the lake is much different. Why don't you take the lead, David?"

"What do you mean?"

"Well, you could invite him to go fishing, or perhaps show him around the lake?"

"Yeah, I suppose..." David looked down, unwilling to meet his grandfather's inquiring eyes.

"There is something you're not telling me, eh?" Carl probed.

"No, it's nothing, Grandpa," David replied. "It's just that... Well... Why didn't you tell me that the Gibsons were Negroes?"

Carl hesitated, surprised by the question. "It never occurred to me that it was important. I have known Nate Gibson for so long, I just never think of him as colored." He studied David's expression, trying to get a sense of his feelings. "Is this going to be a problem for you, David? I do not want anyone to feel uncomfortable."

"Well..." David hesitated. "I just never... I mean, there aren't any Negroes in LaSalle, and I just feel kinda funny being around them."

"When I first met Nathan I felt much like you do now. I was distrustful and even somewhat frightened. Who was this strange man? What did he want? But as time went by, I learned what a good man he was. We worked together in Milwaukee for years. After a while, Nate Gibson became not just a friend, but part of our family. He and his wife were good friends to your grandmother and me when we lived there. Now they have brought their family here to visit. I want you to think about what I am saying, David. I am sure you will find a way to make them feel welcome, eh?"

"I'll try," David replied uncertainly. "I mean I'll do my best."

"That's a good boy. Perhaps now that you know the Gibson children and Angie Bradshaw you will not feel so isolated living out here, eh?"

The mention of Angie's name suddenly reminded David of her morning visit. "Gosh, I almost forgot," He said, rushing to retrieve the package he had left by the boathouse door. "Angie asked me to give this to you. It's from Mr. Bradshaw. Some kind of hood ornament or something."

Carl took the object out of the bag and unwrapped the newspaper to reveal the chrome sailboat inside. "It's for luck," David explained.

"That was very thoughtful of Jacob." He took the ornament and placed it on a shelf by the workbench.

"You look tired, David. Perhaps we should quit for the evening. Help me roll the Barracuda back into the boathouse. Tomorrow I'll add the sheer clamps and deck beams. We will be ready to start decking by the beginning of next week."

## **The Storm**

The Barracuda sat on the trailer just outside the boathouse, its decking uncovered, its cockpit exposed. Before leaving for work, Carl had asked David to continue sanding the hull in preparation for the installation of the fender rails, and for over an hour David had done just that. But his heart just wasn't in the work. His experience with the Gibson boy the preceding day still troubled him. He had promised his grandfather that he would make the Gibsons feel welcome, but that hardly seemed possible after his initial encounter with their son.

Work on the boat could wait - at least for a little while. He walked over to the old bicycle he'd found while cleaning out the shed. The red Rust-Oleum he had applied to the frame of Maddie's old bike was dry now. It was time to reassemble the pieces. He began by reattaching the handlebar stem, and tightening the seat post.

All that remained was to inflate the tires, mount the wheels, and replace the chain on the sprockets. As he re-inflated the tire using his grandfather's hand pump, he stopped frequently checking for leaks. The patch of old inner tube he had glued into place to fix a small puncture in the rear tire seemed to be holding.

As he worked on reattaching the bicycle wheel to the frame, David heard the sound of an approaching boat motor, and looked up to see Angie Bradshaw guiding her father's runabout toward the dock. Angie tied off the runabout and came ashore. She wore a brightly flowered sun dress similar to the one she had worn the day before over her swim suit. If she noticed David at all, she gave no indication. Instead she walked directly over to the Gibson's cabin and knocked at the door. Denise answered, inviting Angie inside.

It was only a short time later that David heard the door open again, and saw Angie reemerge from the cabin, this time accompanied by both of the Gibson children. Like Angie, they were dressed in swim suits and carrying beach towels. David stepped back into the shadows so that he couldn't be seen. The three of them headed down to the beach, throwing their towels over the wooden beach chairs before wading out into the water.

"Race you to the raft," he heard Angie challenge.

David watched as she dove in head first and raced out into the lake. The Gibson girl jumped in next, struggling to keep up with Angie. Having given the girls a good head start, the boy dove in, knifing cleanly into the brisk, cold water. His rapid, powerful strokes propelled him swiftly through the gentle swells, allowing him to quickly catch, and then pass, both his sister and Angie. "Come on, slow pokes," he called back as he pulled himself up onto the raft.

With a feeling of relief, David emerged from the shadows. For the moment he was safe. Now he needed to finish assembling the bike, and leave before the three friends finished their swim and returned to shore. He replaced the front wheel in the bike frame and tightened the nuts on each side holding it firmly in place.

He hooked the chain around the rear sprocket and stretched it to loop around the front chain wheel. He loosened the nuts on the rear wheel axle and moved the wheel back until the chain was taut, then tightened the axle nuts. When he was done, he examined the reassembled bicycle. "Not bad," he said out loud. Too bad it was a girl's bike, but it would have to do. The paint job was a little streaked and a bit bright, but from a distance it looked passable. Certainly an improvement over the rusty frame he had found buried under a pile of car parts. Now for the final test.

There was a brief commotion out on the lake. "Race you back to shore," the Gibson girl called out. She dove in, swimming enthusiastically toward shore, followed quickly by TJ and Angie. David knew it was time to leave. He jumped on the bicycle and peddled quickly up the road, away from the boathouse. By the time TJ, his sister, and Angie reached the dock, David was long gone.

***

"Looks like a storm's moving in," Carl observed looking out the kitchen window as he finished his dinner. "Are you sure you put everything away and closed up the boathouse when you finished working, David?"

The boat! David had completely forgotten the Barracuda when he rode away from the boathouse on his bicycle earlier in the day. He had left everything out, the Chris Craft completely exposed. His grandfather would kill him if he found out. David would have to go down and get the boat under cover without alarming him.

"I'm not sure I locked the boathouse door, Grandpa," he said trying hard not to sound too anxious. "Maybe I better go down and check, ok?"

"All right, go ahead," Carl responded. "But you better hurry. That storm is blowing in fast."

Outside, the western skies looked ominous. Darkness was closing in over the entire lake. Black turbulent clouds billowed across the sky, blotting out what little remained of the setting sun. From his vantage point on the hill, David could barely make out two tiny powerboats scurrying to make their way back to shore ahead of the storm. As the winds began to pick up, the lake waters became rough and choppy. Small white caps danced across the surface, chasing the small fishing boats into shore.

As soon as he was out of sight of the cottage, David broke into a run. He needed as much time as possible to roll the Barracuda back into the boathouse before the storm hit. Lady led the way, barking as she ran down the hill. In the dark David stumbled over a tree root, almost losing his footing, but managed to regain his balance without falling.

As he got closer, he began to hear a banging sound in the distance. David knew immediately what was making the noise. One of the carriage doors had broken free and was being buffeted by the wind, slamming back and forth between the side of the boathouse and the boat trailer.

By the time he reached the boathouse, a light rain had begun to fall. Quickly David grabbed the flapping carriage door and secured it open with a large rock. He then used the trailer dolly to roll the Chris Craft back into the boathouse, closed the carriage doors, and ran back outside to gather up his tools. It was then that he noticed that one of the rowboats tethered to the dock had broken loose, and the boat was smashing violently into the tire bumpers.

David raced toward the floundering vessel, reaching the dock just as a bolt of lightening flashed in the distance. The dazzling display nearly took David's breath away. Wasting no time, he grabbed the loose tether line and pulled the rope hand over hand until he was able to grab onto the rail and pull the boat in toward the dock. He hooked the tether over the mooring post, pulled it taunt, and then lashed it securely in place.

With time running out, he dashed back to the boathouse, grabbing his tools in one hand and the paint cans in the other. He just managed to duck inside the doorway when the gentle rain was replaced by a torrential downpour accompanied by pea sized hail. Sheets of water cascaded across the lake.

David crossed over to the closest window and watched as the storm gathered momentum outside. He looked back and saw that Lady had not followed him into the boathouse, but continued to stand defiantly on the boat dock, barking at the ominous night sky. Lightning flashes darted across the surface of the lake. Great roaring blasts of thunder now followed only moments after the strikes.

"Lady, Lady, get in here," David yelled. The dog turned and ran full speed toward the boathouse. David opened the door and let her in, just as she began to shake, drenching David with water.

He watched as lightning flashes darted across the western end of the lake, creating momentary shadow-scapes frozen in the brilliant strobing glare. Gale force winds churned the water into frothy foam. Flash after flash of lightning blistered the chaotic surface of the lake. Any chance he might have had to return to the cottage had been lost. He would just have to wait out the storm's fury.

David timed the interval between each flash and the accompanying crash of thunder. His father had taught him how to calculate the distance by dividing the time between the lightening flash and the thunderclap by five. "One thousand one, one thousand two, one thousand three...," he counted. By the time he reached twenty he heard the thunderous roar. About four miles.

Another flash. He counted again. This one was closer. Only three miles. Already the far end of the lake was being dotted with the first rain squalls of the storm as the leading edge made its way toward him.

The staccato rhythm of the hail on the roof increased, threatening to tear the shingles off the rafters. Chunks of ice the size of marbles smashed down on the area along the shore, breaking off small branches and pounding the cabins and boats along the beach. Then, as suddenly as the hail had started, it stopped.

With an earth-shaking roar, lightning suddenly struck the upper branches of a nearby oak, rattling the windows of the boathouse. The ground trembled with the violence of the strike. David screamed involuntarily, cupping his hands over his ears to deaden the roar. More flashes came, moving closer across the lake. Each flash briefly illuminated the thrashing waters, burning images of silhouetted trees and lashing waves into David's memory.

Suddenly he recognized the storm. It was the same storm he had dreamed about so many times. It was his nightmare storm. The one in which he had been caught out on the lake. The one in which the waves had shattered his boat, and he had been thrown into the water. And then the monster - the monster that had dragged him to the bottom.

***

As David watched, a blinding flash forked across the night sky. For just an instant, David thought he saw something silhouetted against the backdrop of raging waves. He wiped the moisture from his eyes, clearing his blurred vision. Something was out there. A small boat, no bigger than a dot on the horizon, its occupant struggling bravely to get the craft to shore. The image faded as the flash of light dissolved into the darkness.

Momentarily he thought that he was seeing himself out on the lake fighting against the menacing waves, just as he had so many times in his dreams. But he knew that that was impossible. He concentrated on the area where the boat had appeared. He strained his eyes to see into the darkness, but saw nothing but blackness. The image was gone.

David reached down for a clean rag to wipe off a spot on the window. He knew that his only chance of catching another glimpse of the object was to wait for the next lightning flash. He strained his eyes looking toward where he had seen the image, but only darkness met his gaze. He muttered under his breath, "come on, come on," urging the heavens to throw down another bolt of illumination. Finally another flash.

As the lightning blazed across the lake, David stared in disbelief. The image was closer now and more distinct, silhouetted against the glowing sky. The object was definitely a small craft of some type, the hull curved up at both ends, like a canoe. The canoe's lone occupant stood defiantly in the bow, waving his arms at the heavens and shouting. David knew immediately what he was seeing. The figure could be no one but Little Thunder, returning to his tribal council. David was witnessing an event that had happened almost one hundred years before.

He darted to the door and threw it open so he could get a better look, but the light had already begun to fade. The figure standing in the canoe vanished into the night. David thought he heard a call, or maybe it was a chant, above the thunderous roar of the storm. Then it too was gone.

Already the winds had begun to die down. As the storm subsided, the waters of the lake calmed. Though the rain still beat steadily on the boathouse roof, the raging gale that had threatened to tear the structure apart had been reduced to a gentle breeze. David ran out into the pouring rain and stood on the beach, oblivious to the torrent soaking his clothes and streaming down his face. He gazed intently out over the lake into the darkness. Finally there was another burst of light, but now the lake was empty except for the pounding waves rolling onto the shore. Both Little Thunder and his canoe had completely disappeared. There was no sign of anyone or anything out on the turbulent surface of the lake. Again the night flooded back filling the scene with darkness.

Puddles now dotted the gravel drive and a steady stream of murky water carried mud and debris down the path from the hill toward the lake. David wiped the rain from his eyes and looked down at his drenched clothing. He knew his grandfather would be angry with him for standing out in the rain, but his excitement about the storm and what he had just witnessed overcame any anxiety regarding his grandfather's reaction. Little Thunder was no longer just a legend - he was a reality.

*** 

David dashed up the trail by the road, jumping puddles where he could, and splashing right through the ones he could not jump. He couldn't wait to tell Maddie what he had seen.

Both his grandfather and Maddie were waiting on the porch as David arrived tearing up the path from the lake. "David, are you all right?" Maddie said with concern. "We were worried sick when you didn't come back before the storm. Where were you all this time?"

"Just look at you," Carl scolded. "You are soaked to the bone. Don't come in the kitchen, you'll get the floor wet. Wait here and I'll get you some dry clothes and a towel." Carl left Maddie and David to find some dry things in David's room.

"Here, this will warm you up," Maddie said handing him a cup of steaming hot chocolate. "Goodness, what happened to you anyway?"

"Maddie. I saw him. I actually saw him," he exclaimed taking a big sip of chocolate. Excitement radiated from his eyes, but Maddie just stood bewildered.

"You saw someone out in the storm?" she asked confused. "Who would go out on a night like this?"

"It was Little Thunder, Maddie. I saw him out there on the lake. It was him, Maddie. I just know it!"

Suddenly Maddie's eyes opened in recognition. "You saw Little Thunder? Are you sure it was him?" She seemed almost as happy and excited as David felt.

"Yeah, he was in his canoe and he was chanting to the gods or something. I could actually hear him shouting."

"You heard him talking to you? What did he say? Perhaps the Spirit was trying to tell you something."

"I don't know what he was saying. The storm was too loud, and I couldn't make it out. I tried to move closer. That's how I got soaked. But before I could make out what was happening, everything went black, and then he was gone. I stood out there for a long time in the rain by the shore trying to catch just one more glimpse…"

Before David could tell Maddie any more, Carl reentered the room carrying a towel in his hand. "You had us worried to death," he said tossing the towel toward his grandson. "Here, now, dry yourself off and come in by the fire to get warm."

As David used the towel to dry his face and arms, he considered whether he should mention his vision of Little Thunder to his grandfather. He realized that Carl would not be as receptive to his story of an Indian ghost haunting the lake as Maddie had been. He tried to think of something to tell Carl that he would believe.

David looked over at Maddie, but she gave no indication that he should let Carl in on their secret. Perhaps it would be best not to say anything at all, he decided.

"Well, then get ready for bed now," Carl said. "You've had quite an adventure for one day. I'll drive Maddie down to her cabin, then I'll come back to check on you."

As he removed his wet clothes and changed in to the dry, warm pajamas his grandfather had provided for him, David couldn't get the image of Little Thunder paddling alone across the lake out of his mind. The silhouette of the man in his canoe had been seared into his consciousness. Did Maddie believe him? She must have. But he could never mention the real story to Carl. His grandfather would think he had dreamed the whole thing - or worse, that he was crazy.

    David finished brushing his teeth and got ready for bed. As he pulled the covers up around him, he looked up at the dream catcher swinging over his bed. He wondered what new dreams he would have. After what he had just witnessed, he thought, no dream could possibly measure up.

## **The Aftermath**

"No dreams. I didn't dream at all last night, Maddie." David sat finishing his orange juice at the kitchen table, gazing absently out the window toward the lake. "I thought Little Thunder would come but he didn't. I don't remember any dreams at all," David said disappointed.

Maddie placed two huge oatmeal and raisin muffins, still warm from the oven, on his plate. "Perhaps you were expecting too much. The spirit world does not always work the way we would like."

"But after what I saw last night...," he said. If he closed his eyes, David could still see a solitary figure silhouetted against the angry sky. Little Thunder's spirit driving his canoe through the crashing waves, lightning flashing all around him. The image was etched like a photograph in his mind.

He took an ample dab of butter on his knife and spread it on one of the muffins, watching the butter melt slowly. "I thought for sure the spirit was trying to talk to me. It was Little Thunder. I'm positive, Maddie."

"If the spirits wish you to know their secrets, they will find a way to tell you," Maddie advised.

"David, are you ready?" Carl interrupted. He called his grandson from just outside the screen door to the kitchen. "We should get going. I want to see what damage the storm caused to the cabins. I will need your help clearing up the debris."

David quickly took a last bite of muffin and gulped down the last of his orange juice before dashing out the door to meet his grandfather. "Make sure you two are not late for lunch," Maddie called after him just as the screen door slammed.

When he emerged from the cottage, David was surprised that there was not more evidence of the storm's effect. He expected trees to be uprooted and wreckage to be scattered everywhere. Instead, except for a few small broken branches littering the gravel road in front of the cottage, there was little evidence of the previous night's gale. The dawn had broken clear and bright with almost no trace of the storm's fury.

As they started down the trail toward the beach, Carl looked at David inquiringly. "Do you want to tell me what was going on between you and Maddie in the kitchen when I called you just now?" he said.

"What do you mean, Grandpa?"

"I overheard what you were saying to her. You said you saw Little Thunder out on the lake during the storm. You didn't say anything about seeing someone on the lake last night when I talked to you."

David remained silent, shrugging his shoulders slightly. "I didn't think you'd be interested," he said. "You told me yourself that you didn't believe in Little Thunder's ghost. It's not important anyway."

"It was important enough to tell Maddie, wasn't it?" Carl persisted. "If something is bothering you I would like to know what it is."

"Well, I thought I saw a canoe out there, for a little while, but when I looked again, it was gone," he said, uncertainty beginning to creep into his voice. Already the experience seemed more like a dream than reality. "Now I'm not so sure," he added.

"I am sure there is a logical explanation for what you saw," Carl said. "There is no such thing as a ghost. Come along and I'll prove it to you." Carl motioned for David to follow him. He led David down the road to the boathouse.

Carl directed David to stand beside him on the steps of the boathouse. "Is this where you were standing last night?" he asked.

"Yeah, I came out here at the end. But I stayed inside watching the storm through the window most of the time."

"All right, look out there at the lake right now and tell me what you see."

"I don't see anything out there - just the raft."

"And that's what you saw last night. The raft. That's all and nothing more. But your head was filled with all of Maddie's Indian nonsense, and so you turned a raft being tossed around in the storm into a spirit paddling a canoe to shore. You see? Nothing but a raft in the wind," Carl looked for acceptance from his grandson.

"I guess so," David agreed half-heartedly.

"So, enough of this foolishness," Carl rubbed the top of David's head in a playful manner, messing up his hair. "No more talk of ghosts, ya?" Carl said flatly, ending the discussion. "Shall we see if we can clean up the mess the storm left around here?"

***

As they approached the beach, David could see the extent of the damage along the shoreline. The storm had hit the lakeshore harder than it had the area near the cottage. Several large branches had broken off the old oak and were scattered across the beach. Leaves and twigs were everywhere.

David noted with some satisfaction that, except for taking on a couple of inches of water, the rowboat he had tethered to the dock had weathered the storm without a problem.

Carl led David to the boathouse, checking for storm damage. With the exception of a small area of the roof where several shingles had blown loose, the building and its contents were intact. "I will have to climb up on the roof and fix the shingles this weekend," Carl said. "There won't be a problem as long as it does not rain again before then."

David continued to follow Carl around the property examining the destruction the storm had left behind. One of the lawn chairs had smashed into a fence post, breaking one of its legs. Two empty trash cans had been blown halfway across the compound near Cabin #2.

By far the worst damage was found behind Cabin #4 where a small maple had been uprooted by the storm and fallen onto the rear of the cabin, breaking out a window and damaging the eaves and a flower box beneath the window. Fortunately the cabin stood empty. The father and son fishermen staying in the cabin had returned to their home in Dearborn the previous Sunday.

The fallen tree looked much larger as they got closer. Though many smaller branches had snapped from the trunk and lay strewn on the ground, other, larger limbs clung tenaciously to the trunk, making clearing away the brush a difficult task.

"Hey, Carl, it looks as if you could use some help with that." David looked up to see Nathan Gibson standing on the porch of his cabin.

"Good morning, Nathan," Carl greeted. "Thanks for the offer. We sure could use a hand here."

Gibson made his way around the mangle of branches followed closely by his son, TJ, and his daughter. TJ kept a steady eye on David as they approached. "Boy, oh boy," Nathan exclaimed, "that wind was something, huh? Lucky the power didn't go out."

"That's for sure," Carl agreed. "We have not had a storm like that out here for many years. Nathan, I don't believe you've met my grandson David."

David accepted the man's handshake meekly, profoundly aware of TJ's focus on him.

Nathan turned to his son. "TJ, you've already met Carl's grandson, David, haven't you?"

"Yeah, we met," TJ stated matter-of-factly. "How you doin'?" TJ nodded toward the younger boy, making no attempt to shake his hand.

"Ok, I guess," David nodded back.

"And this is my daughter, Denise," Nathan continued.

"Nice to meet you, Denise," Carl responded. "Have you met my grandson, David?"

The girl smiled demurely and stepped in back of her father. David waved a casual greeting but made no move toward the girl, his eyes focused instead on her older brother.

"Good. Now that everybody's acquainted, let's get to work," directed Nathan enthusiastically. "Carl, where do you want us to start?"

Carl quickly assessed the work at hand. "Perhaps David and TJ can begin cleaning up these branches," Carl said. "In the meanwhile you and your daughter can help me clear up the debris along the beach."

"TJ, get over there and help David with those branches," Nathan directed.

Without protest, TJ walked over and began to pry branches away from the broken window. Hesitantly, David joined him, pulling boughs away from the tree trunk and piling them well away from the cabin. After stacking up several good sized limbs, the boys encountered a branch with the girth of a small tree trunk.

"Ok, on three," TJ ordered. "One, two, three lift..." In unison the two boys lifted the load and unsteadily walked the branch away from the cabin. When they reached the growing brush pile, they released the branch, letting it crash to the ground.

TJ took the opportunity to address David out of the hearing of Carl and his father. "Here's the deal," he whispered, "my father and your Grandpa are friends. I'm not gonna do anything to mess that up, see? So far as they're concerned, we're best buddies. But just between you and me, stay out of my way, ok? Just keep your distance and we'll get along fine. You got that?"

Without comment, David nodded his consent.

"It looks like we will need the chain saw to finish cleaning this up," called Carl. "It's sitting in the shed by the cottage. It'll only take me a few minutes to go get it."

"Hold on a second, Carl," called Nathan. "No need for you to haul something that heavy down here on your own. TJ, you go with Carl and help him with the tools. Denise, come over here and help David with that brush pile while your brother's gone."

TJ dropped the branch he had been carrying with David, letting it fall at their feet. He shot David a threatening glance as he turned to follow Carl up the hill toward the cottage. There was no mistaking the message: "Don't go anywhere near my sister while I'm gone."

***

David heeded TJ's warning, moving to the far end of the brush pile, well away from the approaching girl. She flashed a mischievous smile as she circumvented the pile to come along side him. "Boy, that look TJ gave you could have fried an egg," she said as she walked up to him. "What's goin' on between you two anyway?"

"Nothing. It's not important," David replied, picking up the end of the branch her brother had dropped and pulling it aside. "Let's just keep piling this brush, ok? I don't think your brother wants you talking to me."

"Yeah, he told me. He said you were bad news and I should stay away. But he's not here now. So what gives anyway?"

"We kinda had a misunderstanding, that's all."

"That must have been some misunderstanding. What happened?"

"He kinda thinks I was spying on you guys the day you arrived."

Denise stopped working to observe David's expression. "And were you - spying I mean?"

"I didn't mean to - not really," he replied. "I just wanted to see what was going on. I wasn't trying to spy."

"Look, my brother's a little protective. We live in a kinda rough neighborhood in Milwaukee, so he likes to take care of his little sister. But he doesn't mean anything by it."

"Yeah, well he seemed pretty clear to me. He doesn't want me around you or anyone else in your family."

"TJ can be a real jerk sometimes. He thinks he's a tough guy, but he's really nice once you get to know him. Besides he's just po'ed because dad made him come up here and he's missing the Braves home games."

"I figured he must like baseball - he's always wearing that Milwaukee team cap," David said.

"Yeah, he's a big Braves fan, just like my dad. They go out to County Stadium nearly every week the Braves play at home."

"I don't pay much attention to the Braves," David said. "I'm a Tiger's fan. They're in the American League."

"My dad says if Hank Aaron keeps hitting like he is now, the Braves will win the pennant for sure this year."

"Maybe the Tigers and Braves will play in the World Series," David added. "What about you? Are you a baseball fan too?"

"I go with them once and a while, but I'm more interested in tennis. I want to play like Althea Gibson someday. My dad thinks we might be related since she's a Gibson and all. Anyway, I think she's the greatest."

David looked up to see Carl and TJ returning from the cottage. TJ carried the chain saw, while Carl brought along a hatchet, an ax, and a bow saw. As David watched them approach, he once again moved away from Denise. "Look, I don't want any trouble, so maybe we shouldn't be doing this right now."

"Doing what? Talking?" Denise protested. "TJ's not going to do anything."

"Not to you maybe, but I think I'd better just stay away, ok?"

Moments later TJ and Carl arrived back at the worksite. "Hey, sis, what's goin' on?" he said with an accusatory glance toward David.

"Nothing," Denise replied. "We were just talking, that's all." TJ glared in David's direction, but said nothing.

Carl primed the saw, set the choke, and gave the rope a hefty pull. The saw seemed as temperamental as the Johnson outboard on Carl's fishing boat. After two more pulls, it roared to life and Carl began to carve branches into manageable chunks. As he cut the brushwood into pieces, Nathan, David, TJ, and Denise hauled and stacked the cut sections in a firewood pile.

It took more than three hours for the five workers to finish cutting, collecting, and stacking all of the broken branches from the storm damage. They retrieved the wind-blown trash can lids, and used a temporary two-by-four brace to repair the broken lawn chair.

"That was good work," Carl smiled. "I will go into town tomorrow and pick up what we need to finish the repairs. Until then, why don't we all get some rest."

\*\*\*

David sat relaxing on the screened-in back porch of the cottage, resting in his grandfather's Bentwood rocker, exhausted both mentally and physically from the day's exertion. He clicked off the radio, frustrated by the announcer's recap of yet another loss for the Detroit Tigers, this time at the hands of the Chicago White Sox.

A loud boom crashed through the night, echoing along the shore of the lake. For a moment, David thought another thunderstorm might be on its way. Then he realized that the blast announced the approach of a different kind of disturbance.

"They are a bit early to be celebrating," Carl observed. "The Fourth is still two days away. What should we do to celebrate?"

"Oh, yeah, I almost forgot about the Fourth," David replied unenthusiastically.

"Is there a problem? I thought you would be more excited. It is the nation's birthday."

"I don't feel much like celebrating this year. The Fourth won't be the same without dad and mom and my friends."

"Ah, you are missing your family, eh? Well, I can not bring your family and friends up here, but perhaps we can find a way to celebrate anyway. There will be fireworks over at the park, and then there is the parade, ya?"

"I wouldn't mind going to the fireworks, but the parade sounds kinda boring. Just some old bands and floats and stuff."

"I'm sorry you feel that way. And I am sure Maddie will be disappointed as well. I know she would like you to see her perform."

"Maddie? She's going to be in the parade?"

"Ya, ya. She will be dancing along with other members of her tribe."

"I didn't know Maddie could dance."

"Oh yes every year. It has become a tradition. Didn't she tell you? And there may be other people you know in the parade as well."

"Really? Who's going to be there?"

"You will have to go in order to find out. So, what do you think?

Have you changed your mind?"

"Well, if Maddie's gonna be there, I suppose we could go. I've always wanted to see a real Indian dance."

"That's more like it. We will make it a special Fourth of July."

"That'd be great," David stretched, trying to suppress a yawn.

"You look tired. Why don't you go and get ready for bed. You worked hard today. It's time to get some rest."

"Yeah, I am pretty tired," David replied. "I'll get cleaned up. Good night, Grandpa."

Exhausted from the day's activities, David returned to his room and collapsed on his bed. He reached over and took *Treasure Island* off the nightstand, but before he could read even half a page he lay fast asleep. The dream catcher hung protectively over the bed.

## **Falls Park**

Early the next morning, David waited anxiously on the front porch of Maddie's cabin. Maddie was the only one who believed his dreams were real. He needed her help, but what if she didn't believe him this time? David took a deep breath and was just about to knock, when he heard Maddie's voice.

"Come in, David," she called, "the door is open."

He pushed the door open slightly and looked in. Maddie stood by the kitchen table, a length of ornately decorated blue satin cloth draped over her arm. "How did you know I was here?" he asked.

"No magic," she said smiling at him. "I saw you coming out the window."

David stood at the door, unsure whether to enter or just leave. "You're busy," he said. "I can come back later."

"No, no. Come in please," she replied. "I was just finishing up."

David entered, closing the door behind him. As he moved closer, he saw that the fabric Maddie held over her arm was a skirt adorned with embroidered flowers and hundreds of small metal cones. Each cone had been tied to the dress with a short piece of ribbon.

"Wow, this is really cool, Maddie," he said, gently touching one of the cones. "Is it yours?"

"It's called a jingle dress. Anishinabe women wear them to do the jingle dance."

"Jingle dance?"

"It's a traditional dance of my people. When the cones jingle together, they make music."

"Are you wearing it in the parade?" David asked. "Grandpa told me you'd be in it."

"Come tomorrow. You will see," she replied. Carefully, she hung the dress over the back of a chair, smoothing out the wrinkles with her hand. "But you didn't come here to talk about my dress, did you?" she said. "You want to know about your dream."

"How did you know I had another dream, Maddie?"

"It wasn't hard to guess. You seem to think about nothing else lately. So tell me about it."

"This one was different. It wasn't about the deer this time,"

David explained. "I was in the woods, like before, walking down the same path. And then I saw this glow in the distance, so I walked toward it. The light seemed to keep appearing and disappearing through the trees, but I kept following it till I got close enough to see an old man sitting next to a campfire."

"An old man? Did you see his face?"

"Not at first. He was in the shadows with his back to me. But when he poked at the embers of the fire with his stick, the fire flared up, and I could see that he had dark hair streaked with gray. And he was wearing a vest - leather I think - and a baggy old shirt. It was Little Thunder, Maddie, I know it was."

"But if you didn't see him clearly, how do you know it was Little Thunder?"

"When I got closer, he raised his arm and pointed toward the lake. There was a boat pulled up on the shore. It was the same boat I saw on the lake the night of the storm, I'm pretty sure. Little Thunder's canoe."

"Are you certain it was the same canoe?"

"Yeah, well almost. That's why I have to go to the park, Maddie. I want to see for myself."

"The park? What exactly do you expect to find at the park?"

"Little Thunder's canoe. You said it's over at Fall's Park. It's the only way I'll know for sure that what I saw last night was real."

"But the park is over two miles from here, David. How will you get there?"

"I can ride your old bike. I've been working on it in my spare time. It rides pretty good now. Please, Maddie," he pleaded.

"Well… I suppose... You can take the bicycle, but be careful on the roads - and be back before lunch."

***

Lady ran after the bicycle, barking loudly as David peddled away. "No girl, not this time," David commanded. "You stay here with Maddie." The small golden haired dog reluctantly returned to the cottage steps and lay back down, directing her sad brown eyes at David. "It's all right, girl," he told her. "I'll be back soon."

Falls Park wasn't far from the cottage - only five minutes by car. David covered the two-mile distance in just over ten. He turned off the main road, passing under a massive iron gate bearing the banner

"*Falls County Park.*" He rode his bike along the zigzagging path, through small stands of shady maples, just skirting the water's edge. A number of empty picnic tables and fire pits, placed at regular intervals, lined the park lane.

Rounding a curve in the road, he spotted two young boys playing on a rickety old teeter-totter. One of the boys jumped off the see-saw and ran toward a nearby swing set, followed closely by the other. The rusty chains creaked and moaned as the boys took turns pushing each other higher and higher on the weather-beaten swing. Not far away, the boy's mother sat at a picnic table gathering the remnants of a picnic lunch into a wicker basket.

"Mark and Billy, come along now," she called. "Time to go."

"Do we have to go now, Mom? We just got here," one of the boys called back.

"Get over here this minute or I'm telling your father." This threat brought the two scurrying back to their mother. She herded the two boys toward a dark blue Nash parked beside the road just as David rode by. The younger boy waved and smiled. David waved back.

A low hedgerow extended along the side of the road opposite the lake. David followed the row of hedges until he reached an opening in the bushes. A sign carved out of a cedar plank read "*Ojibwa Cemetery Indian Spirit Houses.*" David stopped momentarily to examine the structures enclosed by the hedgerow.

Row after row of these structures lined the tree shaded lanes inside the cemetery, creating a ghostly housing development of the dead. It was the custom of the Ojibwa to bury their dead in shallow graves marked by small rough hewn houses, two or three feet high, three feet wide, and six or seven feet long. Each burial house had a steeply pitched, bark covered roof and a single window facing out toward the water.

An eerie quiet seemed to surround the deserted grounds. This was no place for the living. Pausing only briefly, David quickly peddled away without entering. He had no intention of upsetting the spirits of the dead by disturbing their resting place.

A short distance further down the road, he dismounted and wheeled the bicycle into the bushes. Nearby, a weathered sign read '*Former Site of Chippewa Indian Village.*'

David left his bicycle and followed a narrow path toward the area indicated by the sign. This was the part of the park Maddie had told him about. Little Thunder and his people had once lived here. David tried to imagine what the encampment must have been like before the arrival of white settlers. In the time of Little Thunder there would have been no houses, nor any power lines, nor any roads. The site had once boasted an entire community of bark-covered wigwams, bustling with activity.

Now only two rundown buildings remained. David walked closer to the dilapidated structures. One of the wigwams had been completely closed off. A sign warning 'Do Not Enter' hung from a rope strung across the entrance of the second. David peeked inside. The interior was empty aside from a crudely constructed sleeping platform built from tree branches bound by rawhide strips. A hide blanket had been thrown carelessly over the platform. A hole in the ceiling of the bark covered structure allowed in light and provided a chimney for the cooking fire in the center of the dirt floor.

David turned away from the wigwam and surveyed the remainder of the grounds. Maddie had assured him Little Thunder's canoe was at the park, but he could see no sign of a canoe anywhere nearby.

He made his way over to an outdoor display case. The case held a site map indicating where the remaining structures in the village had once stood. The case housed posters explaining the exhibit along with several black and white photographs of artifacts archaeologists had discovered when excavating the site in the early 1920s. The photos showed a tomahawk, a wooden bowl, and two crooked knives similar to the one Maddie's grandfather had made.

As David reached the last photo in the exhibit his heart sank. The picture showed a finely crafted canoe. The caption beneath the photo explained that like the rest of the artifacts pictured, the canoe had been removed and taken to the University of Michigan for preservation and study. David examined the photograph more closely. The canoe in the photo was long and narrow, curving upward at both ends. It had carefully carved wooden ribs covered by thin sheets of peeled birch bark. Unfortunately this was definitely not the boat he had seen in his dream.

Lost in his thoughts, David didn't hear a car squeal around the corner, kicking up a cloud of dust, until it was already past him. Barely missing the '*Chippewa Village*' sign, the car screeched to a halt near an unoccupied picnic table. The car, a black 1948 or 49 Chevrolet, looked vaguely familiar, but David couldn't quite place it. Four occupants emerged, seemingly oblivious to the exhibit or anything else around them.

Standing with their backs toward him, David couldn't make out their faces. But he had no trouble recognizing their voices, even from a distance. Sarcastic and aloof, the male voice was the one that had taunted him the night of the great bear hunt. There was no mistaking Terry's mocking tones. David realized immediately where he had seen the car before. It was Terry's car - the one Terry and his friends had driven away from Ike's Market.

But it was the other voice, the girl's unmistakable lyrical laughter, that was the real surprise. At first David refused to believe his eyes. What was Angie doing with Terry?

It wasn't possible, was it? What was it that Angie had said? '*My boyfriend's seventeen.*' Those were her words. Certainly she couldn't have meant Terry. But David didn't have time to consider the implications. The occupants of the car were now walking up the road directly toward him.

*\*\*\**

Quickly David ducked out of sight behind one of the reconstructed wigwams. He certainly didn't want to run into Terry again and even less so with Angie present. He looked toward the bushes. Maddie's bicycle lay partially exposed where he had dropped it. Perhaps the approaching teens wouldn't notice.

The voices were drawing closer. If he didn't act soon, he would be discovered. Acting on instinct alone, David darted past the warning rope into the darkness of an open wigwam.

He glanced around, furtively searching for a place to hide in the dim, sparsely furnished interior. He rushed to the bench platform and slid beneath its low frame pulling the hide blanket down over the edge to conceal his presence.

He could hear Angie and Terry settling down just outside the wigwam. Peeking out from behind the fur covered hiding place, David could just make out the two of them, sitting side by side in the grass, their backs toward him. He was glad that he had decided against taking Lady along on his morning ride. Her presence would have been a dead giveaway that someone else was close by.

A loud bang followed by series of pops shattered the silence. Startled, David jumped slightly, bumping his head on the platform frame.

"What do you think you're doing?" he heard Angie ask, obviously irritated.

"Hey, baby, the guys are just celebrating," Terry replied.

"They're a little early aren't they? Independence Day isn't until tomorrow. Besides you guys started drinking at ten in the morning. Just take it easy on the beers, ok?"

"We aren't doing any harm. We're just having a little innocent fun, that's all."

"Innocent? Is that what you call your driving back there? You scared me half to death. What if there'd been a cop?"

"But there wasn't, was there? I can drive that road with my eyes closed."

"That's what your idiot friend Kenny thought when he hit that deer."

"That was an accident. Anyway, do I look like Kenny?"

"And what about that woman and her kids? You almost ran them off the road, and you think it's funny."

"You saw her - she pulled out right in front of me. Come on, Angie babe," Terry said, trying his best to sweet-talk the girl at his side. "I'm only telling you the truth, and you know it."

David heard another series of loud bangs nearby. He moved around slightly so he could see out of the opening. From his vantage point he could just make out Mike and Jeff tossing strings of fire crackers at some harmless mallard ducks who had ventured too close to the boys.

"Look at your loser friends," he heard Angie say. "All they want to do is drink all day and make trouble for everyone else."

"Hey, maybe you shouldn't be criticizing my friends," Terry answered defensively. "I understand you've been keeping some piss poor company yourself lately."

"What are you talking about?"

"You've been hanging around with that nigger family from Wisconsin down at old man Wertz's cabins."

"What I do and who I see is none of your business," Angie snapped back. "And I don't want you using that language around me. They are not..., well, that word you said. They're Negroes. They're nice people and I really like their daughter, Denise."

"And what about the boy. I've heard about you and him. You been makin' out with that colored boy?"

"You're such an ass, Terry! Just don't try to tell me who I can see and who I can't. You're acting as if we were married or something, for Christ's sake. I can be with whoever I want. Look, you can stay here and act like a fool if you want, but I'm leaving." Angie got up from her place by Terry's side and began to walk away.

"Don't be mad," Terry called after her. "I'll take you home."

"No thanks," she answered without turning around. "I don't need a ride from you - and besides you've had too much to drink already. I can walk."

"Come on, baby, we're cool right? Listen I'll call you. We're still on for tomorrow, right? Fireworks start at ten, so I'll pick you up about eight."

Angie turned her back on him and stomped away, kicking up gravel in the drive as she went.

"Ah, come on, kitten, give me a break," Terry pleaded. "I've made big plans for your birthday next week..."

The comment made Angie stop briefly. She turned, smiling coyly toward Terry. "We'll have to see about that," she replied, then resumed walking away.

David heard a long low whistle. "Man is she ever burned!" Mike exclaimed.

"She'll be all right, don't worry," Terry said reassuringly.

"You still think she'll play along?"

"No problem. When the time comes she'll do whatever I ask."

***

"Look at what I found," someone called out. David recognized Jeff's voice. "I got me a bicycle." A moment later David saw the wheel of Maddie's bicycle appear in the opening of the Indian lodge.

David began to panic. Jeff had found the bicycle where David had dropped it.

"That's a sissy girls bike, you asshole," Mike called out. "Get off before you hurt yourself."

"If there's a bike, the rider can't be too far off," Terry observed. "Take a look around and see if you can find her."

David crouched down and hid while the boys made a half-hearted search of the immediate vicinity.

"Whoever rode this here musta' taken off when we showed up," Mike called out.

"Well, just put it back. We don't have time to mess around," Terry ordered.

"No, wait a minute. Watch this," Jeff called out as he jerked up on the handlebars and pulled the bicycle up so that he was balanced on the rear wheel. "Look I'm a circus star." The bike wavered unsteadily before it came crashing back down to the ground.

"Hey, let me try that," called Mike. He grabbed the bicycle out of his friend's hands, and got on. Holding his beer in one hand and the handlebars with the other, he tried to duplicate his friend's feat. The bicycle came up in the air then went careening off course toward the display case.

David froze in place. Outside there was a horrendous crash and what sounded like shattering glass. David strained to see what was going on from the cramped quarters of his hiding place, but could see nothing.

"Oh shit, now we're in for it," Jeff said.

"Cool it, you morons," ordered Terry. "Don't panic. Nobody saw us."

"Come on, let's get out of here before someone comes," Mike warned.

"Ditch that stupid bike, will ya?" Jeff called. "Hey, Ter, you comin' or what?"

"Yeah, yeah, I'll be right there. Shush up. I thought I heard something."

Someone leaned into the dark wigwam. David hunched down out of sight. He peeked out just enough to see Terry silhouetted in the light of the doorway.

"You didn't see anything, understand?" Terry called softly into the darkness. As if to emphasize his point he held his finger up to his lips in a hushing motion. Then he brought his finger down below his chin and drew it across his neck like a knife blade. It was the same motion he had made at Ernie's Diner talking about Bobber Lane. "Remember what I said," he ordered and then disappeared from the doorway.

David was left terrified and shaking. Terry had known he was there all along. He didn't dare move. Motionless he waited in the darkness. It could have been five minutes or maybe ten, but to David it seemed an eternity. Outside, nothing moved, except the birds in the trees.

Finally David crawled out from under the platform and peered out of the opening of the wigwam. Terry and his friends had gone. No one else was anywhere in sight. David's bicycle lay on its side in the middle of the path directly in front of the display case. Mike had crashed the bicycle into the base of the case crumpling one of the support legs and sending the case crashing to the ground. The case now lay on it's side, its leg shattered, broken glass everywhere scattered in the dirt.

David picked the bike up off the ground. The handlebars were twisted, and the front fender was slightly dented, but no major damage had been done. David glanced around to make sure no one else was watching. If anyone came along at that exact moment, there is no doubt who they would blame for the damage. Quickly he got on the bike, straightened the handlebars and shot off down the gravel road toward home and safety.

# Independence Day

By the time the Falls County Independence Day parade began, David was already roasting in the morning heat. He stood on the sidewalk slightly behind his grandfather, gazing around pensively. He knew that Angie and Terry might already be present somewhere in the crowd. He had no desire to see either of them - especially not Terry. He had said nothing about the previous day's incident to either his grandfather or Maddie. The bicycle damage had been minor, and he thought it best to keep the entire incident to himself. To his great relief he saw no sign of either Angie or Terry.

The throng of people gathered around him was growing impatient waiting for the procession to begin. There had already been several equipment delays, and the crowd was becoming restless. Finally, at ten fifteen, Grand Marshal Emerson Glass, Iron Falls only surviving veteran of the Spanish American War, rode forward astride his bay gelding, signaling the start of the parade. Sweltering in his vintage blue wool uniform and brown wide brimmed hat, Emerson looked as if he might drop out of the saddle at any minute.

Closely behind Emerson came a color guard composed of members of the local VFW post bearing the forty-eight star Old Glory. Behind them, a contingent of veterans from World War One struggled to march in unison. Their dwindling numbers marked the end of an era. David immediately recognized Ike Eisenberg in their midst. Like Emerson Glass, Eisenberg looked stiff and uncomfortable in his heavy khaki uniform.

Next came a unit of World War Two fighting men marching in close formation. Among them, David saw more faces he recognized. Dr. Jacob Bradshaw, who had served at Anzio, and Ray Peterson, who had landed at Guadalcanal. They both managed to smile and wave as they passed by.

The parade swept by quickly. A large delegation of Korean War vets was followed closely by a local Boy Scout troop, wearing khaki uniforms and military style wedge caps. They advanced down the street like veterans of wars yet to be fought. The scouts gave way to the Warrior marching band from Iron Falls High, blasting out John Philip Sousa's *Stars and Stripes Forever.*

Behind the band, David began to make out the slow steady beat of Indian drums, announcing the arrival of the Anishinabe dancers. The men wore ceremonial garb, with elaborately beaded vests worn over colorful shirts of blue, green, and red. Eagle feathers tied on their shoulders or on the sleeves of their shirts indicated their status in the group.

They wore their hair long, woven into braids, with headdresses made of deer tail and feathers along the center of their heads. One of the men beat out a steady rhythm on a hide-covered drum he held slung over his arm. The other two men shook war clubs adorned with sleigh bells, chanting softly as they moved forward.

Maddie and three other women danced behind the men. Carl and David had dropped Maddie off early at the staging area so that she had time to prepare for the festivities. The dancers stamped their feet to the rhythm of the drum beat, occasionally turning full circles or dancing backwards. Like Maddie, the other women wore brightly colored dresses trimmed with fringes of metal cones. As they rotated around, the cones tinkled together creating a pleasant soft jingling sound.

"I don't understand, Grandpa," David said. "Maddie told me how white people forced Indians onto reservations. So why are they celebrating America's Independence Day?"

"Perhaps they are not celebrating the same thing we are, eh? I think it is their pride that makes them dance. The Indians may have lost their land, but they are still proud of who they are."

The end of the parade was now in sight. The Jasper High Diggers marching band attempted to outperform the Warrior band, blaring out another Sousa march, *The Washington Post*, at full volume. The band was followed by the Independence Day float. A seven-foot tall paper mache bald eagle feathered with tissue paper, sat nested on a flatbed trailer covered with red, white, and blue streamers. Embraced in the eagle's wings stood a petite young woman wearing a sash across her frilly pink prom dress declaring her to be "*Miss Liberty 1957.*"

As the float disappeared down the street, the crowd that had lined the route began to filter into the road, milling around and greeting friends and neighbors they met along the way. David followed his grandfather through the throngs of people, gradually making their way to the side street where Carl had parked his station wagon.

"I thought I saw you two standing in the crowd," a familiar voice called out. Both Carl and David turned to see Ray Peterson, still looking uncomfortable in his military attire, walking toward them. "I'm dying in this damn uniform," he said unfastening the top button of his shirt. "Can't wait to get it off."

"Well, I must say, you still look quite dashing, Raymond," Carl greeted. "Your uniform still fits you quite well."

"Nice of you to say so, but it's a lot tighter than I remember. Too much of Rita's home cooking, I guess," Ray joked. "By the way, have you seen her and the boys? They were supposed to meet me after the parade, and I can't find them anywhere."

"No sir," David volunteered

"Well, they're somewhere around here. I can't wait to get back and fire up the grill. I can almost taste those steaks now. Speaking of which, what are you two doing for the Fourth? I know Rita would love to have you come for dinner. The more the merrier as they say."

"I'd love to Raymond, but I still have work to do on the boat David and I are putting together. But perhaps another time," Carl replied.

"Yeah, I heard about that boat you're building. Well how bout you David? Why don't you join us if your grandfather doesn't mind, that is."

"Gee, I don't know," David squirmed like a fish on a hook.

"Actually David won't be able to make it either," Carl interceded. "He's helping me with the decking."

"Oh, that's too bad. But I know how it is when you've got a project in the works," Ray said wiping his brow. "Listen, it's been good seeing you, but I think I better just get out of this uniform before I melt. Maybe I'll see you later at the fireworks show down at the park, eh?"

"Sure, we'll see you there," Carl answered. Ray moved off, continuing his search. Within minutes he had disappeared into the milling crowd.

"Thanks Grandpa," David said.

"What are you thanking me for? I didn't do anything."

"You know. You gave me an excuse for not going out to Uncle Ray and Aunt Rita's house this afternoon."

"You looked uncomfortable when Raymond issued his invitation. Besides Raymond knows you have been helping me with the Chris Craft."

"So do you really want me to help work on the boat this afternoon?" David asked.

Carl thought for a moment. "No, not today," he said. "This is a holiday. I think we could both use a day off. I will tell you what, when we get back I will make us a pitcher of lemonade and I will challenge you to a game of horseshoes."

David glanced back at the group of Indian dancers still gathered in the park at the end of the parade route. "Isn't Maddie coming back to the lake with us, Grandpa?" he asked.

"She will be back later. She is spending the rest of the morning with her tribe. I will drive back into town later this afternoon to pick her up."

***

David grasped the horseshoe firmly around the shank, bent his knees slightly, and swung the shoe back and then forward again, releasing it at the apex of his swing. The shoe arched high through the air, flipping over as it flew, but fell considerably short of the stake in the center of the horseshoe pit. "You win again, Grandpa," said David somewhat dejectedly.

"Yes, but you are getting closer all the time," Carl replied sympathetically.

Carl and David had gone down to the beach almost immediately after returning from the Iron Falls' Independence Day Parade. The temperature was already almost ninety and the breeze off the lake offered at least a hint of relief from the stifling heat. David wiped the sweat off his brow, and took a drink of lemonade from a glass he had sitting next to the portable radio on the nearby picnic table.

Even though the Gibson's Cadillac was not parked in front of their cabin, David kept expecting them to show up any minute. "Where are the Gibsons anyway?" he asked. "I haven't seen them around all day."

"Oh, Nathan told me that he was driving his family up to Bond Falls for a picnic," Carl replied. "Why? Are you looking for more competition?"

David was relieved that he would not have to confront TJ again. "No reason," he said. "I just wondered that's all."

"But don't worry," Carl said. "They will be back in time for us all to go to the fireworks show at the fairgrounds tonight."

The radio crackled with the voice of Detroit play-by-play announcer, Van Patrick. "Two on and two out for Cleveland in the bottom of the fifth," he broadcast, "and that brings up Rocky Colavito. Rocky's gone hitless in two trips to the plate."

"Colavito swings... And there it goes...," the portable radio hissed with static. "Deep to left field... Maxwell goes back... He's on the warning track... It's going... Going... That ball is out of here! A home run for Rocky Colavito!"

David shook his head in dismay. Colavito's homer made the score 3-1 Cleveland. The Tigers had their work cut out for them.

"Maybe it's time for a relief pitcher, eh?" Carl smiled.

"The Tigers can still come back. The game's not over yet. Besides, even if they lose, they can still even it up in game two." Because it was the Fourth of July, the Tigers were playing a double header against their league rivals, the Cleveland Indians.

Carl checked his watch. "It's almost time to go pick up Maddie in town. Do you want to ride along? We can listen to the rest of the game in the car, eh?"

"If it's ok with you I think I'd rather stay here. It's too hot to be in the car. Besides I can practice pitching horseshoes while you're gone."

"I don't know, David," Carl said skeptically. "I hate to leave you here alone."

"I'll be ok, Grandpa. Maddie leaves me on my own all the time. Look around. There are lots of people here."

Carl looked around the grounds. The family staying in Cabin #3 was having lunch nearby under the pines, and the father and his young son from Cabin #2 were playing on the tree swing.

"Well, all right. Go ahead. But just remember what I said about swimming on your own..."

"I know, I know. Don't go into the water unless you or Maddie are there with me. Listen, I'll be fine. So is it ok?"

"Well, I suppose if you're careful," Carl conceded. "I shouldn't be gone long."

David watched as his grandfather drove away, and then resumed practicing tossing the horseshoes more precisely toward the stake some forty feet distant. His accuracy continued to improve. Eventually he managed a couple of 'leaners' and even a lone ringer.

Van Patrick's play-by-play continued on the radio, but the score remained unchanged. In the end, the Tigers fell to the Indians in game number one. David temporarily switched off the radio. It would be another thirty minutes or so before play resumed in game two.

It wasn't long before the boy from Cabin #2 tired of the tree swing and David watched as his father led him back to their cabin. Moments later the family from Cabin #3 finished their picnic lunch, got into a Nash sedan, and drove away. Now no one else was stirring along the entire beach. David was alone.

The area along the shoreline had become uncharacteristically quiet. David tossed the horseshoes into the pit and walked over to the water's edge. The water looked cool and inviting. A power boat towing a tanned young girl on water skis sped by. She smiled and waved invitingly toward David. He smiled back enviously as she shot away. Sliding his shoes off, he ventured cautiously into the water. The waves lapped over his bare feet, cool and refreshing. No swimming alone, his grandfather had warned. But it wouldn't hurt just to wade out a few feet, David thought.

He stripped off his shirt and threw it onto the back of a lawn chair. Walked out into the shallow water wearing only his shorts, he watched as a group of minnows darted away to hide in the shadows of the dock.

He continued to wade into the lake until the water was almost up to his waist. He looked out toward the raft. The water was calm and tranquil, lapping gently against the sides of the metal barrels keeping the raft afloat. It wasn't more than fifty or sixty yards from the end of the dock out to the raft. He could swim that distance easily. If he just took a quick dip, his grandfather would never have to know.

He pushed off from the sandy bottom, kicking out in the direction of the raft.

\*\*\*

Using a steady uneven stroke, David made his way through the water until he was in arm's reach of the raft. The swim to the raft proved farther than he expected. By the time he reached the raft, he needed to rest. He grabbed hold of the ladder and pulled himself out of the water, climbing onto the deck.

The raft rocked back and forth as David walked across the deck boards, looking for a good spot to sit down. He eased himself down along the edge of the raft, dangling his legs over the side. He lay down on the deck, closing his eyes and taking a deep breath. The gentle rolling of the raft relaxed him.

After what he guessed was ten minutes or so, David opened his eyes and sat back upright on the raft. His energy restored, he stood up and walked over to the edge. He looked back toward the shore. He'd have to head back soon, or risk having his grandfather catch him out swimming alone.

Though he was a good swimmer, David wasn't a great diver. More often than not, he ended up doing a belly-flop. He remembered TJ diving off the raft. Graceful and elegant. "If he can do it, so can I", David thought. "Just lean, stretch, and dive." He curled his toes over the edge, leaned forward, and aimed out over the water. He counted to himself, "Three, two, one…"

He sailed away from the raft. Arms extended, eyes shut, toes pointed and knees straight. He glided through the air and sliced into the water like an arrow - straight and true. Perfect, he thought.

He used his momentum to glide as far as possible before coming to the surface. He pushed his arms forward and then brought them back as forcefully as he could against his body while at the same time giving a huge frog kick. He felt like a fish, moving easily through the lake.

Eyes still closed, he again reached out in front of his body to give one more lunge forward. This time however his hand came into contact with something solid directly in his path. "A rock," he thought. "I must be near the bottom." At that moment he felt something tap him on the shoulder.

He immediately stopped kicking and opened his eyes. As his eyes adjusted to the murky water of the lake, David suddenly froze in horror. There, not two feet away from him, staring back at him with an unblinking gaze, were the cold, glazed over eyes of another person. No, not a person. A spirit. The spirit of Little Thunder.

Little Thunder's hand drifted down through the water, coming to rest on David's shoulder. Little Thunder was trying to grab him. Trying to pull him under. Terrified, David involuntarily gasped, inhaling water into his lungs. He gagged and choked. He tried kicking away from the ghostly apparition, but he couldn't move. His arms and legs flailed uselessly. Something held him in place. He looked back and saw the old Indian following him.

David looked down. There was something tangled around his foot, tying him to the ghostly phantom. They were hopelessly snarled together. The ghastly spirit pulled him deeper into the still waters. David reached back, feeling for whatever was holding him in place. He touched something. His foot was tangled in some kind of cord or rope. He struggled to free himself, but the cord held fast. More water entered his lungs, choking him. He looked up toward the surface. Sun light shimmered along the face of the water, just inches above him.

David kicked back with his foot, pushing against the midsection of the ghostly body. His kick caused Little Thunder's mouth to drift open slightly. Bubbles formed around the dead Indian's lips and floated up toward the surface. It seemed as if the spirit was trying to speak to him.

David kicked again. This time he felt something give way. Free at last, he fought to reach the surface. Gasping for air, he emerged from the water. He tried to swim, but his strength was gone. He began flailing his arms, but couldn't hold himself above the surface any longer. He knew now that he didn't have the strength to make it back to the raft. Little Thunder was just behind him, reaching out to grab him and pull him back down.

There was no escape. He took one deep, final breath, and slipped beneath the surface. The shimmering sun rippling above him began to fade. David sank farther and farther down. Someone was calling his name. He could hear the voice distinctly now. Little Thunder was calling him. David felt himself drawn to the voice. Deeper. Deeper.

# Rescued

Dim light filtered in through David's half-closed eyes. He thought for a moment he might be dead. He could remember drowning. He could feel the water filling his lungs. Pain radiated through his chest. There was pressure everywhere. A giant weight was enveloping him, like a vice crushing his lungs. All the air was being forced out of his body.

Opening his eyes slightly, he saw only the boards of the raft beneath him. He was lying on his stomach, his hands drawn up under his head. How had he gotten here? He didn't remember climbing up the ladder to the raft. The last thing he remembered were the eyes - those terrible, haunting, lifeless eyes. They followed him everywhere. Had he just imagined them? Had he imagined Little Thunder?

Someone was kneeling over him, rocking forward, pressing downward on his back, forcing the air out of his lungs. Involuntarily, he choked and gagged. He coughed. Water spewed out of his half open mouth.

The unseen figure now grasped him under his elbows and rocked backward, pulling his arms upward, drawing air into his lungs. What was happening? Who was doing this to him?

He felt the constriction in his chest again. Two hands were pressing down on the middle of his back. Again he coughed, and more water came gushing from his mouth. He raised his head slightly to let the water drain from his nose, spitting up still more of the lake from his lungs. As he rose up, he caught a brief glimpse of the two hands that were pressing the water from him. They were black hands.

David felt a sudden jolt of fear. He jumped to his feet, still gagging and choking, to stand face to face with the person whose hands he had seen. It was TJ - shirtless, shoeless, dripping wet, and wearing only a soaked pair of blue Bermuda shorts.

"Stay away from me," David screamed. "Just stay away." He took a wild, unsteady swing at the larger youth, but TJ stepped aside and caught David's arm, stopping him from falling back into the lake.

"You stupid shit," TJ called out as he wrapped his arms around David's trembling body to keep him from swinging again. "Stop squirming around and hold still, will you. Here I save your worthless ass, and you try to deck me."

"Nobody ask you to help," David protested. "I was doing just fine without you. Let go of me this minute." He continued to try to twist free from the older youth's grasp.

"Now listen, kid. Hold on just a minute," TJ replied, continuing to keep a tight hold on the contentious boy. "I think all that water you sucked in must of addled your brain. If I hadn't come along when I did, you'd still be floatin' face down somewhere out there in the lake. So just calm down and I'll let you go, ok?"

For a moment, David continued to squirm, but gradually he stopped fighting. He soon realized that his energy had been depleted by his earlier struggle to stay afloat. "All right, I give. You win," he stammered.

As the tension in David's body eased, TJ released his hold on his smaller adversary. Once free from TJ's grasp, David staggered exhausted to the far side of the dock, well away from his presumed attacker.

"Stay away from me," he warned. "You better not come near me. I know you're the one who attacked me out there."

"Attack you? Shit, I'm the one who saved your worthless ass. Who do you think pulled you out of the lake anyway?"

"You're the one who pulled me out?" David asked incredulously. He remembered TJ's threat to break him into pieces if he so much as showed his face around the Gibson cabin. Why would TJ ever have bothered to save him?

"Why else would I be out here? I saw you from shore hollerin' your head off and flappin' your arms around like a drowning rat." TJ explained. "At first I thought you were just messin' around, but when you kept screamin', I jumped in and swam out here like a freakin' fish. I almost didn't make it either. By the time I got to you, you were going under for the third time. Shit, what was I supposed to do? Let you drown?"

"But I thought... Weren't you the one who was tryin' to kill me?" David asked confused.

"Kill you? What the fuck are you talking about."

"But when I came to, you were you sitting over me squeezing all the life out of me. My chest still hurts like the blazes."

"For your information, it's called artificial respiration. I learned it from my uncle. But, shit, I never thought I'd have to use it though. So just calm down, will ya?"

"Artificial respiration? You mean you weren't trying to choke me?" David responded, weakly.

"You actually thought I was tryin' to choke you? You white boys are all crazy. I may not like you very much, but that doesn't mean I want to kill you. What the hell's wrong with you anyway? Christ, you're really something else."

David caught his breath and glanced up at the other boy. Without looking up, he spoke just above a whisper. "Ok, I'm sorry. If you're telling me the truth, I owe you an apology," he said reluctantly.

"You're damned right you owe me an apology."

"Well, thanks for pulling me out. I'm sorry I took a swing at you. I mean after the other day and everything you're the last person I expected to risk his neck to save me."

TJ stopped talking and examined David. David was beginning to shiver. His teeth had begun to chatter. "You sure you're feelin' ok?" TJ said. "You're looking mighty pale even for a white boy. Your lips look blue. Maybe you better sit down."

Still shaky from his experience, David did as TJ suggested and sat back down on the edge of the raft. He looked down at himself. Goosebumps were covering his arms. "I'm ok," he managed to reply feebly.

"Sure you are," said TJ. "Just relax. You're safe now. Why don't you just catch your breath for a minute."

In the distance David could hear the shouts of partiers along the distant shore shooting off fire crackers and bottle rockets well in advance of the evening's planned fireworks display. Two or three boats flew through the water, spewing out funnels of waves in their wake. Across the lake he could barely make out the young waterskier who had waved at him earlier.

For several minutes, both boys sat quietly on the raft gazing back toward the shore without talking. David felt an awkward silence growing between them. He knew he should say something, but wasn't sure what. Just a few days before, the boy sitting beside him had threatened to beat him to a bloody pulp, and now that same boy had saved his life.

"Look, if you're still mad about me bein' up on the hill the other day, I'm sorry." David said, looking up, "I didn't mean to do anything to offend you or your sister, ok? So, what do you think, can we just shake hands and try again?" He extended his hand toward TJ.

The other boy hesitated, looking down at David's outstretched hand before reaching out to grasp it with his own. "Sure, why not. Apology accepted." A broad smile spread across TJ's face making David relax for the first time since he had been pulled from the water.

***

Now that a truce had been established, an awkward silence developed between them. The two boys sat side by side on the raft, unwilling or unable to look at each other, each waiting for the other to speak.

At last David broke the silence. "My Grandpa told me your family were all gone for the day. You know, having a holiday picnic or something. How come you were still here anyway?"

"Dad took Mom and Denise for a picnic over at Bond Falls," TJ explained. "They wanted me to go too, but they couldn't get me out of bed. My dad says I sleep like the dead. Anyway they finally gave up and went without me. Good thing for you I stayed behind."

"Look," he offered at last, "whenever your feeling up to it we can start back."

Suddenly David flashed on the old Indian lurking just below the surface, waiting. "I'm not getting in that water again. No way!" he protested.

"Listen, if it makes you feel any better, I'll swim right beside you just in case..."

"You go. I'm stayin' right here," David replied. "Not with that thing out there."

"What 'thing?' What the heck are you talking about now?"

"An old Indian, he was chasing me through the water. You must have seen him. He tried to grab me and drag me down."

"Believe me, there's no one out there. Not a soul."

"It was Little Thunder. I saw him. I swear."

"You saw who?" TJ just stared at him incredulously. "Look, I don't know who the hell Little Thunder is, but the only person I saw flailing around out there was you. Now I'm gonna head back in. You can swim along if you want, or you can sit out here and wait. It's up to you."

"I know it sounds crazy, but there really is something out there. I saw it. I'm not sure what it was, but I'm not going back in the water."

"Well I don't see anything. Look, if it'll make you feel any better, I'll swim out and take a look. If I don't find anything, will that satisfy you?"

David looked back into the lake, contemplating the alternatives. He didn't want to be left alone on the raft - that was for sure. Carl and Maddie would be home soon, and he certainly didn't want them to catch him. "I don't think that's a very good idea. What if that thing is still out there?" he replied cautiously.

TJ got to his feet and moved to the edge of the raft. "Believe me, if I find anything strange down there I'm not about to wait around to see what it wants." Before David had a chance to reply, TJ dove into the water, bobbing to the surface a few feet from the raft. "Ok, just so I know," he yelled up to David, "what am I supposed to be looking for anyway? You said a name before. What was it, 'Little Thunder?'"

David hesitated. His grandfather had already ridiculed him for saying that he'd seen Little Thunder out on the lake. Now he was trying to convince someone he hardly knew that he had not only seen a spirit, but looked it right in the eye and actually touched it. The story seemed far-fetched even to him.

"Believe me, I'm not making this up," he said. "There really is something under water. Right over there." David pointed to a spot in the water directly behind TJ. "About twenty or thirty feet out. It looked human."

TJ suddenly became apprehensive. He was prepared for rocks or even fish in the lake, but the prospect of something human beneath the surface made him slightly nervous. "Human?" he asked checking around himself in the water. "You mean like another swimmer or what?"

"No, not human exactly. I'm not sure what it was," David answered truthfully. "But there's something out there. Really. I'd feel better if you just didn't mess around. Why don't you get back up on the raft? Or just swim back to shore and bring out one of those row boats."

TJ took David's caution as a challenge to his bravery. "Hey, there's nothing out here to be afraid of and I'll prove it." He turned and swam out in the direction David had indicated.

"Just be careful," David called after him.

A few yards out, TJ stopped swimming and looked back toward

the raft. "Is this the place?" he shouted back at David.

"Almost. Maybe five feet or so to the right I think. I'm not sure. I was underwater most of the time."

TJ swam a few feet to his right, before taking a deep breath and diving beneath the surface. David stood up on the raft to get a better view. He counted the seconds in his head. Twenty seconds. Thirty. No sign of TJ. A few bubbles broke the surface. Almost forty seconds. Finally TJ resurfaced and immediately took a deep breath filling his lungs with fresh air.

"Did you find anything?" David yelled.

"Nothing so far. Can't see very much down there anyway. Water's kinda murky. Looks like something's been stirring it up. Let me catch my breath and I'll take one more look."

Again he took a deep breath and then plunged beneath the surface. Again David waited, counting the seconds. Thirty. Forty… Almost one minute.

Suddenly TJ appeared shooting up into the air as he surfaced. He gasped for air and began shouting something. "Holy Jesus," TJ screamed. "There's something down there! It's a fucking body." He swam furiously back toward the raft, as if someone was chasing him.

As TJ reached the raft, David reached down to grasp his arm, pulling him up as he scrambled onto the raft.

"I thought you were full of shit, but there's really a fuckin' body down there," TJ exclaimed gasping for breath. "But you got one thing wrong. That sure as hell isn't any Indian. Whoever it is down there is just as white as you are."

"So you found him? There really is someone down there?"

"Not unless you imagined a ghost dressed up in a plaid shirt and overalls."

A shiver suddenly ran through David's body. He was no longer dealing with the legend of a ghost. This was reality. There was a real body floating just below the surface only a few feet from where he was sitting.

***

"Ok, so if there's really a body down there, what do we do now?" David asked.

"We'll have to tell somebody, I suppose. My folks should be back soon. What about your grandfather? Is he around? He'll know what to do."

"He's not here. He went to pick up Maddie. Do we have to tell him?" David said.

"Sure. He's going to know sooner or later. There's a body out there. Somebody's gonna hafta call the police and report it."

"Yeah, I suppose you're right, it's just that..."

"What's the problem?"

David paused, looking tentatively at TJ. "It's just that I'm not supposed to be out here. Alone I mean. My grandfather'll have a fit if he finds out I swam to the raft without anybody else around."

"Yeah, so?"

"I don't want to get into any trouble. If you say you swam out here with me, my grandfather'd believe you."

"So, you want me to lie for you, is that it? And I suppose you'd just as soon I didn't say anything about pulling you out of the drink either, huh?"

"If he finds out I almost drowned, he'd never let me anywhere near the lake again. Please?"

"I don't know. You're asking for a lot. I bet you never told a lie before in your life."

"Sure I have," David said defensively. "My cousin Kyle and I had to lie to our folks to stay out of trouble when we almost fell into an old mine cave-in by his house." *Stupid Kyle and his dares,* David thought.

"Oh, yeah, and what'd you tell them?"

"When we got back we told everybody a bull chased us and we messed up our clothes crawling through a barbed wire fence to get away."

"Hey, that's a good one," laughed TJ. "And I had you down as one of those straight arrow types. Hell, maybe you're not so bad after all."

"So will you do it? Will you tell Grandpa we swam out here together?"

TJ broke into a broad smile. "Damned," he laughed.

"What's so funny? I'm serious. I need your help."

"It's not that," TJ replied. "I think I finally figured something out."

"Figured what out?" David asked.

"This whole thing. You, me, sittin' out here on this raft. Dead body floating in the water. It's just like a scene from *Huckleberry Finn*."

"*Huckleberry Finn*? What are you talking about?"

"You know Mark Twain?"

David still showed no sign of recognition.

"You've got to be kidding, right? You never read *Huckleberry Finn*?" TJ sounded astonished. "I thought they made every school kid in the country read that stupid book."

"I read *Tom Sawyer* once," David replied. "Mark Twain wrote that didn't he?"

"Yeah, but it's not the same. Huck Finn is about this white kid, who runs away from home and ends up sharing a raft with a slave named Jim. They even find a body in an old house floating down the river. Now here we are sittin' on this raft trying to figure out what to do about a dead guy in the water. Sound familiar?"

"So I'm supposed to be like this Huck guy, huh?"

"Well, maybe not just like him. But the way I figure it, you two have a lot in common."

"Oh yeah? Like what?"

"Well for starters, you're what, twelve maybe thirteen years old? So was Huck. His family's not around, neither is yours. And most of the time he's not very nice to Jim."

"Look, I already told you I'm sorry about the other day..."

"And he makes up stories to get out of trouble. Now here you are askin' me to lie to your grandfather. Maybe I should just start calling you Huck."

"Look, you can call me whatever you want, as long as you tell my grandpa we were together, ok?"

TJ looked serious, and hesitated as if considering his response. "Ok it's a deal. I'll tell your grandfather we were together all afternoon if you want. But I have one condition."

"What's that?" David asked uncertainly.

"You have to swear that you were the one who found the body," TJ stressed to David. "It wouldn't look right if a colored boy had anything to do with finding the body of a white man, accident or not."

"Sure, it's a deal," replied David relieved. "I think I'm ready to swim back to shore now. But you go first, ok?"

"Hell of a way to spend the 4th of July, huh, Huck?" TJ laughed, as he dove into the lake, entering the water as far away from the body as possible.

## The Body

"Good, I don't see my grandfather anywhere. He must not be back from town yet," David told TJ as they waded ashore.

"Yeah, we got lucky," TJ agreed. "Nobody's around." He looked back toward his family's cabin. The Cadillac was still gone, and there was no sign of any activity. "Looks like my folks aren't back yet either."

TJ started up the beach, toward the large willow in front of the dock. "Come on, hurry up. I left my shirt and shoes under that tree next to yours when I saw you strugglin' out there. If we're gonna convince your grandfather that we were swimming together, I better change out'a these shorts before he gets back."

Grabbing his tee shirt and deck shoes from under the tree, TJ continued on toward his cabin. "My mom hung the laundry out to dry this morning," he said, "and I can see my swim suit on the line. All I have to do is put on my trunks, and hang the shorts up to dry."

Hastily TJ led David up to the cabin and grabbed his swimsuit and a towel from the clothesline.

"You can change over in the boathouse," David told him.

"No need," replied TJ. He quickly slipped off his dripping wet shorts, and stood there completely naked. David looked around nervously. It took only seconds for TJ to pull on his trunks, but to David it seemed much longer.

TJ threw the wet shorts over the clothes line. "If mom asks, I'll just tell her I went wading and got the shorts wet. Now we'd better figure out what to do about that dead guy out in the lake," TJ said as he toweled himself off. "Since your grandfather and my folks are gone, we'll hafta try something else. How about that Indian lady who runs the place when your grandpop's gone?"

"Maddie? No that's where grandfather is now - picking her up."

"How bout a phone? You got one up at the cottage don't you?"

"Sure, but shouldn't we just wait for Grandpa to get back?"

"Naw, we better get a hold of somebody pretty quick. No tellin' how long that body's been down there."

The two boys had just started up the road back to the cottage when they saw a cloud of dust billowing up along the access road in the distance.

"I think it's Grandpa," said David anxiously. "Come on, hurry." David led TJ running across the compound toward the approaching station wagon. They reached the car just as Carl was pulling up to the boathouse.

"Grandpa, Grandpa, hurry, hurry," shouted David breathlessly as he skidded to a halt next to the open driver's side window. "Yeah," panted TJ, "you've got to get some help!"

"Whoa! Slow down there boys," Carl said emerging from the car. "What's going on here? Who needs help?"

David and TJ started talking at the same time. "You've got to call the police...", "right away...", "someone's in the lake...", "tell them what happened..."

"Whoa, whoa. Hold on, boys. I can't understand when you both talk at once. One at a time. TJ, you go first - and start from the beginning."

"Ok, Mr. Wertz. When I came out this afternoon, I saw David sitting out here on the beach, so we decided to go for a swim - to cool off you know? Anyway, we swam out to the raft together..."

"That was ok, wasn't it?" interrupted David. "You said I could swim if someone went with me."

"Ya, ya, of course, but let TJ talk. What happened when you went swimming?"

"We got out to the raft, and David decided to try diving in. After he jumped off the dock, he came to the surface almost immediately, yelling about finding something down there, underwater..."

"What do you mean underwater?" Carl seemed confused. "You found something in the lake?" he said turning toward his grandson. "Tell me exactly what you found, David."

"Well, TJ was showing me how to dive, and when I jumped in, there was this person in the water."

"Person? Someone else was swimming out there?"

"No, he wasn't swimming. There's a dead man out by the raft. Underwater. I saw him down there. TJ saw him too."

"My God," real alarm now sounded in Carl's voice. "So. Has anyone called the sheriff yet?"

"We were just headed to the cottage when you drove up," David answered.

"TJ, aren't your parents here?"

"Naw, they went for a ride. I didn't go with them. They could be back any time now though."

"All right, boys, you did just fine. I dropped Maddie off at the cottage. You two can wait with her while I call the sheriff. TJ, be sure to let your dad know what happened as soon as he gets back." There was a pause. "David, are you sure you're ok?"

"Yeah, Grandpa. I'm fine now," David said. For the first time since his dive from the raft, he felt that everything would be all right again.

\*\*\*

"If what you saw was truly Little Thunder, they won't find anything when they search the lake," explained Maddie. She sat with TJ and David at the kitchen table of the cottage while Carl called the sheriff's office. "Spirits only reveal themselves to those they choose."

"But if it was really Little Thunder, how come TJ saw a body down there?" David asked.

"Spirits let us see what we expect to see, David," she said. "You could see him as he really is, but your friend TJ does not yet believe, so Little Thunder appeared in a form he could understand."

"If there's a body out in that lake, it's no ghost," Carl said entering from the living room. "I called the sheriff's office. Sheriff Edmonds is on his way. I've known Les for years. He'll get to the bottom of all this."

While they waited for the sheriff to arrive, Carl made the boys some hot chocolate and tried to distract them from their gruesome discovery. But when a car finally did pull into the access drive, it was TJ's parents returning from their outing. After TJ filled his father in on the events of the afternoon, Nathan went over and hugged his son tightly. "Man, you just never know," he said. "I never thought that coming up here we'd run into something like this. I mean, Milwaukee, maybe, but here? No way."

It was almost an hour before the Falls County Sheriff finally arrived. Sheriff Les Edmonds was a tall, lanky man with thinning blond hair and a pencil thin mustache that gave him the appearance of being a B-movie hoodlum. He emerged from the car confidently, as if to show everyone who was in charge. He walked directly over to Carl, totally ignoring David and TJ. He wiped his brow on the sleeve of his shirt. "Hey Carl. Really got a hot one for the Fourth, eh?" he remarked as if making a social call.

"Yeah, sure is. Sorry to drag you out here on a holiday, Les."

"Part of the job, Carl. So, what's going on anyway? Dispatcher said you found a body out there in the lake. That right?"

"Not me, sheriff, the boys here. They say they found something out there while they were swimming."

For the first time the sheriff turned his attention to the two boys standing nearby. "That so?" he addressed David, giving TJ a suspicious glance. "You boys find something out there?"

David looked back over his shoulder at TJ making sure that the other boy was still there for support. TJ nodded to David as if to say, 'go ahead tell him what we saw.'

"We were swimming out by the raft, and I dove in, and I ran into something. There was this body, and it looked like he was just caught down there or something. There wasn't anybody around when we got back to shore, but then Grandpa showed up, and he called your office."

"Looks like I better get a hold of Roy Farmer," said Sheriff Edmonds. "He's done some diving work for the county in the past. If there's anything down there, Roy'll find it."

\*\*\*

It was another hour before Roy Farmer drove up in his 1954 Plymouth sedan pulling a large power boat loaded on a trailer. By the time he arrived, word had spread and a small crowd had gathered along the water's edge, keeping cool in the shade of the willow tree.

"Afternoon, Roy," Sheriff Edmonds greeted Farmer. "Ann said you were out golfin'. Sorry to interrupt your game."

"That's ok," replied Farmer, a short, wiry man with a muscular build and a eagle tattoo on his left forearm. "I was stuck in a sand trap most of the day anyway," he replied. "What we got here, Les?"

Sheriff Edmonds quickly explained the situation to the diver. "Let's see what's out there," Farmer responded, as if finding a dead body in the lake were an everyday occurrence.

As he backed the trailer down the boat ramp, the sheriff told several spectators to move out of the way. Once past the on-lookers, Farmer maneuvered the Plymouth into position, slowly lowering the boat into the shallow waters of the lake. The sheriff and Carl helped ease the streamlined powerboat into the water while Farmer walked back to his car and opened the trunk. He removed two hefty looking tanks, a diving mask, and a rubberized suit.

Sheriff Edmonds took the boys over to talk to the diver as he pulled on the awkward looking suit, strapped on one of the oxygen tanks, and adjusted the regulator. "Roy here was a Navy diver during the war," the sheriff said, validating the diver's expertise. "He's one of the few guys in Michigan with this kind of equipment. If anybody can figure out what's out there, Roy can."

With Farmer at the controls, David, TJ, Carl, and Sheriff Edmonds were transported out onto the lake. Roy Farmer no sooner fired up the twin Johnson outboards than he had to cut the engines and allow the boat to coast to a halt just short of the raft.

"Tell me where you saw the body," the sheriff said to David. David pointed to a spot about five feet away, and the sheriff decided that they were close enough and dropped anchor.

Roy Farmer slipped over the side or the power boat clinging to the gunwale as he tested his breathing apparatus. Having satisfied himself that everything was in proper working order, he prepared to make his dive. "Ok, let's take a look," he said. He pulled the mask down over his face, adjusted his mouthpiece, and slipped beneath the surface. Soon the boys could no longer see him through the water, and only bubbles indicated his location.

The bubbles moved quickly until they reached almost the exact spot David had indicated to the diver. There, the bubbles stopped and lingered. After several minutes of waiting, Farmer resurfaced, pulling the mouthpiece out and pushing the mask back on his forehead as he swam toward the boat.

"We got a body down there, all right," Farmer exclaimed. "Looks like old Bobber Lane, but he's been down there so long I'm afraid he's kinda messed up."

"Bobber? Jesus, how in God's name...," Sheriff Edmonds said in surprise. "Bobber knew this lake like the back of his hand."

"I drove by his place a couple of days ago," Carl offered, "and he wasn't around. His boat wasn't at the dock, so I figured he was out fishing, or maybe down at Ike's. Why, now that I think about it, that must have been what you saw out here the other night, David."

Carl turned to explain to the sheriff. "David was down on the beach when the storm hit the other night. He said he thought he saw a something out on the lake, but then it disappeared. Tell the sheriff what you saw, David."

David felt grateful that his grandfather had not mentioned his conviction that what he had seen was Little Thunder's ghost. Nevertheless he was nervous about telling Sheriff Edmonds what he had seen. "I came down here to check on the boats," he said. "All of a sudden the storm came up so I ran over and took cover in the boathouse."

"And did you see something out on the lake?"

"Well, there was a lot of lightning out there, and during this one flash, I thought I saw a boat, like a canoe or something, but then when the next flash came, the boat was gone again."

"Think hard David," said Edmonds, "do you remember anything else?"

"It looked like there was somebody standing up in the boat, but I'm not sure about that."

The sheriff looked curiously at David. "You know you should always report anything unusual, don't you? Didn't you think it was kind of strange that a boat was out there on a night like that?"

"Well, yeah, kinda," David replied reluctantly. He didn't want to tell the sheriff that the real reason he didn't think more of his sighting was that he'd been sure it was the ghost of Little Thunder. He looked over at his grandfather who stood waiting to see how the boy would answer.

"At first I thought I must be imagining things," David replied. "And when I moved closer it was gone. I thought my eyes were kinda playing tricks on me. I came down here with Grandpa the next morning, and he thought it was probably the raft I saw out there."

The sheriff looked over at Carl who nodded his head to confirm his grandson's version of the story. "Can you describe anything about the boat or anything else you saw that night, David?"

"It sort'a looked like a canoe floating around out there."

"Yeah, that sounds like Bobber all right. He had that old 15-footer with a motor mount he used to get around the lake. He was probably out fishing late and got caught when the storm came up. Could have been a lightning strike or maybe the canoe began to swamp. Don't know what possessed him to stand up though. He was strange but not stupid. Poor bastard."

"Sheriff Edmonds?" David hesitated. "Do you think..."

"What's the problem?"

"Well, if I'd gone out there, do you think I could have done anything to help?"

"Look, son, if it makes you feel any better, I doubt if there was anything anybody could'a done for poor old Bobber. If you'd gone out there after him, we'd be dragging two bodies out'a that lake and not just one. So don't blame yourself. It's not your fault - just one of those things."

***

When they returned to shore, Sheriff Edmonds used his police radio to call for an ambulance. About an hour later it arrived, and several deputies pulled the lifeless body of Bobber Lane from the lake and loaded him into the ambulance.

For the rest of the afternoon, sheriff's deputies patrolled in powerboats, criss-crossing the lake in ever narrowing patterns. Finally they found what they were looking for concealed in a tangle of lily pads about a half-mile downwind from the cabins. They towed the canoe to shore still containing Bobber's poles and fishing gear, just as he had left it on the night of the storm.

Spectators continued to gravitate to the shore on and off for the rest of the day, looking out on the waters of the lake as if Bobber's body was still concealed somewhere under the surface. They talked in hushed tones, speculating on why the eccentric old recluse had ventured out on such a wildly stormy night. TJ had long since gone back to his cabin to be with his family, and David watched the proceedings from the window of the cottage.

The events of the day replayed again and again in his mind. "We could have dragged two bodies from the lake," the sheriff had said. David thought how close those words were to the truth. If TJ hadn't come along at just the right time, he would have been down there with Bobber. He thought of the blank stare of the old man looking directly at him. How Bobber had seemed to reach out to grab him and pull him under.

For what seemed like hours David lay awake in his bed unable to sleep. Booms from the fireworks display across the lake at Falls Park echoed through the night. The darkness frightened him. The glare of bursting rockets lit up the night sky casting weird shadows just as lightening flashes had on the night of the storm. This was not the 4th of July he had expected.

Bobber seemed to be hiding in every shadow and corner of the room. David was afraid to go to sleep. He was afraid that the nightmares would come back - the storm and the monster in the lake - only this time he knew what the dream meant. And he knew it was no dream - it was real.

David quietly slid out of bed and tiptoed to the door. He turned the knob slowly and quietly so that he would not disturb his grandfather. He pushed the door open just a crack. The light from the hallway barely illuminated the still dim room. He crept back to bed and pulled the covers up to his neck.

The silhouette of the dream catcher was now visible, dangling above the bed in the dim light from the hallway. It twisted slowly casting shadows on the wall behind the bed. The dream catcher looked like a spider's web in the half-light. David stared at it, his eyes getting heavier until he finally drifted off to sleep.

# **Hoops**

Friday it rained all morning. David used the rain as an excuse to stay in bed, pulling the covers up over his head trying to shut out the daylight. Maddie's new dream catcher hadn't done him any good. He hadn't been able to sleep long enough to dream. Every time he closed his eyes, he saw the lifeless body of Bobber Lane staring back at him.

Carl had taken the day off to make sure that David had company after his experience the day before, but his presence did little to comfort the youth. He left his room only for breakfast, insisting that he was ok, but as soon as the meal was over, he returned to his room and locked himself in. He spent the remainder of the morning listening to his record player and sorting out his baseball cards.

It was midway through the morning when Carl called him through the bedroom door. "David come out., Your mother's on the phone. She wants to talk to you."

David hadn't had a chance to talk to his mother since her tearful departure from the lake to return to LaSalle.

"Sweetheart, are you all right?" Helen Bishop's voice crackled through the telephone receiver.

"Hi, Mom. I'm ok," David answered. "Did Grandpa tell you what happened?"

"I just can't believe it. You must have been terrified. It must have been quite a shock. Are you doing any better today?"

"I'll be just fine. But I really want to go home. When are you guys coming up?"

There was a hesitation at the other end of the line. David knew his mother was thinking up an excuse to delay a visit. "Oh, honey, I just don't know. There's so much going on here right now, and that drive takes a lot out of me. Maybe in a couple of weeks…"

David gazed outside. Rain was falling steadily, and the dreary mood of the day was reflected in the tone of the conversation. "Two weeks? How about dad? Can't he get up here to get me? I really need to see you guys."

"I don't know, David. You know how busy your father has been with work lately. But, I'll talk to him about it when I see him. Maybe he can get some time off, but I wouldn't be too hopeful if I were you."

"What do you mean, 'when you see him?' You'll see him tonight won't you?"

Again there was a pause on the line. "Sure, I will. But there's something you should know - I mean you're going to find out anyway. Your father has moved out of the house - at least temporarily. He's taken an apartment downtown - over the bank."

"You and dad are getting a divorce?"

"No, nothing's definite. We just decided it would be better if we separated for a while until we can work things out."

Things had suddenly gone from bad to worse. By the time the conversation ended and David hung up the phone, a climate of gloom pervaded the cottage. The rain continued throughout the morning, intensifying his already sour attitude.

Maddie had tried repeatedly to coax him out of his self-imposed exile, but all to no avail. "I'm too tired," he would reply.

When he returned from Iron Falls late that afternoon, Carl brought along the daily edition of the Iron Falls Herald. The headline read "Local Man Drowns in Spirit Lake." A picture of Bobber Lane accompanied the story. It looked like it had been enlarged from a snapshot of the old fisherman, dressed as he always was in a plaid shirt and overalls. Bobber's eyes looked kinder and gentler than David remembered them. A faint smile crossed his face. David stared at the photo, but saw no need to read the article.

***

It wasn't until the following morning that Carl began to worry. "David, why don't you come out and have some breakfast? Maddie has made your favorite, ham and eggs."

"I'm not feeling very well, Grandpa. Maybe later, ok."

Most of the time he spent reading. When he finally finished Stevenson's *Treasure Island* he began to look for something else to read. He pulled out the box of Golden Classics he had brought along from LaSalle. Rumaging through the box he found a copy of Twain's *Huckleberry Finn*. He began reading the first chapter, but quickly lost interest. The book was even worse than TJ had made it out to be.

Despite repeated attempts by Carl and Maddie to coax him out of his self-imposed exile, David remained secluded in his room.

By midday the rain had stopped and rays of sunshine began to peek through David's bedroom window. Just after noon, someone knocked softly at his door. "Go away," he called out. "I'm not feeling well."

"David?" Maddie's voice sounded concerned. "David? TJ's here. He came to see you. Can you open the door for a minute?"

"Hey Huck, are you in there?" TJ's voice beckoned through the closed door.

"What do you want?"

"I just stopped by to see how you were doing. Can I come in?"

"Yeah, I guess so. The door's open," David replied without any enthusiasm.

As TJ entered the room he glanced around. The room was a shambles. The bed remained unmade, dresser drawers stood open, clothes tossed carelessly on the floor, and books and records scattered everywhere.

"Did my grandfather put you up to this?" David asked.

"Well, to tell the truth," TJ confessed, "he said you were feeling kinda low and might like some company."

TJ picked up the stack of baseball cards David had sitting on his dresser, flipping through them. "Looks like you're a Tiger fan, huh?"

"Yeah, pretty much. I hear you're a Braves fan," replied David.

TJ looked somewhat surprised. "How'd you know that?" he asked.

"Your sister told me when we were cleaning up after the storm. Besides I saw you wearing a Milwaukee ball cap when you got here last Friday."

TJ put down the cards and picked up the book he saw lying open on the nightstand. "*Huck Finn*, huh?"

"Yeah, I just started it. I'm not sure I like it though. It's kinda hard to read."

"Twain meant it as a satire, but if you ask me, it isn't very funny. You gonna keep reading it?"

"Maybe. But right now I don't feel much like reading, or anything else for that matter."

"So what's your problem?" TJ asked David, obviously changing the subject. "Your Grandpa says you refuse to come out of your room. Still thinking about what happened down at the lake? I know the feeling. I'm still creeped out by that guy floating down there, and I'm not the one who found him." David smiled at the older boy's joke. "Is that what's bothering you?"

"Well, kinda," David answered reluctantly. "Look, seeing Mr. Lane's body down there was probably the scariest thing that's ever happened to me. But that's not what's really bothering me."

"No? Than what seems to be the problem?"

"I talked to my mom on the phone yesterday. I figured after what happened, she'd want to come up and get me, you know? But she said she can't make it for another week or two. She said my dad's moved out of the house. I think my parents are getting a divorce. They're being real jerks."

"Damn, that's real crap. So you're stuck up here, huh?"

"So what ya gonna do? You can't spend all you're time holed up in this room. The sun's out now. Why don't we head down to the lake."

"I don't think so. I just can't go back down there yet. I know it's stupid, but I just can't get over the feeling that there's something out there waiting for me. I know it's my imagination, but it seems so real."

"Ok, I'll tell you what, we won't go near the lake. Just come down as far as the boathouse. I saw a basketball hoop down there. We can grab my ball and go shoot some hoops. What do you say?"

"Hoops?" David responded blankly.

"Hoops. You know, basketball?" TJ said. "Why don't we go try it out. It's better than sitting here in the dark."

"I don't know..."

"Come on. It'll be fun. How 'bout it? Ya wanna come?"

"Naw," David replied. "I don't think so. Maybe tomorrow..."

"Look, you're parents are a couple of idiots, ok? You can't do anything about that. But you can't stay in you room forever. You're gonna hafta come out sooner or later. So let's go down and have some fun, huh?"

\*\*\*

David stood in the driveway just outside the boathouse facing his taller, stronger opponent as if he were the biblical David facing off against the Philistine Goliath. Except this time, instead of a sling, David held a basketball in his hands. He looked up. The rusted, netless basket clung tenuously to the building's siding several feet over his head.

He tried to dribble forward, but the still-wet gravel altered the ball's path, almost making him lose control. Seeing a slight opening, he drove for a lay-up, hoping to get the ball off before TJ could react. Too late. TJ had already covered the distance between them, and threw his hand up, blocking the shot and slapping it into the bushes several yards away.

Before David could recover, TJ had retrieved the ball and moved quickly toward the basket. He dribbled effortlessly past David, set his feet, and took a fade-away jump shot. His shot bounced off the boathouse siding, rolled around the rim of the basket twice, and then dropped through the center of the hoop for two points.

Score one for Goliath, David thought.

"That makes twenty-one," TJ said triumphantly. "Looks like I win again. How bout another game?"

"Are you kidding? That's three in a row. I can't keep up. Besides, you're a lot better than me. We could play all day and I still wouldn't win."

"Yeah, but you're getting better every game. Look, we don't hafta play twenty-one if you don't want. How 'bout a game of HORSE instead?"

"Naw, I'm about done in. You win. I quit." David tossed the ball back to TJ.

"TJ? TJ where are you?" Denise called out from the direction of the dock. "TJ, you out here?"

"Hey, Sis, over here, behind the boathouse."

Moments later Denise appeared coming around the corner of the building, followed closely by Angie Bradshaw. Seeing Angie, TJ immediately got up from his seat and moved to greet her. "Hey, Angie, what brings you over this way?"

As usual, Angie was dressed in a one-piece bathing suit, ready for the beach, a towel draped over her shoulders. She removed her sunglasses.

"My dad just told me about what happened yesterday. I'm really upset, about the body and everything? I just can't believe it. It must have been horrible. Weren't you scared?" she directed her comments almost exclusively to TJ, totally ignoring both David and Denise.

"Not really," TJ said with false modesty. "It wasn't so bad, was it David."

David didn't understand TJ's interest in Angie. And why did she keep hanging around TJ anyway. Didn't she already have a boyfriend?

"Listen, David and I were just finishing our warm-up. But we could use a little real competition. Anybody up for a game?"

"I don't know about Angie, but I could use some practice," Denise said. "My game's been getting a little rusty since school let out."

"How 'bout it Angie?" TJ persisted. "You up for a game?"

Although David could tell that Angie hated the idea, she pretended to be interested. "Sure, if you want to," she responded. "But I'm really not very good at basketball."

"That's ok. You'll do just fine," TJ told her. "You can be on my team, and Denise'll play with David, ok?"

The prospect of being on TJ's team seemed to brighten Angie's enthusiasm toward the game. "All right," she replied, "but don't expect too much."

"Great, then let's get started," he said. He tossed the ball to David and moved to join Angie on the other side of the basket.

\*\*\*

The ball arched high, just over TJ's outstretched hand, finding the center of the hoop. "Swish. Nice shot, little sis," TJ conceded. "Looks like you've been paying attention to those lessons I've been giving you."

Denise grinned broadly at her brother's compliment. "We're tied. Next basket wins. Your outs," she said handing the ball to her brother. "Come on David, guard Angie."

With Angie on TJ's team, and Denise playing with David, the competition was heated and the game remained close from the start. David's earlier one-on-one practice against TJ had done little to sharpen his basketball skills. He continued to miss easy shots on a regular basis. Fortunately for him, Denise proved to be a great partner with a fantastic outside jump shot. And even better, Angie proved to be an even worse player than David. She would often just pose on the sidelines and let TJ do all the work. Several times Denise had been able to steal the ball from Angie to make easy layups. And now the score was tied.

TJ took the ball back behind an out of bounds line he had drawn in the dirt. Denise guarded her brother tenaciously, waving her hands wildly in an attempt to confuse him. Seeing that Angie was open, TJ fired the ball inbounds to her, counting on her to return the ball to him once he broke free.

Angie grabbed the inbounds pass, but looked unsure of what to do next. Without thinking, David yelled out. "Over here, Angie. I'm open."

To the surprise of everyone in the game, including David, Angie obeyed, tossing the ball to her opponent. David caught the ball, but the unexpected pass caught him off guard. For a moment, he just stood there looking almost as confused as Angie.

"Shoot the ball, David," Denise yelled. "Go ahead, shoot!"

David could see TJ coming at him out of the corner of his eye. He had only seconds to act. Casually he dribbled the ball once, shifted the ball to his right hand, and made a perfect hook shot to score the winning basket.

"That's game, set, and match," called Denise triumphantly.

"Good game," conceded TJ, but his disappointment was evident on his face.

"I'm sorry, TJ," Angie murmured. "It's all my fault. I told you I wasn't very good."

"That's all right, Angie," TJ reassured her, "they were bound to win one sooner or later. We'll get 'em next game."

"Oh gee, TJ, I'd love to," purred Angie apologetically, "but I've got to go. My dad's expecting me."

"Oh, really?" TJ sounded disappointed. "Well, how 'bout a rematch tomorrow?"

"Sorry, TJ, but I can't make it then either," Angie said. "Tomorrow's Sunday. I'm meeting some friends in town after church. So I'll see you guys later next week," she said. "You'll still be around, won't you TJ?"

"Sure, we'll be here for another week. Maybe we can get together Monday."

"Sounds good. See you then," Angie replied as she turned to go. But she stopped after taking only a couple of steps. "Oh yeah, I almost forgot" she said. "My dad wanted me to invite you all to come over to our place for a grill-out next Tuesday. Dad said that with everything that happened, Mr. Lane drowning and all, nobody had a very good Fourth of July, so he said you and your families should all come over."

TJ seemed to brighten at the announcement. "Really?" he said.

"My dad'll be into it. He was really disappointed that we never got a chance to see the fireworks show in Iron Falls. But what's the occasion?"

"It's kind of a birthday party for me. I'll be sixteen," Angie answered. "Please come. The party was my dad's idea, and I want to be sure that there's at least someone there my own age."

"We'll be there," TJ answered. "In fact, I've got the perfect present in mind."

"No need for presents," Angie said. "Just come. That's all I want, ok?"

She smiled at TJ and turned to leave. Angie again turned away, starting off in the direction of the boat dock. She had gone only a short distance before Denise called after her. "Wait up. I'll walk with you. I'm on my way back to the house anyway."

TJ watched them leave then turned his attention back to David. "Hey, this was fun. I'm glad you decided to come out of your shell."

"Yeah, it was kinda fun, I guess." David replied.

"Look, Huck, I better be going too. Dad will be expecting me, but I'll see you tomorrow, ok?"

"Tomorrow?" David said confused.

"You know, church? Dad says your grandfather invited us to go with him. You're coming, right?"

"Well, I don't know. He didn't say anything to me about it... I usually go to church with my aunt and uncle..."

"Ah, come on. It's just this once. At least if you come there'll be someone there I know. Besides after we get back here, Dad says were gonna help you and your grandpa work on that boat of yours. What do you say?"

"All right, I'll go with you. Maybe then at least I won't have to eat dinner at my cousins' house," David smiled.

"Great, then I'll see you in the morning," TJ replied. The next moment he was gone.

TJ was almost back to the Gibson cabin before David noticed the basketball laying on the ground under the net. "Hey, TJ, your basketball..." he shouted.

"That's ok," TJ shouted back. "You hang onto it. I'll get it tomorrow."

"Thanks, TJ, I need the practice," David laughed.

## **Ghost Stories**

David had never been inside the Iron Falls Lutheran Church before. It was much smaller than the nearby Presbyterian Church - smaller and more intimate. The arrival of a Negro family in the company of Carl and his grandson turned more than a few heads in the congregation. Carl marched down the aisle to the front of the nave, seating himself and the rest of the group in the middle of one of the first rows of pews. "There, that will give them all something to talk about," he whispered to Nathan.

The Lutheran minister, a gaunt stern-faced man with a sharp nose and piercing eyes, couldn't help but notice the newcomers, glancing down nervously at the front pews throughout his sermon. The unwanted attention made David uncomfortable. He tried to slink down into his seat so that no one would notice him.

When it was over, Carl insisted on introducing Nathan and his family to the minister. "Reverend Simmons, I'd like you to meet an old friend of mine, Nathan Gibson and his family."

At first the minister seemed uncertain how to react, but he quickly recovered. "And how long are you folks going to be in town?" the minister asked tentatively.

"Oh, not long. Only for another week or so," Nathan Gibson answered.

Clearly relieved that his guests would not be staying longer, a sigh escaped the minister's lips. "Well it's always good to see new faces," he said without sincerity.

David and Carl left the church parking lot just ahead of the Gibsons, but by the time they arrived at the lake, the Cadillac was nowhere in sight. They waited almost an hour, sitting in the shade of the pavilion, but there continued to be no sign of the Gibsons. As he waited, David began to get restless.

"I wonder what's holding them up, Grandpa?" he said. "I thought they'd be here by now. TJ told me they planned to come right back to the lake. He said they'd be right down after they changed their clothes. Maybe they got lost."

"I'm sure they will be here soon," Carl replied. "They probably just made a stop on the way. But there is no need for us to wait. Why don't we get started, eh? Give me a hand getting the Barracuda out of the boathouse and I'll show you what Nathan and I have done the last few days."

Together David and Carl rolled the trailer containing the tarp covered Barracuda out of the boathouse into the bright July sunshine. Carl loosened the ties on the canvas cover and gave a sharp tug pulling the tarp away from the boat's hull.

David had not worked on the Chris Craft since before the discovery of Bobber Lane's body on Independence Day. The change in the boat's appearance was dramatic. Working together, Carl and Nathan had managed to fit and glue all the deck boards in place and add trim along the gunwales. For the first time, the craft was taking on the appearance of a finished power boat.

"Well, David, what do you think?" Carl probed.

"This looks great, Grandpa. You and Mr. Gibson did a great job," David said running his hand over the smooth newly sanded hull.

"I'm sure you would have done a better job David," Carl said, "but working with Nathan gave us a chance to get reacquainted."

"What's next, Grandpa?" David asked.

"I think we're ready to begin staining the deck boards. Why don't you get out the brushes and we'll get started."

David spread the ground tarp and was about to open up the can of stain when Nathan Gibson and TJ arrived at the boathouse.

"Sorry we're late," Nathan apologized. "We stopped at the Indian village over at Fall's County Park on the way back. Denise wanted to see the Indian cemetery so we took a look around."

"So, TJ, what did you think of our Ojibwa village, eh?" Carl asked.

"It's ok, I guess," TJ answered halfheartedly. "Denise is the one who really likes that kind of stuff. You should ask her about it."

"TJ's just a city boy at heart," Nathan explained. "The only Indian's he's interest in are the Braves back in Milwaukee."

"Aw, come on Dad, I never said that," TJ protested. "It's just that the idea of hunting for my food, cooking it over an open fire, and sleeping on the ground doesn't really appeal to me."

"No, you'd be lost without your television, record player, and telephone," Nathan laughed.

"I would not," TJ answered defiantly. "Heck, I'm a Scout. I earned my camping merit badge."

"And how many times have you been camping since then, huh? Do you really think that being in the Boy Scouts is the same thing as those Indians had to go through? You boys are lucky. You can't compare your life today with the life that they had back then, can you?"

"I don't know, I bet I'd have done just fine."

"All right, David?" Nathan said. "You've been awfully quiet. What do you think?"

"Me? I don't know, Mr. Gibson," David answered. "I mean I really love to hear the stories Maddie tells about how the Indians used to live on this land, but I don't know if I could have done it myself."

"I'm afraid David had a rather unpleasant experience after he first arrived here," Carl said. "He camped out in my old army surplus tent and sleeping bag. David, go ahead and tell the Gibsons what happened."

Though David was somewhat embarrassed that his grandfather had brought up his 'camping experience,' he was grateful that Carl had not mentioned the reason for the ill-fated adventure. "Well, I set up the pup tent behind the cottage, and everything was just fine until a storm came up. The tent started to leak, and my sleeping bag got soaked, so, well... I decided to head back to the house...."

"You see? That just proves my point," Nathan argued. "During the war we spent weeks out in the field sleeping in the worst conditions you could imagine and we never complained about it."

"Aw, come on dad, not another one of your old war stories."

"Hey, don't you lecture me about my war stories," Nathan told TJ good naturedly, smiling as though they had had this conversation before. "I'll bet you boys couldn't survive out here on your own for even one night."

"What'll you bet?" TJ challenged his father.

"All right," Nathan answered, "I've got five dollars that says you two can't last the night out here on your own."

"Five dollars? Apiece?" A skeptical look crossed TJ's face. "You're on. But what do you get if you win, Dad?"

"Oh, let's see, how about if I win you each have to do the dishes and all the chores around the house for the rest of the week."

"Just one night? Are you serious, Dad?"

Nathan laughed slightly. "Carl? What do you think? Can the boys borrow your camping equipment for the night?"

"I'll get it ready as soon as we are done here. It will do the boys good to see what it's like to live out in the wilds, even if it is for only one night."

"Good, then how about tonight? What do you boys say?"

"How 'bout it, David?" TJ asked. "Sounds like easy money to me."

"Well, I guess so - just as long as there's no rain in the forecast," David smiled.

"Good, then it's settled," Carl said. "Now, perhaps it's time to get busy on the Chris Craft, eh?"

*** 

"All right, Huck, how 'bout over here, under these branches?" TJ offered. "It's out of the wind and it's fairly level."

"Yeah, it'll do just fine," David replied with a note of bitterness in his voice. "I'll go get the tent bag."

"Hey, what's up, Huck? We've gotta get going if we want to win this bet. If my dad wins, he'll never let me live it down. So if you have a problem, now's the time to tell me."

"No, it's nothing. Just stop calling me Huck, that's all," David responded. "My name's David."

"Aw, come on, it's just a nickname," TJ smiled. "Didn't anybody ever call you anything but 'David?'"

"I don't get it. How come everybody thinks I need a nickname. My cousins call me 'Davy,' but I really hate that name. And this guy I met on the ferry at the Straits asked me about having a nickname too. But as far as I'm concerned the name David is just fine. What about you? TJ isn't a real name, they're just your initials, right?"

"My birth certificate says Thomas Jefferson Gibson. Pretty corny, huh? I have my sister to thank for the nickname. She started calling me TJ when she was just two, and the name just kinda stuck. Believe me when I think about being called Tom or Tommy, TJ seems like a great alternative."

"Well, at least it's better than 'Huck.'"

"Ok, David, if you insist," TJ said, "but you still seem like a Huck to me. Now give me a hand getting this tent set up."

David began pulling the tent poles out of the storage duffel bag. "Grab those stakes and help me set up the center post," he directed.

Together the boys laid down the ground cloth and within a short period they had the tent staked out and their bed rolls spread out under the canvas canopy.

"You get the fire going while I go up by our cabin and grab some dry logs," TJ said.

While TJ foraged for dry firewood, David cleared a spot downwind from the tent. He carefully arranged a pyramid of sticks and twigs around a wadded up piece of newspaper. When he finished, he used a kitchen match to ignite the pile. Within moments, flames were shooting up from the stacked kindling.

"Nice job," TJ said, rubbing his hands in front of the flames. "Now let's see what mom packed us for dinner." He looked into the picnic basket his mother had prepared. "Looks like dogs on a stick," he told David, pulling out a pack of Armor hot dogs along with buns, paper plates, and potato chips. "At least this way we don't have to worry about washing dishes," he joked.

David thought the hot dogs roasted over the open flames of the campfire were the best he'd ever tasted. He devoured the meal as if he hadn't eaten for days. "I'm stuffed," he managed at last. "I can't eat another bite."

"Yeah, me too," TJ agreed. "If we're done, let's get this mess cleaned up." He tossed the leftover food into a bag, tied the bag to a long rope, and then tossed the rope over a high tree limb. "There, that ought to keep the coons and skunks out of our stuff," he said.

The firelight flickered, occasionally flaring up. David threw another log into the fire and watched the sparks fly up from the embers, bathing the campsite in a warm, reassuring glow. He looked back in the direction of the Gibson cabin. The curtains on the window moved slightly. "I think your dad is watching us," he told TJ.

"Yeah, I know," TJ replied. "He's been sneaking peeks at us for the last hour." TJ picked up the stick he'd used to grill hot dogs and poked a stray log back into the burning coals with it. "I think he's worried I'm gonna catch the whole woods on fire."

David looked out toward the lake. A faint glimmer of oranges and purples still hugged the western horizon. The trees had become black silhouettes framing the deepening blue of the western sky.

***

"Ok, I cooked. Now it's your turn," TJ said. "Know any good

campfire stories?"

"Stories?"

"Yeah, like ghost stories - you know."

"Seriously? After what happened out there on the lake you feel like telling ghost stories? Not me. No way."

"Look, if there were any ghosts out there, they had their chance to get us yesterday, and we're both here to talk about it, right? So who's this Little Thunder guy you kept yellin' about out there? You owe me that much at least. What's his story anyway?"

"Little Thunder's not a story. He's real. Maddie told me. A lot of people have seen him," David explained, moving closer to the warmth of the fire.

"So, fill me in. What'd she tell you?"

"He was a leader of his people," David began, "until one night during a storm, he just disappeared." David relaxed as he talked, enjoying the chance to share the story of Little Thunder and the Anishinabe people. TJ listened with wrapped attention as David related the tale just as Maddie had told it to him.

"So this Little Thunder guy lived right here at the lake, huh?" TJ said when David had finished.

"Sure, he and his entire tribe. This whole area used to belong to the Ojibwa. They had a camp right over at the end of the lake where the park is now. Grandpa says he's found lots of arrow heads and stuff right here along the shore."

"So, do you think Little Thunder's still out there somewhere? Is that why you hung that web thing with feathers over the tent flap?"

"It's called a dream catcher. It helps keep bad dreams away."

"Bad dreams, huh? You mean like Little Thunder's ghost?"

"It's no joke. It really works. Ok, I've told my story. Now how 'bout you?"

"Let me think. You ever hear the story of the Plat-Eye?"

"Plat-Eye? You're kidding right?"

"Nope. The Plat-Eye is real. My grandmother told us the story when my sister and me were just little. The Plat-Eye is the undead spirit of someone who was murdered. And the thing is, a Plat-Eye can take the shape of just about anything. They have huge eyes that glow in the dark. 'Big as a plate and red as blood' - that's what my grandma said. She told us the story of her own run in with a Plat-Eye when she lived down in Georgia. She claimed that she was one of the few people who ever met a Plat-Eye and lived to tell about it.

"She said that she was walking home around dusk one evening, when she passed by a cypress grove near an old graveyard. Her mother told her not to go near the forest, but she went in anyway. In the middle of the forest she came across a cypress tree blocking her path. On top of the log sat a mean looking cat with fire in its eyes. But it was no ordinary cat. The cat had six legs like a spider, and fangs that glowed in the dark.

"She tried to walk around it, but the cat moved to block her way, only now it had turned into a fox with claws five inches long. She backed away, but the Plat-Eye changed again, this time turning into a wolf with silver fur and venom dripping from its mouth. The wolf crouched down and was just about to leap at her throat.

"First, she picked up a broken branch from a tree, and began to hit the Plat-Eye as hard as she could. But the monster kept on coming. So she turned around and ran as fast as she could in the opposite direction, but that old Plat-Eye was right on her heals. She heard a roar, and when she looked back, the Plat-Eye had transformed into the most gigantic, ferocious bear she'd ever seen."

The mention of a bear brought a brief moment of fear to David's eyes. He remembered how frightened he had been when he thought Kenny was being attacked. And how Kenny's friends had laughed at him after he'd run from the 'bear' at the dump. "What'd your grandma do?" he said, "Did she get away?"

"Well, that bear reared up onto its hind legs and ran after her like a man. Just as the beast was about to catch her, she turned around to face the charging creature. She stood up and looked straight into that damned old bears eyes, never once showing how afraid she was."

"And then what happened?"

"That bear just stopped in its tracks, bellowed out a roar that could have been heard in the next county, and lumbered off, never to be seen again."

"Do you think that really happened, TJ?"

"I never knew my grandma to tell a lie. Besides, she gave both my sister and me something to make sure we never get caught by a Plat-Eye. She told us a Plat-Eye can't stand foul odors, and so she made my sister and me special pouches to ward against Plat-Eyes." TJ pulled a small burlap sack out of his pocket and showed it to David.

David took the pouch from TJ and held it to his nose. "Whew, this thing really stinks!"

"See I told you."

"What's in it anyway?"

"Grandma told me it's a mixture of gun-powder and sulfur."

"You mean you actually carry it around with you? You don't really believe it keeps away bad spirits, do you?"

"Well, no, not really, but it's one of the only things I have that my grandmother gave me."

"Like Maddie made me the dream catcher?"

"Sounds like between my pouch and your dream catcher, nothing's gonna get us out here. Besides, it's getting late. We'd better turn in. Help me get this fire out. If my dad sees it still burning, he'll come out to see what's wrong."

After the fire was extinguished, TJ held a flashlight as he and David crawled into the tight confines of their musty tent. "Not much room in here," David said, squeezing into his army surplus sleeping bag. The ground felt hard, but tolerable under a thick bed of leaves.

Once they were settled, David threw open the tent flaps allowing the cool night air to flow in. The stars flickered in and out between the leaves of the maple tree overhead. "TJ? I read some more of that book, you know, *Huckleberry Finn*."

"Yeah, what do you think?"

"You didn't tell me that Jim was a slave."

"Most Negroes were slaves back then. He was a slave. If they'd caught him they'd have sent him back in chains or worse. That's what they did with my great Grandpa."

"Your great grandfather was a slave?"

"And my great grandma too - down in Georgia. My Grandpa tried to escape, but they tracked him down, caught him and whipped him. That's what my mom told me anyway."

"TJ," David proceeded cautioously. "Did anyone ever call you a... Well, you know. The name Huck called Jim in the book?"

"The 'n' word you mean? Yup, and I suspect every Negro boy my age has heard it at least once. I just hope Denise never has to deal with that kind'a crap."

"I would never say anything like that."

"Maybe not. But a lot of folks still think of us that way."

There was a long silence in the darkness of the tent before TJ answered. "No," he said at last. "It's not the same now. Now, go to sleep will ya?"

Neither one of them talked after that. The tent was still except for the sound of crickets chirping outside and TJ's slow even breathing. It took a long time for both boys to get to sleep.

## Bobber's Cabin

TJ was up and out of the tent early the next morning. He had already begun to clean up the camp site when David finally emerged out of his sleeping bag and staggered sleepily out of the tent into the bright morning light.

"What's your problem?" TJ complained. "You were tossin and turnin all night long."

"I couldn't sleep," David said, rubbing his eyes. "Maybe it wasn't such a good idea telling ghost stories before we turned in last night."

"You mean that dream catcher of yours didn't help you sleep."

"Not much. I just can't get over finding that body down there."

"So that's what's bothering you, huh?" he said. "I thought it might be something like that. To tell the truth, I didn't sleep very well either."

"It's not the same," David replied defensively. "You didn't look straight into his cold dead eyes. And you didn't feel his hand reach out to grab you."

"Look, that old man's dead, and that's terrible. But he's gone now, so there's no way he can do anything to us anymore. Once his funeral is over that'll be the end of it."

"I know, but it still gives me the creeps just to think about it."

"Well there must be something we can do to put him to rest once and for all. Listen, I've got an idea. Bobber's cabin isn't far away from here, right?"

"Yeah, not too far. Maybe a mile or so."

"And he lived alone, right?"

"Sure. As far as I know. Why do you ask?"

"Ok, so his place is empty now. Let's go over there and take a look."

"Why would you want to do that? There's nothing to see over there. Grandpa said that the sheriff went and locked everything up."

"Right. That's just the point. There's nothing there," TJ said putting his arm around David's shoulder. "It'll prove once and for all that Bobber's gone for good. Everybody's going to be in town at the funeral, right? So who's gonna stop us."

David remembered visiting Bobber's cabin the day his grandfather drove Bobber home from Ike's Market. There hadn't been much at the cabin. Just some fishing gear, the worm farm, and Bobber's cat, Captain. "Wow, I almost forgot about Captain," David exclaimed out loud. "He's all alone over there."

"Captain? Who the hell's Captain?" TJ asked.

"The old man's cat. He's all alone now. He'll starve unless somebody brings him food."

"Well, sounds like we'd better take care of that, huh? What do you say?"

"Ok," he told TJ, "I'm game. But before we leave there's something I've got to get from the cottage."

TJ followed David to the cottage and waited by the back door as David went inside. In a few moments David returned carrying a can of tuna fish and a can opener. "This ought to do it," he said. "Let's go."

\*\*\*

They walked up the drive toward the main road until David spotted a trail leading off into the forest. "Grandpa showed me this path through the woods," he said. "It's a shortcut to Bobber's cabin. Come on, follow me."

Lady ran ahead of the two boys along the path, stopping occasionally to make sure they were still following close behind her.

"Where the hell is this place anyway?" TJ asked after they had walked about three quarters of a mile.

"I don't think it's too much farther," David replied.

TJ continued to follow David along the overgrown path, stumbling over exposed roots, climbing over fallen tree branches, and being drawn deeper and deeper into the dense forest.

"Jesus, if you got lost back here, nobody'd ever find you," TJ grumbled, brushing a tangled vine away from his face. David and TJ continued through the undergrowth, emerging onto the road leading up to Bobber's cabin. As they stepped out of the shadows of the forest, suddenly the birds ceased singing, and the air became still. TJ stopped short, holding out his arm to hold David back. "You hear that?" he asked.

"I don't hear anything," David replied.

"Exactly," TJ agreed. "Everything got quiet as soon as we walked out of the woods."

"The birds probably took one look at you and flew away," David quipped sarcastically. "You're the one who wanted to come here in the first place, so come on, let's take a look around."

David pushed past TJ, following the split rail fence along the drive to the cabin. The cabin looked empty, but not deserted. A fresh set of tire tracks marked a path in the dust. He continued on toward the porch. A large "No Trespassing" notice had been hung on the cabin door by the Falls County Sheriff's Department. "Grandpa was right, the sheriff's been here already," he observed.

A new hasp and padlock had been installed on the door, barring entry. "Guess they don't want us around," TJ said, moving cautiously toward the cabin. A sudden chill enveloped the forest, filling him with a sense of foreboding. "Look, I know I said we should come, but now I'm not so sure," he cautioned.

"You still got that pouch filled with gun-powder and sulfur your grandma gave you?"

"Yeah, but I'm not sure it covers places like this."

"Sure it does. Come on. Everything's going to be all right," David answered.

He walked around to the side of the cabin and tried looking through the window. The window pane was covered with a cloudy layer of dust and dirt. David pulled his tee shirt out of his pants and used it to wipe a small circle of glass clean. His shirt tail was now covered with soot. Maddie wouldn't be happy.

He peered into the cleared circle of glass, shading his eyes with his right hand to block the reflected glare of the sun. As his eyes adjusted to the dim light, he began to make out pieces of the interior - dishes piled in the sink, canned goods stacked on the shelves. The bed had been left unmade, and a book lay open on a small nightstand as if awaiting the owner's return.

A small creature jumped from the porch, darting for cover behind a stack of firewood. Involuntarily TJ jumped back. "What the hell was that?"

"Relax, TJ, it's probably only Bobber's cat. He must be starved by now. It's been almost five days since Bobber's boat capsized. Here kitty, kitty. Come here boy."

The wind picked up suddenly, ruffling the leaves in the trees, creating a low moaning sound from the surrounding woods. A wind chime hanging from the branch of a nearby pine began to clang eerily in the breeze. TJ thought he saw a movement in the shadows at the corner of the deserted cabin. A chill ran down his spine.

"Look, I might have been wrong about coming over here," he said. "I'm not superstitious or anything, but I *am* cautious. And something's not right about this place. Let's just go, ok? That cat's not comin' out, and I'm getting hungry. If we leave now, maybe I can get my mom to fix us some lunch."

"Thanks, but I'm not hungry. And Captain's around here somewhere. He'll come out if he smells the tuna I brought."

"Ok, just leave him the food and let's get going."

"No, you can leave if you want to, but I'm gonna stay here till I find Captain," David replied. "If you're worried about me, Lady'll stay here with me. She won't let anything happen." David looked down at the dog by his feet. "Will you girl?"

"You sure you know what you're doing? I can wait if you want."

"Naw, I'll be fine, really" David replied. "See you back at the cabins."

David watched as TJ started back down the path. "Come on, Lady," he called. "Let's find Captain." Lady ran ahead, barking toward the back of the shack.

***

"Lady, quiet," David commanded. "You'll scare Captain away if you keep barking like that." The dog quieted down as if understanding the boy's order. "Here Captain. Here kitty, kitty, kitty," David called out softly.

He began circling the cabin, stopping every few feet to listen for the cat, but heard nothing. "I've got some food for you - it's tuna fish," he called. "Here kitty, kitty." David stopped again to listen. This time he thought he heard a faint but distinct purring coming from somewhere beneath the cabin.

Lady ran up to the crawl space and began to growl fiercely. "Lady, Lady, come here girl," David commanded. The dog obediently backed away and returned to the boy's side. "Lay down and stay," he directed. Lady lay down on the road putting her head on her paws.

David knelt down on the ground beside the log cabin wall and peered into the darkness of the crawl space. At first he saw nothing, but as his eyes adjusted to the dim light, he could just make out two eyes glowing in the reflected light.

"Come on, kitty, I won't hurt you." He held out the can of tuna.

"See I've got food for you." But rather than coming to David, the frightened animal turned and scampered off in the other direction, exiting the crawl space at the rear of the cabin.

David quickly moved in the direction the cat had gone. As he rounded the corner, he saw the cat scurry behind a small tool shed. He ran after the cat hoping that the animal would not dart into the woods, where he would no longer be able to find him.

Suddenly, as he arrived at the shed, David stopped short. There, sitting on the stump of a tree, and looking very much alive, was Bobber Lane himself, dressed in the same plaid shirt and overalls he had been wearing when they pulled him from the lake. Lady must have seen it too, for she gave out a frightened yelp and ran back to the protection of the porch to hide.

"What are you doing on my property?" demanded the old man on the stump. "You're trespassing. This is private land."

David stood frozen with fear, unable to move, as if his feet had become planted in the dusty brown dirt. "I'm sorry," he managed to stammer. "We didn't know anybody was here. My friend and I just came to feed Captain." David reached into his pocket and pulled out the can of tuna fish.

"You brought food for Captain, eh?" some of the gruffness went out of the ghostly figure's voice. Bobber reached down and began to stroke the long fine hair on the tabby's back. Unafraid, the cat jumped up onto the tree stump and nestled down into Bobber's lap. The cat began to purr almost at once. "That's mighty thoughtful of you. He's had to forage for himself the last few days, and frankly, he's not the hunter he used to be."

David started to back away from the pallid, ghostly specter.

"Don't rush off," the apparition called out. "Have a seat." Bobber motioned David toward a plank bench near the dock. "Your friend skedaddled out of here in a hurry. Sorry. I didn't mean to spook him. But you don't have to be afraid. I won't bite."

"I'm not afraid..., exactly," David replied, taking a seat on the bench. "It's just that... I don't understand, you're, you're..."

"Dead?" the figure on the stump finished his sentence. "So I am. So I am. And I can't say I like it very much either."

"But, if you're dead, what're you doing here?"

"Yeah, that one's got me puzzled too. Last thing I remember was trying like hell to get back to shore when that damned storm blew up.

My motor cut out and I was left floatin' out there like a sitting duck. Guess I never made it back."

"Uh-uh. I'm the one who found you. The sheriff thinks you fell in and drown during the storm."

"Well, I hope you weren't too disappointed."

"Disappointed?"

"You thought somebody else was caught in that storm, didn't you?"

"You mean Little Thunder? Yeah, kind of. When the lightening flashed, I thought I saw him. I didn't know it was you."

"So instead of an Indian legend, you get stuck with an old codger who lives out in the woods with his cat. Hope you aren't too disappointed."

"I don't know what to think. I mean I never expected to see a real ghost. You are real, aren't you?" David asked confused.

"Why, now that you mention it, I don't really know. I've never been a ghost before - never even seen one that I can recall," the old man replied. "Do I look like a ghost to you?"

"Not really, you look - well normal."

"Normal, huh? Then maybe I'm not a ghost. But, there's another possibility. I might not be here at all. I mean you could be just imagining all of this."

"My grandfather says ghosts aren't real."

"And you? Do you believe in ghosts?"

"I don't know. You're the first one I ever met."

Suddenly Captain jumped up out of Bobber Lane's lap and moved over to David's side, nuzzling against his leg. "Looks like Captain's getting hungry," the ghost laughed. "There's a bowl over there under the back steps."

David went to the porch and found the bowl just where Bobber said it would be. He took the opener and cranked the lid off the can, dumping the fish into the bowl. The cat smelled the juice from the tuna, purring happily and wandering back and forth between David's legs, rubbing against him on each pass. As soon as David placed the food on the porch, Captain sprang to the bowl, greedily devouring the contents.

"Boy, Captain sure must have been starved," David said as he turned back toward the stump. But when he looked around, Bobber was gone.

***

"Mr. Lane's funeral was quite moving, David," Carl said as he sat at the dinner table across from his grandson. "Several people asked about you. That was nice of them, ya?"

David sat uncomfortably at the table. He couldn't tell his grandfather about what had happened at Bobber's cabin. David wasn't even sure he believed it himself. What could he say? That he had seen a ghost? His grandfather would tell him he was just imagining things.

This time he couldn't even tell Maddie about what had happened. She knew about dreams and the spirits of her ancestors. But this was different. This was the ghost of an addled old white man.

"So what did you and TJ do while Maddie and I were gone, eh?" Carl asked.

"Nothing really," David said trying to sound nonchalant. "We just played a little basketball. That's all."

Carl looked unconvinced. "I talked to Nathan. He said that you and TJ went over to Mr. Lane's cabin this afternoon. Are you sure there's nothing you want to tell me?"

"Nothing happened. I just took some tuna fish over for Mr. Lane's cat, that's all. I don't think anyone's been feeding him."

"Ah, so you have been feeding him our tuna fish, eh?" Carl laughed, sounding somewhat relieved. "Well if you are worried about Captain, why don't we go get him and bring him over here? I'm sure Captain and Lady will learn to get along, ya?"

"I don't think so, Grandpa. Lady scared Captain away with her barking. I tried to pick him up, but he ran and hid when I got close." Though David had no desire to return to Bobber's cabin, he needed to know if what he had seen there was real. "Maybe I should go over tomorrow and make sure he's all right," he said.

Carl thought for a moment. "Well, I suppose it won't do any harm if you take care of Bobber's cat, at least for the time being, eh? But no more tuna fish. Tomorrow I'll pick up some cat food in town. And next time, let me know before you go. I wouldn't want anything to happen to you over there."

*Neither would I*, thought David. *Neither would I.*

## Angie's Party

"David, hurry and get ready," Carl urged. "It's almost time for Angie's party and you're still wearing your work clothes. Where have you been anyway?"

"I just stopped over at Mr. Lane's cabin," David replied.

"Weren't you just there this morning?" Carl asked somewhat surprised. "That's twice in one day."

Actually it had been David's third trip to the cabin looking for some sign of Bobber Lane - or his ghost. But his visits had produced no evidence of anything out of the ordinary. No ghosts, spirits, apparitions, or otherworldly beings. Only a lonely, hungry cat. Though David was relieved, he had also been slightly disappointed. If Bobber's ghost wasn't real, then perhaps Little Thunder was just a myth as well.

In any event, David didn't see any reason to mention any of this to his grandfather. "I just wanted to make sure Captain was ok," he replied.

"Well, hurry up and change. We've got to get going," Carl said. "Nathan will be here any minute to pick us up."

"If it's all right with you, I think I'll skip the party, Grandpa. I still don't feel much like celebrating."

"Nonsense! The party will do you good. You've hardly done anything since you discovered poor Robert. I can understand why you did not attend his funeral, but this is different. It should be fun, ya? Now, don't argue. Go get ready. We don't want to be late."

By the time David changed into a clean shirt and shorts, Nathan Gibson had pulled his Cadillac up in front of the cottage, honking to signal his arrival.

"Climb in," Nathan told Carl. "You can ride up front with me. Lillian's not feeling well, so she's staying at the cabin. David, you ride in back with Denise and TJ." David slid into the backseat, squeezing in next to Denise, pulling back slightly when his leg accidentally rubbed up against hers.

The drive to the Bradshaw home took only a few minutes along the dusty back roads. Nathan parked the Cadillac in the driveway right behind Jacob Bradshaw's black Lincoln. Bradshaw's house was a large rambling split-level home constructed in three tiers, like layers on a cake. Carl led the group around the side of the house to a huge stone patio facing the lake.

In the midst of the patio, Jacob Bradshaw stood behind a huge stainless steel barbecue grill sporting an apron announcing "*Genius at Work.*"

"Welcome, welcome," he enthused. "I'm glad you all could come."

"It was kind of you to invite us," Carl replied.

"Well, it's the least I could do considering..." He let the sentence trail off unfinished.

"Quite a spread you've got here," Nathan said, extending his hand toward Bradshaw.

Bradshaw grasped the other man's hand, shaking it vigorously. "We like it here," he replied proudly. "I was just firing up the charcoal. Hope you like steaks. Why don't you gentlemen grab a cold one out of the cooler over there and join me?"

"Where's the birthday girl, Jacob?" Carl asked.

"I think she went down by the boat dock. She's not real happy with me right now. I told her she couldn't invite her friends over for the party, so she's pretty upset. Why don't you kids go down and see if you can round her up, eh?"

David followed TJ and Denise down the hill to the lake shore. Angie was sitting at the end of the dock, her feet dangling in the cool clear water.

"Hey, Angie, what's up?" TJ greeted.

Angie got up and went directly over to him, almost completely ignoring Denise and David. "Hey, TJ, how ya doin'? Guess my dad told you I was down here, huh?"

"Yeah, he said you weren't too happy. So what's going on?"

"I invited some friends from school over, but my dad said no."

David scowled. He knew that one of the uninvited guests must have been Terry.

"You'd think it was dad's birthday, not mine," Angie added.

"Why doesn't he want them to come?" TJ asked.

"He just doesn't like them," she replied.

"Hey, guys," they heard Bradshaw call down from the patio above. "Dinner's on. Time to eat."

"My master's voice," Angie smirked sarcastically. "He's such a jerk," she muttered as she started back up the hill.

\*\*\*

"Happy birthday to you, happy birthday to you," the chorus sang in unison as Bradshaw brought in the lighted birthday cake. Sixteen candles circled the words '*Sweet Sixteen*' carefully scripted in icing across the frosted top.

After filling his guests up on steak, potato salad, corn on the cob, and baked beans, Jacob Bradshaw had moved the party indoors, to the air-conditioned comfort of his recreation room. "This used to be my basement," he explained, "but I had it converted into a playroom."

*Playroom's an understatement*, thought David. Game tables, Green Bay Packers memorabilia, and assorted big boy toys filled the cedar-paneled room. David noted a regulation pool table, a pinball machine, a wet bar, and a player piano among Bradshaw's toys.

"Ok, darling, make a wish and blow out your candles," Bradshaw said setting the Sweet Sixteen birthday cake in front of Angie.

Angie looked embarrassed. "Dad, I'm not a little girl any more."

"But you're still *my* little girl," he replied. "Now blow out the candles. You've got presents to open."

She looked down on the three-layer cake adorned with flowers formed of frosting, took a deep breath and blew.

"Ok now, everybody grab a piece of cake and some ice cream, and we'll get down to opening presents," Bradshaw ordered.

Angie opened the gift from Carl and David first. The box held a Yardley English Lavender gift set that Maddie had picked out. "Thanks, Mr. Wertz," Angie said without enthusiasm. She quickly set the perfume and scented soap aside and went on to the next package.

TJ handed her a flat, square package about twelve inches on a side. "It's an album," he confided. "Hope you don't have it already."

Angie unwrapped the gift. The album, *Here's Little Richard*, sported a picture of the pompadour coiffured singer shouting out one of his songs on the cover.

"I just love R&B music," Angie said. "Little Richard is *so* much better than Elvis." She took a moment to read the album cover. The list of songs included *Tutti Frutti* and *Long Tall Sally*. "It's perfect. Can we play it, dad?"

"All right, but not too loud, ok?"

Angie led TJ over to the entertainment center and put the new album on the hi-fi. "*A wop bop a loo bop a lop bam boom! Tutti Frutti, oh,*

*Rudy...*" Little Richard belted out the opening verse of the first cut on the record. Carl gave a startled look and backed away from the speaker cabinet.

"All right, Angie," Bradshaw said loudly enough to be heard over the music," turn down the hi-fi and get back over here. You've still got one more present to open."

"Is this from you, dad? It doesn't look like a new car to me," she joked.

"Maybe next year," laughed Bradshaw. "Go ahead open it."

Carefully she removed a layer of tissue paper revealing a small leather jewelry box embossed with gold leaf filigree. As she lifted the latch to open the lid, a tiny ballerina popped up and began to turn on her pedestal to the strains of Swan Lake. Angie reached into the box and removed a small pendant hanging from a thin gold chain. The pendant had a large diamond solitaire surrounded by a circle of smaller stones.

"It's your mother's diamond brooch," Bradshaw said. "I had it remounted as a necklace. Your mother always wanted you to have it when you turned sixteen. She would have been so proud. It's called a ballerina setting - you know, shaped like a ballerina's tutu."

David thought he saw Angie's hardness soften momentarily. "Gee, Dad, I don't know what to say. It's really beautiful."

"Here let me help you put it on." Bradshaw walked in back of his daughter and fastened the clasp around her neck.

"Are those diamonds real?" Denise reached out to touch the large center stone as it hung around Angie's neck.

"Sure are," Bradshaw replied. "Center stone's almost two carets. Set me back a pretty penny when I got it for Angie's mom. Really sparkles in the light, doesn't it?"

Angie crossed the room and removed an old photograph from the top of the piano. "It's the same broach mom was wearing in this picture." She handed the photo to Denise. "It's mom and me at my first dance recital."

Denise took the photo and examined it closely. The picture showed Angie dressed as a ballerina standing next to an attractive woman in her late thirties. The woman was elegantly dressed, as if she were attending a Broadway opening. There was no doubt that the two were related. "This is your mom?" Denise asked.

Angie nodded. "It was taken just a few months before she died."

"I didn't know you could dance," TJ said, taking the picture from his sister.

"Yeah, I've taken lessons since I was five. Dad still takes me every Saturday, but it's not the same as when mom was alive."

"She looks so young and beautiful," Denise said.

"She died a couple of years ago." Angie's voice trailed off. For a moment, she looked as if she might cry.

"Angie and her mom were pretty close," Bradshaw said, putting one arm around his daughter's shoulder. "She took her mom's death hard." He was about to continue when the phone rang.

The ringing phone jarred Angie out of her melancholy. "I'll get it," she called as she ran to the counter, lifting the receiver to her ear. "It's for me," she said. "I'll take it in the kitchen."

"Five minutes, and no more! You understand me, young lady?" Bradshaw said.

Angie nodded as she darted up the stairs and disappeared from sight.

*** 

"She'll be gone for a while, if I know my girl," Bradshaw said as soon as Angie had departed. "When Angie gets on the phone you can't drag her away." He walked over to the bar and removed a small tin canister from the counter. He reached inside, and pulled something out.

"While we wait, why don't we pass the time with a little friendly competition, eh?" he said. "TJ, your dad tells me you're quite a pool player, is that right?"

"I'm not too bad, I guess," TJ replied modestly.

Bradshaw held out a ten-dollar bill. "I've got a ten spot here that says Carl and I can take you and your dad in a friendly game of eight-ball," he said. "What about it?"

"Well, I'm not sure, Mr. Bradshaw..."

"How about you, Nathan?" Bradshaw removed a stick from the wall rack and rolled the cue ball across the table in Nathan's direction. "You up for a game?"

"Why not," Nathan answered. He reached into his back pocket and pulled out his wallet. "Ten bucks, huh? I'll take that bet. I haven't played in ages."

"That's the spirit," Bradshaw said, taking Gibson's money. "And just to keep things on the up and up, let's let David here hold the wager. Agreed?"

David took the money and sat down on a nearby bar stool to watch. As Nathan chalked up his cue, Carl and TJ lagged for break. TJ's shot rolled within an inch of the rail. "Your break," Bradshaw told him.

TJ lined up his shot carefully, suddenly feeling the pressure of money riding on his accuracy. The cue ball careened into the pyramid of balls at the other end of the table, sending one of the striped balls into the corner pocket. TJ followed his break by banking in two more balls in rapid succession.

"Looks like we've been hustled, Carl," Bradshaw said good naturedly.

The father, son duo continued their methodical play, keeping Carl and Jacob Bradshaw on the sidelines, until only a few balls remained on the table. Nathan completed the victory by nudging the eight ball into the corner pocket.

"Ok," Bradshaw said. "We concede. You win. Go ahead, David, pay the man."

David handed Nathan the twenty dollars he had been holding just as Angie reentered the room. She had changed into Capris and a sleeveless blouse. Her necklace was gone. "What's going on?" she asked.

"Just settling a friendly wager," Bradshaw told his daughter. "What about you? Why the change of clothes?"

"I'm going out," Angie stated casually. "My friends are coming from town to pick me up."

Bradshaw looked at his daughter in surprise. "Is that so? I don't remember saying you could go anywhere."

"But I told them I'd be ready..."

"You should have thought of that before you agreed to go with them. We've got company. They came to celebrate your birthday. The least you can do is be a gracious hostess."

"But I want to see my friends," she stated stubbornly. "They're probably on their way here now…"

"I'm sorry, Angie, you're not going anywhere until I say so, and that's final. Now go call your friends back and tell them you can't leave."

"You fucker," Angie screamed. The word hung in the air like a bomb waiting to go off. David looked over at his grandfather and Nathan. They both stood frozen in place.

Then the bomb exploded. "That's it," shouted Bradshaw. "You're not going anywhere. Go to your room right now. I'll deal with you later."

Angie burst out of the room, crashing into David and sending him tumbling off the bar stool where he'd been sitting. The soda he was drinking went flying into the air. An icy shower of Hires Root Beer rained down all over David and the chair.

"I'm so sorry," Bradshaw called out, racing to get a bar towel from the counter. "I don't know what's come over that girl," he said, handing the towel to David. "Why don't you go clean yourself up? The bathroom's upstairs, through the living room, third door down the hall to the right."

***

Following Bradshaw's instructions, David climbed the twisting staircase to the living room. Like the recreation room beneath it, picture windows facing the lake lined the living area. Opposite the windows, an immense built-in flagstone fireplace sat idle in the summer heat. A circular white shag rug stretched out in front of the fireplace, covering the solid ebony hardwood floors. In the midst of the rug, a glass-topped coffee table sat before a red mohair sofa with matching end chairs.

David made his way quickly through the living room and down the hall toward the bathroom. At the end of the hallway he could see a door standing partially open. David approached cautiously. Standing just outside the door, he could hear Angie crying quietly inside. He pushed the door open slightly to peek into the room.

The walls were pale pink, bordered with white roses. Lamps, picture frames, and figurines all in pastel colors cluttered the room. Soft, sheer white curtains tied back with silk roses framed the windows. A full-length cheval mirror stood in one corner. An elaborate canopy bed stood unmade, half covered by a lacy pink coverlet. At the foot of the bed, a small cedar hope chest stood open, it's lid resting against the footboard of the bed.

Angie sat at her vanity, her back to him, oblivious to his presence. The jewelry box her father had given her sat open before her on the vanity. She appeared to be writing something, but from where he stood, David couldn't see what it was.

"You ok?" he called out softly.

Angie jumped back, startled, attempting to cover whatever she had been writing. "What're you doing in here?" she said. "You little snoop. Get out before I scream!" Quickly she closed the lid on the jewelry box and then pushed it away.

"I... I'm sorry," David stammered. "I was just looking for the bathroom. Your dad said it was at the end of the hall..."

"Does this look like a bathroom?" she sobbed angrily.

David glanced around. "No... I just thought," he fumbled.

She moved to the bed, pulling the frilly coverlet down to completely cover the mattress, then pushed the lid of the cedar chest closed with her hand. "The bathroom's across the hall, you moron. Get out of here. You're dripping all over the rug."

Embarrassed, David left quickly, making his way rapidly down the hall to the bathroom.

David washed his hands and face, then tried to rinse the root beer stain out of his shirt as well as he could. He made his way back through the hallway. Angie's door was closed.

By the time David returned to the recreation room, Carl and Nathan were gathering their things, preparing to leave.

"Please don't go yet," Bradshaw pleaded. "I'm sure Angie will be back once she cools down."

"Don't worry about it, Jacob," Carl replied. "We should be going anyway. I'm sure Nathan wants to check on Lillian, and I have some things to attend to back at the cabins. But I want to thank you again for having us over. It's been a real pleasure."

"Well, thanks for coming. I just want to apologize again. Angie's been a different person since her mother died. Sometimes I just don't know what to do about her."

"It's just part of growing up, Jacob," Carl reassured. "It's fine, really. We'll talk later. Please say good night to Angie for us."

"Nathan, we'll have to do a little fishing before you head back to Milwaukee, eh?" Jacob said.

As they walked toward the car, TJ and David lagged behind. TJ suddenly stopped short, searching the pockets of his Bermuda shorts. "Damn, I must have left them in the house."

"What's wrong?" David asked.

"My sunglasses. I think I must have left them in the rec room. Look, tell my dad not to wait. I'll walk back to the cabin after I get my glasses."

"You're going to walk? It must be close to two miles along the road."

"Don't worry about me. I'll be ok. Just go ahead. I won't be long."

"You're going back to see Angie, aren't you? Don't bother. She won't talk to you."

"Let me worry about that," TJ replied. "See you back at the cabins, Huck."

## The Attack

Ernie's Diner was almost empty as TJ and David entered. It was the evening after Angie's birthday party. Carl and Nathan had just dropped the boys off at Ernie's on their way to the Upholstery Shop. Carl had been hoping for an opportunity to show Nathan around his shop since the Gibsons first arrived in Iron Falls. Now with only a few days left in Nathan's visit, time was running out.

As TJ and David walked past the counter, David glanced up at the clock on the wall over the soda fountain. It was almost eight. Nathan had told the boys to be ready to leave by nine. *An hour. That should be plenty of time to grab a burger and a malt*, thought David.

A single customer sat at a stool behind the soda bar taking a last sip from his coffee. The man threw fifteen cents onto the counter, and got up from his seat. "See you tomorrow," he said, giving a curt wave to the attendant as he left. The attendant took the money, rang up the purchase, and flipped the coins into the cash register.

David led TJ to a booth in the corner of the diner, sat down, and tried to get the counter boy's attention. The attendant took his time, pulling a cigarette out of the pack he kept in his shirt pocket and lighting it up before ambling over to their table. The attendant wore the standard soda jerk uniform - a grease spattered bib apron and white diner cap pulled back on his head. He took a big drag off his cigarette.

"Hey, you're Kenny's cousin, right?" the attendant said examining David. "You was in here the other day with him. Doug, ain't it?"

"It's not Doug. My name's David, David Bishop."

"David, eh? Ok, so what you gonna have David Bishop?"

"Could we get a couple of those burgers with the Cheez Whiz?"

"Sure thing. You want a malt and fries with that?" the attendant asked.

"Yeah, that sounds great."

As they waited for their meal, David looked curiously across the table at TJ. The two boys hadn't talked since the party at the Bradshaw's the previous evening. "Ok, so what's going on?" David asked. "You haven't said two words since we got in the car. Is something bothering you? Does this have to do with what happened after Angie's party yesterday?"

"How'd ya guess?" TJ replied. "I can't figure her out. When I went back to see her after the party, she didn't want anything to do with me. She said she didn't think it was a good idea for us to see each other anymore. Then she told me to leave. I thought she was my friend."

"It's none of my business, but I think you ought to be careful around her," David replied. "She might not be as good a friend as you think."

"You're right - it's none of your business. And I can be friends with whoever I want. I don't need any advice from you. Understand?" TJ stated with finality.

David saw that it was pointless to pursue the conversation any further. "All right, I'll stay out of it, if that's what you want," he said. He looked over toward the counter and saw the waiter returning with their cheeseburgers and fries. "Great, here comes our food. I'm starved."

The waiter slid the two plates off the tray and onto the table. "That'll be three fifty," he said.

David pulled out the five his grandfather had given him and handed it to the waiter. "Dig in," David told TJ. "You'll love these burgers. They're the best I've ever tasted."

***

The jingle of the bell over the door made David look up momentarily from his meal. Two boys, maybe fifteen or sixteen, had just entered the diner and walked toward the counter. They were dressed almost identically in white tee shirts and tight fitting jeans. The taller of the two boys looked to be slightly older, sporting a flattop haircut and a slight gap between his two front teeth. He scuffed his dirty military style boots across the floor, shooting a hostile glance in TJ's direction before taking a seat at the counter. The younger boy, a callow looking youth with ratty red hair and a bad case of acne, took a puff on his cigarette before hoisting himself onto the stool next to his companion. The two newcomers sat, their backs to David and TJ, talking in hushed tones.

David tried to ignore them, concentrating instead on his cheeseburger. He only had time to take a single bite before the acne-faced boy began to yell at the soda jerk loud enough for both TJ and

David to hear. "Jesus Christ," the boy called out, "something in here smells like shit. You got something rotten in here?" David saw the boy look toward where he and TJ were sitting and pinched his nose with his thumb and index finger to indicate a putrid odor was fouling the air.

The other boy now took up the harangue, holding his nose up in the air and sniffing some imaginary current of air. "It sure stinks in here. You sure you took out the garbage tonight, Walter? Something sure is rotten in here, and I think the smell is coming from over in this direction," he said walking toward David and TJ.

"Hey, look fellas, please don't cause any trouble, ok?" the waiter looked scared. "Mr. Green'll be back in a few minutes to close up, and he's not gonna be happy if you guys leave a mess."

"Don't worry, Walter, we don't want any trouble, do we?" the flat-topped youth looked back at his red haired partner. The younger boy laughed and repeated, "Naw, we don't want no trouble."

TJ sat stoically eating his fries as the boy approached the table. "Is he talking about us?" David whispered to TJ. "What's his problem anyway?"

"It's not about you, it's about me," TJ replied, deliberately not turning his head to look in his accuser's direction. "Just ignore him and go on eating. He's just blowing smoke out his ass. They're not going to do anything. Isn't that right, jerkwad?" he directed his comment to the flat-topped boy who had almost reached their table, but still without looking up in his direction.

The boy stopped short, glancing back nervously toward the redhead, his bravado suddenly tempered by the thought that if a fight did break out, he would be the first one to suffer the consequences.

"Like I said, there's not going to be any trouble," the boy laughed nervously. "Come on, let's split," he said to his friend, motioning toward the door. He took one last drag on the cigarette he had been smoking, threw it at TJ's feet, and crushed it with the toe of his boot. He turned away from the booth and headed toward the exit. "You just be sure to tell old man Green he ought to be more careful about who he lets in, got that Walter?" The bell over the door jingled again as the two left and the door closed behind them.

***

The soda jerk - Walter was the name the two local boys had

called him - continued to glance nervously back and forth between the booth where David and TJ were sitting and the door, as if expecting the teens to return any second. After several minutes of furtive looks, he finally came over to the table, wiping his hands on his apron as he walked. "You guys want anything else, cuz I gotta close in a couple minutes?"

David looked up at the clock on the wall. "It's only eight thirty. According to the sign on the door, you don't close till ten."

"Well, like I told those guys, Mr. Green'll be here soon, and I've got to get the place cleaned up, you know?"

"Don't worry, we were just leaving, weren't we, Huck?" TJ prompted. "Come on, let's get going."

David nodded his head in agreement even though he still had food on his plate. He hurriedly took the last bite of his burger and drained what remained of his malt from the metal mixing cylinder into his glass. He was glad now that he had ordered only a small malt. David wiped his mouth with a paper napkin from the dispenser on the table, and headed toward the door just behind TJ.

On the way to the door, TJ flipped a quarter toward Walter. "Here's your tip," he called out. "At least it's more than you got from those two idiots."

Only moments after TJ and David stepped out of the diner, Walter closed the door behind them, fastened the lock, and flipped the "OPEN" sign over so that it read "CLOSED."

"He's a jerk, but I'd do the same thing if I were him," TJ said. "Let's head down to your grandfather's shop and see if he and my dad have finished the tour yet."

As he spoke, Ernie's Diner went dark behind them. Evening was falling and the sunlight had begun to fade. The two boys hurried down the sidewalk in the direction of Carl's Upholstery Shop.

They had just started past the small alley separating Ernie's from the closed barber shop next door when David felt someone shove him from behind. Before he could react, he was on the ground with his face pressed into the dirt. "What's your hurry," a voice called from behind him. David tried to move, but pressure in the small of his back kept him pinned down. "Does your granddad know you're out wandering the streets with this nigger?" David struggled to get a look at his attacker, but floundered helplessly, unable to free himself.

"Leave the kid alone," he heard TJ call out.

"Shut up nigger," came the reply. David heard a dull thud and listened as TJ winced in pain. "Not so tough now, are you nigger boy?" Was it one of the boys from the diner? David tried to turn his head toward the sound, but two hands twisted his face away, and forced him back down to the ground.

Though he could not see what was happening, David heard the struggle. He couldn't make out exactly how many boys had attacked them, but he estimated six or seven at least.

TJ was putting up a fight, but three or four of the boys now moved in on him, pushing him to the ground. The boys began kicking and stomping him as he lay there helpless. TJ tried to cover up, protecting his face with his arms, but the blows kept coming, and TJ was obviously in pain.

David heard TJ wince again. "Hold him down," a voice echoed in the alley. The voice sounded vaguely familiar. "That's it."

Once or twice, David twisted free long enough to catch a glimpse of the attackers. At first he didn't recognize anyone. Then he saw that one of the boys holding TJ down was the red-haired boy who had assailed them in the diner. Soon he recognized the other boy from the diner as well. He was one of the boys kicking TJ in the ribs as hard as he could.

The beating went on for what seemed like an eternity. Suddenly, Walter, the soda-jerk from Ernie's Diner, came running around the corner into the alley. "You guys better split," he exclaimed. "Mr. Green's back and he called the cops."

One of the boys laughed as the others continued to pummel TJ. David could see blood now streaming from the corner of TJ's mouth. "Nice try, Walt, but I don't think so."

"Naw, really. He just got off the phone. They'll be here any second."

The boy seemed unconcerned, lighting a cigarette. "So what? Those flat-footed clowns couldn't chase the tail on a dog."

David heard the wail of a siren, then the sound of a car screeching to a stop at the curb. A car door opened and slammed shut. "Hey, he's telling the truth," called one of the boys, moving away from the prone figure of TJ. "Let's go - it's the cops."

David looked back toward the street and saw the red glow of a police car flasher reflected off the red brick of the alley wall. Someone grasped David's shoulders tightly, leaning in close to his ear and whispered quietly. "Just remember what I told you in the park." The voice chilled David to the bone. He knew it immediately. The voice was Terry's.

Suddenly the pressure pinning David's arms back was released, and he lurched forward. The attackers were gone. He could just make them out as they darted away into the shadows of the alley.

***

Moments later an overweight, red-faced police deputy lumbered up the alley, panting to a stop as he reached the two boys. The deputy glanced over at David then switched his attention to TJ who had just begun to push himself up off the ground.

"All right, boy, just stay where you are," the big man huffed as he reached over to push TJ's face back down. The deputy placed his knee squarely into the middle of TJ's back and pressed his massive weight down on TJ, causing the youth to cry out in pain. He reached out, grabbed TJ's right arm, and twisted it behind his back. "Don't move and you won't get hurt, you hear me boy?"

"Hey, he didn't do anything," David yelled at the over zealous police officer. But the deputy continued to press down heavily into the small of TJ's back. "He's the one they were beating up, and you're letting them get away."

The deputy looked confused. "Let who get away?"

"The boys who did this. There were at least five or six of them and they ran off down the alley when you pulled up. Didn't you see them?"

"He's right," an older voice cut in, confirming David's version of the story. The diner's owner, Ernie Green, walked up the alley from the front of his store. "I'm the one who called you. I saw them when I got back. They ran off as soon as they saw your squad car pull up."

"TJ and I didn't do anything to them," David confirmed. "They just started beating him. Now you're letting them get away."

The deputy let go of TJ's arm and took the pressure off his back, allowing TJ to catch his breath for the first time in several minutes. "Ok, I'll take a look, but they're probably long gone by now." The deputy took a flashlight out of a loop on his belt and walked reluctantly into the shadows, shining the beam from one side of the alley to the other as if someone might jump out at him at any moment.

Ernie Green went up to TJ and put his hand around the young man's shoulders guiding him into the light of the street lamp. "Let's take a look at you," he said. "You've got some nasty looking wounds there, son. We've got to get you to some medical attention as soon as possible."

Still, it was more than twenty minutes before the deputy returned empty handed. "All right," he panted, completely ignoring TJ's condition. "I'm going to need statements from each of you." He pulled a small notebook from his belt, and began by taking names. "Ok, just what happened here?"

"We were coming out of Ernie's Diner and they jumped us," TJ said.

"Did you ever see them before?"

"Two of them were in Ernie's Diner while we were eating," David replied.

"Did you recognize them?" the officer said. "Were they regulars?" the officer directed this question to the counter attendant, Walter. Walter looked uneasy, shifting his weight from one foot to the other.

"How bout it, Walt?" Ernie Green prodded. "Do you know who they were?"

"Yeah, sort of," Walter answered reluctantly. "I mean I seen 'em around, you know. But I don't know their names."

"What do you mean you don't know their names? They sure knew who you were," TJ interjected accusingly.

"Look, lots of people know my name," Walter answered nervously. "That don't mean I know them."

"How about you, young man?" the deputy redirected his interrogation to David. "Did you recognize any of them?"

David remembered Terry's threat. The same threat he'd made at the county park. And the same throat cutting gesture. David felt the fear well up in him, preventing him from speaking.

"Well," the deputy prompted, "how about it? Did you know any of them?"

"No, I didn't recognize anybody," David lied. He looked down at the ground to avoid eye contact with the deputy or with TJ.

"So nobody saw anything, is that the story?"

Receiving no response, the deputy put away his notebook and turned to the two boys. "Ok, you two, wait here till I tell you that you can go," he said. The deputy turned and walked back toward his car to radio in his report.

Alone, TJ looked at David skeptically. David continued to stare down at the ground. "You know something, don't you?" TJ said. "You know who those boys were."

"No, I don't. I told that policeman. I didn't recognize anybody."

"You're lying. You're a terrible liar. What is it? What didn't you tell that cop?"

"Nothing, I told you. Just leave me alone."

David's fumbling denial was cut short by the arrival of his grandfather and Nathan Gibson. Nathan immediately ran over to his son. "TJ? Are you all right? What the hell happened here anyway?"

"I'm ok, Dad. Just a couple of scrapes, that's all. It was some boys from town. They took off as soon as the police showed up."

"I want whoever did this caught, do you hear me?" Nathan demanded of the returning deputy.

"We'll do everything we can," the deputy replied. "But you have to understand we have very little to go on. Nobody claims to have seen anything, and without a witness, our hands are tied. Look, frankly I need to get back out on patrol, and you need to look after your son," the deputy continued. "Why don't you get him over to the hospital and have those cuts checked out. It doesn't look like there are any broken bones, but those boys gave him quite a going over. No need taking any chances. Now if you'll excuse me..." The deputy brushed past Nathan Gibson and walked back to his patrol car.

"Oh, and one more thing," the deputy added looking back. "You should probably keep your boy out of town. These guys don't like it when somebody new shows up on their turf." He got into his car, turned off the flashing lights, and drove away as if the incident had never happened.

# Wounds

David stood on the dock in front of Bobber Lane's cabin looking out over the calm, tranquil waters of Spirit Lake. He watched as the first rays of the morning sun stretched out over the lake's glassy surface, bathing the pines along the distant shore in a radiant golden glow. A few wisps of smoke drifted up from the houses on the far bank, evidence of other early risers. The pastoral calm of the dawning day contrasted sharply with the senseless violence of the preceding evening.

David had already been up for hours reliving the previous night's events. The trip to the hospital had been bad enough, but then there was the phone call to his parents. His grandfather had insisted on calling, but he left it to David to explain the attack. His mother had been almost hysterical when he told her. After that, sleep had eluded him. His dream catcher had proved powerless against the demons that taunted him. The pills the doctor gave him at the hospital to help him sleep did little to ease his pain or to sooth his conscience.

Unable to sleep, he left the cottage before dawn - before his grandfather awakened, and even before Maddie arrived to fix breakfast. He left a note on the kitchen table explaining that he couldn't sleep and had gone for a walk to think things over. He wanted a place to be alone, to be able to escape the questions that were bound to come. That's why he had chosen Bobber's cabin. It was far enough away from his grandfather, Maddie, and the Gibsons to get some privacy and quiet - for a while at least.

As he stood on the dock, he ran his tongue over his lower lip. He could still taste blood, and the tissue was still tender, but the swelling had gone down. The bruises on his legs and arms hurt more than he had realized at first. But he knew that his wounds were nothing compared with those TJ had received at the hands of their attackers. TJ had put on a brave act in front of his father, but David knew that he'd been hurt worse than he had admitted.

David heard Captain purring behind him and turned to see the cat walking toward him across the dock. "Hi boy," he said, reaching down to pet the tabby cat. Captain cozied up to him, rubbing affectionately against his outstretched hand.

"Looks like Captain still likes you, anyway," Bobber Lane's

disembodied voice called out from the shadows.

"Jesus, you really scared me," David exclaimed. He looked around bewildered. "Where did you come from? I didn't hear anyone."

"Ever hear the expression 'quiet as a ghost?' That'd be me. Besides, I figured you were looking for me. Isn't that why you came?"

"What are you talking about? I didn't come here to find you. I've been here lots of times, and you haven't been here. I thought you'd vanished, or whatever ghost do."

"So why did you come then? Feeling guilty 'bout how you treated your friend TJ last night?" Bobber said stroking, the nape of Captain's neck.

"Hey, look, I didn't do anything to TJ. I don't have anything to feel guilty about."

"How bout what you told the police about the attack? You really let TJ down, you know."

"No I didn't."

"That so? TJ seemed to think you did. In fact he seemed pretty upset."

"Sure, he was angry and he was hurt. But he wasn't mad at me."

"Oh? Is that why he didn't talk to you at the hospital? Or on the ride back to the lake? He was pissed at you all right."

"It was dark in that alley. I couldn't see who grabbed us. Not like that counter guy Walter. I'll bet he knew all those boys. He could of told the police who they were, but he didn't say a word."

"Maybe so, but we're not talking about Walter now, are we? We're talking about you. You knew it was Terry who held you down, but you didn't say a word, did you?"

David remembered Terry's threat, the cruel, unreasoning tone in his voice. "Terry? How do you know about him?"

"I'm a ghost, remember. I know all sorts of stuff. Like how you saw Terry and Angie together over at Falls Park. Or did that just slip your mind? He threatened you and now you're scared shitless."

"I am not. I just don't want to take any chances, that's all."

"I wonder if TJ thought about taking chances before he jumped in the lake to save your sorry ass? As I recall you were about to end up like me when he dragged you up on that dock. Or don't you remember that far back?"

"Yeah, I remember. But what do you expect me to do? Tell the police about Terry? Even if I told them, they probably wouldn't believe me. And if they did, they wouldn't do anything anyway."

"What you tell the police is entirely up to you. It's your conscience. You're the one who has to live with yourself. But if you intend to do something, you'd better do it soon. TJ needs your help now, and he's going to need it even more before long. Now why don't you go feed Captain? He's depending on you too, so don't let him down."

***

"Well, there you are." Maddie stood outside the cottage hanging wet laundry on a clothes line stretched between the cottage and a rusted steel post set into the ground nearby. She removed one of Carl's damp shirts from the basket and hung it over the line. "Where have you been? Your grandfather has been looking for you."

"Nobody was up," David replied. "I couldn't sleep, so I went over to Mr. Lane's cabin to feed Captain."

"Come over here and let me take a look at you," she ordered. Maddie placed her chubby hand under David's chin, lifting it into the light. "Just scrapes and bruises," she said. "No scars." She looked deeply into the boy's face. He was holding something back. "You look upset. Is something troubling you?"

"Naw, I'm just tired. I couldn't sleep. Even the dream catcher you made me didn't help this time."

"A dream catcher can not fix all things, David. There are some things you must do yourself. But just remember, the spirits are always around you. They will help you if you let them."

David looked surprised. It seemed as if Maddie knew about his visit from Bobber Lane. "Do you mean like my spirit guide, like the deer?"

"A deer, a man, a fish, a bird - spirit guides take many forms, David. As I told you, even Little Thunder had a guide. Is this about something that happened over at Mr. Lane's cabin?"

"Maybe, but if I told you, you wouldn't believe me," he said using two clothes pins to fasten a towel to the line above his head.

"You will tell me when you are ready. Now, why don't you go in and tell your grandfather you're here. He's been looking for you all morning. He's inside right now talking to your mother on the phone. She called to find out how you are."

David rushed into the cottage, slamming the screen door behind him. Carl was in the living area sitting on the overstuffed couch. He covered the receiver with his hand. "So, you are back, ya?"

"I just couldn't sleep so I went for a walk."

"Your mother is on the phone. I tried to reassure her, but she's worried about you. Come sit here." Carl got to his feet, making room for his grandson on the well worn cushion of the bulky couch, and handing him the telephone receiver.

"David? Are you all right?" There was some crackling and static on the line, but David could hear the concern in his mother's voice clearly. "I couldn't sleep all night," she said.

"I didn't sleep much either, Mom, but I'm ok," he told her, "just a little sore, that's all."

"Well, your father and I were frantic with worry. That's really why I'm calling. Your dad's on his way up. He's coming to bring you home."

"Dad's coming?" David said confused. He hadn't expected anyone to come so quickly after all the delays of the past week.

"Your father started packing last night just after we talked. He left before dawn. He should be there before dark tonight, if the traffic isn't too bad."

"Aren't you coming with him?"

"No, we decided it was best if I stayed here. Look, baby, I should go now, but I'll see you soon. All right? I love you, ok?"

"I love you too, Mom," David managed before the line went dead.

***

It was almost noon as the tired old Mercury outboard sputtered, puffed, and chugged out onto the lake, carrying Carl and David toward the lily pads in the small cove near Carl's favorite fishing spot. It was one of the few times since arriving at Spirit Lake that Carl had invited David to accompany him on one of his fishing expeditions, but today Carl had insisted. "It will be good for you," he had said. "It will get your mind off what happened."

Carl had been right. Sitting quietly out on the lake had a calming, relaxing effect, making the previous day's attack seem like a bad dream. David sat with his grandfather for what seemed like hours, watching his line for any movement.

"Do you think TJ's gonna be all right, Grandpa?" David asked.

"If you mean will his body heal, yes, he will be just fine," Carl said casting his line. "But not all wounds are physical. It may be some time before TJ recovers from what happened last night."

The boy and the old man remained in silence, their lines dangling idly in the lake, unwilling or unable to share their thoughts. By lunchtime, they had only managed to catch two small sunfish, but in spite of their lack of success they continued their fishing well into the afternoon. It was almost three as Carl maneuvered the old bass boat toward shore, cut the engine, and coasted toward the dock.

"Grandpa? Isn't that the sheriff's car parked over by the Gibson' cabin?" David asked as he pulled the boat up close to the dock.

Carl stopped gathering up the tackle and poles long enough to glance over toward the Gibson cabin. "You're right, David." he replied, "I wonder what he's doing out here. I don't see the Gibson's car anywhere around. I hope everything is all right."

At that moment, Sheriff Les Edmonds emerged from the Gibson cabin. Spotting David and Carl, the lanky sheriff waved a greeting. As they watched, the sheriff headed back to his cruiser, angled his long body into the driver's seat, started the engine, and drove in the direction of the dock.

"I don't know what he's doing out here, David," Carl said. "But it looks like we might get a chance to ask him ourselves."

A minute later, Sheriff Edmonds eased the car to a stop only a few feet from the boat dock. Rolling down the driver's side window, he leaned out. "Howdy, Carl," he greeted.

"Afternoon, Les," Carl replied. "What brings you out this way? Is this a social call or are you here on business?"

"A little bit of both, I'm afraid," the sheriff said apologetically. "First I just want to say how sorry I was to here about what happened to David and his friend in town last night. To think that something like this could happen in Iron Falls...," he let the sentence trail off. Turning his attention to David, he said, "I understand you were pretty shaken up, son. How are you feeling now?"

"I'll be fine, sir," David replied. "I only got a few bruises and scratches. TJ got hurt a lot worse than me."

"That's what I understand. I was hoping to find the Gibson boy at home, but I guess I missed him. His mother said Nathan Gibson took TJ into town to have him checked out by Doc Taylor."

"Is that why you came, Les," Carl said, "to check on the boys? Is there any word on who did this?"

"Nothing that I've heard of. You might want to talk to Chief Benson back in Iron Falls. He'll be able to tell you if they're making any progress on the case."

"If you didn't come about that, then why drive all the way out here? You said you had another reason for coming. I hope it's nothing serious."

"I'm sure it's going to turn out to be nothing, but my office got a report of another incident that might involve the Gibson boy. That's why I wanted to talk to him. I was hoping that he could clear up a few things for me. But it looks like any questions will have to wait till morning. When I explained the situation to Mrs. Gibson and her daughter, she said that TJ and his dad would be here then."

"You need to question TJ?" Carl asked. "What's going on, Les? What's this all about anyway? Is TJ in some kind of trouble?"

"I really can't say anymore right now - not until I have a chance to talk to the Gibsons. But after I've talked with them, I'd like to talk to you and David as well. Why don't I stop by in the morning, if it's all right with you. I can explain everything then. Are you going to be around?"

"We should be here," Carl answered. "David's father is driving up later today, so we haven't made any other plans."

"Good. Then I'll see you in the morning. I can fill you in on what's going on then."

David watched as the sheriff's car drove away, leaving a cloud of dust in its wake. "What's going on, Grandpa?" he asked. "Why's the sheriff acting so strange? What does he want to talk to TJ about?"

From the look on Carl's face, he was as puzzled by the sheriff's visit as David was. "I really don't have any idea, David," he replied "But I don't like the sound of this. Perhaps when the sheriff comes by in the morning we will know more, ya?"

\*\*\*

"Well, it's all set," Donald Bishop said as he entered the kitchen to join David and Carl at the kitchen table. It had been after eight when Donald's Bel Air finally pulled up in front of the cottage. In spite of the late hour, he had made good time, navigating the crowded route north along US 27. Traffic had been light, and he had experienced only a little over a half an hour delay at the Straits. But the trip had exhausted him, and he needed rest.

"I just got off the phone with aunt Rita," he said to David. "She's got room for us to spend the night out there, so why don't you get your things together and we'll get going."

David hadn't expected his father to stay at the cottage, even if there had been room. It was no secret that his father and grandfather didn't get along. Donald's I-like-Ike Republicanism grated against Carl's Wobbly-socialist ideology. Donald's marriage to Helen had been over Carl's strong objection and against his will. Nevertheless, on those occasions when the Bishop's traveled north to visit, Carl and Donald usually managed to maintain a truce. But without Helen to act as a buffer, there was no telling what might happen.

Still, David had no desire to spend the night at his cousin's house again. The bitter memory of his experience with Kenny's bogus-bear practical joke still gnawed at him. "I don't want to go over there. Kenny's a jerk. Besides, Sheriff Edmonds said he'd be coming back to talk to Grandpa and me in the morning."

"The sheriff? Carl, you didn't say anything to me about the sheriff coming out to talk to David, " Donald grumbled. "Why does the sheriff want to talk to him? Is there a problem?"

"Sheriff Edmonds didn't say," Carl answered, "but I'm sure it isn't anything. Why doesn't David stay here with me tonight, and you can pick him up after the sheriff leaves."

"This is all about that Negro boy, isn't it? Carl, I can't believe you let David play with his sort. What were you thinking?"

"TJ is not guilty of anything. Donald," Carl protested. "The boys were just minding their own business. It's not TJ's fault that they were attacked. Nathan has been my friend for years, and..."

"And what?" The veins had begun to stand out on Donald's neck. "Look, I don't care who you're friends with, but where it concerns my son, I draw the line."

"Dad, stop it. Just stop yelling," David interjected. "TJ's no different than you or me. He plays basketball and goes to Braves games..."

"Stop right there, young man," his father demanded. "You don't understand these people. You're still young, but when you're older you'll know what I'm talking about. That kind of boy just invites trouble."

"There's nothing to understand, Dad. TJ's not 'that boy.' He's my friend. If he hadn't pulled me out of the water that day we found Mr. Lane's body in the lake, I might have drowned. He saved my life, ok?"

Donald and Carl both looked at David astonished. "What are you talking about?" Carl managed to utter at last. "You never said anything about this before."

"I didn't want to get into trouble," David replied. "I was out there alone and when I found that body under water, I must have panicked. TJ saw me struggling and swam out to pull me up onto the raft."

"Is this true?" Donald struggled to accept what his son was telling him.

"It's the truth, Dad, I swear. Now do you see? TJ saved me."

"Did you know about this, Carl," Donald directed an accusatory glance at his father-in-law.

"I had no idea, Donald," the elder man replied, "believe me."

"I don't know what to say, David."

"You could start by saying you're sorry, Dad."

"Look, I may have been a bit hasty in jumping to conclusions. If that's the case I apologize. It's been a long day, and I'm sure we're all tired. Why don't I head over to your Aunt Rita's. You can spend the night here, and I'll give you a call in the morning."

# **Missing**

There was a soft knocking at the back door - knocking just loud enough to interrupt David's restless sleep. He checked the wall clock. 7:15. Who would be coming to the cottage at this early hour, he wondered. Too early for the sheriff. And he was sure his father wouldn't be up yet.

He went to the window and looked out. The only car in the drive was his grandfather's station wagon. Whoever was knocking had not come by car. They were on foot. The soft knocking came again.

David got out of bed and went to the bedroom door, opening it just enough to look into the kitchen. He could just make out his grandfather pouring himself a cup of coffee before returning the pot to the burner on the wood stove. "All right, just a minute. I'm coming," he heard Carl call out.

David listened from his doorway as Carl went to the kitchen door and opened it. "Denise, what a pleasant surprise," Carl greeted. "What brings you out at this early hour?"

"Good morning, Mr. Wertz," David recognized Denise's polite greeting. "I'm looking for my brother. Has he been here?" She glanced around the room nervously, more hopeful than expectant.

"TJ? Why no, dear," Carl answered. "I haven't seen TJ since yesterday. Why? Is there anything wrong? You look upset."

"But I thought...," she stammered. "Are you sure he hasn't been here? I've just got to find him. Maybe David's seen him..."

"Seen who," David said, stumbling half asleep into the kitchen. "Hey, Denise, what's going on?"

"It's TJ. He's gone and I don't know where to look. Dad said he's probably out taking a walk to clear his head, but I'm afraid he might have run away."

"Run away?" Carl said bewildered. "Why on earth would TJ run away? Come in sit down and tell us what's going on."

Denise was so upset she was almost shaking as she took a seat at the kitchen table. "Let me get you a cup of hot cocoa," Carl offered, walking to get the hot water kettle from the stove. "It will help settle your nerves," he continued. He stirred two spoonfuls of cocoa mix into a steaming cup of hot water and handed it to the anxious girl. "All right," he said, "just take your time, and tell us what happened."

Denise hesitated, as if unsure how to respond. "It's the sheriff," she said at last. He came to the house yesterday while TJ and dad were in town."

"Ya, ya," Carl responded. "We saw him leaving your cabin when we got back from fishing. But I still don't understand. What did he say to you that made you so upset, my dear?"

"When he came to our cabin, he said he wanted to talk to TJ about something, but he wouldn't say what it was. Then he started asking me all kinds of questions about what happened on the day of Angie's birthday party."

"Angie's birthday?" David asked incredulously. "What does Angie's birthday have to do with TJ?"

"That's what my mom wanted to know. She told the sheriff we weren't answering any more questions until he explained exactly what was going on. That's when the sheriff told us why he had really come. He said that Dr. Bradshaw had called the Sheriff's Office and reported that Angie's diamond necklace and some money were missing from his house after her party." Denise paused before continuing. "The way he was talking, it was obvious the sheriff thinks TJ took the necklace and Mr. Bradshaw's money too."

"That's crazy," David said. "TJ would never do anything like that."

"That's what I told the Sheriff Edmonds, but he said that according to Angie, TJ was the last person to leave the Bradshaw house before the necklace turned up missing. Then the sheriff told mom he wanted us to stick around Iron Falls, at least until he could talk to TJ and dad. That's why he's coming back this morning."

"I don't suppose TJ took it very well when you told him," David said.

"I've never seen him so mad," Denise replied. "When mom told him what the sheriff said, TJ almost blew up. He just kept pacing back and forth saying how everyone up here hated Negroes and he wished we'd never come."

"So where's TJ now?"

"That's just it. I don't know. He was still up last night when the rest of us went to bed, and when we got up this morning, he was gone. We waited around for almost an hour, then dad sent me up here to see if I could find him. If he's not with you, where could he be? What if the sheriff comes back and TJ's still missing?"

"Listen, Denise," Carl said calmly. "I'm sure TJ is just fine. He's probably back at your cabin already. Why don't the three of us head back down there now?"

David hesitated. "Why don't you two go ahead," he told them. "I've still got to get dressed and there's something I want to check before I come down."

"Is it about TJ?" Denise exclaimed excitedly. "Do you know where he went? Cause if you do I want to come with you."

"I don't think so," David protested. "If he's where I think he is, it'll be better if I go alone."

Carl looked reluctant. "Are you sure you know what you're doing, David?" Carl cautioned. "TJ's already missing, and I don't want to have to worry about both of you."

"I'll be fine, Grandpa," David replied. "I promise that I'll be careful."

"All right, you go look for TJ," Carl said. "I'll take Denise down and wait with her parents. But if you don't find him, I want you to promise to come right down to the Gibson's. Do you understand?"

"Yes sir," replied David. "I'll get ready and leave right now."

\*\*\*

David stood on the porch of Bobber Lane's cabin looking out over the calm waters of the lake. The morning fog had not yet lifted, enveloping the scene in an unearthly stillness. The dense layer of mist deadened the sound, making the already placid lake strangely quiet. Not even Captain came begging for his usual morning meal. David walked toward the rear of the cabin, alert for any sign of recent activity. He felt as if Bobber were somewhere nearby watching.

"You can come out now," David called into the fog. "I know you're here."

For what seemed like an eternity, nothing moved. Everything remained quiet and still. "Look, I know you're still mad at me, but you've got to come out. Your folks are worried about you." Still there was no answer. David was almost ready to turn around and leave when he heard a voice call out from the mist.

"What you doin here, Huck?" TJ asked, emerging from the veil of fog.

"Looking for you," David answered. He paused to examine the older boy more closely. TJ looked tired, but otherwise he seemed in good spirits. "Denise came to the cottage this morning. She told us about what happened with the sheriff yesterday. Your folks got up this morning and you were gone, so they panicked. Denise thinks you ran away."

"That figures. My sister always assumes the worst."

"She said your folks are pretty upset too. Nobody has any idea where you went."

"Yeah, I suppose I should have left a note. But I figured I'd be back before they knew I was gone."

"So, what happened?" David asked. "Why'd you take off like that?"

"I just had to get away by myself for awhile," TJ replied. "I couldn't sleep. I just kept thinking about what the sheriff told my mom. The more I thought about it, the madder I got. Angie must have lied to the sheriff about what happened to her necklace, and now he thinks I'm guilty. Nobody else was up, so I decided to take a walk."

"But how'd you end up way over here?"

"Somehow I must of gotten turned around in the dark. My goddamned flashlight died, and I had no idea where I was. Then I saw a light shining through the woods. I thought it must be the cabins so I started walking toward it."

"You followed a light through the forest?" David asked. It was like his dream, he thought. The dream in which he'd followed a faint light through the forest to find Little Thunder.

"Yeah, there was a light, but it kept moving, then all of a sudden it disappeared. It was pitch black and I was totally lost. But then I stumbled over a fence rail along the road. I remembered the split rail fence leading up to Bobber's cabin, and realized where I was. I forgot how creepy it is over here. It's really spooky, especially at night. I knew I'd never find my way back in the dark, so I decided to wait till morning."

"You mean you stayed here the whole night? Weren't you scared?"

"Scared and a little hungry. I thought if I could get into the cabin, maybe I could find a flashlight or something to eat. The door was padlocked, but when I tried the window, it opened right up. Weird. So I crawled in and fumbled around in the dark for awhile before I found the old man's cot. I must'a been exhausted, cuz I passed out as soon as my head hit the pillow. Next thing I knew the sun was pouring in through the window and this mangy old cat was purring in my face." TJ said reaching down to pet the purring tabby at his feet. "I was about ready to head back when I heard you calling. How'd you know where to find me anyway?"

"Just a lucky guess," David replied. "I remembered what you said when we were here before, that 'if you got lost back here, nobody'd ever find you.' So I took a chance. Besides, this is where I come whenever I need to be alone and think."

Suddenly a blur of motion darting through the woods caught TJ's eye, attracting his attention. It wasn't until the blur rounded the bend in the road and pulled into the drive that TJ recognized the car and its driver. "Did you tell anybody else you were coming here?" he asked.

"Nobody. Not a soul," David replied.

"Then how'd the sheriff know where to find us?"

"The sheriff?" The words were barely out of David's mouth when he heard the sound of a car crunching along the gravel drive behind him. He turned around to see the Falls County Sheriff's car approaching. Sheriff Les Edmonds eased the car to a stop just a few feet from the spot where David and TJ stood. The sheriff got out of the cruiser, and walked toward them with deliberate slowness, a self-satisfied smile on his face.

***

"Good morning, boys," Sheriff Edmonds said, striding toward David and TJ. The sheriff took his time, looking around the misty grounds of the deserted cabin. "Kinda eerie out here, don't you think? This place gives me the willies - especially in this damned fog. I'd never have thought of looking for you two over here if it hadn't been for your grandfather, David. He's the one who thought you might have come over this way."

"Grandpa told you we were here?" David said nervously.

"Yup. Guess he knows you pretty well, eh? Last time I was over here was the day you boys found poor old Bobber Lane out in the lake. That was a terrible thing. It must have been quite a shock discovering Mr. Lane's body like that. You both handled it very well. I know that it couldn't have been easy for either of you. Funny, us meeting here now - this being his place and all.

"Well, now that I've found you, I'd better radio into my office and let them know. There are a lot of people looking for you two boys. My office can call over to the cabins and let your folks know that you're ok." David and TJ watched as Sheriff Edmond's headed back toward his car. The tall, lean sheriff eased himself behind the steering wheel and pulled the radio mic from beneath the dashboard. The car's radio squawked as the Falls County Sheriff's Office acknowledged his report.

When he finished reporting in, Edmonds returned to spot where he'd left the two boys. Apparently anxious to put an end to the small talk, the sheriff turned his attention to the reason for his visit. "Now that that's out of the way, why don't we get started." he said reaching into his shirt pocket to withdraw a small note pad and a blue mechanical pencil. "You're a hard guy to track down, young man," he told TJ, his voice showing no trace of hostility. "Guess you already know why I'm here, eh?"

"You want to talk to me about what happened at the Bradshaw house," TJ replied. "My mom told me some things were missing after Angie's party."

"That's right. I hate to put you through this, but some serious allegations have been made. I hope you understand I'm only doing my job."

"You think I had something to do with taking her necklace. But I didn't do anything. I swear." TJ answered defensively.

"All right then, help me out here. I just want to find out the truth. What went on over at the Bradshaw place? Maybe you or David saw something that will help us find the missing items. Let's start with the necklace. Were you both present when Dr. Bradshaw gave it to his daughter?"

"Sure," said David. "We all watched Dr. Bradshaw help Angie put it on. She seemed really surprised. She told us the necklace had been her mother's and showed us a picture of the two of them."

Sheriff Edmonds took a moment to jot something down in his notebook. "Then what happened?"

"Then the phone rang, and she left the room to take the call," TJ said. "Dr. Bradshaw told us she'd be gone awhile, so he said maybe we could play some pool to pass the time. He bet he and Mr. Wertz could beat my dad and me in a game."

"You bet money on the game?"

"Yeah, a few bucks. He went over to the bar and got ten dollars out of a canister sitting on the counter."

"So you saw where he kept his money?"

"You mean that cookie jar? The only money I saw was the ten dollars that my dad and I won. After we finished the game, Angie came back so we quit playing."

"Was she wearing the necklace?"

TJ thought for a minute before answering. "I don't think so. She'd changed into a blouse and some slacks. She said she was going out with some friends. That's when the argument started, and..."

"There was an argument?"

"Yeah. Angie and her dad got into a big fight when he told her she couldn't go out with her friends," TJ explained. "She was really steamed."

"She almost knocked me over when she ran out of the room," David added.

"And was that the last time either of you saw her before you left?"

"Well, I kinda saw her again - by accident" David answered. "When Angie ran out of the room, she spilled root beer all over my shirt. I had to go to the bathroom to clean up, but I must have made a wrong turn. Anyway, I accidentally walked into Angie's room, and she was sitting at her dressing table."

"Any sign of the necklace?"

"No. She got real mad when I walked in and told me to get out, so I left. I didn't see anything. By the time I got back, everyone was getting ready to leave."

"And you all left the Bradshaw house at the same time, is that right?"

"Everyone except me," TJ confessed. "I forgot my sunglasses so I went back to get them. I just wanted another chance to talk to Angie."

"You went back to the house alone?" Edmonds made another note in his little pad.

"That's right. But when I got there, Angie wouldn't even talk to me," TJ explained. "When I told her I needed my sunglasses, she opened the door and let me in, but she was acting real nervous and followed me around everywhere while I looked."

"Was Dr. Bradshaw present?"

"No sir. Only Angie and me. Once I had my glasses, she told me to get out."

"So she never left you alone, is that your story?"

"My story? What did Angie tell you? Did she say that I took her stuff?"

"No, son, but she said she discovered the necklace was gone just after you left."

"Sheriff? Do you think I took the necklace?"

"I'm not making any judgments right now, just gathering facts.".

"Then I'm not under arrest?"

"Arrest? No, There's not really any evidence that a crime's been committed. From what I've been able to determine, that necklace and the money might just as easily have been lost or misplaced. Hopefully they'll turn up soon, and this whole matter will be forgotten. In fact, if the necklace and money were suddenly to be found, I'm pretty sure there'd be no more questions asked."

The sheriff sounded sincere, but TJ was sure he was just fishing for a confession. "Well, unless you have something to add, that's about all I have right now," Sheriff Edmonds said. He scribbled something else in his notebook, then slipped it into his shirt pocket. "You've both been a great help. Why don't you two get in the car and I'll drive you back to the cabins. Your folks'll be waiting."

***

If either David or TJ thought that they would be greeted as heroes upon their arrival at the lake, they were sadly mistaken. First of all, Nathan Gibson was furious with TJ for wandering off in the middle of the night. "What the hell were you thinking?" he demanded. "You had your mother and me worried sick."

Then, when Donald Bishop arrived on the scene, David's father was equally irate. Initially Donald was upset that Sheriff Edmonds had questioned his son without him being present. But it was when the sheriff insisted that Donald and David remain in Iron Falls until the matter of the missing items was resolved that the situation started to turn ugly.

"What do you want with my son?" Donald protested. "He doesn't have anything to do with any of this. He's the one who was beaten, and now you're treating him as if he were a criminal."

"Nobody's accusing David of anything, Mr. Bishop," the sheriff replied. "Right now, I'm just investigating a complaint. As soon as I'm done, I'm sure we'll get this whole thing straightened out and you'll be on your way."

"And how long's that gonna take?"

"No more than a day or two."

"A day or two? Jesus, you must be out of your mind. I can't afford to sit around here waiting for you to decide we can leave. I've got a job to get back to."

"I'm sorry, Mr. Bishop," Edmonds replied, "I understand your concern. But until this matter is resolved I'm afraid I'm going to have to insist. Until I'm done with this investigation, you and your son will be staying here in Iron Falls."

## Break In

It wasn't until that evening at the Peterson's that Donald began to calm down. Things might have remained tense if it had not been for the intervention of David's uncle Ray. It was Uncle Ray who was able to convince Donald to accept the delay, relax, and enjoy the weekend. "Look, I'm off tomorrow. Why don't we take a ride out first thing in the morning and get in 18 holes. It's just what you need."

When Donald agreed to the golf outing, David was relieved. With his father gone, David had the opportunity to spend the morning at the lake alone, and more importantly, it gave him a chance to visit Angie and hear her account of events first hand. Though he really didn't think talking would do any good, he had to at least try.

David took a deep breath and knocked on the glass patio door of Jacob Bradshaw's home. At first, no one answered, so he knocked again. He used his hand to shade his eyes, peering through the plate glass window into the recreation room. After waiting for several minutes, he saw movement on the curving staircase, indicating that someone was coming.

Soon Angie appeared at the sliding door. She didn't look surprised to see David. "What do you want," she said harshly, opening the door just a crack.

"I want to know why you lied about TJ."

"I didn't lie. I told the sheriff what happened, that's all."

"So you didn't tell the sheriff that TJ stole your things? 'Cause that's what everybody thinks."

"I didn't say he took anything. But my necklace and the money were missing after he left. What else was I supposed to think?"

"If you thought TJ took your necklace, why'd it take two days before you had your dad call the sheriff?"

Angie smiled as if she'd been anticipating David's question. "I didn't want to believe anyone I knew was a thief," she said. "When I first realized the necklace was missing, I thought I might have dropped it or misplaced it. So I looked all over and still couldn't find it. That's when I began to think something else might have happened. When dad discovered the money missing from the cookie jar on the counter, I started to suspect someone might have taken the necklace and the money."

"So why TJ? We were all here. Any one of us could have taken your stuff."

"It must have happened when TJ came back to get his glasses. You and the rest were already gone. He was the only one who could have done it."

"Just because he came back doesn't prove anything. TJ told the sheriff you never let him out of your sight when he was in here."

"That's not true. He could have picked up our things when I wasn't looking."

"And I suppose it's also a lie that you were nervous, like you were expecting somebody. That's what TJ said."

"It's no secret. I was expecting some friends from town. You remember, I called them before my dad got all crazy."

"Is that why you were so anxious for TJ to leave? It would have been pretty embarrassing if your boyfriend Terry had caught you with TJ still here, wouldn't it?"

"What?" Angie gasped, obviously frightened. "What are you talking about? Who's Terry?"

"Terry. You know, the guy I saw you with over at Falls Park. He was the one you were expecting that night, wasn't it? I'll bet he was the one you were talking to on the phone before you had that fight with your dad too."

"You're crazy. Terry didn't have anything to do with..."

"So it was him," David exclaimed.

"That's none of your business. Just keep my friends out of this. They have nothing to do with my necklace being stolen or the missing money."

"Do you expect me to believe that there's no connection between your so-called missing necklace and that jerk Terry."

"Look, I don't have time for any of this. I've got dance class in thirty minutes, and I have to get ready. Now get out of here before I call my dad. Or maybe I should just call the sheriff."

"Do what you want," David said, "but you know what really happened." He stood on the patio starring directly at Angie as she slid the door shut and went back inside.

***

David found a secluded spot behind a stack of firewood near Dr. Bradshaw's tool shed and settled in to wait. If he peeked through a crack in the stack of split logs, he could just see the doctor's Lincoln from his hiding place. He felt a tingling sensation run up his spine. The morning air was chill, but it was fear that made David shiver.

It was Angie who had given him the idea when she mentioned that her father was taking her to dance class. If she wouldn't tell him the truth, he'd have to find out for himself. David had hoped that Angie would be honest with him, but her continued lying left him little choice. If he could find evidence that she'd lied about the necklace, the sheriff and everyone else would have to believe him.

He glanced down at the Timex on his wrist. It was quarter to ten. He sat down on the ground, propped his back against a nearby oak tree, and made himself as comfortable as possible. It was another twenty minutes before he heard Angie calling to her dad as they left the house. "Come on, Dad. We're going to be late."

David crouched down as far as he could behind the wood pile, listening as the Bradshaws got into their sleek sedan. He heard a car door slam shut, then another, and finally the sound of the engine starting up. He peeked through the crack in the wood pile and watched as the Lincoln turned around and headed away down the long drive. David listened as the sound of the car's engine receded into the distance. They were gone.

For several minutes David remained in the shadows, concealed behind the wood pile, his heart racing. He feared that any movement might sound an alarm and the sheriff's car would come racing into the drive, siren blaring and light flashing. He worked up his courage before cautiously peeking over the top of the wood pile. The house sat silent and the pines whispered softly overhead.

Finally, he crept forward across the driveway, tiptoeing so that he would not be heard even though he knew this precaution was foolish. Avoiding the patio, David chose instead to try the side door on the second floor near the kitchen. No one ever locked their doors in Iron Falls. It was not necessary. No one would ever think about breaking into someone else's house. But that was exactly what David intended to do.

Hesitantly he tried the door knob, pushing gently as he did so. He half hoped the door would be locked and he would be able to tell himself that he had at least tried to get in. But the knob turned and the door creaked open just far enough for David to peek inside.

"Hey, Angie, you here?" he called into the kitchen. "Dr. Bradshaw? Anybody home?"

The lack of any response emboldened him to move tentatively into the room. If he were going to do this he would have to be quick. He pulled the door closed behind him, making sure that the latch did not accidentally lock. Quickly he crossed the living room and was about to start upstairs to Angie's room when he again thought he heard the sound of a car engine. He stopped, standing perfectly still.

He listened closely. Only the wind and chirping birds. *Must be my imagination*, he thought. Again he moved toward the stairway.

Then there it was again, only closer this time. A car engine definitely. The sound of tires rolling over gravel. Someone was driving up the Bradshaw's drive. David darted to the nearest window. He peeked out between a slit in the blinds. The Lincoln was back, and pulling to a stop just outside the house.

David began to panic. He glanced around furtively. There was no place to hide. His point of entry was blocked. If Angie or Dr. Bradshaw caught him inside the house, it would be all over. He'd go to jail. The windows were all shut and sealed, blocked to allow for the air conditioning. He heard footsteps on the gravel in the drive. Not much time.

He remembered a narrow ventilation window in the bathroom. If he could get there, he might have a chance. Quickly he darted down the hallway and dashed into the bathroom. He unfastened the window latch and tugged on the handle. The window slid open easily. David looked out. The drop to the ground was only a couple of feet down. As David climbed up onto the windowsill and slid out, he could hear the patio door slide open. There was no time to try to close the window behind him. Hopefully they hadn't returned to use the bathroom. He slipped behind a nearby lilac bush to hide. His heart pounded. Nothing to do now but wait.

"Got it dad," he heard Angie call from somewhere inside the house. "I'll be right out."

***

David listened as the sound of the car's engine receded down the driveway and then disappeared entirely. They were gone at last. His heart rate began to return to normal. Quickly he climbed back in through the window and made his way upstairs and down the hallway to Angie's room.

The door to Angie's room was closed. David eased it open and peeked inside. The drawers of Angie's dresser had been pulled out, and clothes were scattered across the room. A pair of shorts hung on the closet door knob and a tank top lay rumpled on the floor. David directed his attention to the other side of the room, where Angie's jewelry box sat on top of the vanity.

David slipped into the room, crossing quickly to the vanity. He reached over and picked up the jewelry box, careful to note its position. Before leaving he would have to be sure to replace everything exactly where he found it. With a small breath of anticipation, David lifted the latch and opened the top of the box. The tiny ballerina sprang to life, dancing to the tinkling strains of Swan Lake. David threw a small switch on the bottom of the box stilling the miniature dancer. The music stopped.

David searched inside the box, raking his fingers through the contents. Nothing but costume jewelry. The necklace was not inside. Angie was lying about the necklace being stolen. David was certain of that. But what if she had been telling the truth? Then that would mean TJ was the liar. And David knew who he believed.

The necklace had to be somewhere in the room. David thought back, trying to remember what he had seen the day of the party when he'd come into the room. When he had arrived, she had been sitting at the vanity and seemed to be writing something. She had closed the lid on her jewelry box and then pushed it away.

If the necklace wasn't in the box, where else could it be? He looked around the room. The bed stood unmade from the night before. What was it Angie had done when she saw David enter? First, she had reached over to pull the dust ruffle over the mattress and box spring. Why had she done that?

David walked over to the bed, lifted the dust ruffle and knelt down to look underneath. Nothing. What else had Angie done? The cedar chest at the foot of the bed. She'd pushed the lid closed when he came in the room. He went to the foot of the bed and checked the chest. It was closed and locked. What was it that Angie didn't want anyone to see? Without a key, he would never know.

He suddenly flashed on something he had seen as he rummaged through the contents of the jewelry box. Amidst all the rings, necklaces, and earrings there had been a key. Quickly he returned to the vanity and opened the box. The key lay under a rhinestone brooch. He pulled it out, and headed back to the chest. The key fit easily into the lock. With a simple twist, the lock snapped open. David was in.

He opened the chest slowly, as if he expected something to jump out at him. On top of the chest was a picture frame turned face down on top of the pile of items. David picked up the frame, turning it over to look at the photo held inside. The gilded frame held a sepia toned photo of a woman in her late twenties or early thirties. It was the same woman he had seen in the photo Angie showed her guests on the day of her party. The woman's eyes and mouth left David with no doubt that the woman in the photo was Angie's mother.

He set the picture aside and picked up an album filled with old birthday cards, post cards, letters, and newspaper clippings. David flipped through the pages briefly, noting nothing of value to his search, and was about to set the album aside when an old newspaper article from the *Iron Falls Herald* caught his attention. The paper was dated September 18, 1954. The headline read: "*Local Woman Dies in Mine Collapse.*" Below the headline was a grainy black and white photo of an unidentified police officer standing next to his patrol car near what appeared to be a gaping black chasm in the ground. David began reading the article:

*"A woman died early yesterday morning around 8:45 from injuries she received when her car, a 1953 Mercury, drove into a collapsed mine shaft which opened up beneath the road along Route 5, two miles west of Iron Falls. The dead woman has been identified as Victoria Bradshaw, wife of prominent local doctor, Jacob Bradshaw. Moments after Bradshaw's car plunged into the abandoned section of mine, another car, driven by Vern Harper of Eagle River also skidded into the open sinkhole. Mr. Harper escaped injury when his vehicle came to rest at the edge of the opening. The cause of the collapse is still under investigation."*

David felt a shiver run down his spine. It was the same mine shaft cave-in he and Kyle had almost fallen into. The woman that Kyle had told him about, the one who drove her car into the sink hole, had been Angie's mother. He felt guilty somehow about knowing something he wasn't supposed to know. This was a piece of Angie's past she hadn't shared. But learning this secret didn't change why he had come. He carefully folded the article back up and replaced it in the album, then closed the book.

David suspected that if Angie had hidden anything of importance in the chest, it would be at the bottom. So he kept sorting through Angie's treasures. He dug deeper into the contents of the chest. There was a small book with blank pages containing pressed flowers. A small wooden box contained a variety of foreign coins and stamps. There was a volume of Elizabeth Barrett Browning's poems.

At last he reached the floor of the chest. There he found a pair of black and white saddle shoes covered by a frilly white blouse. *Shoes are a funny thing to put into a chest containing all the most important items Angie owns,* David thought. He picked up one of the shoes and turned it over in his hands. Nothing unusual. He replaced the shoe and lifted the other, examining it as he had the first one. Something jiggled in the toe of the shoe. He reached inside and pulled out a small leather pouch tied securely with a piece of rawhide. David loosened the binding, reached in and pulled out the missing diamond necklace. There had been no robbery. It was as he had suspected. Angie had lied, and now David had the proof.

But there was still the matter of the missing money. There were several envelopes in the chest that might have contained two hundred dollars, and David methodically opened and searched each one. There was a letter from Angie's aunt in Phoenix, another from a girlfriend who had moved to Chicago, and several from her mother, but none containing so much as a dime.

A small leather bound book with the initials "AB" on the cover caught David's eye. It was the only thing remaining at the bottom of the chest. David picked it up and examined it closely. He had never read a girl's diary before. David flipped through the pages until he reached the entries starting with the arrival of TJ and his family.

David had reached the end of his search. The chest was empty. He put the necklace in his pocket, put some of the coins he had found in the box into the empty pouch, and carefully placed the remaining items back into the chest exactly where he had found them.

## **Confrontation**

David sat uneasily at the end of the pew frequently glancing back toward the doors at the entry to the sanctuary. A few stragglers were filing into the nave of the Iron Falls Presbyterian Church, waiting until the last moment to take their seats before the pipe organ blared out the opening cords of the processional. Still, the person he was waiting for had not yet arrived. Angie Bradshaw and her father should have been here by now. David was beginning to worry. The service was about to start, and there was still no sign of the Bradshaws. Maybe they weren't coming. Maybe Angie had already discovered that someone had invaded the privacy of her room.

He reached into the pocket of his suit coat, feeling for the small package that seemed to burn like a hot coal through the fabric of his jacket. The packet was still there, both a comfort and a curse. David felt a tap on his shoulder. He flinched, half expecting to see Sheriff Edmonds standing over him. Instead he looked up to see his father looking down at him from the seat next to his on the pew.

"Take it easy, David," Donald Bishop whispered. "What's going on with you this morning. You've been fidgeting around in your seat since we got here. Just settle down, will you?"

"Sorry, Dad," David replied. "Guess I'm still just a little jumpy after what happened the other night."

"It's ok, pal," Donald said good naturedly, rubbing his hand through his son's hair. "You're safe in here. Just take it easy, ok?"

David tried to remain cool, calm, and collected, but he continued to survey the new arrivals for any sign of the Bradshaws. He could hear his Aunt Rita's voice in the background, raising above the din of the gathering crowd. He looked down the pew just past his father to see the Peterson clan sitting in a row like birds on a wire. Aunt Rita chirped away at her brood, happy that she had at last succeeded in getting her husband to attend a church service. For his part, Ray sat uneasily between his wife and brother-in-law, looking uncomfortable in his unfamiliar Sunday plumage. He pulled at the knot on his tie as if it were a noose strangling him.

David was glad Ray had overcome his reservations and accompanied his family to church. Ray seemed to have a positive effect on David's father. Ever since their golf outing the previous day, Donald Bishop's attitude had improved. Somehow Ray had managed to calm his father's hostility. For the first time since his arrival, Donald appeared to be in good spirits. It was curious that a simple round of golf had enabled him to leave worries about his job and an uncertain marriage behind. Ray had even convinced his brother-in-law to delay his departure for LaSalle until Wednesday. David only hoped that three days would be enough time to get Angie to change her story.

The first strains of the processional were just filling the air in the sanctuary when Dr. Jacob Bradshaw and his daughter arrived. Bradshaw entered through the main door from the vestibule, sauntering casually down the central aisle of the nave as if the entire congregation were waiting for his appearance for the service to begin. Close behind him, dressed in pale yellow ruffled dress came Angie Bradshaw. She didn't notice David staring at her as she passed the row where David and his family were seated. As one of Iron Falls most respected citizens, it was important for Dr. Bradshaw to sit where he could easily be seen by his fellow parishioners - in one of the frontmost pews. Bradshaw excused himself as he squeezed past a rather hefty woman near the front of the congregation. Angie smiled briefly at the woman as she slid past her to take a seat next to her father.

The service proceeded at a painfully slow pace. Even before Reverend Nathan Goodall began his sermon, David was ready for the service to end. But Reverend Goodall wasn't about to let David and the rest of his congregation off so easily. He stood in front of the assembled crowd preaching about the moral dilemma faced by Job in questioning God's wisdom. David glanced around, noting that more than half of the parishioners appeared to be either sleeping or on the brink of nodding off. Reverend Goodall droned on, oblivious to the plight of his parishioners.

David sat patiently waiting for the service to conclude. He was biding his time. As he listened to the seemingly endless sermon, David kept his eyes glued to the spot in front of him where Angie sat dutifully beside her father. Angie didn't seem to have a care in the world. Not yet at least, David thought.

\*\*\*

"May the Lord bless you and keep you. May the Lord make his face to shine upon you, and be gracious unto you. May the Lord lift up his countenance upon you, and give you peace." Reverend Goodall prayed from the rear of the nave, ending the service.

The congregation was dismissed a row at a time, meaning that Angie and her father were able to make their way down the aisle and out into the vestibule before David could move. Once released, David hurried out ahead of his father, anxious to locate Angie before she vanished into the crowd. As he made his way to the back of the church, and passed through the double doors into the late morning light, he spotted her just as she was about to disappear down the steps.

David took a quick look to check what his father was doing. He saw Aunt Rita cheerfully pulling Donald Bishop and Uncle Ray toward Reverend Goodall's greeting line. She couldn't wait to show off her family to the Reverend. It was the perfect opportunity for David to slip away. He rushed down the steps toward the retreating figures of Dr. Jacob Bradshaw and his daughter.

David had gone over what he would say to Angie time and time again in his head. He had hardly slept all night anticipating this moment. Now rehearsal time was over. It was time to put his plan into action.

"Hey Angie, wait up," he dashed up to her side out of breath.

Angie turned around slowly to face David. It was obvious by the look on her face that she was not happy to see him. "Oh, hi David," she said apprehensively. "What do you want?"

"Can I talk to you for a minute?"

"I don't think I've got time." She looked over at her father who was engrossed in conversation with a rather distinguished looking woman wearing a pale lilac dress with a matching purple hat. "We're leaving just as soon as dad's done talking to Mrs. Goodall," Angie said.

"It's important, Angie," David said. "I need to talk to you - privately." He motioned toward the flower arbor at the rear of the church.

"Is this about TJ? Cuz if it is, I already told you what I saw. I don't want to talk about it anymore."

"You might change your mind after you see what I have to show you."

A touch of concern flashed across Angie's face. For the first time she began to show an interest in what David was saying. "And what's that exactly?"

"You're a smart girl. I'll bet you can figure it out. Have you checked your hiding place lately?"

"What are you talking about? What hiding place?"

"You know. The chest at the foot of your bed. The place where you put everything you don't want anybody else see."

Angie's face sank as she realized the implication of David's words. Had he actually seen what she had hidden away? Had he violated her private things? "How did you...?" she managed to stammer. "When?"

"Take a walk with me and I'll tell you."

Angie went over to her father who was still engaged in his post-sermon conversation with Reverend Goodall. "Hey, Dad, I'm going to take a walk with David in the flower arbor, OK?"

Her father glanced at his watch. "All right, but don't be too long. We're due at the Carpenter's for lunch at 12:30, and I don't want to be late."

A small shrine containing a cement statue of Jesus holding his arms out in blessing was recessed into a cove in the wall. On either side of the cove ran rows of day lilies and garden roses. Along the gravel path in front of the statue stood an ornate cement bench - a place where worshipers could come and meditate in peace.

David led Angie into the church's gardens, down the gravel path before the cement shrine, and sat down on the bench, motioning for Angie to join him. Reaching into his pocket, David pulled out the small packet containing Angie's diamond necklace. Carefully he unwrapped the package, revealing the necklace to Angie. "I thought you might like this back, since you say it was stolen."

Angie tried to look indifferent, but David thought he saw a flash of panic in her eyes. "Ok, so you have the necklace," she said. "So what? What's to keep me from telling the sheriff that you were in on it with TJ all along? After all, you broke into our house, so I wouldn't be lying, would I?"

David merely shrugged. "Go ahead, say whatever you want. I don't want the necklace. Here, take it," David said, tossing the necklace toward Angie. "You're going to need it anyway."

Angie reacted quickly, catching the dazzling piece of jewelry in her outstretched hands before it could fall to the ground. Like David, she quickly moved to conceal the glittering diamond necklace. "What do you mean, I'm going to need it?"

"You'll need it when you go to your father and tell him it was all a mistake about TJ - that he didn't do anything, and that you mysteriously found the necklace - and the money."

"You took the money too?"

"No, I couldn't find it. I sure hope you didn't spend it, cuz you're going to need it now."

"Why would I do that? You've just given me the only thing that proves that TJ didn't do it. What's to stop me from hiding it again? If you go to the sheriff, it's just your word against mine, and I've lived here all my life. My father's a respected doctor. Nobody'll believe you."

"They don't have to take my word. But they'll probably believe you." David reached back into his pocked and pulled out a scrap of paper. "I wanted to get your exact words right, so I copied them down." David began to read from the paper he now held in his hand.

*"Terry called again and told me that if I didn't do what he wants, he'll tell everyone I made love to TJ. Terry's such an ass. I don't know what to do. I hate this. TJ and his sister are nice, but Terry says I have to prove myself to him. He wants me to accuse TJ of stealing from me and my dad. He says that if I don't do what he wants, he'll make sure my reputation is ruined."*

"You bastard! You stole my diary!" shouted Angie almost loud enough for someone to overhear. Realizing she could not afford to be overheard, Angie quieted her voice to a hushed, though still livid outburst.

"Wait, there's more. This one's even better, but you know that better than I do."

*"I just found out that somebody attacked TJ and David last night. I feel so terrible. It had to be Terry and his buddies, that shit!!! I don't know what to do. I HATE HIM!! I hate myself too."*

"Where is it? Where's my diary? Give it back right now, you hear me?"

"Don't worry, your diary is safe. You'll get it back when TJ is in the clear."

"And what happens if I don't do what you want me to do?"

"Well, I figure both Sheriff Edmonds and your father might be interested in reading what you wrote. Then everyone in town will know you're a liar."

"I might be a liar, but you're a thief! If you go to the sheriff, he'll know that you broke into our house and stole it."

"Maybe so, but even if I get into trouble, it won't help you. No matter what else happens you'll be the laughing stock of all your friends. And I don't think you want that to happen."

"Shit," Angie exclaimed. "Shit, shit, shit!" Though her words were still bitter, Angie's tone had changed to one of forced resolve. "And exactly how am I supposed to explain to my father how I just 'found' the missing stuff without sounding like a liar, a fool, or both?"

"That's not my problem, but I'm sure you'll figure out something. Maybe you forgot you borrowed the money, or maybe you found the necklace under your bed. I don't know. Be creative. Your dad will believe anything you tell him."

"Angie," Angie's father's voice cut across the church grounds, "come on. We've got to get going."

"It's up to you," David finished.

"Damn you, David. Damn you to hell," Angie hissed as she tucked the necklace into her purse and closed the latch. She glared at David, then turned toward her father. "Coming dad," she shouted, and ran off toward him.

David smiled to himself. For once he knew he had done the right thing.

***

David had become something of an expert at surviving Sunday after-service dinners at the Peterson's. Since he'd arrived, he had weathered the storm after the mine cave-in debacle and endured the embarrassment following the great bear hoax. So it came as somewhat of a surprise to him when today's Sunday dinner was relatively uneventful.

Maybe it was concern over the attack on David, or maybe it was the presence of his father, or maybe it was just a coincidence. Whatever the reason, both Kenny and Kyle remained subdued throughout the family meal. Even Uncle Ray seemed more restrained than usual. David suspected that Aunt Rita was responsible for the change. By hook or crook she had somehow managed to convince both her sons and her husband to avoid snide remarks and sarcastic

# Dream Catcher

comments for the duration of the Sunday meal.

Although David was thankful for the reprieve, he had other things on his mind. Ever since he and his father had left church, he couldn't stop thinking about his conversation with Angie. Had he said enough? Too much? Would she call his bluff? Would she do as he asked? David spent most the dinner poking at his mashed potatoes and nibbling his meat loaf.

After they had eaten, Donald drove David back to the lake so that he could finish packing for the trip home. The drive seemed to take longer than usual. David knew that eventually he would have to talk to TJ even if Angie failed to come forward, and he wasn't looking forward to the conversation.

But as they arrived at the cottage, David knew something was up. The sheriff's car was parked in the drive, and Carl was standing next to it talking to Sheriff Les Edmonds. Though David sensed that sheriff had come to deliver some new information, he had no idea whether the news was good or bad.

"Now what?" Donald said as he pulled up next to the sheriff's car. "This is getting ridiculous."

"Glad to catch you," the sheriff said as Donald got out of the car. "I wanted a chance to talk to you."

"Look," Donald replied, anger rising in his voice. "I've tried to cooperate with you, but there are limits to my patience."

"Actually, Mr. Bishop, I just stopped by to inform you that you and your son are both free to leave."

The unexpected news brought an immediate change to Donald's demeanor. "You mean we can go?"

"Today, if you want," the sheriff answered.

"Ok, what's the catch? Why the sudden change of heart?"

"It seems that Angie found her missing necklace."

David, who had been quietly looking on, suddenly came to life. "Really? That's great," he exclaimed, as if he'd been expecting the news.

Though Donald and Carl did not seem to notice the boy's reaction, the sheriff did. "Not only that, but the missing money turned up at Dr. Bradshaw's home as well," Edmonds said.

"I'll bet she just forgot where she put that stuff," David offered.

"Maybe," the sheriff agreed. "But it still seems to me kind of strange how the items just turned up like that. Don't you think so,

David?"

David shuffled his feet and looked down at his shoes to avoid the sheriff's eyes.

"Anyway," Sheriff Edmonds continued, "I just told the Gibsons that their boy had been cleared of any suspicion and that they are free to go. Sounds like they plan to leave as soon as they finish packing."

"They're leaving so soon?" David said concerned.

"Ya, ya," Carl said. "Nathan is due back at work tomorrow, and it will take them at least six hours to drive to Milwaukee. If they leave this afternoon, they can still make it back before dark. If you want to see TJ before he leaves, you had better head down to the cabins, ya?"

"Thanks, Grandpa. I'd better go catch him." Before his father or the sheriff could object, David was already halfway down the path to the cabins.

## **Loose Ends**

When David arrived at the Gibson's cabin, TJ was busy loading two suitcases into the trunk of the Cadillac. They were the same two suitcases David and Angie had watched him unload just two weeks before.

"I heard you're leavin'," David panted as he ran up to TJ.

"Yup. The sheriff was here this afternoon and said we were free to go. Dad's inside right now helping mom pack up. We're leaving as soon as the car's loaded. To tell the truth, I can't wait to get out of here. Nothing good has happened since we arrived."

David looked slightly hurt by TJ's comment, "Yeah, I guess it's been kinda rough for you."

TJ stopped working for a minute and looked directly at David. "You know, there's still one thing bothering me."

"What's that?"

"Angie's sudden change of heart. Funny how that missing necklace and money turned up all of a sudden. Things don't just disappear then reappear again like that. Don't suppose you know anything about that, do you?"

"Me? What would I have to do with it?"

"That's what I'd like to know. Just before the sheriff showed up here, your grandpa came down to tell me I had a call up at the cottage. It was Angie. At first she tried to give me some half-hearted bullshit apology. She sounded about as sincere as a snake."

"She's probably just sorry about causing you so much trouble," David said. "But what does that have to do with me?"

"It was the way Angie acted on the phone. She seemed more interested in making sure you knew she'd found her stuff than apologizing to me. She said something about talking to you after church this morning. The whole thing sounds fishy if you ask me."

"Hey look, I talked to her. I even asked her if she'd looked everywhere for her missing stuff. But that's all I did."

TJ looked skeptical. "Ok, if you say so. But whatever you said to her, it worked. So thanks," TJ extended his hand toward David.

David reached out to accept the handshake. "Hey, I'm just glad things worked out," he said.

"Oh yeah, there was one more thing Angie wanted me to tell

you. She said if you're done reading that book she loaned you, she'd like it back. Since when did you start reading girl books anyway?"

"It's nothing really. Just something Angie thought I might be interested in. But to tell the truth, it was kind of boring. I'll make sure she gets it back before we leave."

"So I suppose you'll be going home soon too, huh?"

"Yeah, dad has to get back to work, so as soon as I'm ready we'll probably leave."

"Come on, TJ," Nathan Gibson called from inside the cabin. "Hurry up out there. We've got bags to load, and we have to get on the road if we're going to get home tonight."

"Look, Huck," said TJ. "I'd better go or my dad will have a fit. So I guess this is goodbye. You think you'll ever make it over to Milwaukee?"

"I'll ask my dad, but I doubt it... Not unless Detroit plays the Braves in the Series this year, that is."

"Hey, it could happen. But that reminds me, I've got something for you." TJ took off his Braves cap with a large block "M" embroidered on it and handed it to David. "Here, so you'll remember who the next world champs are going to be."

David took the hat and looked at it appreciatively. "Thanks," he said. "This is great, but now you'll need a replacement." He reached up and took off his Tiger's hat with the old English "D" and handed it to TJ. "It's a fair trade. Besides I can always get another one."

"Thanks," said TJ accepting the cap and placing it on his head. Suddenly he reached out and grabbed David, hugging him tightly. "Strange thing is I'll probably miss you - for a white boy, you're ok."

***

David stood alone by the boat dock at Bobber Lane's cabin watching the sky turn glistening shades of orange and red as the sun slowly set over the gentle swells of the lake. He had hoped - no expected - to find Bobber himself at the cabin. Bobber seemed to appear whenever something was troubling him, and this was one of those times. By all rights he should have felt self-satisfied. After all, his plan had worked perfectly. Angie had succumbed to his not so subtle attempt at blackmail, and TJ and his family had been allowed to leave Iron Falls.

Still David couldn't help feeling empty and alone. TJ was gone.

"Shouldn't you be back at the cabin packing?"

David turned around, startled by the sudden intrusion into his meditation. He faced Maddie, who stood only one or two feet away. She had come up behind him so silently that he had not heard a sound.

"Maddie, how'd you know I was over here?"

"It wasn't hard to figure out. It seems like you're always over here lately. What about the packing?"

"Dad's not planning to leave till Wednesday now, so I've got some time."

"You seemed to be in deep thought when I got here. Is everything all right?"

"Yeah, I'm OK. It's just TJ. He left so soon, I hardly had a chance to say goodbye."

"I saw you talking to TJ before the Gibsons started home. You both looked very serious."

"There are some things I needed to tell him. But now he's gone..."

"Maybe it's not too late. TJ and his family are gone, but you can still clear your conscience, eh?"

"Clear my what? Why do you think my conscience is bothering me?"

"Something happened after the attack, didn't it, David? Something you should perhaps have told the police?"

"How'd you know it was about the attack, Maddie? Did TJ say something to you?"

"No, but you two hardly talked to each other after it happened. It was obvious that something was going on between you two."

"Yeah, TJ thought I knew the boys who attacked us."

"And did you?"

"Well, yeah. Their leader. I recognized him. I should have told the deputy the night it happened, but I was afraid to say anything."

"That is serious, David. But you still have a chance to make it right. You and your father aren't leaving until Wednesday, eh?"

"You think I should tell the police, is that it?"

"What you do is up to you," she replied. "But if you decide to talk to the police, are you going to tell them about Angie as well?"

Maddie's assertion caught David off guard. "Angie? What does she have to do with any of this?"

"I'm not sure, but I think you do. It can't be a coincidence that the day after her party you and TJ were attacked, and then the day after that her necklace went missing. It is not good to keep the truth hidden, eh?"

"I know, Maddie. I'll do the right thing, I promise."

Maddie looked into the distance, across the lake. The sun was just touching the horizon, its reflection on the water almost blinding. She held up her hand to shield her eyes from the glare.

"Tell me what you see," Maddie said.

David followed her gaze, looking into the bright reflected brilliance. "There's someone out there," David replied. "Looks like someone in a canoe."

"Is he the one you visit here? The one you see when you come to feed Captain?"

The sun danced across the water, momentarily obscuring David's view of the canoe. He raised his hand, shielding his eyes as Maddie had done. In the brilliant reflection of the sunset, the lone occupant of the canoe turned slightly toward them, and David recognized Bobber Lane paddling away into the distance.

"Can you see him, Maddie?" he asked the Indian woman. "Do you see Bobber out there?"

"Of course I see him, David," she said. "But look again."

David turned to look again into the blazing sunset. The canoe was still there silhouetted against the brilliant sky, but he no longer saw the face of Bobber Lane. This time it was the weathered face of an old native warrior, dressed in buckskins, a single feather braided into his flowing black hair.

"Is that..."

"Little Thunder? Yes. He has come to say goodbye."

"But how...?"

"It's as I told you, spirits let us see what we expect to see, David," she said. "When you came here after you discovered Mr. Lane's body, you weren't ready to see an old Indian brave. Little Thunder appeared in a form you would understand."

David looked back out into the lake, but the canoe and its lone occupant were gone. "Do you think he'll be back, Maddie?" he asked.

"Perhaps, but not today. Come along David, it's time to go. It's getting late."

***

David sat anxiously in the outer office of the Iron Falls Police Department sandwiched between his father and grandfather, waiting to be summoned in to see Chief of Police Darryl Benson. His talk with Maddie had convinced him that, no matter what the consequences, he would only be able to leave Iron Falls with a clear conscience if he reported the truth to the local police.

The outer office of the Iron Falls Police Department felt a lot like the waiting room at the doctor's office in La Salle, except that instead of the doctor's receptionist, there was a uniformed officer sitting behind the desk. They had been waiting for over fifteen minutes before the deputy rose from his desk and walked over to the group.

"The chief will see you now," he said. Carl, Donald, and David followed the deputy into the sparsely furnished confines of Chief Benson's office. The deputy closed the door securely behind them as he left the room.

A forty-eight star American flag stood unfurled on a pole set in a stanchion in the left corner of the room, while a Michigan flag occupied a similar position in the right hand corner. Between the two flags, on the wall above the chief's desk, hung a portrait of G. Mennen Williams, commonly known as 'Soapy,' heir to the Mennen deodorant fortune, and perpetual governor of Michigan.

Behind the desk a burley, gruff looking man dressed in the uniform of the Iron Falls Police Department sat in a slat-backed chair. The large man did not bother to rise from his seat to greet his guests. "Sorry to keep you waiting," the chief said. "I'm Darryl Benson, Iron Falls Chief of Police."

The big man made David nervous. He hesitated, standing back close to the door. "Don't be afraid, son," the chief stated quietly. "Come on in." Chief Benson extended his hand toward David. "You must be David Bishop, eh? Your grandfather said you wanted to see me. Please, have a seat," he said, gesturing toward a row of slat-back wooden chairs against the far wall of the office.

Donald pulled one of the chairs forward and pushed it toward David, before pulling up one for himself. Carl also grabbed a chair and sat down next to David. As soon as all three guests were seated, the chief got right to the point. "I assume this has to do with Thomas Gibson," he said.

"Yes sir," David said. "It has to do with what happened at the diner..."

"Before we begin, let me just say that I hope we aren't letting our emotions get the best of us here," said Benson. "What happened to you and the colored boy is just terrible, mind you, but you have to understand that we're not used to dealing with coloreds up here. Not like they are in the South. Makes you understand why they have Whites Only places down there, if you know what I mean." Benson paused, expecting some sort of affirmation for his assertion.

When the only reaction he received was a weak smile from Donald Bishop, Benson continued unphased. "A couple of days ago, I had a talk with Walter Jacobs, Ernie Green's counter helper over at the diner," he said. "After a little arm twisting, Walter finally fessed up. Turns out he knew the two boys who came into the shop that night. It was Pete and Tony Mitchell - you know 'em, Carl. Their dad works over at the Jasper mine?"

Carl nodded.

"Anyway, yesterday we brought in the boys for questioning. The Mitchell boys owned up to being in the diner that night, and even admitted saying a couple of things they shouldn't of in the heat of the moment. But they denied having anything to do with the attack on David and the colored boy."

"That's not true," David said. "They're lying. They were both there in the alley. I saw them. The one with red hair, he was holding TJ down while his brother was one of the boys who was kicking him."

"Well, this is the first I'm hearing of it," Benson said. "I thought you told my deputy you didn't recognize any of the boys who attacked you in the alley."

"I just caught a glimpse of them. Someone was holding me down, and it all happened so fast... I was confused. I guess it must have slipped my mind..."

"Then you're not sure, is that right?"

"I'm as sure as I can be. Ask that counter guy, Walter. He must have recognized them."

"When I talked to Walter he didn't say anything about those boys being in the alley."

"Well, how about that other boy - the one who held me down? Walter must have seen him. He's the one who ordered the others to attack TJ."

"You saw him give the orders?"

"Well, I didn't actually see his face, but his voice was... well, I recognized his voice. His name is Terry. I never heard his last name, but Walter knows him, and so does my cousin Kenny."

"You recognized his voice?" Chief Benson said incredulously. "So what you're saying is you're basing your identification on a voice you heard in a dark alley, is that right? And you never actually saw his face."

"If my boy says he's sure, he's sure," Donald interjected. "What I'd like to know is what you're going to do about it. When can we expect an arrest?"

"I've got to be honest with you, Mr. Bishop, as far as my office is concerned, the investigation is over. It would be a waste of time to have my deputies chasing around town looking for these boys. Even if Walter Jacobs could identify this Terry, or any of the others involved, there's really not much we can do. The only people who really know what went on in that alley were David and his friend. The Gibson boy's already left town, and you're about to leave yourself. So without either of you boys around to make a positive identification, I can't press charges. There's not much I can do.

"I know the Mitchell boys, and their families. They're basically good kids - just a little headstrong and impulsive, that's all. I'm sure that if they were involved, they didn't mean any serious harm to David. It'd be a shame for something like this to spoil their good names."

Chief Benson got up from his chair, indicating that the interview was over. "It's been a pleasure meeting you folks. I hope the next time you're up this way you'll be able to avoid any unpleasantries." It was obvious that Chief Benson had no intention of pursuing the investigation.

*** 

David looked over the trim lines of the Chris Craft and ran his hand along the smooth surface of the hull. He took pride in the hard work he had put in on the Barracuda. Now the project was nearing completion. The deck and hull had been primed and coated with a glossy burgundy marine paint. In a few days, the boat would be ready to set in the water for a trial run. But now David wouldn't be here to see it.

"I thought I might find you here," Angie's voice was soft and almost humble. She did not have the arrogant attitude she had exhibited the last couple of times they had met.

"Yeah, I thought I'd come down here one more time to check out the Barracuda before we leave for home," David replied.

"When are you going?" Angie asked.

"Dad says we have to leave Wednesday. I was hoping he'd want to stay a while longer now that things have settled down. But he says he has to get back."

"I heard that TJ and his family left already."

"Yeah, they went just after the sheriff told them they could. TJ told me that you called him just before he left. Did you mean what you told him?"

"If it makes any difference, I'm really sorry about the way things turned out. I wanted him to know how terrible I felt. Believe it or not, I didn't mean to hurt anybody. I actually liked TJ and Denise. A lot. It's just that Terry..."

"Yeah, I figured he was behind all this. But that still doesn't make what you did right."

"Look, I'm not as bad as you think I am. I know it was a stupid thing to do. I never thought it would go this far."

"Here, I've got something for you." David picked up a small package wrapped in brown paper and tied with binding twine from the work bench and handed it to Angie. "I was going to drop it off at your place as soon as I was done here."

"Did you read it?" Angie asked.

"No, just the parts I told you about at church. The rest is none of my business. Look, you should know, I talked to Police Chief Benson this morning."

A brief look of panic crossed Angie's face. "Did you say anything about..."

"About you lying about your stuff being stolen? Naw. You kept your word, so I kept mine. I thought about it though."

"Thanks for keeping quiet. My dad would kill me if he found out."

"But I did tell him about Terry. You knew it was him and his buddies who attacked TJ and me in that alley, didn't you?"

For a moment David saw a faint look of surprise in Angie's eyes. "Terry? That bastard. I figured he had something to do with it, but when I confronted him he denied it to my face."

"I don't think Terry has anything to worry about. The cops aren't going to do anything about it anyway. Chief Benson as much as said so. You could do better, you know."

"Better?"

"Better than Terry. He's a real loser."

Angie just smiled.

## Goodbyes

When David arrived at Bobber Lane's cabin the following morning, he was surprised to find a Dodge sedan towing a U-Haul trailer parked out front. He had come to feed Captain - perhaps for the last time. His father planned on leaving soon, and once David was gone, there would be no one left to take care of the old tabby. He had asked his father if he could adopt Captain, but his father was allergic to cats and said it just wasn't possible. *Maybe I can convince grandpa*, David thought.

"Hi there. Can I help you?" an unfamiliar woman asked as she stepped out of the cabin carrying a small night stand.

David looked confused. "No, not really," he said. "Well, I just - I just wanted to make sure that the cat was ok." The sound of David's voice brought Captain out from under the porch, and he came over to David, nuzzling against his leg.

"Well that explains the mystery," the woman said. "I was wondering who was taking care of my brother's cat." She walked over to the U-haul and put the night stand down inside. "Does he have a name?"

"Yeah, that's Captain. He was Bobber's - er, Mr. Lane's cat," David replied. "Did you say Mr. Lane was your brother? I didn't know he had any relatives living around here."

"I'm sorry. I should have introduced myself. I'm Ellen Dawson, but my maiden name was Lane. I'm Robert's sister." The woman moved forward extending her hand toward David. He took her hand and shook it somewhat hesitantly. "I was out of the country when my brother died, and I just learned of his death when I got back last week. My husband and I have a home just outside of Traverse City in the Lower Peninsula. I just wish I had been here for the funeral. Did you know my brother?"

"No, not really... I mean kinda. I met him a couple of times - down at Ike's store." For a moment he thought he should tell her that he was the one who had found him dead in the lake, but decided that news would just upset her more. "My grandfather knew him - he bought worms and stuff from Bobber."

The woman laughed. "Bobber. I heard that that was what they called my brother around the lake here. That's a fishing term, isn't it?"

"Yes ma'am. It's a float that keeps the line from sinking."

"Bobber. That's kind of clever, really. My brother's full name was Professor Robert Kevin Lane - quite a mouthful isn't it? Robert was once head of the Department of History at Northern Michigan University. Did you know that?"

"No, ma'am, I didn't know that."

"Please don't call me ma'am, it makes me feel so old. Please call me Ellen."

"Ok, Mrs... er, Ellen."

"You probably thought my brother was a little strange, huh?"

David did his best to pretend that he hadn't been bothered by Bobber's behavior. "No, not really, he was ok."

"You're not a very good liar, son. Now you know my name, but I don't think you ever told me yours."

"I'm David, David Bishop."

The woman seemed surprised for a moment before continuing. "David - that's a nice name."

"Come on in here for a minute. I want to show you something." She led David into the shack. The cabin was just as he remembered from his previous visit with Bobber. Simple, austere, and rustic.

Ellen led David over to a desk set back in the corner that he had not noticed before. On top of the desk sat two photos in wooden frames. She picked up one of them and held it out so that David could see. It was a black and white picture of a smiling man with short dark hair and glasses wearing a neatly tailored dress shirt, tweed suit, and tie. David didn't recognize the man in the photo.

"My brother was a handsome man back then, wasn't he?" she asked, putting the picture back on the desk.

"You mean that was Mr. Lane? He sure looked different."

She picked up the second photo, again showing it to David. "You might recognize him better in this one," she said.

David looked at the second picture. Bobber was dressed in a simple plaid shirt and khaki pants. Standing next to him was a young boy about David's age. Bobber had his arm around the boy's shoulder. "Who's the boy standing next to him?" David asked.

"That's his son. His name was David too."

"David? He had a son named David?"

"That's right," she said. "That's why I reacted so strangely when you told me your name."

"That was a long time ago. Where's his son... I mean David, now?"

For a moment Ellen looked at the framed photo thoughtfully then placed it back on the desk. She sat down on a nearby chair, knowing that the conversation had suddenly taken a turn she had not intended. "There was an accident," she said softly.

"An accident?" David probed, looking somewhat confused. "What kind of accident?"

"It was a car accident, David. A long time ago. Robert was driving to his home in Marquette one evening in winter. His car hit a patch of ice and went out of control. The car skidded off the pavement and flipped over." She paused and took a deep breath as if remembering. "Robert suffered a head injury and was in a comma for weeks. When he came to, he had no memory of the accident or what had happened.

"David was about your age when it happened - he had just turned thirteen. He was Robert's pride and joy. The whole thing is so sad. You see David died in the accident.

"At first we didn't tell Robert - his recovery was slow, and we were afraid the news about David might cause him to have a relapse. Robert would never have done anything to hurt David. Anyway, when he finally learned what had happened, he couldn't stop blaming himself for David's death. I'm afraid Robert never recovered."

"But you said it wasn't his fault."

"No, but no one could tell my brother that. He was inconsolable. Because of his memory loss, Robert could no longer teach, and eventually the university had no alternative but to terminate his position. After he lost his job, my brother began to drink heavily. For a while dad's second wife, Marie, put up with his self-pity, but when she couldn't take it anymore, she finally left him.

"After that he just kind of withdrew from everything and everybody. I tried to let him know that I loved him, but he just pushed me away. I finally stopped trying. He decided he needed a change. That's when he sold his house and moved out here. After that we just lost touch. Now I wish I'd kept trying.

"It's all such a shame, really. My brother was actually quite a brilliant man. Would you believe Bobber even wrote a book once? In fact, he wrote about this very lake."

She walked over to the bookcase behind the desk and began

scanning through the volumes on the shelf. "Here," she said pulling out one of the books, "I thought I saw this copy here earlier." She blew the dust off the jacket and turned the book over, showing the photo on the back cover to David. It was the same portrait as the one which he had seen earlier on the desk. Beneath the picture were the words *Professor Robert K. Lane.* David took the book from the woman and turned it over to see the cover. On the cover, the weathered, wrinkled portrait of an elderly Indian man had been superimposed over the placid picture of a lake at sunset. Bold print splashed across the top of the cover announced the book's title: *The Legend of Spirit Lake.*

"While he worked at the university, Robert spent almost every summer here at the lake," Ellen explained. "He was doing research on the history of this area and of course Chief Little Thunder. He finished the manuscript just a few months before the accident. I remember how proud he was."

She noticed how interested David seemed to be in the picture on the book's cover. "Do you suppose this is really Little Thunder?" he asked intrigued.

"I don't know, David, but I know Robert used to have a ton of pictures of people who used to live around here. As I remember, there's a whole section of photos somewhere inside the book. Are you interested in the history of the lake?"

"Yeah, kinda. I mean I've heard about Little Thunder. My grandfather's housekeeper, Maddie, told me the story when I got here."

"If you'd like to read the book you can take that copy with you. I have one or two copies at home anyway. I'm sure my brother wouldn't mind - especially since you've taken such good care of Captain here," she reached down and petted the cat that had wandered into the shack after them.

"Thank you, I'd like that," David replied, opening the cover of the book. His face must have expressed his astonishment at what he saw, because Ellen immediately reacted. "What is it dear? Is there something wrong? I hope my brother didn't write any profanities in there. He wasn't always the most pleasant man, and I never thought that he might have inscribed..."

She took the book back from David and opened the cover. "Oh, my," she sighed as she read what was inside the cover:

*David,*

*Wherever your life leads, may you always find the peace and serenity I have found at Spirit Lake.*

*Love always...*

"He must have intended to give this to his son David. This inscription is to him. But it is quite a coincidence, isn't it - your name being David and all? You're not superstitious, are you?"

"Maybe... Maybe I shouldn't take the book - I mean if he meant it for his son."

"Nonsense. You take it," she insisted, handing the book back to the boy. "I'm sure Robert would have wanted you to have it."

"Thanks, Ma'am... I mean Ellen," David hesitated for a moment. "I was just wondering..."

"Go ahead David, what's bothering you?"

"I was just wondering, well, I'll be going home in a few days, and I just wanted to know... Well, Captain's going to be left here all alone..."

A sweet smile spread across the older woman's face. "No, dear," she said. "You needn't worry about Captain. He'll be coming home with me to Traverse City. I have two cats of my own, and Captain will fit right in."

Captain was now rubbing his back on David's pant leg, just as he had the first time he'd met the curious tabby. David reached down and picked up the cat. "I'm going to miss you, old boy," he said. "But Mrs. Dawson... er, Ellen... will take good care of you." David petted the cat as Captain licked his hand.

"It's his way of saying goodbye to an old friend," Ellen said. "Here, let me give you my address. That way you can write to me and see how Captain is doing. Or better yet, come up and visit us. I'm sure my brother would have liked that."

***

David stumbled slightly, tripping over an unseen tree root on the ground under his feet. "Careful," said Carl taking a firm grip on his grandson's elbow and leading him forward. David used his free hand to feel for obstacles in his path. A bandana had been loosely tied around David's eyes, preventing him from seeing where he was going.

"Where are you taking me, Grandpa?" he asked.

"You will see," Carl answered. "It's just a bit further now."

David continued to walk unsteadily over the uneven ground guided only by his grandfather's hand and the barking of Lady as she ran on ahead of the duo. The branch covered ground beneath his feet eventually gave way to sandy beach and then to the boards David recognized immediately as the boat dock. Finally Carl brought him to a stop.

"All right, we have arrived. "You can take off the blindfold now."

David removed the blindfold tenuously, unsure what lay in store for him. What he saw was something he hadn't expected. There, standing on the dock, were Maddie and Ike Eisenberg. They were both grinning from ear to ear and pointing down to what appeared to be the completed hull of the Barracuda, floating gently in the calm swells of the lake. A tarp was spread across the deck and cockpit making it impossible to see the entire craft beneath.

Behind him David heard a chorus of voices calling out in unison, "Surprise!" He turned around to see a small group of people gathered on the beach. His father was there, standing next to Aunt Rita and Uncle Ray. And just behind them were his cousins Kenny and Kyle looking like they'd rather be anywhere but there.

"I thought we should have a small ceremony to celebrate the launch of our little craft," Carl said. "So I invited a few people to join us."

"But it isn't finished yet, is it, Grandpa?"

"Almost. There are still some finishing touches that need to be done, but nothing that I can't take care of after we try her out. So I thought you might like to have a little ride before you leave, eh? Besides, the launch wouldn't be the same without my entire crew present."

"But I thought you promised Mr. Eisenberg the first ride, Grandpa."

"He sure did," responded Ike Eisenberg. "And I intend to have him keep that promise. So on the maiden voyage, I'll be your captain, ok sailor?"

"Now, would you all like to see what David and I have been so busy working on?" Carl asked his guests. His question was greeted with a rousing cheer from those gathered along the shore. With that, Carl pulled off the tarp revealing the freshly painted Chris Craft beneath. The gleaming burgundy hull glistened in the summer sun. Along the side, painted meticulously in white letters just above the water line was the power boat's name: *Bobber Lane*.

"It was Maddie's idea," Carl explained. "She did the lettering."

"Bobber would have loved this moment," Maddie said. "After all, this was his lake."

A brand new 35-horse Johnson outboard hung off the transom. "The poor old Mercury engine needs a rest, ya?" Carl said. "We still won't be able to keep up with Doctor Bradshaw's Catalina, but it should be enough to get us around the lake pretty well."

"Well, who wants to take a ride?" Ike Eisenberg called out.

"How about just the main crew on the first run?" Carl offered.

One by one Carl, Ike Eisenberg, David, and Maddie boarded the boat for the maiden voyage. When Carl started the engine, the big Johnson roared to life - a far cry from the noisy, temperamental sputtering of the old Mercury. After easing out into the lake, Ike Eisenberg gunned the engine and the Barracuda zoomed off around the lake. For the next twenty minutes they flew from one end of the lake to the other. For David it was the best day of his entire trip.

***

"Hey David, ya got a minute?" Kenny asked. The older boy led David behind the boathouse, out of hearing of the remainder of the group who continued to congratulate Carl on the success of his Chris Craft project.

"Look, I just wanted to say I'm sorry about what happened - you know, with Terry and your friend. I didn't know anything about what Terry and the rest were planning. You've gotta believe me. I hear your friend's already gone, huh? Too bad he left before the cops brought Terry in for questioning."

"The police arrested Terry?"

"Not exactly, but they brought him in for questioning. Mike told 'em it was all Terry's idea - the attack and everything. Said he was pissed at that Negro boy for hanging around with Angie all the time. Wanted to teach him a lesson."

"So what's gonna happen now?"

"Probably nothing - especially now that your friend left town. Without him to testify, I doubt if there'll be any charges. But if Terry thinks everything's gonna go back to the way it was, he's got another think comin'."

"Why? What's changed?"

"Angie for one thing. She did what Terry wanted, and now she's in trouble with her dad, and the sheriff's still thinking of charging her with making a false police report. I figure he's just trying to scare her, but she doesn't know that for sure. Anyway, she'll kill Terry if she ever gets a hold of him. So are we square?"

"Square? What do you mean?"

"The bear? What happened over at the dump? You know, that was Terry's idea too. He said we should try and scare you a little. The rest of us just went along with it cuz we thought it'd be funny. A practical joke, you know. But I guess it wasn't so funny, huh Davy?"

"Not really. But thanks for the apology, Ken. And just for your information my name is David. Not Davy. It's David. Ok?"

"Sure, whatever. So, David, are we square?" Ken held out his hand.

"Sure, why not," David answered taking his cousin's hand. "Guess I'll see you the next time we're up, eh? By then your truck should be all back together, huh? Maybe you can give me a ride."

Kenny laughed. "Sure, why not."

***

Carl took a package from the table and handed it to David. David tore off the wrapping, revealing a small box beneath. Inside he found a beautiful hand-tooled leather belt with an engraved silver buckle.

"It is the belt you started the night you arrived here, ya?" his grandfather said. "I know you wanted to finish it yourself, but I thought you wouldn't mind my helping out a little."

"Thanks, Grandpa," David said. "This belt is fantastic. I could never have made anything this beautiful."

"I have something for you as well, David." Maddie reached into her pocket and removed a small thin object. She extended her hand toward David, and he reached out to accept the gift. When he looked down he recognized the bent blade and carved haft of Maddie's crooked knife. "But Maddie, I can't take this," he said. "It's the knife your grandfather made. It belonged to your father."

"And now it is yours," she replied. "It is a man's knife, David, and now you are a man. My grandfather would be proud for you to have his work. I know that you will take good care of it and treasure it. And when you look at it, you will remember me, and the spirit of the lake."

"But I have nothing to give you in return," he said.

"You have given me an even greater gift, David. Without you I might never have had a chance to witness the spirit of Little Thunder. Now I know he is real."

Donald loaded David's bags into the trunk of the Chevy for the long drive back to LaSalle. "You about ready to go, kiddo? Why don't you say goodbye to your grandfather and Maddie and we'll be on our way, all right?"

Saying goodbye was harder than David imagined. He felt the tears welling up in his eyes, but fought to keep from crying in front of the others. "I'll miss you, Grandpa," he said, reaching out to shake Carl's hand.

"No handshake," replied his grandfather sternly. "I want a hug, eh?" The old man reached out and pulled David in, wrapping his arms around the boy and squeezing him tightly. A slight blush of embarrassment reddened David's cheeks, but quickly passed.

"Don't I get a hug too?" Maddie asked, holding out her chubby arms toward him. David laughed, then leaned down, threw his arms around the plump little woman, and gave her a big kiss on the cheek. "Don't forget me, Ok?" she said.

"All right, David," Donald Bishop told his son. "Time to hit the road." David waved as he slid into the passenger's seat of the Bel Air, and his father started the engine. As they drove away, David continued to wave to Maddie and Carl until they disappeared from view.

But as Donald turned off the dirt road onto the highway into town, David knew he had one more thing to do before heading home to LaSalle. "Dad? Would it be all right if I ask a really big favor?" he said uncertainly.

"A favor?" his father replied. Well, that depends. Just what did you have in mind?"

"I was just wondering... instead of going home across the Straits like we usually do, would it be ok if we drove back home through Wisconsin?"

"You mean drive all the way around Lake Michigan? That's quite a bit out of our way, David. Why on earth would you want to do that?"

"There's somebody I want to see in Milwaukee."

A serious look crossed his father's face. "Milwaukee? Does this have anything to do with that Gibson boy?"

"I really have to talk to him, Dad. I owe him an apology," David said.

"I'd like to help, David, but I really can't. I should have been back at work two days ago. And what about driving in Chicago traffic?"

"Please, Dad. It's real important. Besides, taking the long way home will give us time to talk. Ok?"

A smile spread across Donald Bishop's face as he pulled up at the single traffic light in downtown Iron Falls. For a few moments he sat parked there thinking, then, reaching a decision, he pulled out, turning south toward the Wisconsin border rather than east along US 2.

"You know it's been a while since I visited Milwaukee," he said. "Hell, I don't suppose another day's gonna matter one way or the other anyway. And considering the week you've had, I guess you've earned a reward. Besides, I think you're right - it's time we had a real father-son talk."

"Thanks, Dad. I'd like that." David smiled back at his father. "It's good to be going home."

## About the Author

Phil is a retired high school teacher originally from Kalamazoo, Michigan. Ten years ago Phil and his wife moved to Tumwater, Washington in order to be near their family. In addition to enjoying time at their cottage on Lake Cushman in the foothills of Olympic National Park, Phil and his wife love to travel, having visited much of Europe, parts of South America, and China. Though he loves living amid the magnificent mountains of the great Northwest, Phil has fond memories of the many summers he spent as a boy visiting relatives in the western part of the Upper Peninsula.

Made in the USA
Columbia, SC
23 November 2017